"Deborah Simmons never fails to please her fans."
—*Romance Reviews Today*

"Simmons is rapidly climbing to the top peak of the historical romance genre." —*Affaire de Coeur*

"Humor, sensuous love, and tremendous characters."
—*The Literary Times*

"Deborah Simmons is an author I read automatically. Why? Because she gets it right. I can always count on her for a good tale, a wonderful hero, a feisty heroine, and a love story where it truly is *love* that makes a difference."
—*All About Romance*

"Excellent, enchanting, and exciting . . . I couldn't put it down." —*Rendezvous*

"Filled with wonderful sensuality and a basic joy of living." —*Under the Covers*

"Wonderful . . . funny and sexy." —*The Romance Reader*

"Simmons . . . delivers characters that steal your heart."
—*Bookaholics*

"Thrilling, fast-paced romance . . . Simmons guarantees the reader a page-turner." —*Romantic Times*

A Man of Many Talents

DEBORAH SIMMONS

BERKLEY SENSATION, NEW YORK

A MAN OF MANY TALENTS

A Berkley Sensation Book / published by arrangement with the author

PRINTING HISTORY
Berkley Sensation edition / June 2003

For information address: The Berkley Publishing Group,
a division of Penguin Group (USA) Inc.,
375 Hudson Street, New York, New York 10014.

ISBN: 0-425-19070-6

A BERKLEY SENSATION™ BOOK
Berkley Sensation Books are published by The Berkley Publishing Group,
a division of Penguin Group (USA) Inc.,
375 Hudson Street, New York, New York 10014.
BERKLEY SENSATION and the "B" design
are trademarks belonging to Penguin Group (USA) Inc.

PRINTED IN THE UNITED STATES OF AMERICA

10 9 8 7 6 5 4 3 2 1

PROLOGUE

SHRIEKS, LOUD AND shrill, echoed through the old hall, sending Abigail up from her chair in an instant. She knew they could mean only one thing.

The specter was out and about.

Hurrying in the general direction of the shrieks, now joined by the sound of running footsteps, Abigail entered the foyer just in time to see Mr. Wiggins, the prospective buyer of the property, rush past her toward the doors.

"Mr. Wiggins! Please, wait!" Abigail called, but the gentleman only glanced in her direction, his face pale, his expression one of absolute terror. Although she suspected there would be no reasoning with him, Abigail was not about to concede defeat.

"Mr. Wiggins!" she called again. Stepping outside, she gave chase, but encumbered by her skirts, she stood little chance of reaching the man at the speed he was going. Pausing to retrieve his fallen hat also slowed her, so that by the time she finally neared him, he was already climbing into his carriage.

Abandoning all decorum, Abigail flung herself at the window of the conveyance. "Mr. Wiggins, if I might have a word with you about the property," she said a bit breathlessly.

"I have no interest in a—a haunted house!" he sputtered, out of breath himself. "Do you know what I saw in there?"

"Well, I gather—" Abigail began.

Mr. Wiggins cut her off. "It—it was a ghost, a disembodied spirit swooping through the air right toward me! Why, it nearly attacked me!" No doubt that explained his headlong flight from the place, as well as his shrieks.

Although Abigail tried once more to gain his attention, Mr. Wiggins turned his head away and shouted for his driver. She had just a moment to thrust the man's hat through the open window before the carriage rolled into motion, leaving her standing in the drive.

"He was not attacked! Why, what nonsense!" A female voice, sounding rather bemused, came to her ears, and Abigail turned to find her cousin Mercia behind her. The elderly woman had been giving Mr. Wiggins a tour of the house, but obviously was unable to keep up with him, for she only now reached Abigail's side.

"Sir Boundefort simply made contact with us," Mercia said. "It was quite thrilling! Why, Mr. Wiggins ought to feel privileged. I certainly don't know why he left so suddenly."

"And at such speed," Abigail remarked dryly.

"Yes, he did seem to be in quite a hurry, didn't he?" Mercia said. "Perhaps he had some other pressing appointment."

No doubt his next stop would be an angry meeting with her solicitor, Abigail thought as the vehicle carrying away her hopes raised a cloud of dust before disappearing into the distance. For a moment she was disheartened, but she swiftly banished the sensation. If only she could banish the specter as easily, she mused, and the thought gave her pause.

"This situation cannot continue," she said aloud. Unfortunately, today was not the first instance in which a grown man had run past her, out the door, and away in broad daylight, but she vowed that it would be the last.

Ever since her arrival at Sibel Hall, Abigail had heard rumors of a mysterious specter, supposedly the spirit of some long-dead ancestor rising from his grave to make an appearance. The ghost, apparently manifesting itself as a wispy white form, had already driven off most of the servants, the solicitor, and another interested party.

But the fright's reign of terror, or at least its reign of annoyance, was soon to end. Abigail didn't care whether the thing was a relative or not, she was in desperate straits. She needed to sell Sibel Hall, and she had suffered enough interference from its resident haunter. Any further dallying on her part would only result in the property's acquiring an adverse reputation, making its eventual sale impossible. Therefore she must act, before it was too late.

"What do you intend to do, dear?" Mercia asked.

Abigail's mouth tightened. Having already exhausted nearly all potential avenues of dealing with the problem, she knew that only one possibility remained.

It was time for the Last Resort.

Chapter One

❦

HE WAS SICK to death of ghosts.

In fact, Christian Reade, Viscount Moreland, heir to the earldom of Westhaven and a man who could hold his own in any situation, had gone to ground at the family seat in order to avoid them. Or rather, to avoid the invitations that bombarded him to variously observe, debunk, or verify them.

Much to Christian's annoyance, the general public viewed him as an expert on the phenomenon, thanks to friends who had dragged him on a lark to the famous haunted house in Belles Corners. Of course, the so-called ghost had been nothing more than a couple of poor sods hoping to profit from their antics, and in an action he had begun to rue, Christian had been the one to prove it. As a result, he was inundated with reports of specters, apparitions, appearances of the dead, and assorted haunted objects, including bells, drums, and stones, as well as spirits of animals, which apparently manifested themselves most often as fiery-eyed dogs.

None of them interested him in the slightest.

The only good thing to come of the situation was that in an effort to escape such pleas he had returned to his childhood home for a long-overdue stay with his grandfather. Having arrived too late the night before to spend much time with the elderly earl, he was looking forward today to a cozy visit—and a respite from all things ghostly.

After a leisurely breakfast, Christian wandered the familiar rooms of his youth, coming finally to the long gallery, where portraits of his ancestors lined the walls and the earl was ensconced in a comfy chair by the fire.

"I thought I'd find you here," Christian said with an affection born of both blood and respect. But his smile was tempered by unease as he watched his grandsire rise unsteadily to greet him. Only force of will kept Christian in his place, along with the knowledge that the proud gentleman would not welcome his assistance. Having taken a fall from his horse last year, the earl was looking every one of his seventy years, and the thought made Christian's heart catch. The old man was all the family he had left.

Silently he vowed to spend more time with the earl, who had been resting here since the injury. For many months Christian had let himself be kept away by petty business and travel. Well, not that petty. His own house had burned to the ground last year, and while making plans for a new structure, Christian had found himself developing a genuine interest in building. Since then he had been observing different country homes and meeting with architects, but now he berated himself for his absence. His grandfather wasn't getting any younger.

As if echoing his thoughts, the older man spoke in a deceptively casual voice. "So, how long are you planning to grace us with your presence, dear boy?"

Taking his seat, Christian accepted the sting of guilt that came with his grandfather's words, for he fully intended to change his ways. "I think I'll linger awhile this time," he answered, just as casually.

The earl glanced up at him in some surprise. "But what of your plans for Bexley Court?"

Christian shrugged. "They can wait."

The old man's white brows drew together in thought, and Christian braced himself for argument. The earl, ever generous, would probably insist that Christian pursue his project without delay, but he was just as determined to resist and spend a little time with his grandsire. Whatever the earl was about to say, however, was interrupted by the butler, who entered with a small tray.

"Ah, the post," the earl said, grinning. "One of the highlights of my day." The words made Christian frown as he thought of the old man, once so vital and busy, reduced to cherishing the reading of correspondence over any real activity. But there was no doubt that the earl perused the arrivals with more than the usual interest.

"Here's some new letters from your architect cronies," he said, tossing a couple of missives toward Christian. "And a packet from your steward, sent on from London." He paused to hold up another piece of mail. "But what's this? A letter from Devon! And in a lady's handwriting, I do believe. I used to know a young lady from Devon," his grandfather said, waxing nostalgic.

Christian suspected the missive was from some builder who had heard of his plans. "Go ahead and open it," he suggested with a smile. He felt a pang that the earl, eager for some vicarious enjoyment of a love affair, was bound to be disappointed. Certain in his suppositions, Christian could only be dismayed when he heard his grandfather's next words.

"Why, it *is* from a lady," the old man murmured. "A lady in distress!"

Christian rolled his eyes. Most of the females he knew were more capable of *causing* distress than being a victim of it. But before he could voice that disparaging remark, the earl was looking up at him, a grave cast to his features. "Good Lord, Christian, she's being plagued by some sort of phantom. And she is begging you to drive it from her home. Why, this is a most serious business. You must help her!"

Christian groaned. Not again! Most of these absurd appeals arrived at his town house or were directed to his own estate, but it seemed someone had the wherewithal to approach the family seat with the nonsensical reports. Although tempted to snatch the missive from his grandfather's hands and toss it into the fire, Christian showed admirable restraint. He didn't snatch it—he asked for it politely.

"Let me see," he said, leaning forward to receive the foolscap. He paused in surprise at the expression of expectation on his grandfather's face, then dismissed it, distracted by a faint whiff of pleasing scent. Lifting the letter to his nose, Christian drew a deep breath. Lilacs. He struggled against an unwelcome warmth. Something about the flowers always made him feel good.

Perhaps he equated them with home. Someone had brought the plants over from the Continent years ago, and there were several enormous old bushes clustered near the orchard. He had often played beneath them in his childhood, so it was no wonder that he liked the smell. And yet, why did the once-familiar odor rouse his interest so strongly as to border upon anticipation? Christian shook his head even as he shook out the letter.

My Lord Moreland, it began, and Christian noted the beautiful hand, *it is with deep regret that I write to impose upon you.* Deep regret? He'd never heard that particular tone before.

However, I find myself in a difficult situation, which I feel could benefit from your expertise. I'll just bet, Christian thought cynically.

I have recently inherited Sibel Hall, a small manor that I am attempting to sell. Sadly, I have attained little success because of the sudden and unpropitious appearance of a specter. Probably the specter of spinsterhood, Christian decided.

Although presumably of interest to men of science as an

unusual phenomenon, the phantom is disrupting my plans for the house, and I am rather anxious for its departure. That particular phrasing made Christian laugh outright.

Having recently become aware of your experience in these matters through reports of your activities in Belles Corners, I am convinced that you would be able to provide invaluable assistance in dealing with the disturbance here. Thus, I am writing to request that you visit Sibel Hall at the earliest opportunity and draw your own conclusions. Unfortunately, Christian had already drawn them. And he found the correspondence most notable for its rather dry character—hardly the desperate plea of a damsel in distress that his grandfather had described.

I would not normally appeal to you, of course, but circumstances being what they are, I would appreciate your aid in routing the ghost. Hopefully, this can be accomplished swiftly and with minimal inconvenience. It was signed by a Miss Parkinson, Sibel Hall, Devon, and since unmarried ladies did not, as a rule, write gentlemen, Christian was even less inclined to look favorably upon the missive.

With a low sound of annoyance, he turned to feed it to the fire, but the earl was still quick, despite his years, and managed to seize it.

"Christian!" he scolded, eyeing his grandson askance. "You cannot mean to ignore this! Why, this poor woman, this *Miss Parkinson*, is in most desperate straits."

Aren't they all? mused Christian sardonically. Women had always plagued him—for his title, his money, or his attentions. And he could just envision Miss Parkinson. Either she was the kind of henwit who was frightened by nightly noises, the type constantly being revived from faints with burning feathers, or she was just another in a long line of schemers out to snare herself an eligible nobleman.

Considering the tenor of her so-called plea, Christian was betting on the latter, and he had no intention of being forced into wedding such a creature. In fact, marriage was the furthest thing from his mind right now. Lately, he had made no time for dallying with women at all, preferring to focus his attention on the planning of Bexley Court. "I'm afraid I can't help the lady," he said.

"But she says you are an expert," the earl protested.

Christian grimaced. "That business at Belles Corners was so obvious that anyone with a modicum of sense could have uncovered it. Personally, I think most of the people who paid to see the ghostly visitation simply wanted some entertainment. And the fellows who were putting on the show certainly provided it," he added dryly.

"Now, Christian, you can hardly blame this poor young woman," the earl said. "She appears to be a victim of circumstance, having inherited the phantom along with the house. And there's no need to be so contemptuous. Why, she doesn't sound the least bit foolish or naive."

Christian lifted his tawny brows in a manner that bespoke his skepticism, but the earl appeared unmoved. "It's your duty to come to this lady's aid," he insisted.

"My duty? Do you know how many of those entreaties I have received since the Belles Corners affair?" Christian asked with a pained expression. "Right now, I just want to rebuild Bexley Court, and I certainly don't have the time to trot about the country, exposing haunts that the gullible public seems happy to embrace."

"Your plans for your house are admirable, and, as you know, I heartily approve of your initiative. However, as a gentleman of the realm, you are obligated to protect the weaker of the sexes," his grandfather intoned in his most patriarchal voice.

Weaker? Christian snorted. In his experience, that was a misnomer, for the women he knew were wilier than men, with a deep-rooted instinct for self-interest. He opened his mouth to point that out, but the earl had donned a pensive expression and began muttering to himself.

"Sibel Hall. I do believe I've been there. A striking bit of Greek Revival architecture with a modern interpretation," he said, tapping the letter on his chin. "You really ought to take a look. Go over there and kill two birds with one stone, sort of thing."

Christian frowned, but the hint of an interesting edifice had hooked him like a fish to bait. "Just how striking?" he asked.

The earl grinned. "Ought to have thought of it before, really. But now you have the perfect opportunity to see for yourself. And you can report to me on how you like the style—and the ghost." His grandfather waited expectantly, his eyes shining, as if with renewed interest in life itself, and Christian didn't have the heart to turn him back into a bored old man whose daily highlight was the arrival of the post.

But if the earl was that enamored of the idea, perhaps he could be persuaded to go along. Not having been inundated with spectral tales, the old man obviously was curious about the haunting, and Christian would enjoy his company on the trip. Truth be told, he wouldn't mind having a chaperone along to stand between him and the potentially marriage-minded Miss Parkinson.

"I've an idea. Why don't we both go?" Christian suggested. But the earl twitched suddenly as if his hip pained him, and the light in the old eyes dimmed.

"If you don't mind, I'll bow out this time," he said, putting a brave face on his failing physical condition. "Not quite feeling up to it."

Christian's brow furrowed instantly in concern. "Then I should stay here with you."

"No!" His grandfather's head jerked upward. "Now, Christian, you've a responsibility to live up to your noble forefathers and rescue this poor lady in distress."

His forefathers were a pack of pirates, not knights-errant, but Christian politely refrained from pointing that out.

"Besides, I want a full report on your impressions of Sibel Hall. I've an interest in Bexley Court myself, you know."

He looked so eager, so vital again, that Christian wavered, even though he had come home specifically to avoid

the supernatural and to enjoy a nice long, leisurely visit with
his grandfather. But how could he refuse such urging? Finally, he nodded his assent and was rewarded with his
grandfather's hearty grin.

"That's the spirit!" the earl said.

Christian wasn't sure if the pun was intentional or not,
and he was even less certain about his own feelings. For
even as he basked in his grandfather's approval, Christian
had the vague suspicion he had just been manipulated by a
master.

ONE LOOK AT Sibel Hall confirmed Christian's earlier conjecture with a vengeance. With a groan of disgust, he
glanced across the coach at his valet, Hobbins. "Obviously,
Grandfather is having me on," he noted unnecessarily.

"I wouldn't know, my lord," Hobbins answered with his
usual decorum. Having been his father's valet as well, Hobbins was getting on in years, but to Christian he was a
steadying presence, as well as an excellent body servant. Although the man had a standing offer of a cozy retirement, he
refused to abandon his employer to what he termed the "im-
pertinent incompetents" of the younger generation and
stayed on, quietly efficient and immune to all manner of dis-
turbances, from bad roads to unaired bedding.

"The earl always manages to get his way, through a variety of means, but this time he has lied outright, though he
will never admit as much," Christian said. "If I tell the crafty
old gentleman that Sibel Hall definitely isn't a unique example of Greek Revival or, indeed, of the slightest architectural interest, he'll get that pensive look, as if his memory is
failing—even though we both know he is sharp as a pin and
just as prickly when crossed!"

"If you say so, my lord," was Hobbins's noncommittal
answer.

With a sigh of frustration, Christian again studied his destination, a rather nondescript building overgrown with trail-

ing vines. If he hadn't been so tired and hungry, he would have set his coachman to turning round. But the nearest inn was miles behind them, and should he abandon his quest, he would no doubt never hear the end of it from his grandfather, who would swear he had missed viewing some extraordinary piece of interior decoration. Unfortunately, Christian figured his chances of finding *anything* of interest at Sibel Hall were minimal.

He turned back to Hobbins and lifted his brows, struck by a sudden suspicion. "I don't suppose the earl shared with you his reasons for promoting this little jaunt?" Christian asked.

"I'm sorry, my lord, but I am not privy to his lordship's innermost thoughts," Hobbins replied.

Christian tried not to snort at that statement. Hobbins knew more about what went on in both his and his grandfather's households than anyone else, including himself. But if the loyal retainer was aware of the details of this venture, he certainly wasn't talking, and nothing short of torture would get it out of him.

Heaving another sigh, Christian stepped out of the coach, ignoring the delightful aspect of a June afternoon to turn a jaundiced eye upon the north face of Sibel Hall. Although not especially ugly, it was one of those jumbles of ragstone, timber, and brick of various ages, with pitched roofs and crenellations, that didn't have much to recommend it. It looked to be rather neglected as well, both the house and the grounds giving evidence through overgrown hedges, broken shutters, and the ever-present vines.

What was his grandfather thinking to send him on this wild-goose chase? Christian found it hard to believe the old man had been taken in by some female's tale of ghostly activities. He shook his head, knowing that he might never understand the sometimes eccentric ways of his grandsire. Indeed, it seemed that the old man's peculiarities had increased since the accident, and Christian wondered if the fall had affected something other than his bones. He felt a sudden pang of dismay, for the earl had always been as clever as a fox. He would hate to grow senile.

Christian dismissed the thought as he approached the entrance while Hobbins supervised the unloading of the coach. Whatever his grandfather's reasoning, he was here and he would have to make the best of it, at least for the night. He just hoped that for his pains he would receive a decent meal and a comfortable bed—and that Miss Abigail Parkinson didn't plan to ensconce herself in the latter.

When the door finally opened to admit him, Christian frowned to see a wide-eyed maid. The lack of a butler bespoke straitened circumstances at Sibel Hall, and his concern over Miss Parkinson's motives grew with his discovery. The little maid led him through a rather dark interior that needed a good airing. He wondered cynically if the dimness was supposed to lend atmosphere to the ghost tales.

The furnishings were heavy and dark as well, and rather threadbare, confirming Christian's initial opinion as he made his way through several rooms toward, he presumed, his hostess. He half expected Miss Parkinson to be draped over a couch bed in dishabille, prostrate from terror as she waited for rescue, whether from the haunting or from her straitened circumstances, Christian wasn't sure. But to his surprise, when he was shown into what appeared to be a study, the only other occupant of the room was seated, straight-backed, behind a massive mahogany desk.

And instead of looking terrified, she looked rather terrifying, with a severe expression, hair pulled back from her face, and an ill-favored gown of unrelieved black. Reminded of one old governess who had run roughshod over the household in his youth, Christian shuddered. He turned to glance behind him, looking for someone else as well, but they were alone. Surely this female was not Miss Parkinson, but some employee or dependent relation? He arched a brow in question, even as he nodded slightly in greeting.

"My lord Moreland, how good of you to come so quickly. I trust your journey was not too taxing," the somber woman said, rising to her feet, as a subordinate would. Although the windows were behind her, keeping her face in shadow, Christian could tell she was tall for a woman, though not as old as he would have guessed by her clothes and demeanor.

Squinting, and urged on by a sudden, sharp curiosity, Christian was tempted to tell her to move into the light. He caught the scent of lilacs, though the window was closed, and felt the resulting sensation of both comfort and excitement, along with the stirring of some long-dormant interest. *Did he know this woman?* "The trip was satisfactory. Miss . . . ?" Christian trailed off, lifting his brows.

"Miss Parkinson," she answered, her own, darker brows rising slightly.

Christian hid both his surprise and his disappointment. For a moment she had seemed oddly familiar, but he shook off that feeling, only to frown in puzzlement. Surely she could not be the woman who had written to him. He had expected someone younger, more appealing, and certainly more accommodating. Indeed, he had the strange sense that this Miss Parkinson did not approve of him in the slightest. Perhaps, then, she was only representing another.

"I do appreciate your prompt reply and timely arrival," she said, though her tone belied the expressed gratitude. "I assume you are called upon often to perform these sort of . . . duties."

Christian shrugged. "Well, I certainly don't answer every summons that comes my way." That was true enough, since he'd never answered *any* summons before. He glanced around. "Perhaps your employer could explain the problem more fully?"

Miss Parkinson stiffened, a black silhouette in the dim light. "I fear you are laboring under a misapprehension. I am not employed by anyone here. I am the owner of this house, and as I explained in my letter, I am having difficulties finding a buyer for it."

This time Christian could not hide his surprise as easily, for why would a female of any means take on this one's appearance? He supposed there were women in the world who knew so little about fashion and deportment that they resembled governesses without actually going into that line of work. Perhaps they were born that way, stiff and menacing in their cradles, in preparation for a career of wearing caps and dour expressions, Christian mused.

Again, he shook off his thoughts and tried to pay attention to Miss Parkinson's speech, despite a certain, nagging inquisitiveness about her. "Specter," she was saying, and Christian leaned forward in a pose of concentration. After all, the apparition was why he was here, wasn't it?

"There seems to be little interest in such a phenomenon from the science community, so I was hoping that perhaps you, with your, uh, particular abilities, might be able to aid me," she said.

Christian frowned. For someone who was asking for his help, Miss Parkinson wasn't making up to him very well. Indeed, he kept catching the hint of disapproval in her voice. Did she want her ghost routed or not? He began to wonder whether she was a little too involved with the haunting, just like the fellows at Belles Corners.

"My dear Miss Parkinson, if you want me to take a look at this thing, I'll give it a go. But if you're hoping for some kind of notoriety or a lot of gullible visitors, then I'll just turn around and save us both a waste of time."

In an instant her expression changed from one of vague distaste to outrage. Well, the feeling is mutual, Christian thought. "I assure you that I wish to be rid of the creature, not to perpetrate some hoax upon the public!" she protested.

"Good," Christian said. "And while we're speaking plainly, Miss Parkinson, let us understand each other. I am here for no other purpose than to have a look at your so-called phantom." Although he couldn't imagine this sour female cozying up to him, Christian supposed that anything was possible, and he wanted to put an end to any such notions immediately.

However, she was already taking umbrage at his words.

"My lord, there most certainly is a phantom. Whether he is real or not is for you to determine," she retorted, with the look of an overtaxed teacher about to deliver a stern set-down to a pupil.

Christian held up his hand to stop the lecture he anticipated as forthcoming. "What I mean is that I am not here to entertain you or your guests, nor to be matched with any eligible young ladies."

Despite her resemblance to a tutor, Miss Parkinson didn't appear to be too quick to comprehend his meaning. Indeed, she managed to stare at him in a way that conveyed both shock and befuddlement.

"I will not countenance any flirtations or compromising situations," Christian explained. "I have a reputation as a matrimonial prize, though well exaggerated, to be sure. And I want your assurance that no one here"—he eyed her meaningfully—"has fixed her sights on my title—or anything else."

Perhaps he should have phrased that with a little more tact, Christian thought belatedly. The Governess, as he thought of her, drew herself up to her rather impressive height with such fierce dignity that he took a step back, half expecting a rap on the knuckles for his impertinence. Her cheeks flushed, her eyes bright, and her jaw rigid, she glared at him, and for some unknown reason Christian felt his pulse kick in response.

"I have no interest in marriage, and if I did, your sort would be the last I would consider," she answered, with such scorn that Christian was momentarily ruffled.

"I assure you that handsome rogues of your ilk are not my dish of tea," Miss Parkinson added.

Had he been insulted? Christian blinked in surprise. Most women either cozened him in a positively sickening manner or else treated him as boldly as a stallion at stud. Against his better judgment, he found the Governess rather refreshing. He wondered just what sort of man would fill the bristling Miss Parkinson's . . . dish.

She continued to hold her ground with a fierce look, and Christian was seized by an impish mischief he hadn't known in years. "Just as long as we understand each other," he said, grinning.

Miss Parkinson made a noise low in her throat as though she didn't trust herself to speak, and when Christian lifted his brows innocently, she cleared her throat. "I'll have Becky show you to your room. We keep country hours, so supper will be early for you, I'm sure."

Christian ignored the little jab. He was too busy watching Miss Parkinson step toward the door, the movement giving him tantalizing glimpses of a lush figure hidden beneath the ill-fitting gown. And as she walked past him, the faint whiff of lilacs sent a rush of blood to his head. Nearly dizzy with it, he had to steady himself.

When his thoughts cleared, he realized the Governess was saying something about the ghost again, and he forced himself to follow, pretending attention. "Ah, yes, when can I view the, uh, specter?"

For the first time during their brief interview, Miss Parkinson seemed at a loss. Her hand upon the latch stilled tellingly before she swung the door open, and for once she did not meet his gaze with her direct one.

"That, my lord, remains to be seen."

Chapter Two

CHRISTIAN FOLLOWED THE little maid up a surprisingly handsome staircase, past a wonderful stained-glass window and into a sour-smelling chamber. Although he rather expected to meet the infamous specter around each new corner, the only thing waiting for him in his room was his trunk. He told himself he ought to be glad that no conniving female lurked behind the moldy bed hangings, but the thought of the Governess lying there held a kind of perverse appeal.

Obviously, the stifling atmosphere was going to his head. Walking across the threadbare expanse of carpet, Christian dragged aside the heavy curtains and opened the window to take a deep breath of fresh air. Sibel Hall was oppressive enough to house a restless spirit, though he had bedded down in worse places. He glanced outside, where the sun was lowering above the bedraggled grounds. Undoubtedly supper would be served soon, which was just as well, for he was hungry after the long hours of travel. He had just enough time to rid himself of the dust of the road.

A distinctive knock on the door heralded the arrival of
Hobbins with a pitcher of water, which he set upon a heavily veneered chest of drawers. One look at his valet's face
made Christian grin. Clearly, he was none too pleased with
the accommodations either.

"How bad is it?" Christian asked.

"It appears that the upper floors have never been piped
for water, my lord," Hobbins said, with a definite air of distaste. "So those wishing to wash must either make do with a
primitive tub or adjourn to a plunge bath located outside in
the, uh, garden area. If you would care to repair there, I can
bring you fresh clothes," Hobbins suggested, politely de-
clining to elaborate upon the lack of other amenities.

"I'm not sure I have the time," Christian said, keeping in
mind his hostess's dictum about an early dinner. Although
he was tempted to be late just to annoy her, his lack of
luncheon was wearing on him, and he knew his grandfather
expected him to be on his best behavior. Definitely a wrong-
headed notion on the earl's part, but Christian figured he
ought not stir up the Governess any more than he already
had. The thought made his lips curve in an odd sort of anticipation.

"I expect I'll have to make do with the pitcher for now,"
Christian said.

"Very good, my lord. Then I will return when you wish
to dress," Hobbins replied.

With a nod of agreement, Christian turned back to the
window. Taking another long, deep breath, he paused,
vaguely aware of a sense of disappointment when the air
carried no hint of lilacs.

FRESH CLOTHES IMPROVED Christian's mood as he
headed down to the main rooms once more, keeping an eye
out for any signs of ghostly inhabitants. Miss Parkinson had
proved oddly reticent about the whereabouts of the phantom, and against his better judgment he found his interest

piqued. So it had been at Belles Corners, Christian reminded himself ruefully.

The dining room was just as gloomy as the rest of the place, with dark tapestries and curtains and only a few candelabra to provide light. Christian had a suspicion that the dimness was intended to aid the haunting, either by adding to the atmosphere or by hiding any human manipulations involved, and he was tempted to call for some oil lamps or more candles. But he realized that the sorry state of Sibel Hall's finances might prohibit the luxuries to which he was accustomed, so he braced himself for an evening of squinting at Miss Parkinson. Surprisingly, his pulse kicked up again, and he frowned.

He had surely been too long without female companionship if he was excited about a meal with the Governess. Christian shuddered. Still, his eyes seemed to search the room of their own accord. For ghosts, he told himself. The only occupants of the room that he found were human, however, and not the one he was looking for, either.

An older woman was seated in an armchair near the fireplace, a fleshy sort of fellow stood beside her, and a young man leaned against the mantelpiece. Disappointment stung Christian at the sight of the others, though he could hardly expect to stay alone and unchaperoned in Miss Parkinson's home. And why should he want to? he asked himself. No answer was forthcoming except a rather vague notion of curiosity about the woman.

Catching a whiff of lilacs, Christian turned unerringly toward his hostess, drawn, he told himself, by that luscious scent and nothing else. Still, he couldn't help smiling as Miss Parkinson approached him in greeting, for surely no woman had ever looked less welcoming. Christian had to stifle a surprised bark of laughter. She definitely was back in her governess guise and performing a repugnant duty as well.

"My lord, you honor us with your presence," she said, and Christian really would have laughed at that charming falsehood had they been alone. And suddenly it annoyed him that they weren't. Just so they could spar, of course. Take off the gloves, so to speak. Not necessarily anything else.

"May I introduce my cousins, Miss Mercia Penrod, Colonel Averill, and Mister Emery Osbert?" she asked, drawing his attention reluctantly back to the group.

If Miss Parkinson appeared less than cordial, Cousin Emery looked positively hostile, and Christian wondered just what had roused the young man's enmity. Perhaps the scrawny fellow simply possessed an ill nature and disliked Christian on sight. Or maybe it was Christian's mission here that disturbed him. Interesting.

Miss Penrod, Colonel, *Emery*," Christian said, deliberately using the boy's first name. Although presumably an adult, Emery had a mulish expression that made him seem positively childish and fully deserving of the familiarity.

"My lord," he acknowledged with a sullen nod.

"My lord, we have been looking forward to your visit with much anticipation," Miss Penrod said, glancing up from some sort of needlework. Her words were kind enough even though Christian knew she couldn't possibly be speaking for anyone else, considering the pall that had settled over the group. The colonel actually snorted in disagreement.

Miss Penrod looked up at him over the top of her spectacles. "Now, Horace, you have to admit that something must be done."

The colonel snorted again. "Stuff and nonsense!" he muttered, a scowl evident beneath his thick white mustaches.

Christian sent him a look of polite inquiry.

"You are wasting your time here, my lord," the colonel boomed.

"Oh, I don't know," Christian said with a sidelong glance at his hostess. Her eyes widened, and he wondered what color they were. The dim light made it impossible to tell, but he felt a nagging urge to discover for himself.

"You certainly won't find things here as you did at Belles Corners," Emery put in, in a churlish tone.

"Ah, my reputation precedes me," Christian said, without

moving his gaze from Miss Parkinson. Unlike any other female, she did not seem at all flattered by his scrutiny. In fact, she frowned. Christian grinned.

"Ah, such an interesting case at Belles Corners! You must be commended," Miss Penrod said. "But, what Emery means is that our specter is an authentic one. In fact, he is one of our very own, an ancestor, Sir Berold Boundefort," she noted with apparent pride.

"And I can't imagine him taking kindly to outside interference," Emery said.

Was that a threat? Christian eyed the callow youth more closely. "Ah, and you are on such intimate terms with the shade that you know his very thoughts? Or perhaps he has conversed with you on the subject?"

Emery flushed and stammered a denial.

"I think what Emery is saying is that some members of the family feel the ghost has a right to haunt the premises and that we should not attempt its ouster," Miss Parkinson said. Obviously she did not share that opinion, for her governess disapproval was evident despite her even tone.

Christian smiled slightly. "On the contrary, I imagine Sir Boundefort would enjoy a challenge. Dreary business being a specter, I should think."

The colonel laughed, a startlingly loud sound in the quiet of the dim room. "Well, if anyone can set the business to rights, I expect it shall be you, my lord," he said. "Though I hate to see you kick your heels here for nothing."

"Oh, I'm sure Lord Moreland has nothing else pressing him for his time," Miss Parkinson noted, in a rather acerbic aside, and Christian turned toward her in surprise. Really, the woman was presumptuous, especially since he was long past the days of answering to a governess's scrutiny. Abruptly he felt the need to prove both his age and gender to her.

"Well, it was good of you to come. No matter what Abigail might think, I know you young bucks have more to do than poke into dusty corners," the colonel said, smacking

Christian on the back. He dipped his head close. "Ladies, you know. Have to humor them."

"Dinner is served," Miss Parkinson said with a dubious smile. Clearly she had overheard the colonel's remark, and Christian's lips quirked in reply. He couldn't imagine anyone humoring his hostess. He was tempted to try, though. Just for the sake of a challenge, of course.

In keeping with the general mood of Sibel Hall, the meal was a rather dreary affair, the food plain and none too plentiful, and the conversation stultifying. The colonel appeared to eat a prodigious amount, while Emery pushed his small portions around on his plate, still apparently sulking. Christian couldn't decide if his manner simply reflected an insecure youth's wariness of an outsider or something more sinister.

Or maybe the colonel's booming voice put him off his food. Somehow, the old fellow managed to do most of the talking as well as most of the eating, telling long tales of his military career that nearly set Christian to nodding off. The stories had nothing to do with Sibel Hall, its inhabitants, or the alleged specter, and Christian wondered if that was the man's intention—to distract him from the matter at hand.

Finally, when the colonel had just taken a huge bite of some sort of fowl in a nondescript sauce, Christian cut in. It was time to get down to business. "Please, tell me about the ghost," he urged the table in general.

From the colonel's response, he might as well have called for high treason. The old fellow looked like he was going to choke, and Christian considered slapping *him* on the back. Emery made some indistinct sound of contempt, whether directed at the subject or at the colonel Christian wasn't sure, while the colonel swallowed hastily.

"Well, that's the thing, my lord," he said, without spewing too much of his food. "Don't like to discuss it. Upsets the ladies," he added in that loud undertone of his, as though the women were deaf or absent.

Miss Parkinson was neither, and Christian prepared himself for the anticipated setdown. But before the Governess could bang the old man's knuckles, either figuratively or literally, Miss Penrod spoke.

"Nonsense, Colonel. I, for one, am quite fascinated with our most famous ancestor." She turned to Christian. "Sir Boundefort was a pious man who took up the cross to fight in the last Crusade and returned to establish this family. Indeed, he—"

Emery cut in, rather curtly. "Most of what we know is just hearsay. I've been unable to verify any details."

"Emery is our resident scholar," Miss Penrod explained. "He has been doing his best to research the history of the family."

Emery scowled, as if his duty were a necessary but painful one. Or perhaps he was simply bilious from the indigestible meal.

"And have you discovered just why he has taken to haunting the place?" Christian asked.

Unfortunately, scholarly Emery chose that moment to study his food, but Miss Parkinson stepped into the breach, much to Christian's delight. "The theory is that he is against the sale of Sibel Hall," she said.

"Has he said as much?" Christian asked.

"Of course not. He doesn't speak," Miss Parkinson replied, adopting her disapproving tone.

"How do you know? Have you tried to converse with him?" Christian asked.

That appeared to fluster her. "Certainly not! I've never even seen him."

"I have! And I tried to communicate with him, but he only moaned and waved his arms, as if in distress," Miss Penrod said.

"I see," Christian said, steepling his hands together. As Miss Penrod was hardly what he would call a reliable witness, he wondered just who else had viewed the apparition.

"Emery has seen him, too," the colonel boomed out in

answer to his silent query. Now why hadn't he guessed that?

Christian glanced toward the young man, who stammered and sputtered. "I *thought* I saw him. It may only have been a trick of the light," Emery protested.

"But you were quite sure before," the colonel argued loudly. "Said he held up his hand in warning."

"I saw something. I'm not certain what it was," Emery snapped.

"Perhaps the solicitor and the two gentlemen interested in purchasing the manor can provide you with further descriptions, for they both saw the specter," Miss Parkinson said.

"Chased them out of the place, I daresay!" the colonel exclaimed, chuckling heartily.

"I must admit that he seems to be rather selective as to when he shows himself and to whom," Miss Parkinson noted, looking none too pleased at the observation. Perhaps, as hostess, she was feeling left out.

"And just where does he appear when he deigns to do so?" Christian asked.

"Oh, he's choosy in that regard as well," Miss Penrod said, with the enthusiasm she seemed to display in all matters ghostly. She dropped her voice dramatically. "I cannot say for certain, but I suspect that he is confined to his earthly domain."

"And where might that be?" Christian asked. Despite his better judgment, he was becoming fascinated.

"Why, in the great hall, of course," Miss Penrod answered. "These rooms you see around you were all added later on to the original structure, which Sir Boundefort built himself."

Christian tried to express the appropriate awe at that announcement without revealing any of his contempt for the structure itself. Turning toward his hostess, he asked, "Might I have a look?"

"Certainly," she said, pushing back her chair with her

usual authority. Unfortunately, everyone else rose, too, even the colonel, who was still chewing. Snatching up a last date from a nearby bowl, he hurried to keep up with the rest of them, while Christian swallowed his disappointment.

Compared to the great houses of the nobility, Sibel Hall wasn't large, but it was a decent size, and as Miss Parkinson led him through a series of rooms, Christian realized that the original core was much older than he had suspected. He reached out to touch a painted wall, faded and dusty, but in truth he was far more interested in the pair of hips ahead of him, swaying in an almost imperceptible rhythm. Almost. Luckily, he was a very perceptive sort.

Now, if only he weren't surrounded by the cousins, a thundering herd certain to ruin a mood, as well as scare off any respectable ghost. Behind him Mercia was chattering away happily about her own encounters with the specter, while the colonel was loudly expressing his reservations, and Emery was shuffling along wearing a mutinous expression. Suddenly Christian was seized by a devilish urge to turn around and yell bloody murder. Just for his own amusement, of course, certainly not to get rid of them so he might be alone with the Governess.

The great hall was not that vast, but it was big enough to be cold and drafty and dark—the perfect spot for a haunting. "I'm told this is where he appeared to the first interested buyer and the solicitor, who refuses now to return. The second man was being shown about by Cousin Mercia," Miss Parkinson said.

"Oh, yes, this is his place," Mercia said, in hushed tones, just as though she were communing with the spirit as she spoke. Christian glanced about. Although the hall itself might be original, over the years someone had made improvements. The old hearth had been abandoned and a large fireplace installed along the exterior wall. A heavy wooden screen at one end probably concealed the old kitchens, which must have been turned to new use or abandoned.

As if following his gaze, Miss Parkinson said, "That's the

spot." Christian felt unaccountably delighted that she was watching him, but tried to assume a serious pose as he perused the area. He thought the "spot" rather conveniently located near the edge of the screen and wondered if that was deliberate, so that the ghost might hide behind it when not making an appearance.

Christian stepped closer, but he saw nothing except gaping blackness behind the open-worked wood. He felt no chills beyond the drafts inherent in old stone spaces and heard nothing above the booming voice of the colonel, who was commenting volubly and loudly enough to frighten anyone, human or not.

"Yes, this old place probably housed a few knights in its day!" the former military man was saying. "Our ancestors may have fought with different weapons, but some of their tactics are still used today, I'll warrant. Can't say that I see any of the departed fellows here, though."

"Perhaps Sir Boundefort doesn't care for a crowd," Christian remarked dryly.

"Nonsense!" the colonel blustered. "A specter that's afraid of people? Why, I've never heard of such a thing!" He paused, his mustaches swaying, then swung his gaze toward Christian as if struck by doubts. "Have you?"

Christian shrugged. He wasn't about to admit that he knew nothing whatsoever about hauntings, outside of the counterfeit one at Belles Corners.

"Still, perhaps we should leave Lord Moreland here to do, uh, whatever he has planned," Miss Parkinson suggested.

Christian was amenable to that notion, as long as she stayed behind as well. Solely as a witness, of course. As for his plans . . .

Emery sniffed, apparently disgusted by the very idea that any proper ancestral shade could prefer a stranger's company to that of one of its heirs. "I'm going to study in my room," he announced, turning on his heel.

You do that, Christian thought. He half expected the so-called scholar to return draped in bed linen and couldn't decide if the pleasure he would get from trouncing the boy would compensate for the abrupt end of his little adventure if he did so. Suddenly he wasn't sure he was ready to unveil the ghost just yet and thus cut short his visit with the intriguing Miss Parkinson.

"Well, you just shout if you need any help, my lord," the colonel said. He looked about the room rather apprehensively for someone who didn't countenance ghosts.

"Oh, I don't believe Sir Boundefort would actually harm anyone, do you?" Cousin Mercia asked. "I think he's just protecting his home."

"Or warning against interlopers," Emery muttered over his shoulder.

A rather startled silence followed the young man's remark, broken only by his retreating footsteps, until the colonel coughed out a nervous-sounding laugh. Christian wasn't certain whether the ghost or Emery himself was making the old gentleman wary, but he was inclined to dismiss both.

"Well, I daresay Lord Moreland shall get to the bottom of it all, eh?" the colonel said, now obviously eager to be gone. Cousin Mercia nodded pleasantly in agreement. The Governess, Christian noted, gave no response. She was self-contained, that one. Perhaps that was what drove his curiosity. It certainly wasn't her scintillating conversation.

"Let us go so that he can get to work, then," the colonel said. Waving jauntily, he took Cousin Mercia with him, leaving Christian, much to his delight, alone with his hostess—and any phantoms, of course.

Christian's pleasure was short-lived, however, as Miss Parkinson soon turned to depart as well. "I shall leave you to your task, my lord, with my thanks," she added, a bit grudgingly, in Christian's opinion.

His lips quirked as he thought of several witty replies. Instead he found himself saying only, "Stay," softly, and with more feeling than he intended.

His hostess, already moving away from him, stopped to stare back at him, wide-eyed. "What?"

Christian regrouped quickly. "I thought you would want to remain here and see things for yourself," he said, stepping toward her.

Miss Parkinson's startled expression vanished, replaced by one of dismissal. Why did he get the impression that she disapproved of everything he said?

"Well, you could at least keep me company," Christian complained. He wondered, with no little amazement, whether he was actually whining. And for what? The society of a governess? His brain must be addled. He took a deep breath but only felt dizzier as he inhaled the scent of lilacs. Lush and heavy and full of promise.

"I hardly see how that will aid your . . . efforts," Miss Parkinson said, sounding as if she didn't believe he was going to do anything at all. Well, he wasn't, Christian admitted. But only to himself.

"You could assist me," he suggested.

"How?" Miss Parkinson asked, lifting delicate brows that did not look at all governess-like.

That was a good question. Christian glanced about, but there was still no sign of the ghost. His gaze was drawn to the blackness beyond the heavy wooden screen. "I'd like to look around, but I'll need a lamp or lantern."

"I'll have one sent back to you," Miss Parkinson said. Glossing over the whole assistance business, she appeared as eager to leave as the old colonel was, but for entirely different reasons. Didn't she want his company? How exceptional, Christian marveled.

It was time to take off the gloves. Fixing her with a direct gaze, Christian asked, "Are you afraid of the ghost, Miss Parkinson?"

She drew herself up stiffly. "Certainly not!" she snapped. "However, you'll forgive me if I decline to remain here with you, unchaperoned, when you made it quite clear that you did not want to be put into any compromising situations. Good night, my lord!"

With that she turned on her heel, leaving Christian to rub his chin ruefully. It seemed that Miss Parkinson already knew how to take off the gloves. With amused respect, he watched her go, ignoring the slight pang that struck him as the scent of lilacs faded from the air.

And then he was alone. Christian almost called her back, before coming to his senses. What the devil was the matter with him, beyond some bizarre obsession with spring flowers? He shook his head. It certainly wasn't the hall that disturbed him, for he harbored no fear of the dark or the unknown. Indeed, when his hostess's footsteps had ceased echoing upon the old tiles, Christian turned toward the site of the haunting and stared, more perplexed than anything else. He was rather at a loss.

At Belles Corners, the ghostly happenings had been linked to a bed, where knockings and banging had erupted with great force and frequency, disturbing the tenants of the house, reportedly because of some past grudge. Christian had simply examined the furniture more thoroughly than any of the other enthralled witnesses had and pried open a side of it to reveal a boy in midknock. The young member of the household claimed he had been urged on by his elders, who, unable to afford their lodgings any longer, had come across the unique idea of charging admittance to the haunted room.

And that, as his grandfather liked to say, was that. Christian's entire experience with the supernatural boiled down to less than an hour with a hoax. Now he had the distinct suspicion he would be adding greatly to that span of time. Very greatly, considering the fact that so far he hadn't seen a thing. With a sigh, he began a slow study down the length of the hall, pausing to admire the old curved timber construction of the roof, then peering into corners and behind moldering tapestries.

"Come out, come out, wherever you are," he called out

whimsically at one point, echoing the childhood game. But Sir Boundefort remained stubbornly unavailable even as the hall settled into darkness. The wide-eyed maid finally arrived with a lantern in each hand, visibly trembling as she delivered her burden, then removed herself from the place as quickly as humanly possible, leaving Christian alone once more in the silence.

Outside, the wind picked up, causing old shutters to rattle somewhere and setting one of the tapestries to fluttering in a stray draft. A veritable feast for those craving a gloomy atmosphere, Christian thought. But apparently Sir Boundefort was not sufficiently impressed. With an eye on the spot where the screen ended, Christian lifted the lantern high and stepped behind the fretwork.

He had hoped to find, if not a boy with a knocker, at least a sign that someone had been there, but the tiles beneath his feet were clean. Moving forward in the narrow passage, he discovered a door that looked to be a later addition. He rattled the latch hopefully, but it was stoutly locked. Further along, he came across another door, this one probably original to the structure. Presumably it had led to a buttery or to the old kitchens, but the heavy oak wouldn't give way now, and he made a mental note to demand all of the keys tomorrow.

Abruptly, a vision of palming the instrument of entry to Miss Parkinson's room danced before him, but Christian dismissed that odd fancy. Really, he was becoming far too interested in the Governess. He ought to finish this ghost business as soon as possible and be on his way, focusing his attention back on his true passion, the rebuilding of Bexley Court. Unfortunately, *passion* was not the best word to distract him.

With a sigh, Christian emerged from behind the screen and wandered over to the dais, where the lord of the manor had once presided at his high table. Sinking down, his lantern beside him, he prepared to wait for *something* to happen. He hoped it wouldn't take too long and firmly ignored the sense of displeasure that struck at the promise of an early departure. After all, he could always plant some lilac bushes under his new windows. That would be a lot easier than indulging his curiosity about his hostess.

But somehow less satisfying.

Chapter Three

AFTER A LONG and fruitless vigil through much of the night, Christian finally took himself off to bed, only to awaken all too soon to the ceaseless drip of rain. He wandered down to the dining hall to find the sideboard bare. Apparently he was too late for breakfast. Considering the fare to be had at Sibel Hall, he decided that was probably just as well. He would have to bide his time until luncheon and hope for the best.

The overcast skies made the interior of the building even darker and more conducive to a haunting, at least in Christian's opinion. Unfortunately Sir Boundefort didn't seem to share that view, and Christian began to lose patience with the specter as he stalked the silent rooms, hoping for a glimpse of the fellow—or at least his hostess. But he saw no one except the occasional maid until a loud shout heralded the arrival of the colonel.

"Ho! There you are, my lord! I've been keeping an eye out for you! When you didn't appear at breakfast, I asked your valet if you'd made it to bed. Didn't want to think the specter had made off with you!" he said with a wink.

How comforting to know that the colonel was keeping such close watch on his habits, Christian thought with no little sarcasm. Not that he didn't plan to be in his own bed every night, but polite country house behavior, of which the colonel seemed to be ignorant, precluded an interest in such things as who was sleeping where. And with whom.

Completely oblivious to Christian's lack of enthusiasm, the colonel gave him a hearty smack on the back, which made him wonder if he ought not to brush up on his boxing moves in Gentleman Jackson's rooms. He needed to react more quickly if he was going to dodge the old fellow's clouts, no matter how well intentioned they might be.

"Yes, glad to see you up and about," the colonel said. "But I say, that valet of yours is rather a tight-lipped fellow, isn't he?"

Christian stifled the bark of laughter that threatened. The colonel was no match for Hobbins. Christian only hoped the military man hadn't tried to slap *him* on the back. With as sober a visage as he could manage, Christian replied, "He takes his duties quite seriously."

"Ah, yes, well, you look none the worse for a night with our own Sir Boundefort or, uh, whomever," the colonel said.

Christian's lips quirked as he tried not to explore the possibilities in that statement. The colonel, it appeared, had a gift for double entendre.

"You *are*, uh, none the worse?" the old fellow persisted.

"Yes, I'm fine," Christian said, surprising himself. Despite his hunger, weariness, and longing for better accommodations, he did feel exceptionally good. He was fairly certain, however, that his mood had nothing to do with the ghost. "I'm afraid I didn't see or hear a thing," he admitted.

"Good! Good! Ha! Just as I thought! Not a thing to worry about," the colonel said, his behavior serving to focus Christian's attention. Why was the old fellow so relieved that

Christian hadn't seen anything? Was he wary of a real ghost, or was it something else?

Christian had no time to probe the matter, for they had reached the withdrawing room, where the other residents were gathered. If he felt a spark of anticipation upon entering, it was strictly because he was curious as to what guise his hostess might be wearing today. Or at least, that's what Christian told himself. He soon discovered that Miss Parkinson was not in attendance. He tried to stifle a surge of disappointment, but who could blame him for remarking her absence? She was the only member of the household who was the slightest bit interesting.

Cousin Mercia tendered an absent greeting before returning to her sewing, while Emery sat immersed in a book, pausing only to eye him with a sullen expression. Suddenly, the thought of being trapped here with the cousins was a dismal prospect indeed.

"Where is Miss Parkinson?" Christian asked, hoping the desperation didn't show in his voice.

"She is closeted in the study again with correspondence," Mercia replied.

Correspondence? More likely the Governess was hiding, but from him or the cousins? Christian wondered wickedly. Only momentarily deterred, he tried to think of a reason to beard her in her den. A report of his uneventful night? He grinned at what might be made of that. But his pleasant musings were interrupted by Mercia.

"Well, my lord, have you made contact with Sir Boundefort?" she asked, without even glancing up from her needlework.

Before Christian could answer, the colonel declaimed loudly—and cheerfully, "His lordship didn't see a thing!" Apparently he thought Christian's experience an affirmation of his own theories on the matter. Although Christian didn't see how his dull evening proved anything one way or another, the others were also swift to judge. Emery grunted in self-satisfaction from behind his book, while Mercia expressed her skepticism.

"Perhaps you nodded off, my lord," she said.

"I did not nod off," Christian answered as evenly as possible over the chortling of the colonel, who appeared to think that suggestion the height of humor.

Thankfully, Miss Parkinson chose that moment to make her appearance, and though not on the level of a phantom sighting, Christian greeted it far more enthusiastically. Perhaps that was her intention. If she locked him up in a roomful of these characters long enough, she would seem a paragon, if not marriage material. But since she approached him with her usual disapproving expression, Christian relaxed—his hopes, or rather his suspicions, swiftly routed.

"I see his lordship has decided to grace us with his presence at last. Just in time for luncheon," she observed. Although couched in a smile, her words made Christian arch a brow. She might be the Governess, but she was not *his* governess. He hadn't reported to anyone since he was a toddler, and he was not about to start now.

"He was up late, keeping watch in the hall," the colonel explained.

Christian remained silent. It was bad enough that the colonel felt free to check up on his whereabouts, but now the old fellow was making excuses for him. Christian didn't know whether to laugh or complain. He wasn't about to explain his hours to his hostess. Nor was he going to rise with the roosters just because she kept bizarre country hours. Governess hours. Christian wondered just what time she went to bed, before deciding he really ought not pursue that line of thought.

"And I assume our infamous phantom is making himself scarce?" his hostess asked as the group rose and moved toward the dining room. Although she barely glanced at Christian, her tone held some sort of subtle accusation, as if the ghost's absence were somehow his fault.

"I believe you wanted me to get rid of him, not draw him

out," Christian noted. "Perhaps I've succeeded already." He smiled at her and was pleased when she answered with a frown. Getting any reaction at all from the Governess was an accomplishment, though he could think of some other responses he would prefer. Yet somehow he couldn't quite imagine Miss Parkinson in the throes of passion.

He tried to. He really did. He pictured her letting that hair down. What would it look like? Feel like? And as for the voluptuous form hidden beneath her shapeless gown . . . Christian attempted to conjure a vision, but all he could see was dull black crepe, while his pulse thundered as if he had just gone a couple of rounds with Gentleman Jackson.

Cousin Mercia, oblivious to the undercurrents, said as she took her seat, "Perhaps Sir Boundefort doesn't feel that Lord Moreland is a threat to him."

Or perhaps he does, Christian thought, tearing his attention away from Miss Parkinson's bodice. And that is exactly why he is hiding.

"After all, Lord Moreland is not interested in buying the manor," Mercia said, causing him nearly to swallow his tongue instead of the watery soup that was served. He couldn't think of anything less inviting than the purchase of this hideously mundane structure, dim, dark, and depressing as it was. Except for the Governess, of course.

"And being a man of means himself, he would hardly be interested in the treasure," Mercia added.

"Treasure?" Christian said, turning with mild curiosity toward his hostess. It was as good an excuse as any to eye her.

"Apparently it's an old family tale, though I've never heard of it," Miss Parkinson answered, with the vaguely disapproving skepticism that Christian was beginning to think came naturally to her. So why did he feel like making her believe, if not in old family tales, then in other, more tangible delights?

"According to Cousin Mercia, there is quite a legend associated with our resident haunting," she said.

"Legend? Why, of course there's a legend! Can't have a good haunting without a story behind it, now, can we?" the colonel said.

"I hardly think Lord Moreland would be interested in old rumor and gossip," Emery commented, looking up from his plate to glare at them all.

"Nonsense! Ripping good story, if nothing else," the colonel said.

"Hardly! A bit of meaningless mumbo jumbo," Emery argued. He immediately applied himself to pushing his food around again, as if to dismiss the subject entirely.

"Oh, I don't think so. I like to believe there might be a clue to the treasure hidden in the words," Mercia said, her eyes bright with the enthusiasm she normally reserved for the ghost.

Christian was beginning to think the woman kind and harmless, but hopelessly dotty. He turned to his hostess once more and waited for clarification.

"There is an old rumor that our ancestor returned from foreign climes with a fortune, which has lain in wait for the right descendant to discover it," Miss Parkinson explained.

From the line of her mouth, Christian could tell that she didn't lend credence to the story, though she refrained from spoiling Mercia's fun by denying the possibility outright. Obviously she wasn't all bad, for she behaved well enough toward the cousins. So why was she singling him out for the misbehaving-pupil treatment?

"And we've even got a clue!" the colonel boomed, startling Christian from his musings on his hostess. "How does it go, Mercia? Tell his lordship about the poem that's supposed to lead to the prize."

"I cannot believe you're perpetrating this nonsense," Emery said with a tone of derision that bordered on desperation.

"I thought you were interested in the legend, Emery," Miss Parkinson said, giving him a questioning look.

There. Better mind the Governess, Christian thought, glad to see someone else being reproved. He nearly grinned.

Emery's ears pinkened as he sputtered, "It's silly. I thought it was amusing, that's all, but I can find no basis in record. As a scholar, I am interested in facts, not fancies. There is no reason to believe that old rhyme has anything to do with anything!"

Emery's sudden and fierce dismissal of the so-called legend piqued Christian's attention. "I would think a scholar would find such things of interest, whether they be myth or actual history, especially when applied to one's own antecedents," he said.

Emery colored further and mumbled something intelligible, but Christian's instincts had been roused, and he studied the young man more closely.

"How's it go, now, Mercia?" the colonel called out loudly, and Christian nearly jumped again. He was going to have to muzzle that man.

Mercia smiled eagerly, and began to recite.

My grief is such I cannot bear,
So must my worldly goods despair.
All my treasure sacred keep
In stone abode and darkness deep.

There shall they rest in blessed care
'Neath the angels singing fair,
Untouched by all but she who wear
Mine own love token in her care.

Thy ring when set against its mate,
Sweet kiss! Shall unlock the gate
For only her, all others spurning
Until my lady's love returning.

Christian listened with half an ear while watching Emery, who kept his attention firmly focused on his plate. To hide what? Interest or indifference?

"What do you make of it, my lord?" Mercia asked when she had finished, and Christian turned to find her studying him with bright eyes.

"Sounds like some kind of love verse," he said, with a shrug. He had never been much for poetry. Byron gave him hives.

"I fear whatever meaning the phrases might once have had has been lost over the years," Miss Parkinson said.

"Perhaps if we all put our minds to it, we might come up with an answer, and a clue to our ghost's behavior as well," Mercia suggested.

Christian stifled a groan. If there was anything he hated worse than poetry readings, it was playacting and guessing games. He had hoped that the adjournment to luncheon meant he would have some decent conversation, preferably with Miss Parkinson. She was more intelligent than the average female, Christian knew with utter certainty, though how he wasn't sure. Whether it was her likeness to a tutor or just the fact that she held herself slightly apart from the rest of the rabble here at Sibel Hall that convinced him, he didn't know.

She was intriguing, and Christian couldn't remember the last time any woman had roused his curiosity. She had an innate dignity that wasn't compromised by the most outlandish tales of the company, and he guessed she would be steady and sensible in all situations. Perhaps that was what he found appealing about her—besides the lilacs, of course. Obviously, it wasn't her warmth or her looks.

"Well, who has an idea?" Mercia prompted.

An uncomfortable silence followed, broken by the colonel's hearty laugh. "I'm afraid I'm not very handy with rhymes."

Emery remained silent, though he appeared to sit up straighter in his seat, alert despite his preoccupation with his food, and Miss Parkinson simply shook her head. Nevertheless, Mercia persisted, and finally everyone except Emery threw out a few feeble suggestions. But after a good quarter of an hour even Mercia settled into silence, while Christian stirred himself from his stupor, having nearly nodded off during that boring exercise. Now, thankfully, the issue appeared to have died away and he could turn his attention to the only real point of interest here: his hostess.

Christian found himself wondering how she had come to head up this household of eccentrics, for it was obvious that she was in charge. Had she been born to lead them or had she simply fallen into the role? More important, what color were her eyes? Perhaps he could get close enough today to find out. And why did she smell so damn good?

"Well, that was quite a lively meal, I must say! But now I think I'll pop into the old hall, just to see if your specter's about," the colonel said, clearing his throat loudly. "Care to join me, my lord?"

Startled, as always, by the colonel's voice, Christian was taken unawares by the invitation. He glanced at Miss Parkinson, who gave him a look as if to ask why he was hesitating. After all, the ghost was the only reason he was here, wasn't it? Resisting the temptation to scowl, Christian rose to his feet. "Certainly. If you'll excuse me, ladies? Emery."

Once they stepped out of the dining room, the colonel hurried Christian along, then motioned for him to come closer with a conspiratorial air. "I've been doing some research of my own, in a bit of effort to help our dear benefactress," he confided in a low voice.

"Benefactress?" Christian echoed.

"Cousin Abigail," the colonel said. "She's generously allowed us all to stay on here, at least for the time being."

Christian felt the first stirrings of real distrust—not that he was by nature a suspicious person. Like hell, his grandfather would say. He had been born with the instincts of his pirate ancestors, a useful trait that had enabled him to keep his pockets full amid London vices that destroyed the fortunes of many another young man. It was those very instincts that had told him something at Belles Corners wasn't as it should be. And now he wondered just what was happening at Sibel Hall.

"Stay on?"

"Well, ahem, yes. You see, Emery and I were living here when Bascomb passed away. Or rather, Emery was here on an extended stay, after being at school. Wanted to study his heritage, and all that."

"And Mercia?" Christian asked.

"Oh, she has her own household, but she has remained here to help Abigail," the colonel said.

Yes, she was a real help with her ghost sightings and weird lore, Christian thought cynically.

"As I was saying," the colonel began. Obviously, he was trying to get back to his point, but Christian wouldn't let him.

"And *Abigail*," Christian cut in, only to pause to mull over the name. It struck some chord deep inside him, like a treasure long buried or a memory since forgotten. He drew a breath. "And *Miss Parkinson* was living here as well?"

"Oh, no. She came after the funeral. I expect she didn't even know about Bascomb's death until the solicitor contacted her about the bequest."

"I see. So she was willed the house?" Christian recalled something like that from the letter, but he hadn't been paying much attention at the time. Now it seemed more important.

"Yes, ahem, and most gracious she has been about it," the colonel said, obviously uncomfortable with the path of the conversation. "But, as I was saying, I've been doing some studying of my own." He drew himself up, his mustaches bouncing. "Ghosts, you know."

"Ghosts?"

"Yes! Can't say I knew much about them before. Not my line, so to speak," he said, chuckling heartily. "But I've been looking through the large library here at Sibel Hall. Bascomb was quite the scholar, you know. Runs in the family," he added, preening. "Though I must admit that heretofore I have not been one of those so inclined."

"And what have you discovered?" Christian asked, now desperate for the old man to get to the point. If there was one.

"Well, it seems they're a product of their times," the colonel pronounced.

"What?"

"Ghosts, my lord! Back in the old days, you didn't hear much about them because the early church fathers didn't take to such things. But then, when the stories do start cropping up, they pretty much echo the teachings of the period— punishments and rewards after death, that sort of thing."

The colonel paused to stroke his mustaches thoughtfully. "In the late Middle Ages, sightings became much more prevalent, with most of the apparitions supposed to be from purgatory, a sort of waiting area between death and their final reward. They often required the living to do penance for them or buy indulgences from the clergy. But, of course, the Reformation did away with all that.

"Now we get things more on the order of poltergeists, possessions by the devil, knockings, flutterings, and abominable cases like your Belles Corners business. Of course, you probably know all this!" the colonel exclaimed. "After all, you are the expert here and should be lecturing me, eh?"

Christian shrugged, suddenly uncomfortable with his ignorance. He didn't know which was worse, the implicit faith granted him by Mercia, the manly reasoning imputed him by the colonel, Emery's scorn, or the vaguely disdainful expectations of Miss Abigail Parkinson herself. As Emery had noted, this was not Belles Corners, and that lark was rapidly losing whatever amusement it had once possessed, if any.

Christian wondered whether he ought to brush up on his spectral knowledge, but the thought of closeting himself in a library was only slightly more palatable than reciting poetry. Muttering imprecations about a certain interfering earl under his breath, he wished the cursed phantom would make an appearance, so he could get out of here and back to the business of Bexley Court.

Instead, he was being treated to a lecture on paranormal manifestations. "How about ghostly animals?" Christian asked suddenly, in an attempt to sound more knowledgeable than he felt. "Why do they always appear as black dogs with red eyes and slavering lips?" He had received plenty of correspondence on that subject.

For a moment the colonel appeared taken aback, then he laughed in his deep, resonating way. "Just so! You do know your stuff. So, what is your opinion as to the cause of these aberrations? Cases of people wanting attention, or simply those open to suggestion? Is it some kind of mass hysteria or just singular attacks of mental illness?"

Christian blinked, a bit overwhelmed by the colonel's views. "Are you saying Mercia's a bit queer in the upper story?" he asked, tongue firmly in cheek.

"Eh, what? Oh, no! Certainly not. Obviously, there must be something behind whatever she saw," he said, clearing his throat and ducking his head.

"Or *someone*," Christian muttered under his breath as they entered the old hall.

It was dim and quiet, the rain a distant rhythm against thick glass set high up in the walls. Christian roamed the perimeter, but to his disappointment, the place looked just as it had during his evening vigil, the overcast day cloaking the room in a pall that made him long for some proper lighting. He wondered idly if he would ever get a good look at the space. He prowled restlessly about while the colonel kept up a steady stream of commentary, pausing beneath a wall of what appeared to be ancient weapons, which he had barely noticed the night before.

Christian studied a battered helmet, a broadsword, some rather nasty-looking daggers, a brace of old pistols, and a pair of foils and wondered if they might come in handy at some point. Unfortunately, anyone might put them to good use, and he made a mental note to watch his back even as he kept an eye out for the phantom. The thought made him glance toward Sir Boundefort's favorite haunt, with the hope of seeing something—anything—but only darkness yawned behind the wooden screen.

With a frown, Christian stepped behind the partition. Nothing awaited him there except shadows and the outlines of the two doors along the wall. He moved toward the first, then paused, his eyes narrowing as he contemplated the floor. He had been here before, last night, and yet there was no sign of his footprints. Crouching low, he put a finger to the dank tiles, swiping them, but no telltale dust marked it. Considering the state of housekeeping in the rest of the house, he wondered just how this area seemed to be so clean. Reason told him that the unused parts of the house would be even more dirty than the rest of the place, but that was not the case here.

Interesting.

He came to his feet just as the colonel's loud voice erupted nearby. "My lord?" Christian turned to see white mustaches bobbing around the fretwork.

"Ah! There you are! Thought for a moment you'd disappeared into thin air!" the man said a bit nervously. Christian wondered if the old fellow perhaps wasn't quite as sanguine about the spirit as he claimed to be. Or maybe he had other reasons for his odd behavior.

"Do you know where these doors lead?" Christian asked. He tried the first one, but it was locked just as tightly as the night before.

"To the old kitchens, I presume, long gone now, of course," the colonel answered. "And to the cellars, perhaps. I've never had cause to go down there."

Christian turned toward the older man with a questioning look.

"Well, not really my house, you see," the colonel explained gruffly.

Christian checked the other door, but it wouldn't budge

either. He swung round to the colonel again. "I'd like to have a look behind them. Do you know where the keys are?"

"Well, I seem to recall a set hanging in the kitchen—housekeeper's, I imagine, but she's no longer with us. Complained that she kept hearing noises after Bascomb died. Thought he'd come back to haunt her. Handed over some pilfered silver and fled, without even asking for her references!"

A search of the kitchens didn't turn up any keys, nor did the young maids who were all that remained of the staff admit to any knowledge of them. The colonel frowned at such negligence, but a slow smile stole over Christian's face as anticipation stirred his sluggish blood.

"Miss Parkinson must have them," he said.

The Governess, he suspected, was totally organized. She probably had every key labeled and tucked away in careful order. And the thought of getting his hands on them was what made Christian grin, surely not the prospect of seeing his hostess again.

Nonetheless, his pace quickened, taking him swiftly to the entrance to the drawing room, where, for one brief moment, he was able to watch his quarry without her knowledge. Now that he had hints of the form beneath her gown, he knew just where to look to search out each curve and dip, and he was just tracing the slim column of her throat when the colonel called out a greeting from behind him.

Christian bit back a curse as Miss Parkinson, *Abigail*, immediately glanced toward them. Her mouth tightened, and she adopted a guarded expression that seemed to convey some sort of displeasure at the mere sight of him, which he found positively baffling. After all, he was here at her request, wasn't he?

"Back so soon?" she asked.

Christian frowned in surprise at the rebuke implicit in her words. If he hadn't known better, he would have thought she didn't want him around. He did know better, didn't he? Why wouldn't she want him around?

"Looking for some keys, I'm afraid. I don't suppose you have a set?" the colonel asked in an apologetic tone.

"I assume you have keys to all the rooms?" Christian said more pointedly.

The Governess stood, and Christian tried not to admire her utter grace in doing so. How could a woman so seemingly severe move with that certain tantalizing sensuality? He tore his gaze from her hips and decided he was imagining things. He'd been cooped up too long in the ghost house, no doubt. Obviously it was affecting him. Adversely.

"I was given a ring of keys by the solicitor," Miss Parkinson acknowledged rather warily. "Why do you need it?"

"There are a couple of doors in the hall that seem to be locked. Thought we'd take a look," the colonel answered rather sheepishly.

Christian said nothing, simply lifted his brows in silent query at his hostess. Would she thwart his simplest efforts to investigate? Why had she sent for him, if not for this purpose? Had he ever known a more frustrating female?

"I'll fetch them," she said with a brisk nod, and Christian stepped back to allow her to move past him. As she slipped by, he caught a whiff of lilacs, and he nearly reached out to draw her back. Gad, sometime he was going to plant himself next to her and just *breathe*. Or plant himself *inside her*. It was a startling thought that he immediately dismissed. Miss Parkinson definitely was not his sort of female, and besides, he had no intention of bedding a seemingly virtuous governess-type. Despite his pirate ancestry, he still had some honor.

But a man could dream.

Christian sighed, then tore his eyes away from those gently swaying hips long enough to turn toward the colonel. "I'll be right back," he said. Ignoring the older man's sputtering questions, he followed his hostess, albeit at a discreet distance. When she disappeared up the main stairway, he waited, hoping to catch her alone at the bottom when she returned. Strictly for business purposes, of course.

She was efficient, naturally, and was back in good time, only to pause when she became aware of Christian standing at the bottom. He smiled cordially and held out his hand, ostensibly for the keys. She ignored it, managing to sort of sidle past his arm and stop a few steps away, so that she was positioned just a little bit higher than he. Christian's pirate instincts urged him to toss her over his shoulder, but unfortunately the veneer of civilization precluded such antics in this day and age. In England, anyway. Perhaps a visit to the East Indies was called for . . .

"Yes, my lord?" Miss Parkinson said, looking down her lovely nose at him.

Christian savored the words, imagining them in a different context entirely. He held out his hand again. "I've come for the keys."

"Yes, well, I'm not sure which is which, you see," she said, prevaricating. Obviously, she didn't want to accompany Christian to the dim great hall. Alone.

"I'll just take the whole ring. I shall need the keys to all the rooms, anyway," he said, flashing a smooth smile.

"I think not!" his hostess protested.

Christian admired the delicate rose color that bloomed in her cheeks. Was she thinking what he was thinking? Probably not. Unfortunately. "How else am I to . . . expose the specter?"

"I assure you that the ghost has never been seen in my rooms!" she answered tartly.

"Still, you want me to explore all avenues, don't you?" Christian asked innocently. "What if he should appear there?"

"Then I shall deal with him!" she replied in her best Governess voice, and for some reason Christian delighted in the frown she gave him. Really, he must have been fawned over far too much in his lifetime, if he found her behavior stimulating. Yet somehow he did.

He sighed his disappointment as she brushed by him, but if he was not to have the keys, at least he would have her, since she would not part with them. "Unless I am mistaken, the hall is this way," he said, turning in question.

But his hostess ignored him. "Colonel!" she called in a rather panicked fashion as she headed back toward the drawing room. Christian watched with a smile. Now, why was his stalwart Governess running like a scared rabbit? Did the thought of being alone with him so unnerve her?

Christian shook his head as he followed, tagging along as she rather breathlessly brandished the keys at the colonel, while still hanging on to them for dear life. Then they all trudged back to the great hall, where Christian stood as close as politeness allowed while Miss Parkinson tried one key after another, in one door and the next.

None of them worked.

"May I?" Christian asked.

His hostess was not pleased, giving him a frown that told him so in no uncertain terms, but she finally pushed the keys toward him. Biting back a smile, Christian went through the same motions, just to assure himself that none truly did fit. He used more strength perhaps than Miss Parkinson, but he couldn't manage to unlock either door. Ignoring her I-told-you-so expression, he tendered the ring to her with a gallant bow.

"It appears that the necessary keys are missing. Are you certain that you received no others when you took possession of the property?"

"Quite sure," she answered firmly.

Christian turned to the colonel. "Do you have any idea where another set or any loose keys might be?"

"I'm afraid not, my lord. Can't say that I've ever known anything to be locked up around here. Perhaps you might find them among Bascomb's personal effects?" He sent a glance toward Miss Parkinson, who shook her head.

"Perhaps a set has been tucked away in the study," the colonel suggested. When the Governess gave him a tentative nod of assent, he set out in that direction, followed by Christian and his hostess.

Miss Parkinson appeared to take great pains to avoid her companion, hurrying forward to catch up with the colonel, and Christian wondered yet again just what made her so intriguing to him. All good reason told him to decry everything about her, so why did all his other senses stir to life at the very sight of her? Hell, at the very *whiff* of her?

"I say, this is turning out to be quite a mystery, isn't it?" the colonel called out over his shoulder.

And Christian, though he remained silent, could only agree wholeheartedly.

Chapter Four

CHRISTIAN'S SECOND VIEW of the study was a bit more thorough than the first, although his attention still wandered to his hostess. When she moved toward the desk, he couldn't help watching as she bent over a drawer, his reward a delightful view of a gently curved posterior. Unfortunately, the object of his interest chose that moment to turn and glare at him, making him wonder if she had the same preternatural senses possessed by many a governess.

Flashing her an innocent smile, Christian quickly returned to his task, looking for any place where keys might be absently tossed or hidden away. Much to his irritation, the disorder made the task difficult, for mounds of papers littered the surfaces of a Baroque side table, a Tudor chair, and an ugly bureau. This Bascomb obviously had no taste and was messy besides.

Approaching the table cautiously, Christian lifted an old account book, dislodging a pile of what appeared to be personal correspondence and old receipts. Hell, anything could be hidden under all this rubble. "Was it always so cluttered in here?" he wondered, sifting through some letters in case the keys had been tossed among them.

"I say, it is a bit of a muddle, isn't it?" the colonel said as he stepped behind the desk to survey the area. "I wasn't in here very often, it being Bascomb's private study, but I don't recall it looking so haphazard. Usually, he was quite organized. Everything and everyone in its place, so to speak."

Christian found that hard to believe.

"Well, it was worse than this when I arrived," Miss Parkinson commented a bit defensively, though certainly no one had accused her of creating the confusion. "The ordering of it all has kept me very busy."

No wonder she looked so annoyed all the time. Christian nearly suggested that she toss the entire load into the nearest fireplace and move on to some more rewarding activity. He was sure he could think of something that would qualify, but he didn't expect his hostess to agree. With a sigh he went back to his search, mindful that were he anywhere else, he could hire someone to do the chore for him. No doubt the earl, whom Christian held responsible for all his discomforts here, would be highly amused.

Although he cast frequent glances at his hostess and tried to inch close enough to catch another whiff of lilacs, Christian found the work tedious and didn't complain when, with a sound of exasperation, the Governess began shooing the two men from the room, insisting that she would complete the task herself.

The colonel seemed as relieved as Christian and shrugged away any concern about the aborted mission. "Can't think that anything's behind those doors anyway," he said, with a chuckle that might have been hearty or nervous. Christian couldn't decide which.

But Christian wasn't about to dismiss the closed-off areas as easily. After all, that was why he was here, wasn't it, to investigate? He wondered whether he ought to pick the locks or even break down the doors, if things came to that.

It seemed like a lot of effort for what should have been a lark, but nothing about Sibel Hall was turning out to be easy. With another glance in his hostess's direction, Christian considered lingering behind and consulting privately with her on the matter, but she appeared to be in a hurry to be rid of him.

He cocked a brow at that. His suspicious nature made him wonder what the devil she was up to, summoning him here and then avoiding him. After all, she was his employer, he thought, pausing momentarily at the singular notion. He had never been employed in his life, let alone at the beck and call of a woman. Normally, he would have rejected the very idea, but there was something about the Governess that made it rather titillating.

Christian shook his head at his own perversity. Next he'd be wanting her to rap his knuckles. And she looked inclined to oblige when she caught him eyeing her. Frowning, she moved to shut the door behind him, sending the dizzying scent of lilacs his way, and Christian leaned against the jamb, rather like a boy heady from his first flirtation. Perhaps it was his pirate blood, stirred to life by a female's seeming disdain, but Christian felt positively invigorated.

Drawing a deep breath, he straightened and pushed away from the jamb with new resolve. He might have to go out and swash some buckles . . . or at least rout a ghost.

THE EUPHORIA THAT sent Christian charging back to the great hall with eagerness gradually dissipated in the absence of either the specter or his hostess, and he was soon kicking his heels, bored beyond reason by the colonel's military tales. When the dinner hour arrived, he felt like a condemned man granted a reprieve, but the somber atmosphere, the bizarre company, and the poor provisions turned his mood once again.

Christian wondered if he might find sustenance in a village nearby. Surely there was an inn or tavern of some sort that provided food. If so, he was determined to escape there on the morrow for luncheon—or perhaps for every single meal from now on. That he would still be staying at Sibel Hall was not in doubt at this point. His mission was clearly going to take a lot longer than he had anticipated.

Not even the sight of his hostess did much to cheer Christian, for she greeted him with her usual lack of enthusiasm. Not close enough to smell her perfume or to receive a rap on the knuckles, he felt a kind of restless frustration at her aloofness. And the desultory conversation at the table did nothing to enliven the gloomy gathering.

"Did you find the keys?" Christian finally asked, since the Governess had made no mention of them. Had she even looked for them? Were they in her pocket all along? Perhaps a search of her person was in order . . .

"No, I did not," she answered in clipped tones, as if the question annoyed her, and Christian decided the cousins were just as weary of him as he was of them. Miss Parkinson seemed displeased by the very sight of him, and even the colonel was less voluble than usual. Having set aside his vaunted studies long enough to eat, Emery had joined them, but he continued to glare at Christian with no little enmity.

Christian smiled evilly in return. "Perhaps Emery can put his considerable intellect to the problem," he suggested.

"What?" the young man said, glancing about with some alarm.

"We seem to be missing some keys!" the colonel announced in his booming voice.

Emery sputtered, his face flushing. "Why should I know anything about any keys?"

"Because you've been living here for some time," Christian answered.

"The colonel's been here longer than I have!" Emery protested. "Besides, I don't bother myself with the running of the house. I have my studies."

"Emery is quite the scholar, my lord," Mercia declared,

though Christian remained unconvinced. She looked up from her plate with curiosity. "What keys are missing?"

"Oh, nothing to worry about, just looking to open an old door or two in the hall," the colonel said.

Emery snorted. "Those keys probably were lost years ago. I believe the passages were blocked up. Old stone, rotting foundations. Too dangerous," he said dismissively.

The boy's comments sounded plausible, Christian realized. He knew from his own experience, however, that many a building older than Sibel Hall remained solid, and from what he could see the place was dreary but firm. Perhaps Emery's theories were based on misinformation or perhaps he had his own reasons for putting them forth. After all, blind passages and crumbling cellars made for a convenient home for the ghost or its minions.

Emboldened by the silence that followed his pronouncement, Emery hastened to embellish it. "Indeed, the original portion of the house is in terrible condition, as anyone with any knowledge of architecture can attest," he said with a superior air.

Christian opened his mouth to argue the point. After all, he knew quite a bit about buildings himself. But the smirk on Emery's face stopped him. No matter how galling, perhaps it would serve him better to keep his expertise to himself, at least for now.

"Indeed, I would be careful wandering about the old part of the house, my lord. I'm sure such places are not your normal venue. You might be struck by falling stone," Emery added.

Christian lifted his brows. Was that a threat?

Miss Parkinson made a low sound of dismay. "I had not realized the building was in such poor condition," she said. Was she worried about his safety? Christian flashed her a smile, but she quickly became engrossed in her food.

"I have never seen any loose stones," the colonel observed, only to become flustered by Emery's glare. "But architecture is not my forte," he hastened to add.

"Of course, the area itself is not the only danger," Emery said, warming to his topic. "There is also the ghost to contend with."

"But I thought he wasn't harmful," Miss Parkinson said in her usual practical tone, a tone that Christian was beginning to relish beyond all good reason.

Emery smirked again. "Who knows what the specter is capable of doing when provoked?" His words, ringing out in the dimly lit room, were punctuated by a great lash of rain against the windows. Very effective, Christian mused, though no one at the table seemed to notice. Perhaps they all thrived on the dismals.

Emery was certainly thriving in his role as unchallenged expert. "Indeed, one wonders exactly how you intend to rout the spirit, my lord?" he asked, eyeing Christian directly.

As much as Christian would have liked to wipe the sneer off the obnoxious pup's face, he didn't have an answer to that question. He had no idea how to rout or even rouse a real specter. All he could do was watch and listen for some kind of worldly connection, but so far he had caught no one knocking. And he had no intention of sharing that information with the so-called scholar.

Emery practically drooled into the ensuing silence. "I mean, you cannot have put any study into the matter, eh, my lord? It's not as though you are a man of science or a philosopher, is it?" he asked, looking quite triumphant.

Christian was tempted to lunge over the table and give the scholar a good taste of his specialty, but he told himself the boy wasn't worth his while. Besides, he was supposed to be on his best behavior as gentleman and rescuer of Miss Abigail Parkinson, which meant not giving in to his more uncivilized impulses. Or even his boxing expertise. He gave a casual shrug.

"Indeed, my lord, I am hard-pressed to see what qualifies you to be here, beyond a chance encounter at Belles Corners," Emery persisted.

Obviously, the boy thought Christian to be just an idle

nobleman out on a lark. Well, he was, really. Or rather, he was a nobleman (not necessarily idle) coerced by his elder into forsaking the comfort of clean, luxurious surroundings for this definitely non-larklike experience. Christian opened his mouth to point that out, but the Governess rushed to his defense.

"Emery, please!" she said, and Christian bit back a smile of pleasure, absurdly heartened by her concern—until he heard her next words. "I believe I told you that none of the men of science I contacted would consider our case. Lord Moreland is our . . ." She paused, as though unwilling to continue.

Christian sought to supply the missing word, in his own mind, at least. *Savior? Champion?* He grinned, but found his hostess unable to meet his eye. Was that a blush on her cheeks? Christian decided that she needed color and exposure to wind and sunshine instead of this gloomy tomb of a place. For one giddy moment, he felt like leaping over the table and sweeping her off her feet, as his ancestors might have done. Except he didn't have a ship. Hell, right now he didn't even have a house of his own.

Miss Parkinson cleared her throat and began again. "What I meant to say is that Lord Moreland has been kind enough to answer our summons. If you feel you have some expertise that he lacks, then you should aid him as best you can, Emery."

Emery sniffed, dismissing Christian's skills as too limited for consideration. Annoyed, Christian opened his mouth to note that he had attended Oxford, after all. If he hadn't quite finished, there was no need to mention that, was there? But Emery's smirk stopped him once again. Why not let them believe what they would? His chances of discovering any nefarious goings-on could only be improved if the villain, whether ghostly or corporeal, underestimated him.

So Christian just smiled, content in his own self-knowledge, yet aware that he probably looked like an idiot.

•   •   •

PERHAPS HE *WAS* an idiot. Christian could find no other explanation for his current behavior. After another evening spent kicking his heels alone in the great hall, he had retired to his room, hoping that the specter would decide he was off guard, at least for the night. And after waiting an appropriate interval, to make sure everyone else was asleep, he had sneaked out again to roam the dark rooms like some kind of housebreaker.

He wasn't quite sure what he expected to find. Sir Boundefort floating through the moonlit passages? The three cousins engaged in some sort of skulduggery? Or Miss Parkinson . . . Well, better not to think about his hostess lying abed. Still, he couldn't help wondering where her room was. But then he shook his head. Really, she wasn't his type at all. He leaned more toward sophisticated blond widows who knew how to please a man than to stern, dark-haired women who looked like menials, no matter how luscious their form. Setting his teeth, Christian tried to focus instead on a less corporeal figure.

Slipping through the house with a stealth bred in the bones, he was disappointed to discover that all was still and silent within. Outside, the rain had whipped itself into a full-fledged storm, including thunder and lightning, but it appeared that even the perfect setting couldn't lure Sir Boundefort out. Christian even checked in the shade's favorite spot in the hall, but he could find no sign of the medieval spirit or any earthly accomplices either.

Having kept the small, shuttered lantern he had been given earlier, Christian peered behind the fretwork, but all seemed unchanged. Of course the doors were still locked. A lengthy search of several of the main rooms after dinner hadn't turned up anything except a lot of dust, and although Christian had asked Hobbins to poke around the servants' quarters, his valet had given him a look that stated most equivocally that such duties were below his station. Now, as Christian studied the heavy oak, he wondered if perhaps

Emery was right. The stout portal looked like it hadn't been opened in years.

And that was when he heard it.

Catching his breath, Christian paused to listen. There it was again. Far and above the lash of the wind and rain outside, this was a more rhythmic sound, as if someone were tapping. Or knocking. Silently, Christian walked the length of the passage behind the partition, then the hall itself, where the noise was definitely fainter. Still, he was fairly certain of the direction it was coming from: below.

He was just wondering if there was some other entrance to the old cellars that presumably lay beneath the hall when he caught sight of a light. No flash of lightning illuminating the windows, this was a steady bob of brightness that came from within the house. Unless Sir Boundefort glowed as he floated along, someone else was approaching. Swiftly extinguishing his own lantern, Christian ducked to the side of the doorway, where he waited silently to see who felt the need to visit the great hall in the middle of the night.

Whoever it was moved quietly but not with the noiselessness of an expert, and the light was a beacon that announced the advance. With a smug smile, Christian was inclined to guess the visitor was Emery, the not-so-intelligent scholar, and he nearly stuck out a booted foot in order to trip him. Accidentally, of course. But another sound stopped his movement, a gentle swish that he well recognized from his rather dissolute youth: the sway of a lady's skirts.

And so Christian stood still, watching, as a circle of light came into view, accompanied by a firm but soft tread and a glimpse of dark, utilitarian fabric. The Governess! Christian jerked in surprise as his employer walked into the cavernous room, her lantern's glow practically swallowed by the vast shadows around her. With a frown, Christian leaned against the cold stone, crossed his arms over his chest, and spoke just loud enough for her to hear him.

"Looking for someone?" he drawled into the darkness.

To her credit, she did not flinch, but turned toward him, her lamp held high. Brave woman, Christian thought.

"Yes, actually, my lord. I heard footsteps earlier, and I thought I would investigate," she replied in a matter-of-fact fashion hardly in keeping with their surroundings.

Brave or incredibly foolish, Christian amended. He pushed away from the wall. "Have you gone mad?" he asked in a conversational tone.

"I hardly see how my mental state can be any concern of yours, but, no, I consider myself quite sane," she answered.

Christian found himself growing more than a little annoyed at her wit, as well as her self-possession. "Pardon me, but when you entreated me for help," he said, enjoying her slight wince at his words, "you made yourself and everything here my concern, and I hardly think that wandering about here alone in the dark is a clever decision."

For some reason he was becoming angry, so he drew in a deep breath in an effort to shrug it off. He was normally the most easygoing of men, and he did not intend to let the Governess and her bizarre behavior alter his temperament.

"You would have me confined to my room, unable to walk through my own house?" she asked in her sharpest tone. Her expression was accusatory, even though she was the one acting like a lunatic.

Christian blew out a breath in exasperation. "During the night hours, yes! Didn't you hear the claims at dinner that the great hall isn't safe? What if you are struck by falling stone? What if this ghost of yours attacks you?" With every question he uttered, Christian stepped forward, while she held her ground, her head high.

"I have noticed no debris in the hall," she answered. "Nor do I think any phantom capable of seizing a person."

"And what if your specter is man-made? How will you fend off a human attack, with only your lantern and . . ." Christian trailed off. He was standing in front of her now, quite close, in fact, and realized that she was wearing a robe.

". . . in your nightclothes?" he croaked, his voice suddenly tight, his breeches more so.

Christian swallowed, trying to gather his wits. It wasn't as though she were lounging about in some diaphanous shift. Indeed, her robe appeared to be plain and serviceable and not the slightest bit enticing. So why, then, was he enticed? He let out his breath, trying not to focus on the folds of the material, where a bit of pristine white showed at her throat.

"So you believe that one of my cousins might murder me?" she asked. Her tone was her usual firm one, and yet Christian noted a certain breathy quality in it that he had never heard before.

"Perhaps. How well do you know them?" he asked, his gaze moving up her pale neck to her hair. Let it be loose, he thought. Let it be loose. "Or the footsteps you heard might belong to anyone—a housebreaker, a turned-off servant bent upon revenge, an old enemy of the family . . ."

Again Christian's voice trailed off as he saw that her hair fell neatly down her back in a plait, but was not pulled as tightly from her face as during the day. In that moment of delicious discovery, he decided that he had never seen anything quite as alluring as that long, heavy braid. He shifted his gaze to her face to find her usual severe expression gone. Her eyes, he realized, were a gentle blue that reminded him of something. Lilacs. Christian loosed a low sigh of pleasure at the discovery, while she stared up at him with wonder . . . or was it alarm?

Suddenly thunder boomed outside, a ferocious roar that made her hand dip and the lantern sway. But, to Christian's great disappointment, she didn't jump into his arms as a typical female might have. Instead, she seemed to recover her equanimity with distressing swiftness. Drawing a deep breath, she appeared ready to launch into one of her lectures, but Christian held up a hand.

"Shhh! Did you hear that?" he whispered. The rhythmic

sound was back, or perhaps it had never stopped, Christian having been too distracted by his hostess to notice.

"Of course I heard it! One would be deaf not to," she snapped, though she pitched her voice low.

"Not the thunder, the tapping," Christian replied.

Frowning at him suspiciously, Miss Parkinson cocked her head, and he could tell the moment at which she discerned the sound. Instead of evincing the slightest bit of unease, she turned unerringly toward the fretwork. "Perhaps it is Sir Boundefort," she whispered.

Christian lifted his brows ever so slightly. "What's he doing? Walking with a cane?"

"How would I know? You're the ghost expert."

Christian opened his mouth to argue, then promptly shut it again.

"It sounds like knocking," Miss Parkinson whispered.

Oh, good. That *was* his area of expertise. Unfortunately, the knocking didn't seem to be in answer to anything, nor was it emanating from a bed of any kind.

"And it's coming from underneath us," his hostess said in a hushed voice, rife with excitement. Christian stared at her, momentarily nonplussed by the lack of governess-like expression upon her face. In fact, in the soft light, with her cheeks flushed and her eyes bright, she looked positively . . . beautiful. Christian sucked in a breath as she swung the lamp lower and bent over to examine the old tiles. "Perhaps there is some sort of trapdoor," she said.

At her words Christian jerked his attention from the intriguing curve of her backside back to the business at hand. "If so, you won't find it tonight," he replied. And if, by some miracle she did, he wasn't about to use it. He didn't care if ten men and a boy were down there banging.

"Why not?" she asked, glancing up at him sharply. Christian began to realize that the lovely Miss Parkinson did not like to hear any negatives. This was one determined woman. Too bad he couldn't redirect that steely resolve in a different direction . . .

Christian tried to look just as resolute. "Because it's too dark and far too dangerous. Do you have any idea what's below?"

"No," she admitted.

Christian shook his head at her recklessness. Brave and foolish. "There could be any sort of old cellars, dungeons, passages, and steps, all of them crumbling, and I for one don't care to be entombed down there when either we fall or our knocking friend, who already knows his way around, locks us up!"

At last he seemed to have gotten through to her, for she stopped her searching and straightened, visibly disappointed. And for some reason, seeing that slight droop to her mouth made Christian feel an urge to remedy it. "Aren't there any plans to the house, made perhaps when the additions were built?"

"How would I know?"

"Well, you *are* the owner of the place." When she looked nonplussed, he felt a pang. The Governess obviously wanted to act immediately, and without a firm and immediate plan, she appeared a bit lost. "Tomorrow we'll start searching the library," Christian promised.

Miss Parkinson nodded, tight-lipped. "I just hate to give up now when we've finally made contact. Do you suppose he is trying to direct us to a specific spot?"

"I don't think so. The rapping doesn't seem to be affected by our movements." In truth, he didn't believe the sound had anything to do with Sir Boundefort, beyond a judicious use of rumors about the old fellow's appearances. Someone was trying to scare them away, or, worse, was involved in something nefarious. In either case, Christian thought it prudent for the brave and foolish Miss Parkinson to be safely away.

"I'll walk you back to your room," Christian announced.

"There is really no need," she replied, wariness in her gaze and a certain chill back in her voice.

"I insist," Christian said, inclining his head. Although his hostess looked as though she would like to refuse, there was really no polite way for her to do so. Thankfully, the Governess usually observed the social niceties, so with a stiff nod she stepped forward. Christian grinned as he walked beside her, amused by her reluctance. Was she still concerned about his warning that he would not be caught in a compromising position? Christian wasn't. Indeed, he was beginning to find the notion appealing.

And although he had never been the fanciful sort, moving through the shadowed rooms of the house, alone in their circle of lamplight, was rather novel and inviting. Of course, the fact that she was dressed in her nightclothes, however utilitarian they might be, didn't hurt. And then there were the lilacs. Every few steps a stray draft would send the scent wafting over him until it was all he could do not to seize her—just to see if she was really as delicious as she smelled.

His pulse pounding, his senses roused, Christian discovered their little nighttime stroll was an exercise in restraint, an unaccustomed experience for him, to be sure. The very act of disciplining himself only seemed to heighten his interest in a sort of vicious cycle. By the time they reached the main stairway, all he could think about was rolling around in a big bed draped with lilac blossoms—and Miss Parkinson.

When she halted at the bottom of the stairs and turned, her hand upon the railing, the lamplight gilded her lovely features and Christian was hard-pressed not to touch her. His palms were as damp as a lad's and his breeches tighter than they had been in years. But the object of his attentions held her lamp before her like a weapon, and Christian wouldn't put it past her to clout him with it.

"There. You have seen me to the steps. I assure you that I can find my way to my room," she said in her severest voice. Given his perverse bent since his arrival here, her tone only titillated him further.

"I have no doubt of it," Christian answered, enjoying the flicker of relief in her eyes, especially considering what he planned to say next. "But I will accompany you nonetheless."

She looked nonplussed, opening her mouth as if to speak, and Christian decided that her lips were very tempting when they weren't pursed tightly in disapproval. He would have liked to keep them open, and at that moment fate stepped in and gave him the opportunity. Before she could protest, thunder crashed loudly outside, followed by a great lashing of rain and a gust of wind that rattled the windows and sent a draft swirling around the lantern, fortuitously extinguishing it. As Christian's own lamp was shuttered, they were plunged into complete and utter darkness.

For once, Miss Parkinson seemed to lose her aplomb. She made a sound rather like a squeak, so Christian set down his lantern and reached for her, his hands closing about her shoulders. They were soft and supple beneath his fingers, the material of her robe worn and smooth. Lilacs, faint yet poignant, invaded his senses, and he pulled her closer. A bolt of lightning illuminated her face, wide-eyed and gasping as he gazed down at her.

And then he kissed her.

It was certainly not his usual encounter, staged in the black bleakness at the bottom of Sibel Hall's main stair, nor his usual partner, for Miss Parkinson was no experienced widow or mistress. And yet, for some reason, perhaps his heightened senses, energy surged through him as though diverted from the lightning outside. He felt a certain power in his own attraction to her, to be sure, but that was not all of it. In truth, he couldn't explain it, and couldn't be bothered to. He was too busy enjoying it.

Her lips were lush and sweet, the swift intake of her breath an invitation to explore the richness of her mouth. Heady. Exciting. They fit together perfectly, as if he had been searching for her all of his life, and want flowed through him like life's blood, urging him to press her tightly to him, to carry her up to his bed, to claim her as his own. This night. Every night. *Always*.

Unfortunately his partner didn't seem to feel the same way. Christian gradually realized that she was pushing at him, not in a manner designed to get them closer but to move them apart. He was so startled that it took a while for his brain to process that astonishing development: he was kissing a woman who didn't want to be kissed, at least not by him.

Since such a thing had never happened to him in his lifetime (hell, he was accounted quite a catch and a good lover as well), again he hesitated. Rather desperately, he suspected that if he just kept kissing her, she would come around. Eventually. It was only after she practically unmanned him that he realized his actions could be construed as forcing himself upon her. In the meantime, her knee came into contact with his groin, causing him to groan aloud and release her.

In the darkness he could hear her rapid breaths above his own ragged grunts, and for a long moment they remained thus, only a hairbreadth apart yet as distant as the moon. As Christian grappled for some thought beyond his uncommonly fierce desire, some explanation for such unfathomable behavior, the Governess finally spoke.

"I realize that professional seducers of your ilk feel the need to practice their wiles on any female in the vicinity, but I thought we had an agreement to avoid this . . . type of thing. In fact, I believe that you were the one who made it quite clear upon our acquaintance that ours was to be strictly a business arrangement. Indeed, you demanded that I avoid any situation that could be misconstrued. I might not be your social equal, my lord, but I feel I am entitled to the same courtesy."

Christian nearly recoiled at her biting tone. She hadn't kicked him that hard, but he was beginning to ache. And not just in the groin area. When had he failed so miserably with a woman? Hell, when had he ever failed at all? And then, as if to add insult to injury, she spoke again.

"Believe me, I have been prey to your sort before, the idle, rich young gentlemen of the *ton* who make a jest or game out of trying to ruin the governess or the companion or any other poor female struggling to make a living who chances to fall into their orbit. Perhaps I was powerless before, but I will not stand for such abhorrent behavior in my own household."

Christian flinched, her accusations paining him far worse than any blow. And then, as the gist of her words sank into his muddled mind, Christian stared at her in horror. Was she truly a governess?

"You're a *governess*?" he croaked.

"A companion," she corrected.

Christian gaped, dumbfounded, as he realized that he knew nothing at all about this woman who so intrigued him—and so aroused him. She was a gentlewoman, he was sure of that, but beyond her birth and her straitened circumstances, he knew little enough, and that discovery made him feel even more uncomfortable.

"How? When? Where?" Christian asked, seized by sudden trepidation. Had he met her before? Treated her cavalierly in some long-forgotten encounter? That would explain her scorn. He shifted uneasily. How many dowdy, unassuming figures had he greeted in passing over the years without a thought to their difficult existence?

In response, his hostess drew herself up stiffly. "After the death of my parents, I took a position with Lady Holland, whom I served until just recently, when I learned of my inheritance."

Lady Holland? Christian couldn't place the name, so it was with some measure of relief that he dismissed the possibility of a previous meeting with Miss Parkinson. He could not so easily dismiss his new knowledge of her life, however. Although Christian initially had believed her to be a dependent, the confirmation disturbed him, as did the discovery of her vulnerability. It was one thing to imagine the imperious Governess slapping the wrists of her young charges, quite another to picture her fending off the importunities of full-grown males.

The idea enraged Christian, and the blood that had been

heating his cheeks began to pump through his body, fast and furious. "Who? Who dared touch you?"

"It was nothing, I assure you, and that is how I view it," she answered, dismissing him as easily as she had his kiss.

"Who? Name them, and I shall see they never bother another defenseless female!" Christian said, seized by a sudden wild need for revenge upon the nameless, faceless males who had dared touch this woman. He took a step forward, only to note the soft tread of her slippers as she moved up the stair into the blackness.

For a long moment Christian thought she wasn't going to answer him, and then it came to him, that voice, positively dripping with contempt, floating from somewhere above him. "Why, Lord Moreland, the most recent miscreant was . . . you!" Then he heard her continue lightly up the steps, obviously unafraid of the darkness.

Or of him.

Chapter Five

CHRISTIAN SLEPT LATE, having spent an unusually restless night. He never wasted a lot of time pondering things,
especially his actions. He usually did what he liked within
reason, while adhering to the prescribed codes of honor and
civility that were his birthright. But something had gone
wrong last night, and it left a sour taste in his mouth.

It was not the remnants of the kiss, for that lingered beneath the bitterness like a sip of heaven. In fact, despite his
best efforts, Christian couldn't rid himself of that tantalizing
memory. It had been a long time since he'd been so affected
by a simple kiss. Oh, who was he fooling? He lifted a hand
to rub his face. Hell, he'd *never* been so affected.

Impossible, he told himself. There could never have been
such heat between an experienced man like himself and . . .
Miss Parkinson. He must have imagined it all, his fierce response merely a product of the darkness and the storm and
the tension between them, a desperate diversion from the

gloom that was Sibel Hall. Or was it? He stalked across the room and shouted for Hobbins.

Normally, such thoughts wouldn't give him a moment's pause, let alone cost him a night's sleep. He would simply seek out the lady and prove to himself whether he'd been drunk—perhaps on too much ghostly atmosphere—or dreaming. But in this case there was little chance of a return engagement. For once in his life, he couldn't proceed as he wished. And because of what? A misstep on his part? Miss Parkinson's overreaction?

Splashing some cold water on his face, Christian snapped the towel and jerked on fresh linen, his even temper upended by a surge of frustration, a heady mix combined with his underlying guilt and outrage. Only the entrance of Hobbins, wearing his usual stoic expression, stopped Christian from swearing aloud.

"Difficult night, my lord?" the valet asked, after Christian ruined his second neckcloth.

"No," Christian lied. "And what does it matter how the damned thing is tied? It's not as though anyone will notice in this dismal place."

"One has a responsibility to one's appearance," Hobbins pointed out, as he presented a third strip of linen.

Christian frowned but took it, drawing a deep breath as he once again attempted a fashionable knot.

"If I may say so, you seem extraordinarily tense this morning," Hobbins commented, obviously having observed his employer's ill temper.

Christian sighed. He knew the old retainer would not be satisfied until he gave some sort of explanation, and an unsatisfied valet made for chilly relations. "For your information, Hobbins, I find this task extremely onerous," Christian said, willing to admit that much. After all, it was the truth. As far as it went.

"The ghost, or at least someone, finally decided to make himself heard last night, but I couldn't even reach him, let alone discover who or what was behind his antics." He slanted a glance at Hobbins. "I don't suppose you found the missing keys?"

"No, my lord," Hobbins answered without hesitation.

Had the valet even looked? Christian had no idea, but he knew better than to get the old fellow's back up by asking him.

"I presume the *antics* occurred behind the locked doors?" Hobbins said.

Christian nodded. "Or least *below* them. The noises we heard were definitely coming from beneath the great hall, but there doesn't appear to be any other entrance to the old cellars."

"*We*, my lord?" At Hobbins's dry tone, Christian hesitated, his fingers halting their movements before he recovered himself and finished the knot as casually as possible. It was not his usual skillful design, but it would have to do. And, in the end, what was the difference? There was no one here of note to see him except Miss Parkinson, and she had made her feelings quite clear.

"Miss Parkinson," Christian muttered, half in bitter recognition of his thoughts and half in answer to Hobbins's query. "She came down to investigate my footsteps."

"A redoubtable female," Hobbins remarked.

"An idiot, more likely," Christian retorted. "She's lucky I wasn't some housebreaker intent upon the silver. Or her virtue." The minute the words were out of his mouth he flinched, for they were much too close to the truth for comfort. He paused, struck by a sudden doubt, and slanted a glance at his valet.

"Hobbins, do you think I'm conceited?" he asked.

"Certainly not, my lord!" Hobbins answered, suitably affronted by the very suggestion.

Christian was slightly mollified. He had never thought so either. After a lifetime of being pursued, however, he found the notion that a woman might actually refuse him rather startling—and mystifying. It seemed to him that from the moment he had assumed the title, barely out of his boyhood, the female population had been enamored of him. Too enamored, he thought sometimes. It was one thing to enjoy a choice of willing partners, quite another to be the object of marital traps and scheming mamas.

Although Christian had always complained about such treatment, now he wondered if it might be preferable to rejection. The novelty of the sensation did nothing to diminish its impact, and just the thought of his ignominious defeat kept his mood sour. He shrugged, trying to shake it off, but it clung, intensified by her implication that he was no better than some randy old lecher attacking the household help.

"Surely Miss Parkinson did not accuse you of being conceited?" Hobbins asked.

"I stole a kiss, that's all," Christian muttered, once again engaged in a dialogue with himself as well as his valet. As far as he was concerned, Miss Parkinson was making entirely too much of it. Unfortunately, it seemed as though he was making too much of it as well, for the memory of that little encounter remained incredibly powerful. The body that had been pressed to his oh so briefly was more luscious than he had imagined, and her mouth—Christian set his teeth, knowing that it was better not to think about her lips. He had a feeling that that brief taste would haunt him far more thoroughly than any specter.

"If you don't mind my saying so, my lord, Miss Parkinson is not your usual sort," Hobbins said.

"How well I know it!" Christian said.

"What I mean, my lord, is that she seems to be a genteel young woman, despite her circumstances, and might not be accustomed to the flirtatious behavior of the *ton*," Hobbins clarified delicately, using a polite euphemism for the sort of dallying that was rampant among the social elite.

"Well, she needn't act as though I were forcing myself upon her! I'll be damned if I'm going to apologize for one little kiss." The more Christian thought about it, the more annoyed he became, and the prospect of facing his hostess did nothing to ease his temper.

As he stalked across the room, he decided it would be

best to dismiss the entire episode and get on with the task of ridding the house of the alleged specter. Then, when he returned home, he might just have to break the *other* leg of a certain interfering earl, who was responsible for his grandson's sudden dose of humility.

As he stalked toward the door, a gust of wind from the open window sent a burst of moisture his way and set his teeth on edge. He swung toward his valet in exasperation. "And why does it always have to be raining here?"

Hobbins, stoic as ever, refrained from replying to that question. "Breakfast time has long passed, but I managed to retain some items on the sideboard for your repast," he said, dismissing Christian and his ill mood with the ease of long service.

THE DINING ROOM was deserted, much to Christian's relief. Yet the very notion that he should be relieved to escape some woman's censure annoyed him further. Though he was not about to hide himself away just to avoid her, he could not ignore the fact that his hostess had always looked at him with some semblance of disapproval. Now that she seemingly had a reason, he could just imagine the reception he would get. Christian scowled as he put the little remaining meat upon his plate, along with some stone-cold toast. He had never let anyone else's judgment, true or false, affect him before, so why did he care what the Governess thought, especially when she seemed to prefer the negative view?

Perhaps he ought to give her something to be really angry about, Christian thought with a sudden grin. While he ate, he conjured up several delightful plans, ranging from simply tossing Miss Parkinson over his shoulder to finding the key to her room and using it. That would give her plenty to squawk about, he decided. Then, just as he was trying to imagine what he would do there, the object of his musings came into the room. He could tell because the temperature dropped several degrees. Well, that, and the whiff of lilacs.

Christian didn't even turn around. "You need not fear any further lapses on my part," he said, determined to get the business over with as quickly as possible. "You were perfectly right. I don't know what came over me." In truth, he was not lying. Why this composed, dowdy sort should be the one to stir his dormant passions, he still had no idea.

Perhaps it was her very unavailability. After all, his ancestors weren't remembered for stealing off with tavern wenches. It was the forbidden ones who aroused their lust, the very women who had become his ancestresses, Christian thought.

These days, he was expected to tryst with the ladies of the demimonde or bored widows of the *ton* and to marry one of the young ladies of nobility who were foisted each year upon the marriage market. Gentlemen did not give their attentions to those under their protection, menials and employees, and most especially not to decent, penniless women of good background. Such females were not for marrying or dallying. So, naturally, his piratical nature made him want one of them.

"Well?" he asked into the silence. Had his hostess no comment? No lecture to give him? With a sigh, Christian turned around to face not just Miss Parkinson, who had flushed a lovely shade of rose, but her cousin Mercia as well.

"Oh, my lord, we are so excited that you have finally made contact!" the older woman trilled.

Christian blinked. Was she talking about what he was thinking about? No wonder the Governess was blushing.

"With the specter," his hostess said hastily. "Cousin Mercia is glad to hear that Sir Boundefort is stirring."

"We have set the colonel to watch, but so far he has heard nothing. Perhaps the storm roused our ancestor," Mercia suggested. "Or perhaps our ancestor roused the storm. Emery claims it was a manifestation of his anger."

"Whose, Emery's or the phantom's?" Christian asked.

For a moment, the older lady eyed him blankly, then she giggled. "Oh, my lord, you are too clever."

"Isn't he, though?" the Governess asked in a dry tone that put a decidedly different meaning to her words. Indeed, she was wearing her disapproving expression, and Christian was tempted to stick his tongue out at her . . . or in her . . . He rose abruptly.

"Are you going back to the great hall to coax him forth?" Mercia asked breathlessly.

"I'll do my best," Christian drawled. "But you go on ahead. I want to speak to my, uh, your cousin for a moment," he added with a grim smile.

Nodding, the little woman left the room, leaving him alone with his hostess, who looked anything but pleased by the prospect. Christian could only stare in amazement at her unhappy visage. Why, of all the women in the world, did this one so affect him?

"I can't think of a thing we have to discuss privately," Miss Parkinson said, tilting her nose into the air as if he even smelled bad. Christian took a deep breath just to prove to himself that he didn't.

"Can't you?" he asked, stepping forward and grinning wickedly at his nemesis, er . . . hostess. She held her ground, brave, foolish creature that she was, but Christian could see the hesitation in her eyes. She wanted to flee. Good. At least he had some power over her.

"How about the little fact that you seem to have announced to the world at large our rendezvous . . ." Christian paused, enjoying the shocked look that crossed her face. ". . . with Sir Boundefort?"

To her credit, the Governess recovered herself quickly, her expression changing from outrage to rather annoyed inquiry. "And why shouldn't I speak of what happened last night? I thought that was the reason you were here, to banish the ghost?"

Ignoring her little dig, Christian leaned against the doorjamb and crossed his arms over his chest. "And just suppose this spectral fellow is really made out of flesh and blood?"

"Isn't that for you to find out?" she asked, arching her dark brows just a little.

"Well, it would be a bit easier if we were more circumspect with our knowledge, using whatever information we come across to our own advantage," Christian replied. He didn't necessarily suspect any of the cousins of knocking about down below. Indeed, he couldn't imagine the colonel or the scholar or the little old lady skulking in the cellars making odd noises, but just in case one of them, most likely Emery, was behind it, any element of surprise was gone.

Watching the play of expression upon her face, Christian knew the moment she understood him. "Are you accusing someone in this house—my own cousins—of perpetrating a fraud?"

Christian shrugged. "I'm not saying one of them did it, but now everyone in the whole house, in the whole countryside probably, will know what we discovered. And will have a chance to cover their tracks."

The look she gave him next was priceless, a kind of reluctant admiration, as if she wanted to apologize for her blunder but couldn't quite bring herself to do so. That made two of them. Christian grinned in response, which of course ruined the effect at once.

Suddenly his hostess became brisk and businesslike. And accusatory. "Well, you should have warned me not to speak of it if you wanted to pursue that course." Dismissing her own culpability with apparent ease, she eyed him with expectation. "Now what do you intend to do?"

Christian wanted to say, Kiss you again, but tamped down both the words and the urge. "I had hoped to look for some plans to the house, but now I suggest we find a way below the hall without delay, before our phantom can remove evidence of his activities."

Miss Parkinson nodded stiffly, and Christian decided that one thing, at least, he had not imagined the night before. She really was lovely in a unique sort of way. But that hair! It was too tight by half. The Governess needed loosening up in the worst way. Christian imagined himself pulling out the pins, one by one. His breath caught for a moment before he dismissed the vision with a vengeance. If he touched that coiffure, he'd probably get a poke in the eye for his trouble.

With a frown, he turned his attention back to the ghost. "Let us call for some lanterns. We shall probably need them." When she nodded again, he summoned the audacity to take her arm for a stroll toward the hall. "So, tell me, how did everyone react to the news?"

Pointedly stepping away from his touch, the Governess gave him a reproving look. Did she have any other kind?

"They reacted as anyone would," she said.

"And how does *anyone* react when informed of strange knockings below their residence?" Christian asked, amused.

At that she had the grace to appear chagrined, but only, Christian suspected, for a moment. "Well, I certainly didn't tell everyone, as you so rashly assumed," she said. "I saw no need to inform the servants, as it would only . . . confuse them."

"Frighten more of them into fleeing, you mean?" he asked.

The Governess looked at him with annoyance, and he nearly laughed aloud. So much for her brief chagrin. "And as for your cousins?" he prodded. "No one turned red in the face or appeared to be disturbed by the news?"

She shook her head. "I'd like to know upon what you base your supposition that someone here is the cause of haunting."

Christian shrugged. "If, as I presume, the ghost is man-made, then it stands to reason that anyone in the vicinity would be a suspect."

She seemed affronted. "With that sort of reasoning, then even I could be responsible!"

Christian shrugged again, enjoying her outrage. She was

so easily riled. "But I know you weren't directly responsible because you were there."

"Yes, I was there," she echoed, and they both fell into silence, the sparring mood between them chased away by the memory of what else had befallen them the night before—when they were alone together.

Miss Parkinson cleared her throat as they neared the great hall. "As for the reactions of the others, the colonel was most surprised. He doesn't seem to believe in spirits."

"Though he doesn't quite disbelieve, either," Christian said.

Miss Parkinson nodded. "Cousin Mercia was most excited, being rather a proponent of Sir Boundefort's."

"And Emery?" Christian prodded.

She slanted him a glance. "Emery is a scholar, and as such he keeps an open mind."

"Ah," Christian noted. He couldn't very well say anything more, as they had reached their destination, where he found all three cousins eyeing him expectantly, Mercia with obvious glee, the colonel more warily, and Emery with his usual ill will. Christian decided he just couldn't wait to tell the earl how much he had enjoyed this little jaunt the old man had sent him on.

And then they all began talking at once.

Christian silenced them with an upheld hand. "Does anyone know where a copy of the plans for the house might be?" he asked. When they all shook their heads, he turned to Emery. "What about you? Surely, in all your research, you have come across some mention of the original building or additions?"

Emery glared at him. "No, my lord. I'm afraid such things hold no interest for me," he answered with a sniff.

Christian narrowed his eyes for a moment, then decided against argument. "Well, I guess we will just have to open the doors and discover what we may."

"B-but you can't!" Emery protested.

"And why is that?" Christian asked, finding the young man's reaction most interesting.

"Well, I thought the doors were locked!" the colonel blustered.

"It's dangerous down there. Any fool can see that—else why close off the cellars?" Emery said with a snide superiority that was beginning to grate on Christian's nerves.

"I didn't think anyone knew exactly what lay behind the doors," Christian commented with narrowed eyes.

"Perhaps Sir Boundefort wants us to go down below," Mercia suggested.

"More likely he is warning us against it," Emery said.

"I say, all this discussion is moot unless you plan to break down the doors," the colonel said. He paused. "You don't plan to, do you?"

"No, I don't plan to break them down," Christian said. "But I'm hoping to pick the locks."

That little announcement silenced the entire hall, the arguing and the chatter dying away in a heartbeat as everyone stopped to stare at him, presumably dumbfounded that a viscount of the realm would even suggest such a thing. Christian grinned. His pirate heritage came in handy at times, though it was a friend of rather dubious talents who had taught him this trick years ago. Unfortunately, he was not in the habit of using the skill and so wasn't too certain of his success.

But he was rarely plagued by doubt, and so he turned to his hostess. "One of your hairpins, please?" he asked, holding out his hand. He would like to remove all of them, but he didn't see how he could justify that request.

For her part, Miss Parkinson simply stared at him in horror. Was she that attached to her hideous coiffure? She looked positively flummoxed for a long moment, and Christian wondered if she needed some sort of assistance. Of course, he would happily provide some, of a physical nature . . .

"Am I to understand you can enter through locked doors?" she finally asked.

Christian shrugged. "I'm going to do my best."

Miss Parkinson opened her mouth as if to launch into one of her lectures, but shut it again as she looked around the room at the avid faces of her relatives. Perhaps she feared that he would pick *her* lock? Christian felt his body's immediate interest in that idea and firmly quelled it.

Obviously the Governess did not approve of his skill, no matter how helpful it might turn out to be, but what choice did she have? The only other way to get through the locked doors was to take an ax to them, and Christian didn't feel like expending that much energy. He waited, expectantly, until she finally lifted her hands to her hair and removed one pin of the far too many that he was certain were lodged there.

She dropped it, still warm from her touch, into his hand, and Christian drew in a sharp breath. Just to catch a whiff of lilacs, of course. He stared down at it for a moment, unaccountably affected, and realized there was something about the Governess that seemed to destroy his usual composure. Loosing the breath, he walked toward the fretwork. "Colonel, could you bring one of the lanterns?"

"Aha! Most certainly," the old fellow said, following close behind. They all did, filling up the narrow passage, but Christian was rather glad of it. He liked having every one of them where he could keep an eye on them, just in case. Halting before the farthest door, he knelt, carefully bent the metal of the hairpin, and inserted it in the old lock. He made a few delicate maneuvers and with gratifying swiftness he heard a click.

Someone gasped, and the colonel slapped him a bit too heartily on the back. "Well done, my lord, well done!" he exclaimed. Christian slanted a glance at his hostess. Her expression remained what he would call dubious. He grinned, then pulled the handle.

The heavy wooden door swung inward easily, and Christian was not surprised to find the opening clear. No cobwebs hung in his face, no crumbled stones impeded his path, and no centuries of dust lay thick upon the floor. Someone had found a way in here, and recently, for the stone flags looked to be swept, just like the tiles in the hall itself.

Christian lifted his lantern with anticipation, only to find himself facing a stone wall. For a moment he wondered whether the whole area had been bricked up, but when he peered further inside, he saw that the passage continued to the left. A relatively even surface stretched in that direction, but he could see no sign of steps. Perhaps this way led to the old kitchens instead of to the cellars.

"Well? What's there? What do you see?" Various voices assailed Christian as he was crowded forward, and now he wished that all the residents of Sibel Hall were not present and bearing down upon him. He would prefer just Miss Parkinson, he thought, his lips curving slightly. Turning, he glanced her way. Unlike the others, she was not straining to see, but standing calmly nearby, waiting. The image struck him forcefully. How long had she been waiting? And for what?

Christian shook his head at such whimsy. His hostess was just keeping her distance, as was her wont, but he had no doubt that she would charge ahead into the darkness at the first opportunity. Christian let his gaze rove over her figure, taking in the drab gown of some indeterminate shade. Any other woman would have insisted upon changing her gown or donning an apron before entering the passage. Of course, few other women would even have wanted to go. Against his will, Christian felt a sharp surge of admiration, as well as an odd dose of kinship.

"Well?" she asked him sharply, thereby breaking whatever spell was upon him.

Christian sighed. "I suppose you are determined to come along."

"Of course," she answered.

"Well, then, watch your skirts," he said. He glanced

around at the others. "Colonel, would you please stay here, in case we get into any trouble?"

"Certainly, my lord!" The man actually looked relieved not to have to venture into the blackness, and Christian bit back a smile. It faded when Emery stepped forward.

"I'll have a look, if you don't mind," he said in a proprietary manner.

Actually, Christian *did* mind. "I thought you were concerned about the dangerous state of the building," he said in a subtle taunt.

Emery flushed. "I still think it's unsafe to go blindly rushing in there, but since I have the most expertise, I'd better go along."

"I thought you didn't know anything about the plans of the house," Christian said.

"Nevertheless, Emery's knowledge can only serve us well," Miss Parkinson said, effectively ending the standoff, and Christian's questioning as well. He frowned at her, but she was already moving past him, holding her lantern high.

"I'll wait here," Mercia trilled from behind him. "As much as I would like to explore, I suspect I would only impede your progress."

"Perhaps we shall catch a glimpse of Sir Boundefort, as you roust him from his den!" the colonel called jovially from behind.

Stepping ahead of his hostess, Christian reached out a hand to keep her back and adopted one of her reproving looks. "Please stay behind me," he said, including Emery in that bit of advice. Although Miss Parkinson appeared a bit surprised, apparently she decided not to argue, which was a good thing for her. Sibel Hall might be her house, but he was the ghost . . . router.

With his newly acquired architectural eye, Christian studied the walls of the passage, but the structure seemed sound enough. Indeed, he was hard-pressed to determine exactly why the whole area had been closed off, but his wondering came to an end when he reached another door, even larger and thicker than the earlier one.

"It goes nowhere, just as I thought," Emery said with a snort. Christian was inclined to point out that the alleged scholar had never tendered such an opinion, at least publicly, but he held his tongue. Again, the door was locked, and Christian reached into his coat to retrieve his hostess's hairpin. He stroked it absently, aware that his possession of such a personal object bespoke an intimacy that they did not share.

"Can you do it again?" Miss Parkinson said, from over his shoulder, and Christian tried not to imagine those words in any other context.

"I'll do my best," he managed, his lips curving involuntarily. But whether his hostess harbored a new admiration or simply a continued disgust for his skills Christian couldn't tell. Setting down his lantern, he concentrated.

"Oh, this is ridiculous!" Emery said, stomping about and kicking up dust.

"Could you please stay in one place?" Christian asked.

"What seems to be the problem?" his hostess asked.

"Patience, my dear Miss Parkinson. These things take time. You can't rush true talent. Ah! Patience is rewarded," he said with a grin as the lock clicked.

Pocketing the hairpin once more, he rose to his feet, but when he grasped the latch and pushed, the old door barely budged. Perhaps the ghost or his minions had not passed this way? Christian didn't know whether to be encouraged or disappointed by the thought as the creaking hinges protested and the heavy oak swung open at last.

Disappointed, he decided as the heavy smell of rain and damp fresh air struck him. Unless this was some sort of primitive conservatory, the passage led outside. Reaching up to push aside a bough of some sort, he saw that they were in a tiny courtyard, surrounded by the additions and outbuildings of Sibel Hall.

"I imagine this route led to the old kitchens, which presumably were detached and either burned down or were torn apart years ago," Christian said. He stepped aside, but not too far, in order to allow Miss Parkinson a view. Unfortunately she managed to keep her distance while peeking out.

"A waste of time, just as I told you," Emery crowed, triumphant.

"I believe you claimed the place was dangerous," Christian muttered. "Not dismantled."

But Emery was already hurrying back the way they had come. Shrugging, Christian secured the exterior door and turned to follow.

"But the noises were coming from below the hall, not outside," Miss Parkinson said from her place beside him.

"Yes. Perhaps we shall find a way down through the other locked door," Christian said, slowly retracing his steps. He was in no particular hurry, since he was closeted rather closely with his hostess in a dark passage and found the possibilities intriguing. When he lifted his lantern high, however, he saw that Emery was positioned near the entrance, waiting for them.

Christian frowned. Too bad a crumbling stone couldn't fall on the scholar's head—but the passage appeared perfectly solid. Perhaps he ought to dislodge one, Christian thought wickedly. If he could come up with that idea, though, presumably so could Emery, which was not a comforting notion. Christian vowed to keep himself alert to any dangers, accidental or man-made, especially since the white-faced youth viewed him with his usual degree of rancor—and something else. Some sort of agitation?

Christian looked around the passage carefully before proceeding but could find no evidence of ghosts, real or manufactured, or anything that would stir up the so-called scholar. Emery continued his nervous behavior, however, gesturing for them to precede him in an attempt to rush them out the door. What was he up to?

"You go on," Christian suggested, when Emery seemed determined to usher him through.

"No, no, you go ahead, my lord," Emery argued, but his sudden attempt at civility was not convincing.

Christian remained where he was and moved his lantern to view the young man closely. Emery appeared a bit panicked by the bright light, but it wasn't the boy's expression that arrested Christian. Indeed, it was what lay behind him that was interesting. Above the youth's blond head there was a faint yet unmistakable glow of light. And Christian was guessing it wasn't a halo.

Inching forward, he felt a slight draft of cooler air that confirmed his suspicions. Whether Emery's position was innocent or deliberate, he stood directly in front of another opening in the passage.

Chapter Six

WHEN EMERY JUST stared at him in a belligerent manner, Christian was tempted to knock him out of the way. But he restrained himself nobly. For his hostess's sake.

"Would you please step aside?" he asked as politely as possible under the circumstances.

"Why?" Emery said, his eyes darting nervously between Christian and the Governess, who stood nearby.

"So that I can find out where this opening leads," Christian explained. He paused to flash the young man a smile. "Unless there's something in there you don't want me to see?"

While Emery sputtered a denial, Christian moved past him into a large room, with Miss Parkinson not far behind. The pale light of a gray day entered through a tall window set high in the stone wall, casting the space into gloom that the lantern did little to dispel. But even in the dimness Christian could tell that the place was empty of anything except cobwebs and dust.

Despite Emery's dire warnings, Christian noted, the floor was solid and the ceiling seemed intact, as well as the walls. He walked the perimeter, searching more closely, but no other passages or doors were visible. And there were no stairs to take them beneath the old tiles.

"This is probably the old buttery," Christian said to his hostess, who was standing in the center of the room, gazing about curiously.

"But why close it off?" she asked.

Christian shrugged. "Perhaps because it was part of the old kitchen passage, but you could certainly open up the space and utilize it," he added, though he had no idea what for, especially since the great hall itself appeared to get little use.

"I? I have no intention of making any changes in the house," Miss Parkinson said. "But I will certainly mention the fact to anyone interested in buying the place." She paused to give Christian a rather accusatory look, as though the public would be clamoring to purchase this wretched building if only he would complete his task and rout the ghost. Ignoring her implicit scold, Christian made a gracious bow and gestured for her to precede him.

Emery remained at the door, seemingly uninterested in viewing the old buttery. Perhaps because he had seen it before? But if so, why had he acted so anxious, as though he were concealing the place from view? Christian could only shake his head. Perhaps he was growing too suspicious.

"See, it's nothing. Just an empty old room," Emery said with an air of triumph.

"Spoken like a true scientist," Christian noted dryly as he passed. He had not failed to notice the boy watching both Miss Parkinson and himself like a hawk. Either Emery was hiding something or he had some other reason for his strange behavior. Christian frowned as a thought struck him that was far more insidious than any specter. Did Emery covet Miss Parkinson for himself?

Christian swung around to glare at the young man with a

new enmity. Normally he was an even-tempered sort, and he certainly had never come to blows over a female. But right now he felt like one of his ancestors, ready to do murder over a woman who had caught his eye.

He wondered just how distant the cousins were. Of course, the boy was too young for Miss Parkinson. Not that she was old. She was probably younger than she looked, for those dowdy clothes and tightly wrapped hair surely added years. Christian turned an assessing glance upon her and guessed her to be a nice, ripe twenty-two. But Emery looked like a gangly sixteen. And as far as Christian could tell, the boy had no home, no money, and no prospects. Perhaps he intended to leech off his cousin permanently.

The notion roused some previously dormant protective instincts, and much to Christian's surprise, he was seized by a determination to save Miss Parkinson from herself—or at least from Emery. But short of packing the boy off or pummeling him into submission, Christian was at a loss as to just how he could accomplish that task, especially when his hostess would no doubt fail to appreciate his aid. Nor would she heed any warning he might tender, being the most stubborn woman he had ever encountered.

Scowling at her back, Christian shut the door but left it unlocked. There was no point in tripping the mechanism again when the passage didn't lead anywhere particularly interesting or dangerous. And just in case someone tried to hide there, Christian wanted to have easy access. The lack of dust had revealed that he wasn't the first person to explore the area.

When he turned once again toward the group, Miss Parkinson was explaining their meager findings to Mercia and the colonel. Watching her speak, and contemplating her slender form dressed in the drab, ill-fitting gown, Christian knew a surge of possessiveness, followed by an equally absurd conjecture. What if Miss Parkinson looked with favor upon that fledgling?

Christian shook his head, unable to conceive of such a

thing as any female preferring Emery to himself. She certainly didn't seem to show the upstart any regard, but then, would the Governess actually display any such emotions? And wasn't she always mentioning Emery's supposed scholarship, as if she positively revered his mind? A mind that left Christian singularly unimpressed.

Lost in his brooding, Christian needed a moment to realize that the hall had grown silent, and he discovered that the others were eyeing him expectantly.

"Don't be discouraged, my lord," Mercia advised him with a kindly pat on the arm. "I'm sure the next door will prove to be more rewarding. Perhaps you shall find Sir Boundefort in his earthly prison! Wouldn't that be lovely?"

"Quite," Christian muttered, stifling a shudder. Rather than see the specter, he would prefer to get his hands on it, especially if Emery were responsible. With that cheering thought, Christian knelt before the second door, pulled out the hairpin, and set to work.

The lock soon gave a satisfactory click, and he pocketed the hairpin once more, without bothering to return it to his hostess. After all, he might need it again, Christian thought. It was not as though he intended to hold on to the thing as a keepsake or any such sentimental nonsense.

Grasping the latch, Christian pushed on the door, and it swung open easily, suggesting that someone else had been this way as well. He lifted his lantern and glanced downward, seeing the telltale sweep of comparatively clean flags at his feet. This was no passage, but a room, though not quite as large as the old buttery. Perhaps it had once been a stillroom or pantry. Holding the light high, Christian moved forward, letting his gaze rove over the old stone walls and the litter of cast-off furniture and items long forgotten.

Was it nothing more than a storage place? Christian felt a surge of disappointment, but continued searching. His eyes probed the darkness until . . . *there*. At the rear on the right, a deeper blackness gave him hope. He stepped forward, even as he heard Emery braying warnings behind him, until he stood before an arched opening, where at last he found stairs leading downward.

A wave of dank air and darkness met him, but no whiff of danger, and despite Emery's cautions, Christian could see that the steps were wide, smooth stone. Now, if only the young pup didn't try to push him down them . . . Christian moved toward the wall, keeping it nearly at his back as he descended. And finally he found himself at the bottom, looking upon the old vaulted cellars.

A quick lift of the lantern revealed that no dungeons or worse awaited him. The floor appeared even and free of debris, and the massive stone arches, a masterpiece of architecture, certainly were in no danger of collapsing. So much for the scholar's opinion.

Christian turned his head to point that out, but the youth was not behind him. Instead, he found himself looking into Miss Parkinson's face, deliciously near. Drawing a sharp breath, he swallowed his snide comment and swung back around to study the cellars, though he would have preferred to study his hostess.

Below the great hall the vast space was divided into two compartments, which was not unusual for buildings of this age. In more-fortified early structures, such an area might have been used for housing soldiers, and even here that purpose might have been served at one time long ago. More likely it had always been used for storage, as was the case now, for a jumble of old furniture, crates, and assorted items lined the walls, including what appeared to be a full suit of armor.

"That might be worth something to the antiquarians," Christian observed, nodding toward the piece. But when Miss Parkinson followed his gaze, she started. Perhaps she was not quite as fearless as she pretended. Christian bit back a smile at the realization.

"Easy. Don't fall," he said, seizing the opportunity to reach out and steady her. He was so close he could feel the heat of her body, and his hands itched to close over her narrow waist. He half hoped that the ghost would make an appearance, if only to send her skittering into his arms. Nothing too frightening, of course. Christian didn't want her incapacitated, just a little clingy. But he could not imagine the Governess ever clinging, no matter what the provocation.

As if to prove him correct, she slipped from his hold, moving past him to wander the stone floor. She seemed to be a bright spot in the darkness, and Christian wondered rather wildly whether she possessed some inner glow. When he saw that she held her own lantern, he felt a measure of relief, along with chagrin at his own foolishness. Clearly he was smitten beyond reason.

Holding her light high in a steady hand, Miss Parkinson seemed to have recovered herself, for she showed no signs of quailing before a shadowy figure of medieval prowess, whether it be the armor or Sir Boundefort himself. Once more she appeared to be a fearless warrior woman, protectress of scholars, benefactress to shiftless relatives, and nemesis to specters. Better get out of the way, ghosts, Christian thought, grinning.

"It looks to be all a jumble down here," she observed. "What do you suppose caused the noises we heard?"

"Probably some old shutter, or the wind," Emery said with a sniff. The sound of the young man's voice, coming close behind him, made Christian jerk around in surprise. When had Emery joined them? Christian realized he had better quit mooning over his hostess and keep his wits about him—or he might find himself with a knife in the back, either figuratively or literally.

"As you can see, there's nothing unusual down here except a mess that is liable to fall upon you," Emery said.

"A mess that might bear looking into," Christian replied as he stepped forward. Indeed, it appeared that some of the items had been hastily pushed to the side, and recently, from the looks of the marks upon the stone floor. *Interesting.* The sweeps of dust were so revealing, in fact, that Christian wondered if he might actually find a footprint somewhere that could give him an idea who had been down here.

"Emery's right," Christian said then, his lips quirking at the lie. "These things might not be too stable. Better stay in the center, away from them all."

His advice was met with a questioning look from Miss Parkinson. Obviously, she was wondering how an eight-foot-tall cupboard that looked like it was carved out of solid oak might suddenly come crashing down upon them. Too smart for her own good. Maybe even for mine, Christian thought. With a shrug, he worked his way forward, keeping an eye surreptitiously on the stone flags at his feet. But he was not so preoccupied that he failed to notice the figure darting ahead.

"Going somewhere, Emery?" Christian called, even as he hurried his own steps.

"I—I . . . No. I'm just looking around."

"Well, let's stay together, shall we?" Christian said, giving the boy a significant look. He walked to where Emery stood, at the opening to the second chamber, and lifted his lantern, only to nearly drop it to the floor in surprise.

"What's this?" Christian said, hurrying into one of the large bays. There several old casks stood in a corner, covered with dust and cobwebs, as though undisturbed for centuries, but Christian barely glanced at them as he moved past, heading toward the gleam of old glass glinting in the lantern light. Setting the lamp down, he dusted off one dark bottle, hardly daring to hope, then lifted it. The nearly noiseless swish of liquid inside made him loose a long, low breath of satisfaction.

"What is it?" Miss Parkinson called from the other chamber.

"A wine cellar!" Christian said. "We shall drink well tonight!" Perhaps a finely aged Bordeaux would improve the taste of Sibel Hall's dreadful fare.

The casks, of course, had long gone bad, if they even still

held their contents, but the bottles, properly corked, promised untold delights.

Although Christian was tempted to seize his hostess and swing her round in celebration, Miss Parkinson looked singularly unimpressed. Her dubious expression and a sound from across the room prevented him from indulging in at least a quick taste, if not a quick toss. Instead, he turned toward the noise just in time to see Emery moving suspiciously among some old crates.

Christian bit back a curse at his own inattention. *Again.* While he had allowed himself to be distracted by his find, Emery no doubt had trampled or erased any footsteps that had existed, whether by deliberate act or carelessness it was impossible to say.

"What are you doing?" Christian snapped at the young man.

Emery jerked around abruptly. "N-nothing," he stammered. Ever suspicious, Christian stalked to where Emery stood and held his lantern high. At first he could see nothing out of the ordinary, but as he leaned closer he saw that something had been moved. One of the crates, perhaps? Pushing past Emery, he ignored Miss Parkinson's protest and set his lantern down, intending to investigate the area. But just as he knelt, his lamp went out, plunging him into blackness.

In the total silence that followed, all Christian could hear was his own breathing, followed by Miss Parkinson's gasp and a rustle of movement. Quickly he ducked away from where Emery had been, just in case the fellow was bent on putting him out of commission for good.

"Lord Moreland!" Miss Parkinson's calm voice was a reassurance.

"Over here," Christian called, even as he moved a bit more to keep Emery confused. His bearings were good, so he figured he could find his way back to the stairs even in the dark, but he would rather not attempt it. Especially with Emery lurking about. So the glow of Miss Parkinson's lantern, when it arrived, was most welcome.

"What happened?" she asked.

"Emery kicked over the lantern," Christian said, hazarding a guess as he looked down and saw the lamp on its side.

"If you hadn't practically knocked me down, it wouldn't have happened," Emery said, effectively confirming Christian's speculation. The young man was responsible, all right, but was the mishap accidental or deliberate?

"I did not practically knock you down," Christian said, not bothering to hide his contempt. "And you're lucky these crates didn't catch fire and send the whole place up," he added, as he righted his lantern.

Emery blanched but made no further excuse or argument, perhaps stunned to silence by what might have happened. Christian could only hope the peace and quiet would last more than a moment.

"Perhaps we should remove all these old things to prevent such an occurrence," Miss Parkinson said. The Governess looked a bit shaken but game, as always, and Christian spared a moment of admiration for her fortitude.

"I don't see why you must come down here and muck about, anyway," Emery said in a petulant tone. He had recovered his tongue—and his ill temper—all too quickly. "So far all you've done is filch some wine."

Christian straightened himself to his full six feet two inches and stared down his nose at the boy in his best imitation of the earl's most regal pose. Then he lifted his brows ever so slightly, daring the youth to say anything more. The boy paled again and started sputtering.

"Emery!" Miss Parkinson cut in. "I realize that our nerves are strained by the falling lantern, but there is no call to insult his lordship."

"There was no call for him to push me, either!" Emery said mulishly.

Christian had to stifle the urge to turn to the Governess and proclaim, "He started it!" Instead, he tried to stand on his dignity or whatever noble mien he was supposed to possess. It was the correct recourse, apparently, for Emery soon sputtered an apology.

"I beg your pardon. My lord," he added, in a less than sincere tone.

But having his bellyful of dramatics, Christian had already turned his attention back to his investigation. Before Emery could do anything to stop him, he reached out to shove the nearest crate out of the way. And what he saw made him smile grimly. Stepping back, he gestured to his hostess with a sweep of his arm.

"I'm guessing this is what caused the noises we heard last night," he said. To his gratification, Miss Parkinson moved closer and peered downward, then looked up at him with at least a modicum of admiration. Christian fairly preened . . . until Emery spoke.

"Nonsense!" he blustered in a poor imitation of the colonel. "Why, those tools could have been here for centuries!"

Christian glanced down at the hammer and chisel, then back at the flustered Emery. "If so, why is there no dust upon them?"

"B-because you blew it away!" Emery said, his mouth a petulant curl. Christian figured the boy might break down and bawl at any minute. Or, better, take his tools and go home.

Nearly smiling at the thought, Christian squatted down to get a closer look. When he set his lantern nearby, the marks upon the old stone could be easily discerned in the lamplight. "What the devil were you doing?" Christian asked idly.

"I . . . I? What do you mean?" Emery said, foiling Christian's attempt to catch him at his game. Apparently the scholar was not quite as stupid as he seemed.

"What is it?" Miss Parkinson said, bending over to gift him with a whiff of lilacs, especially delightful among the must of the cellars. Christian drew a deep breath, then tried to steady himself. Now was not the time to become distracted again, even if his hostess was leaning close.

"Someone was hammering at the foundation," she murmured. "But why?"

Christian ran his fingers over the indentations. "I imagine whoever it was is looking for something," he said. He glanced up at her. "Perhaps your family treasure?"

Both Miss Parkinson and Emery scoffed at that, but Christian continued to study the damage. "Look. These were not made at random. It appears as though they were trying to loosen a stone in the wall." To what purpose? A hidden room behind? Some sort of secret storage place? The thing looked rock-solid to him, as only medieval foundations could be.

"Well, I certainly don't understand it," Miss Parkinson said.

Of course not. You're far too prosaic to go knocking about for clandestine booty, Christian wanted to reply. And that was all to the good, for there was nothing he disliked more than women who swooned over a bit of fancy.

The Governess would never swoon.

"Most likely it is some housebreaker intent upon gaining entry to the main building," Emery said.

Christian rose to his feet. "I would think he'd do better to go through a door or a window than chip away at the cellar walls. The only thing he is likely to find behind there is good Devon dirt," Christian noted with a nod toward the stone. He turned toward Miss Parkinson, only to discover, to his delight, that she stood so close that he could breathe in lilacs and her. "Well, there's your ghost."

Her reaction to his words was almost comical. But a hairbreadth away, she looked up at him, her eyes wide and her lips forming an "O" as if in dismay. And then, abruptly, Christian realized just what he had said. If the specter was no more than some furtive hammering, then his work here was done. He could leave. He could be done with the blustering colonel, the mystical Mercia, and the supremely annoying Emery forever, as well as the only woman who had ever disdained his kiss. Christian stared at her. She stared back. And then they both started talking at once.

"But, of course, we have yet to discover the perpetrator," Christian said.

"But, my lord, you haven't really routed the ghost," Miss Parkinson protested in a rather breathless voice. "This can hardly be construed as physical evidence, one way or another, of the specter's presence or disappearance. After all, the potential buyers and the solicitor saw *something* they described as a phantom in the great hall itself."

"You're right. I still have to take care of that," Christian said. And when he looked down into the luscious lilac-colored eyes of his hostess, he forgot about the ghost, about Emery, even about how she had spurned him. Of course, it was hard to remember the spurning when her eyes were all soft and warm with something other than disdain, something almost like . . .

"Well, I think it's all nonsense!" Emery said loudly, breaking the spell that had held them both. "How you can possibly equate some old tools from a foiled housebreaking that probably occurred years ago to the specter that has haunted Sibel Hall these past weeks is beyond me!"

He turned to Miss Parkinson. "I told you that this . . . *nobleman* would know nothing of such things!" Emery practically spat out the words, then turned on his heel to march away. But his grand exit was spoiled by his lack of a lantern.

"Cousin Abigail, would you please light my way?" he asked stiffly.

Recovering the wits that had temporarily deserted him, Christian didn't know what to make of Emery's exit. Did temper actually drive the boy, or was he trying to divert attention from the cellars? Or, worse yet, was he trying to separate Christian from his hostess? Christian's eyes narrowed. It appeared that Miss Parkinson had no choice but to lead the boy away, but Christian had no intention of leaving just yet. Indeed, he wanted to explore the place more thoroughly, to see if there were any other marks or evidence of tampering. And, of course, there was the old wine cellar . . .

"I think I'll stay here and have a look around," Christian said, though he couldn't deny his disappointment at her departure, especially when she stood there, gazing up at him for a long moment, as though undecided. "Why don't you give Emery your lantern and stay here?"

Christian knew the moment the words had left his mouth that he had pushed too far. His hostess assumed a wary expression and took a step back. "I will leave the, uh, investigating to you, my lord," she said rather stiffly, though she again hesitated. "Are you sure you'll be . . . all right?"

Christian couldn't decide whether her question constituted a slur upon his manhood or heartfelt concern, but he nodded. "I'll be fine," he said. As long as Emery doesn't cause any more problems. He gave the belligerent youth a warning look, then watched the boy and Miss Parkinson move toward the steps, two figures in a pool of light that drifted through the cavernous space.

As he caught himself mooning again, Christian decided that it might be best if Miss Parkinson didn't return. He had a feeling he would need all his wits about him down here in the bowels of Sibel Hall, where any manner of trouble might be lurking—and not all of it involving a specter.

Chapter Seven

❧

ABIGAIL MOUNTED THE stone steps with mixed feelings, struggling against an unaccountable urge to slow her pace. For one wild moment she wondered if there actually was some otherworldly presence behind her, tugging at her skirts, pulling her back down toward the cellars—and Lord Moreland.

"I told you this viscount would be of no use to you!" Emery grumbled, dragging her from her thoughts. Any other time, she might have been grateful for the interruption, but not here, not just now, and not to hear the same old litany. Her cousin had made the same complaint so many times that Abigail was heartily sick of it.

"And I told you that no one else would come," Abigail said, wearily repeating her defense yet again. Emery knew Lord Moreland had not been her first choice, for she had explained her actions to all three of her cousins, even as she undertook them. After the specter's initial appearance, she had sought out the learned community, those scholars at Oxford and Cambridge who, by their reputations, would be trustworthy seekers of knowledge.

They had failed to respond to her letters more often than not. And the men of science, even those who once had been her father's friends and colleagues, had proved equally uncooperative. The Royal Society, that most august of bodies devoted to new fields of study, had dismissed her entreaties outright, and most of the individual members she had contacted had scoffed at her request. Those who had not had demanded an exorbitant sum before venturing forth in the name of study. Offended, Abigail had replied that if she had that sort of money, she wouldn't need their services in the first place.

With the pool of qualified gentlemen shrinking, she had been forced to seek aid from, well, the Last Resort, or so she had deemed him. Lord Moreland was not a researcher in any sense of the word and certainly not a scholar, as Emery kept reminding her. Indeed, from what she could ascertain, the man was an idle, titled rogue, a rake even, the type she held in the utmost contempt when she considered such fellows at all, which was as infrequently as possible. Worse yet, he appeared to have a penchant for notoriety that she did not care for in the least. But that notoriety was what had brought him to Abigail's attention. Hadn't he exposed the most famous ghost of the decade, perhaps even the century, as a hoax? He must have some sort of . . . affinity for such things.

"I just don't understand why you had to call in an outsider," Emery muttered.

Abigail stifled a sigh. Of course Emery didn't understand. Sibel Hall wasn't his house, so to him the phantom was an object of interest, while to Abigail the thing was a nuisance. It was most vexing. Abigail had been toiling away in virtual servitude when out of the blue she had been gifted with the Hall, a rambling country home that she deemed worth a small fortune. But just as soon as she took possession of the property, she began to hear tales of a ghost that was frightening away the servants and, worse yet, prospective buyers as well.

The cousins claimed the apparition had been in the family for years, making an appearance only when he was displeased with the actions of his heirs, which might, they suggested, include her plans to sell the place. But as far as Abigail was concerned, she and her cousins were distant connections at best, so why would they be any more palatable than a stranger? And, if the spirit were protesting her efforts, why didn't he show himself to her personally? Then at least she could try to reason with him.

Abigail was well known for her ability to soothe, if not the savage ghost, then a variety of annoying persons, including her rather astringent godmother. Unfortunately, the specter, legendary or no, appeared only to other residents of the manor, the servants, and prospective buyers, who took one look at the ghastly white form and lost interest in Sibel Hall. Permanently.

It all seemed an excessive waste of energy, for surely anyone, dead or alive, could see that neither Abigail nor any of the threadbare residents of the manor could afford to maintain it. Indeed, she was hard-pressed to keep those servants who hadn't fled, for her bequest did not include the wherewithal to actually live at the Hall for any length of time.

Not that Abigail was complaining. No one could have been more surprised at the news of her inheritance, especially since she had met her great-uncle Bascomb exactly once in her life, at her parents' funeral. He had appeared duly unimpressed with her, warning her that she would have to make her own way in the world, as he was already supporting enough destitute relatives.

Of course, Abigail had no intention of foisting herself off on a man she didn't even know. Instead, she had taken a position as companion to her godmother, who, though not exactly what one would call a termagant, nonetheless had reminded Abigail often enough of the charity involved in her action.

Abigail had already spent many long years attending the lady, and indeed had seemed destined for a life of stifling duty, when she received notification from the solicitor about Sibel Hall. It was a veritable godsend. Although far too large for her alone, the property could be sold, providing enough money to allow Abigail to set up her own household. Nothing grand, mind you, but a place of her own, a tidy little cottage where she could do as she pleased and never have to wait upon anyone except herself. It had seemed too good to be true.

And so it was. The buyers had fled, the larder was increasingly bare, and the man she had asked for help seemed to do little more than disturb the tenants of the place, especially herself.

"Well, obviously the fellow is accomplishing nothing," Emery said, as if reading her thoughts. "Just tell him to be on his way, and let's be rid of him!"

The suggestion sent a frisson of horror through Abigail that could not be explained away in terms of foodstuffs or potential sales, and she reached for the brooch that hung on a chain beneath her gown, absently running her fingers over the surface while she tried to understand the odd sensation. Naturally, she did not want Lord Moreland to leave while the threat of the specter remained, she reasoned. After all, nothing had been proved to her satisfaction concerning its existence.

But her dismay went far deeper, and Abigail knew it. Truth to tell, her sudden anxiety had nothing to do with the ghost and everything to do with Lord Moreland. Abruptly aware of what she was doing, she took her hand from her throat, only to find it was trembling, a strange reaction indeed. Halting her steps, Abigail drew in a deep, steadying breath.

Inviting Viscount Moreland to Sibel Hall had seemed a logical conclusion to her problem when she had penned the letter to his family seat. But the reality of the situation was something else entirely. From the moment he entered the study, he had upended all of her expectations. How could she have imagined he would be so handsome, so witty, so very alive? Abigail told herself that such attributes were what made him a rake and what made such men appealing to less-discerning women. Nonetheless, she had never felt more plain, more dull, and more dead inside.

As had become her habit in the past years, Abigail sought to arm herself with the facts, and the facts were that this promising young nobleman had accomplished nothing in his life beyond the typical *ton* pursuits of gaming and attracting females. Abigail reminded herself constantly of his failings, seeking them out and latching on to each one tenaciously. And yet . . . it was far more difficult to disapprove of someone in person than when reading what accounts she could find of his dissipations.

"You may rest assured that he will find nothing else," Emery insisted, interrupting her thoughts once more, and Abigail scolded herself for her inattention. It was not like her to be so impolite, and yet Emery was straining her patience with his constant whining. It reminded her all too well of her godmother and years spent in less pleasant circumstances. "I am not wholly convinced that those items that he claimed as evidence are indicative of anything at all, let alone the ghost. Spurious logic, indeed!"

"Perhaps," Abigail admitted. Somehow, she could not envision the misty form of Sir Boundefort brandishing hammer and chisel. After all, wouldn't a specter use more deadly implements if it were intent upon violence? Or wouldn't it possess otherworldly powers that made such objects unnecessary? Abigail shook her head. "But those tools undoubtedly caused the noises we heard last night."

Emery snorted. "Spurious logic again! I tell you, any loose board could have been rattling in the wind. And as for Lord Moreland's purported find, I wouldn't put it past him to have placed them there himself, so that he would look good in our eyes, instead of wholly ineffectual!"

Abigail gasped at such an accusation, taken aback that Emery would so malign their guest, but her cousin didn't appear the slightest bit remorseful. "After all, he made quick work of the locks," Emery pointed out. "Who is to say the man had not opened those doors before today?"

Abigail frowned, prepared to defend Lord Moreland, no matter if he was her last resort, but she had to admit that his knowledge of burglary skills had shocked her. And there was no denying the possibility that he might have gained access to the doors before today. But why? Although Emery's suggestion that he wanted to appear effective sounded absurd, much of Lord Moreland's behavior made no sense to her.

As they reached the great hall, Abigail was forced to abandon her conjectures and Emery his argument, for the colonel and Cousin Mercia crowded close, eagerly bombarding them with questions.

"Well, what happened? What did you find?" the colonel bellowed.

"Did you see Sir Boundefort?" Mercia whispered eagerly.

Abigail was surprised, as usual, by the older woman's enthusiasm. She only wished she herself took such delight in the specter, or anything else, for that matter. Catching the tenor of her thoughts, Abigail rebuked herself. Soon, when Sibel Hall was sold, she would have her heart's desire, her own household, and then she would delight in her garden and her peace and quiet each and every moment.

"No," Emery grumbled. "It was a useless venture, just as I predicted. Now, if you will excuse me, I am going to my room to engage in some real scholarship, not idiotic, and might I add highly suspect, theories!" He stormed off in a petulant fit, but since the others, presumably inured to Emery's sometimes rude behavior, ignored him, Abigail made no attempt to call him back.

Instead she turned toward her other cousins, who were, for all their eccentricities, far better behaved. "Lord Moreland found some tools that he thinks may have been used to make the noises we heard in the evening," Abigail explained. "From the looks of it, someone was hammering at the cellar walls," she added, though the explanation sounded feeble even to her own ears. Doubt crept into her thoughts again. After all, what did she really know of the viscount? Could he be trusted? He had already demonstrated an alarming tendency to ignore her wishes, and even his own decrees.

"Hammering at the walls? Whatever for?" the colonel exclaimed.

"Lord Moreland suggested they were looking for the treasure that you spoke of in the, uh, legend," Abigail said.

The colonel, a dear old fellow, looked so dumbfounded that Abigail had to bite her lip. "Odd business, indeed! I have lived here for years and never heard tell of any of this," he said, shaking his head.

"That is because you have never been interested in the family history," Cousin Mercia said. "Perhaps Sir Boundefort is determined that someone at last should discover his riches! It is fortunate that we need not suspect Lord Moreland of seeking out our hidden hoard."

Abigail turned to stare at Mercia in surprise. Of course her cousin was right. A rich nobleman would hardly have designs upon some mythical cache, and yet . . . The colonel had a point, too. Everything seemed to have come to a head at once—right after Lord Moreland's arrival. Suspicion surged through her, driven by her own doubts about her guest.

But her innate logic quickly asserted itself. How could Lord Moreland have been below, pounding on the walls, when he was with her in the great hall? Even a man of the viscount's dubious charms could hardly be in two places at once. But what if he had directed someone else to do the chore—such as his valet? Abigail frowned at that far-fetched notion. She had seen his lordship's body servant, and the thought of that stiff gentleman picking away at the foundation of the house was ludicrous. She was letting her imagination get the better of her, an imagination that had been nonexistent until her arrival here at Sibel Hall, home to ghosts, legends, and fanciful relatives.

"Well, I don't like the idea of anyone down in the cellar, let alone someone chipping away at the foundation," the colonel said. "Perhaps we should call in the authorities."

Abigail stifled a smile at the thought of what the local magistrate would have to say about a mysterious chiseler below Sibel Hall. "I doubt they would take us very seriously. All we can say for certain is that we found some tools that might have been used the night before to hammer at the walls." She refrained from mentioning the specter, which could only hurt any case they might attempt to make.

"Yes, well, I see your point," the colonel muttered. "Although I still don't like it. Perhaps we ought to set one of the servants to watch down there."

Sometimes Abigail wondered if she was the only resident of the hall in touch with reality. Between Emery's outlandishness and Mercia's flights of fancy, she had thought the colonel the most firmly grounded of the cousins, but even he often seemed blind to the facts. Who did he think would take on such a task?

"I fear that Sir Boundefort, or at least the rumor of him, has driven away all but a few desperate young women, hardly the sort to guard against housebreakers," she said. "But perhaps you might find some hardy lad in the village—unless you wish to take on the task yourself?"

The colonel appeared startled by the suggestion, then laughed loudly. "Oh, I think not, my dear! My days of keeping watch are over." He cleared his throat, then lowered his voice, as though to confide in her. "Though I would dearly love to be of use, these old bones can't stand the damp, which I fear must surely be the case below."

Abigail took pity on the old fellow. He really was sweet,

if a bit loud. "It is probably just as well, for we should miss your company, wouldn't we, Cousin Mercia?"

"Indeed! No one tells a story quite as well as the colonel," Mercia said.

Stepping around the fretwork, Abigail felt a small measure of relief to be out of the darkness and in the airy great hall once more, but Cousin Mercia and the colonel were slow to follow. When they finally joined her, they looked puzzled.

"Are you going to leave him down there, by himself?" Mercia asked, as if astonished by the notion.

"Yes, that seems rather, uh, unaccommodating to our guest," the colonel added.

Abigail tried not to frown in response. "Lord Moreland is not simply a guest. He is here to do a job." A job, she might add, to which he seemed to devote precious little attention. "He felt it would be beneficial to his . . . inquiry to search the cellar."

"Alone? Hardly seems fitting," the colonel muttered.

"You are welcome to join him," Abigail said.

"Oh, no, not I! Dampness," he said with a shudder. Abigail eyed the old fellow and wondered, not for the first time, if he was afraid of the ghost he professed not to believe in. "And I suppose you ladies don't want to be mucking about down there!" he added with a loud chuckle.

Abigail pursed her lips. It wasn't the specter or the prospect of mustiness or even the dreadful clutter that kept her from returning below. She had no intention of joining Lord Moreland, especially in a darkened cellar. Why, the very thought— Abigail reached for her throat as an unwelcome frisson of excitement coursed through her.

"Well, I'm sure that his lordship will inform us of any interesting finds," Cousin Mercia said.

"Yes," Abigail agreed aloud. "I'm sure Lord Moreland will keep us abreast of his discoveries." And yet, always wary, Abigail wondered. Was her Last Resort actually applying himself to his task, or was he pursuing another investigation entirely his own?

Knowing such thoughts could reach no logical conclusion, Abigail tried to put the viscount out of her mind. Excusing herself, she retreated to the study, where she continued sorting out all the bills and correspondence her great-uncle had left behind. But the room that had once served as her refuge from her well-meaning, yet sometimes overwhelming cousins no longer gave her the solace it had. She could see *him* here, ostensibly searching for keys but more likely caught gazing out the window.

There! Abigail seized upon the memory with something approaching desperation, for didn't it prove her poor opinion of the viscount? That was just the sort of behavior she expected from a pampered nobleman who had accomplished nothing during his gilded existence. He had made such a fuss about the keys when in the end he hadn't needed them at all. Meanwhile, he had demanded that everyone drop all other responsibilities to look for them, yet he had barely glanced about the room. In fact, his eyes, more often than not, had seemed to be upon Abigail herself.

The recollection of that particular conduct, though just as damning as his habit of staring out the window, somehow produced a different reaction in Abigail. Flushing with an unaccountable heat, she snatched up some papers from a nearby stack and sat down hard in her chair. Still, she felt a surge of dizzying euphoria, presumably at the notion that the man was looking at her more than he ought. Oh, folly! Abigail tamped down the errant sensation and set herself to work. Well accustomed to disciplining herself and her thoughts, she welcomed the normally distasteful chore of sorting Bascomb's papers with quiet determination.

And as for the viscount . . . he was relegated to last place in her set of well-ordered priorities.

•   •   •

IT WAS ONLY when the shadows began to lengthen that Abigail leaned back and put a hand to her aching neck. And just as quickly as she realized that she had finished for the day, anticipation swept through her, making her heart beat faster and her face flush. She told herself that she was relieved to be finished going through quite a bit of material and that after spending so many hours in solitude, she could hardly be blamed for looking forward to joining her cousins, no matter how eccentric they might be.

It was certainly not Lord Moreland that made her pulse quicken so. If she harbored some expectation in connection with her guest, it was simply that of the successful completion of his task. With that fact firmly established, Abigail rose and smoothed her skirts. It was an automatic action, but when she caught herself reaching up a hand to pat her hair, she stopped abruptly. She had never fussed over her appearance, and she was not about to start now. Dismissing an unbidden wish that she might change for dinner, she headed toward the drawing room, deliberately keeping to a modest pace.

Abigail had barely stepped into the room when the colonel boomed out a greeting, surprising her, as always, with his welcome. He was standing beside Mercia, who was seated and working on her ever-present needlework. The older woman nodded in response to Abigail's greeting, but Emery, slumped nearby over a book, barely glanced up from his reading. Obviously, she was still out of favor with him, for she caught a glimpse of the same sullen expression he had worn ever since Lord Moreland's arrival.

Lord Moreland. Abigail's gaze swept the room, but her guest was not present. The happy bubble of anticipation that she had refused to acknowledge now deflated, and instead of being relieved she felt perversely annoyed. Frowning, she told herself that his lordship's perpetual tardiness was a good thing, for such bad habits did well to remind her of his irresponsible nature.

No doubt rakes spent an inordinate amount of time

preening before the mirror, which made them late for their appointments, Abigail surmised. That righteous observation didn't have its intended effect, however. Instead she became oddly tantalized by the image of Lord Moreland standing before a mirror, his handsome form reflected in all its beautiful detail . . . perhaps while he changed for dinner. Or bathed . . . Taking in a swift breath, Abigail reached toward the neck of her gown, nervously touching the brooch beneath as she tried to put such thoughts out of her head.

"So, did you have a good rest, my dear?" the colonel asked.

Abigail blinked at him stupidly, then berated herself for her inattention. It was a recent fault, for usually she was awake on every suit. A companion needed to be in order to follow the politics of a large household and anticipate the demands of those she served. Of course, Abigail no longer served anyone exactly. Still, there was no cause to let her mind wander. It was impolite, as well as an exhibition of poor self-discipline.

Abigail cocked her head toward the colonel. "I'm sorry. What did you say?"

"Did you have a good rest, dear?" he repeated, so loudly that Abigail cringed. She wasn't hard of hearing, simply distracted.

And what did he mean by "rest"? The old fellow seemed to be under the impression that she did nothing but lie about, her life one of leisure. Abigail gently corrected him. "Actually, I've been going through some of Bascomb's correspondence and bills."

The colonel cleared his throat. He didn't approve of discussing finances and was quite comfortable ignoring the truth of the current situation and continuing on as always. Although the solicitor had told her that all three of the cousins were left small stipends in the will, they remained here, availing themselves of the room and board to be had at Sibel Hall. Abigail didn't complain, for she enjoyed the company, but she alone seemed concerned for the future.

She had tried to explain that the household could not carry on indefinitely with no real income to support it, but no one was willing to listen.

What kept them here? Habit? Camaraderie? Abigail could see they might be attached to what had been home, to the colonel at least. Perhaps it was a place of memories. Not being the romantic sort, she found that rather hard to understand. Or they might have become accustomed to the larger house, with its amenities, though she failed to see many of those in the rather gloomy atmosphere, the threadbare furnishings, and the lack of servants.

Abigail would much prefer a cozy little cottage, and as soon as the thought entered her mind, the dormant longing rose up in her, fresh and fierce. Years of lost hope had beaten it down, but now it was revived, stronger than ever. Indeed, sometimes it seemed more important to her than breath, this wish that she could have a place of her own, tiny and tidy and blissfully peaceful.

The house need not even be as large as her childhood home. Her father, the younger son of a younger son, had come into a piece of property that was not at all grand, nothing like Sibel Hall, but it had enabled him to marry and to raise his daughter in comparative contentment while pursuing his interest in the sciences.

Abigail's mother had made the house a cheerful place, and the little family had existed in a warm, loving atmosphere full of books and ideas and experiments. Unfortunately, the property had been entailed, and since he died without a son, it had gone to another relative.

Abigail sighed at the memory, but she knew she could not recapture the world of her childhood. A few simple rooms would suit her, with a garden and no servants beyond a day girl. Perhaps she would even have a cat or a little dog to keep her company, Abigail thought, smiling wistfully. There she would relish a life with no one to cater to or wait upon except herself—and no guests beyond the occasional visitor.

As soon as the idea formed, Abigail scolded herself.
Compared to her godmother, her three cousins were no
trouble at all. It was just that she yearned for some privacy,
a bit of space and time to call her own, without having to
concern herself with another's needs or wants or fancies.
She felt obligated, as owner of the Hall, to serve as hostess.
And having been displaced herself, she harbored a bit of
guilt over her inheritance, which made her do her best to
please them all, as well as to help them plan for the future.

She had tried to broach the subject, if only to suggest
that the colonel, at least, should be looking for a place to
let. Emery, she assumed, would return to school, and Mercia to her own household. Presumably they could still visit
each other, so the breakup of the party should not be so
wrenching. And, with their stipends, no one would be left
out in the cold, as she had been after her parents' death.

But Abigail's efforts had yielded no fruit. Someone always managed to change the subject. She had quite given
up trying to discuss the matter, putting things off until the
sale of the house, which now seemed delayed indefinitely.
And so they continued, the four of them. Abigail had to
admit that most of the time she was grateful for her cousins'
presence in the rambling old house. And if they departed,
she would be quite alone . . . with Lord Moreland.

The thought came to her with sudden startling intensity,
and she flushed, trying not to remember what had happened
the last time the two of them had been together . . . unchaperoned. Abigail could feel her face flame and cursed her
pale complexion. Someone of her advanced years should
not be blushing at the memory of a simple kiss. But it had
not been simple at all. Complex, sweet, passionate, giving,
taking, it had been unique.

Of course, Abigail's experience had mostly consisted of
encounters with so-called gentlemen who had visited her
godmother and thought to importune the help. Although
initially she had placed Lord Moreland in that group, her
experience with him was not at all similar to those horrid,

sloppy attempts. Instead, the touch of his lips against hers had resembled some kind of ignition, a wholly, new scientific discovery of spontaneous electrical combustion occurring between two people.

Abigail had been so startled she had gasped, only to feel his tongue invading her mouth. And it wasn't the sickening, thick thrust of mucus that Lord Randolph's nephew had forced upon her. Rather, Lord Moreland's mouth was warm and rich and tantalizing, reminding her with vivid intensity of one other kiss, which she had long ago dismissed as a product of youthful imagination and childish romantic nonsense.

And yet hadn't she recaptured that sensation of rightness, of joy, of destiny? Oh, folly! Abigail shook her head, determined to discourage such fancies. Nor should she be belaboring, even in her own mind, that moment of sheer madness on the stairway. At the time she had been so stunned she had nearly fainted, despite her famous fortitude. And when he had held her close, she had nearly given way to him, which would have been disastrous.

Not only would her capitulation have fed Lord Moreland's already excessive confidence, but she knew better than to succumb to any nobleman's advances, especially in the darkness of night. There in the shadows, did he even know whom he kissed? The thought, however fleeting, had been piercing enough to awaken her from her daze.

And Abigail was glad of it. Else where would she be now? Tucked up in his bed like some doxy? No longer mistress of this house, she would be mistress to a man? Having managed to hold on to her virtue for the long, dull years of her near servitude, Abigail had no intention of giving it away now that she was free, not even to Lord Moreland. Especially not to Lord Moreland.

Abigail took a deep breath. She would do well to remember that the viscount, no matter what his behavior, past or present, was a member of the *ton*, and as such moved in a world apart from the rest of humanity. He was part of the elite of society, wealthy and revered, even though his talents appeared to be limited to womanizing, gambling, and routing ghosts.

Struck by a sudden·thought, Abigail turned to her cousins. "Did Lord Moreland discover anything else in the cellars?"

The colonel and Cousin Mercia, who had been immersed in conversation, raised their heads to give her inquiring looks.

"We haven't seen him, my dear," Cousin Mercia said.

"I thought he would have reported to you," the colonel said.

Abigail felt a small twinge of panic. "Perhaps he has gone up to change for dinner." But it was nearly time for the meal now, she realized, after a quick glance at the clock.

The colonel cleared his throat loudly. "Uh, perhaps I should check with the servants, just to make certain."

"Yes, perhaps you should," Abigail said, trying not to appear too concerned about their guest. She told herself that he was probably fine, and yet she couldn't help thinking of all sorts of disasters that could transpire in the cellars. He could have fallen, or something could have fallen on him. Indeed, right now he could be trapped beneath a heavy timber! Inhaling deeply, Abigail tried to stem the flood of visions produced by an imagination that seemed to be making up for years of inactivity.

With a nod, the colonel made his exit, leaving her to take up the conversation that she had aborted. But she was too busy conjuring possible calamities to think of idle chatter. As if she sensed Abigail's dilemma, Cousin Mercia smiled reassuringly.

"I'm sure Lord Moreland has not met with any difficulties," she said.

"If he has, he has only himself to blame," Emery said.

Her cousin's callousness so startled Abigail that she turned a furious glare upon him. Even if he harbored no liking for their guest, perhaps he would have a care for his own skin. "I fear that Lord Moreland's grandfather, the earl of Westhaven, might not agree with you," she said. "Indeed, I imagine he would be quite distressed should anything happen to his heir."

Emery blanched as her words struck home. Apparently he was not so lost in his studies as to ignore the power of the nobility and the fate awaiting those who trifled with them.

"I'm sure Sir Boundefort harbors no ill will against Lord Moreland," Cousin Mercia assured Abigail, just as though the only danger below lay with a specter.

Abigail frowned at that reasoning. "If Sir Boundefort is so particular, I wonder that he didn't do something about whoever was down there chipping away at his domain," she said.

"Indeed!" Mercia said. "But perhaps he did. After all, we have discovered no further sign of the trespassers, have we?"

She uttered this rather alarming conjecture with an equanimity that caused Abigail to blink in stunned surprise. It was one thing to claim the ghost chased away potential buyers but quite another to suggest it disposed of unwanted intruders. Abigail had just opened her mouth to protest, albeit politely, when the colonel arrived, huffing and puffing as if he had run all the way from Lord Moreland's rooms.

"I say, his lordship's valet claims he hasn't been seen since late this morning," he announced.

"Oh, dear," Mercia said.

By the time the words were uttered, Abigail was already halfway out of her seat.

"I suggested that we have a look for him, but the valet didn't seem to think much of that. Said it wasn't his job to search down his lordship!" the colonel said, obviously disgusted by such a show of disloyalty.

Even as he spoke, Abigail was heading out of the room. "I say, with or without the fellow's help, we should try to find the viscount, shouldn't we, eh?" the colonel continued.

But Abigail only heard the words from behind her as she hurried to the great hall. Heart in her throat, she regretted all that she had said to the viscount. It seemed apparent now that she had done little except complain about his lordship, at least to herself, and that she had barely been civil to him to his face, let alone grateful for his prompt response to her plea. Perhaps, while awaiting his arrival, she had wished for more, but she could not blame him for her childish fancies. He had come to help her, and she had snapped at him all too often, most especially last night!

Although not an hour before, Abigail had been cataloguing his faults, now the thought of never again looking upon his handsome visage filled her with horror and dread and a sorrow so deep that it dispelled all else. She could barely keep her feet to an even pace while she fought an urge to run, heedless of her skirts, to the cellar door. Her godmother would never have countenanced that, and even her cousins would surely think her mad, but Abigail Parkinson, known as the soul of reason and discretion, was beyond caring.

She was out of breath when she reached the passage behind the fretwork, where the heavy oak door still stood open. Had someone else gone down there? What of the miscreants who had been hammering? What if they had been hiding in some corner only to emerge and attack an unsuspecting Lord Moreland? Grabbing the lantern she had left behind, Abigail plunged into the darkness.

Behind her, she was dimly aware of the colonel, huffing and puffing and urging her to caution in a breathless voice. He managed to catch up with her, halting her progress at the top of the cellar stairs.

"Let's see if he answers first, shall we?" the colonel suggested. Without waiting for her reply, he called Lord Moreland's name more loudly than ever, but his bellow was swallowed up by the darkness and muffled by the old stone, making even the prosaic Abigail uneasy.

Suddenly the steps that seemed so innocuous this morning appeared positively evil, a dreaded stair leading to some blackened crypt from a gothic novel. Abigail waited as the last traces of the colonel's shout echoed around them, but as from the depths of a tomb, only silence answered.

Chapter Eight

⁂

THE STILLNESS WAS deafening. Above it, Abigail heard only the sound of her own breathing coming loud and fast as panic began to beat a frantic rhythm in her blood. And then, beside her, she heard the colonel clearing his throat.

"Perhaps we should summon the magistrate," he said.

Abigail turned to stare at him in disbelief. He would wait for some fool from the village? To do what? One glance at his nervous expression told her that the military man might have faced the enemy on foreign battlefields but he was not prepared to brave the cellar of his own home.

Abigail had no such qualms. Right now nothing could keep her from Lord Moreland. Shaking off the colonel's restraining arm, she hurried downward. Grasping the lantern in one hand and her skirts in another, she was forced to watch her steps, so she did not see the shadowy figure until it loomed up in front of her. Abigail drew back with a gasp, wondering if she had met the phantom at last, but then it spoke, and not in some high-pitched wail but in the low, heady voice of Lord Moreland.

"Whoa!" he said, grasping her shoulders to steady her, and for one long, dreadful moment, Abigail felt like weeping. She, who rarely showed emotion, who hadn't cried since the death of her parents, felt the hot pressure rise up in her throat, stinging her eyes. She stood, shaking, seized by a fierce urge to toss down her lantern and throw her arms around his waist, to press herself against him tightly and never let go.

And who could blame her? She was so glad, or rather so thankful, to hear his voice, to see him before her, seemingly unharmed, to smell that wonderful, unique scent that was his alone, coupled with . . . wine? Since she had been sniffing rather fitfully, holding back tears, Abigail could not ignore the distinct, telltale odor. She stepped away from him, her dizzying elation swamped by suspicion.

"What have you been doing? Didn't you hear us call?" she managed, her voice sharp.

Lord Moreland lifted one well-manicured hand to his tousled hair. "I came up as quickly as I could. You can't exactly move at great haste down there, even equipped with a lantern."

"Obviously not," Abigail said dryly, considering the amount of time he had spent below. "Would you mind telling me what has occupied you all day?" The alarm that had wrung her out like a wet glove now turned to outrage. How could the viscount have caused them all such grief with his thoughtlessness?

"I've been exploring," he said, explaining nothing even as he reached out to escort her up the steps.

Abigail slipped away from his touch. She could walk quite well on her own, thank you, and she demonstrated as much by turning her back on him and stalking up to the little room, where the colonel greeted them both in his usual jovial manner.

"Ah, I see you've found him. Good show! I say, we were

a bit worried about you, my lord, when you didn't appear for dinner," the colonel said, giving the errant nobleman a hearty slap on the back.

Abigail did not stay to share in the exuberant welcome, but hurried into the great hall. Her heart was still pounding frantically in the aftermath of uncharacteristically violent emotions, and she was tempted to keep on walking all the way to the drawing room. But good manners, along with an urge to give the miscreant a piece of her mind, made her turn and linger. She did not have long to wait, for the colonel and the viscount soon emerged.

As she watched, the latter brushed at his dusty clothes with perfect grace, then straightened to his full, glorious height to appear casually confident and handsome, his tousled golden hair only enhancing his appearance. Abigail, who had a feeling she looked flushed, harried, and untidy, felt a slow surge of resentment. By what miracle of birth and circumstances had he lived in privilege and arrogance, idling away whatever wits and talents he might have, neglecting to pursue any worthwhile occupation of his thoughts or skills, while she had been forced into drudgery, her mind all but dulled by the demands upon her time and person and energy?

He had strolled into Sibel Hall, assuming command, oozing condescension, and ordering her not to consider herself his equal. Fine. She had tried to stay out of his way, hoping that he would conduct his . . . business quickly and be gone. But it seemed that at every opportunity he was approaching her, eyeing her, or standing beside her, far too near. And then, last night, he had given her the ultimate insult, disregarding her wishes and her person, tendering her no respect by treating her just as he would any servile, powerless female.

And no matter what heady sensations his actions had produced at the time, there was no denying the pain of her discoveries—not only that he thought so little of her but that he was the type of man who would prey on an unprotected woman, using the skills he had no doubt honed on many others. Wenching and drinking must be the viscount's sole areas of expertise, for instead of ridding her house of the specter, he appeared to have spent the afternoon imbibing from the wine cellar.

Abigail made a low sound of disgust. She had never understood the *ton*'s penchant for guzzling everything from claret to champagne with gusto, the men bragging about how many bottles they could drink in one sitting, the women boldly tippling as well. Personally, she held them all in contempt and considered such activities a sign of weakness—or an excuse for ill behavior. More often than not, the only time "gentlemen" noticed the companion was when their breath reeked of alcohol. And as for her godmother . . . Abigail shuddered at the memory of putting the woman to bed, smelly and belligerent, far too many times.

Abigail felt something inside her, some final dream or last lingering hope, disintegrate at the thought that Lord Moreland was no different. The Last Resort? More likely he was no resort at all, an utterly useless rogue who was eating her food and stealing kisses, probably from the servants as well, while accomplishing nothing. She crossed her arms in front of her. "And did you rout the ghost?" she asked, knowing full well the answer.

"Rout him? I never even saw him," the scoundrel admitted.

And would he have seen any phantoms had they paraded past him, or had he been slumped over a barrel below, drunk and insensible? Abigail pursed her lips. "And just what did you achieve?" she demanded.

He grinned. "I found a lovely old claret. Shall I fetch a bottle for dinner?"

Abigail, who never had been given to bouts of temper, had to restrain herself. "Dinner," she said through gritted teeth, "is already waiting." Then, her patience exhausted, she stalked past the arrogant nobleman, not trusting herself to say anything else.

• • •

CHRISTIAN WATCHED THE stiff, retreating back of his hostess and fought an urge to toss her over his shoulder and carry her off to his room. The impulse had come upon him when he ran into her on the stair, his body bumping up against hers all too briefly, her face flushed and glowing in the lantern's light with an expression on it that he didn't recognize. Why was she always on the step above him? Though he wouldn't mind her being on top . . .

Christian sighed. Obviously a day in the cellars had not improved his taste—except in wine. He shook his head, sending up a faint flutter of dust, and decided that late or not, he had better change for dinner.

He found Hobbins waiting for him with a welcome pitcher of water and a basin for washing as best he could. He would have liked to try the plunge bath, but considering the time and his hostess's mood, that was out of the question. He greeted his valet with a curt smile.

"Ah, there you are, my lord. One of the hall's residents sought me out, looking for you," he said, his tone heavy with disapproval.

"I see that the possibility of my coming up missing didn't alarm you," Christian remarked wryly, with one glance at his valet's stoic expression.

"Of course not, my lord. I believe you to be eminently capable of taking care of yourself."

Was that a thinly veiled insult or a compliment? Christian grinned as he began stripping off his coat.

"Taking care of your clothing, however, appears to be a different matter," Hobbins said, grasping the discarded garment between two fingers and holding it away from him as though it were some sort of rotting carcass.

"But Hobbins, that's your job," Christian said, laughing.

"Hmmm. Yes, so I see," the valet murmured, eyeing the coat and his employer critically. "Apparently the housekeeping here is even more negligent than I thought."

Christian laughed again. "I was in the cellars all day."

"Ah," Hobbins commented, unfazed, as always, by that announcement. "And did you enjoy yourself, my lord?"

Christian paused in the act of removing his waistcoat. "Actually, I did," he answered, surprising himself. "It's a fine example of medieval vaulting and still solid except for some odd sorts of tampering at various points in the wall. Although not much of the furniture and stored items is worthy of attention, I found a wine cellar that is beyond price, with the most beautiful champagne from the Abbey of Hautvillers, probably bottled when Dom Pierre Perignon himself was alive."

Christian sighed at the memory of the taste, a just reward for a day spent below. Or so he had thought. One look at the Governess had shown him that she did not share his opinion. Apparently his efforts, which he deemed quite estimable, were all too easily dismissed. Christian frowned in annoyance. What did she expect him to do, drag the specter forcibly from the woodwork?

"I take it Miss Parkinson does not share your appreciation of fine wine," Hobbins said.

Christian glanced at his valet's impassive countenance and wondered, not for the first time, if the man was omniscient. Perhaps *he* could call up the ghost? "Yes. She was . . . unimpressed."

"That appears to be her general attitude where you are concerned, my lord," Hobbins observed. "Rather refreshing, I might add. Probably good for you."

Christian sent him a look. "Undoubtedly you think a day in a dark, dusty cellar, with no thanks for my trouble, promotes intellectual growth."

"Hardly intellectual."

"Ah, spiritual, then?" Christian asked, snorting in amusement.

"So, it's fawning you want?" Hobbins asked as he laid out fresh clothing.

"No," Christian said, annoyed. "But I wouldn't mind a little gratitude."

"For drinking the champagne?" Hobbins asked.

Christian's eyes narrowed. Although he was good-natured, he did have his limits, and he was becoming increasingly tired of Sibel Hall and its inhabitants. He wasn't known for his store of patience, which was rapidly running thin with both the ghost and his hostess, who treated him as if he had some sort of communicable disease that prevented her from coming too close to him. Since the house party was small, that left him with the cousins, a fate from which an afternoon in the cellars had seemed a reprieve.

He didn't need his valet adding to his troubles. "Perhaps you are overdue for retirement," he suggested without heat.

"I beg your pardon, my lord." Hobbins dipped into a bow that might have been an apology—or a mockery.

"You ought to welcome the chance," Christian said. "I, for one, am more than ready to leave this wretched place."

"And forgo your duty, my lord?" his valet asked.

Christian shrugged. "I'm serious, Hobbins. Maybe we should just throw in our hand on this one."

"Perhaps you are right, my lord. After all, you have given the business your best and, sadly, have failed in this instance. There will be other challenges." Hobbins spoke with no perceptible inflection. So why did disapproval ring in every word?

Christian glared at his valet, who continued his duties as if he had not used an extremely repugnant word.

"Failure is usually not a part of my vocabulary, Hobbins."

"I beg your pardon, my lord," Hobbins said, appearing not the least bit remorseful. "How would you phrase it?"

Christian mulled that one over. "Well, I certainly tried, but circumstances—mainly a lack of phantoms—have prevented me from completing my mission," he said, only to frown at Hobbins's impassive face. Regrettably, no matter how you put it, the end result was the same. If he left now, he would go trailing home having accomplished little beyond retrieving a few tools—and some lovely wine—from the cellars of Sibel Hall.

Of course, Christian couldn't heed just his own desires in this case. He could imagine the earl's distress, whether real or feigned, all too clearly as the old gentleman accused him of abandoning a lady in distress. Christian rolled his eyes at that one. He could hardly explain that Miss Parkinson was no lady but some kind of governess, who appeared equal to anyone and anything, including a medieval specter, without any assistance from him.

But despite appearances, she had asked for his help, so if he left now, he would be abandoning her—at least in the earl's eyes. "Oh, very well, I suppose I can give it a bit longer," Christian muttered, half to himself and half to his manservant.

But kicking his heels with nothing except a bit of fine wine to keep him occupied wouldn't do either. He let his valet help him into a fresh coat. "If only I knew why someone is chipping away at the cellar," he mused aloud.

"I suspect they are looking for something," Hobbins conjectured.

Christian nodded absently. "But there's no sign of anything down there," he murmured. His first thought had been a hidden room, but the cellars had been built before the need for such places arose. There was a chance that the medieval owner had built a hiding *space*, just large enough to store his wealth. Christian had spent some intimate time with the foundation walls, however, and he hadn't found one single sign of anything beyond the recent tampering.

Again, Christian wished he had the plans or some sort of record of the building. "Tomorrow I suppose I'll search the library and see what turns up." He could think of other things he would rather search, primarily his hostess's person.

That thought carried him through a swift exit from his room down to the dining room, where he found, to his dismay, that the rest of the company had failed to wait upon him. For an instant he was so outraged that he opened his mouth to protest, but the look on his hostess's face made him decide not to risk it. And what had he missed, anyway? No doubt the fare was as bad as ever. Just colder. Wincing, Christian excused himself and hurried back to the cellars to fetch a lovely old bottle imported from France by some former resident of Sibel Hall. Since then the line had clearly gone downhill.

So did his evening.

By the time he returned, the wretched meal was stone cold and his hostess colder still. He couldn't even enjoy the delightful Bordeaux because of the evil looks the Governess sent his way. Christian felt as though he was stealing her wine, especially since she refused even a taste. Only the colonel seemed happy to join him in a glass, slurping so enthusiastically that Christian felt compelled to limit the old fellow's share.

The conversation was practically nonexistent, and what there was of it proved unpalatable. Christian decided it had reached the absolute nadir when Cousin Mercia asked him about his afternoon's explorations. At the very question the Governess sniffed. *Sniffed!* Christian could not recall ever having been the object of such censure. It was all he could do to retain some semblance of politesse when he wanted to lunge across the table and wipe away her scowl. Of course, at this point, he was wondering if any man, even a fellow of his previously admired talents, could put a smile on her face.

As if that weren't bad enough, Emery decried Christian's every observation about the cellars, including the glaring truth that someone had been down there trying to find something. The boy actually sneered at the facts!

"Next you shall be claiming that Sir Boundefort himself was floating about, chipping at the walls," Emery mocked, again testing Christian's resolve not to dive over the dinner settings. But in Emery's case, his objective would be to draw blood, not a smile.

And just when Christian thought he'd heard it all, Cousin

Mercia seized upon Emery's sarcastic conjecture as entirely probable, postulating that her knightly ancestor was trying to escape his earthly boundaries by hacking away at the foundations of his own house. She then launched into yet another recitation of her wretched couplets.

Christian stifled a groan.

When the beastly affair was over, he excused himself to seek an early retirement, eager for any escape from the dreadful company. But his room seemed small and stifling, so when all was quiet, he once again left it to prowl around the house during the night, listening for noises that never came. And a hostess who, unfortunately, never appeared in the darkness, clad only in her nightclothes and suffering a change of heart about her gallant rescuer.

Bored and restless and weary of being cooped up inside dreary Sibel Hall, Christian finally trudged back to his bed, which had never seemed emptier.

HE WAS GROWING irritable. He admitted it. Although not quite as surly as Emery, he reminded himself of one of the earl's gouty old cronies. And he didn't particularly care for it. But who could blame him when he was now into his fourth day at Sibel Hall, with little enough to show for his stay except a bad night's sleep and poor company?

And, in his misguided search for plans to the house, he had been trapped in the dusty old library seemingly forever, which in itself was enough to ruin anyone's mood. Wasn't it? Christian slanted a glance at the colonel, cheerfully humming away as he thumbed through moldy old volumes, then toward the governess, who seemed content enough until she caught him staring and glared at him.

Christian sighed. He was not a reader. He never had been, having scraped through his school days by doing as little of it as possible. He had always preferred the out-of-doors, escaping whenever he could, and his tastes had changed little over the years. An afternoon spent surrounded by books at

Sibel. Hall was the stuff of nightmares as far as he was concerned. But what else was he to do? He was the one who had insisted on looking for some clue to the original construction, the so-called treasure, or Sir Boundefort himself.

And so far he had found books on every conceivable subject *except* those. Indeed, there seemed to be a notable dearth of any sort of family history, so notable as to make Christian suspicious. Had someone actually gone through the place and removed anything that might be pertinent? It seemed like a great deal of trouble—and to accomplish what?

Christian shook his head, which was too full of dust and stultifying writings to think clearly. Hell, he could hardly even breathe. He had sneezed twice, yawned innumerable times, and ogled the derriere of his hostess whenever he got a chance. But as much as he enjoyed sneaking those glimpses, Christian found himself growing impatient for some kind of activity that did not involve dry old tomes.

The possibility of a rousing haunting seemed extremely remote at this point, for Christian had come to the conclusion that if there ever had been a phantom, it wasn't about to show its spectral face when he was around. And if actual corporeal beings were involved in the happenings here, then his discovery of tools in the cellar had effectively scared them off as well. But his family had never been known for their inaction, and Christian had reached the limit of his.

It was time to do something to flush out the fellow.

Replacing an unpromising volume on families of the north country on its shelf, Christian turned around and dusted off his hands purposefully. "I'm going into the village to post a letter. To my grandfather," he added, to forestall any protest from his slave-driving hostess. She could hardly object to a familial missive, nor could she tell him to send one of the servants, considering the lack of help about the place.

Christian glanced toward her, expecting at least a mild protest, but whatever complaint she might have lodged was interrupted by the colonel's booming voice. "I'll come with you! Dash it all, I haven't been to the village for some time."

Christian conjured a smile with some effort. So much for his escape. He might manage to get away from Sibel Hall, but not from the cousins. As for the letter, he hadn't even written it yet, and it certainly wasn't to his grandfather. He would just have to make sure the colonel didn't see the direction.

"All right. Why don't you call for the carriage while I run up and fetch the letter?" Christian asked.

"Very good! Very good!" the colonel said, his obvious delight in the journey robbing Christian of any ill will.

Christian turned to his hostess. "Perhaps you would care to join us as well?" he asked, trying not to look too hopeful. If he was going to take one cousin, why not another—more specifically, the best of the lot?

For a moment she appeared tempted, but then shook her head firmly in rejection. Christian decided she needed tempting more often. Luckily, he considered himself quite good at providing that sort of thing. "Are you certain? It looks as though the day will clear off," he added.

Unfortunately the colonel spoiled the effect. "Yes, do join us, Abigail. We shall have a fine time, I'll warrant."

Miss Parkinson turned toward the colonel then, much to Christian's disappointment. "I'm sorry, but I have more correspondence to go through, as well as continuing my search here."

That last barb obviously was directed his way, but Christian ignored it, taking the high road instead. "Is there anything I can get for you while I'm out, or do for you, Miss Parkinson?" he asked. Like kidnap you? And carry you off?

As if reading his thoughts, his hostess drew herself up sharply. "No, thank you, my lord." He thought she would follow up with a stern warning to return in a timely fashion, and indeed, she looked as though she might speak, but only tightened her mouth into a thin line and nodded toward him in a deferential fashion. Christian frowned. He would rather have a reprimand than that, unless, of course, she was deferring to him . . . in bed.

With a sigh for that impossibility, Christian hurried to his room, where he quickly penned a note, closed it with his own personal seal, and strolled downstairs and out the main doors. The air was still damp, but the rain had finally stopped, and Christian drew in a deep draught, a delight after the musty atmosphere of the hall.

No scent of lilacs flavored the breeze, but the sun was peeking out from behind the clouds, and he was doing something at last besides kicking his heels, frustrated with both his hostess and her ghost. So, with one last glance at the building behind him, Christian headed down the steps to the drive, only to find his own coach waiting for him.

"Thought you'd be more comfortable with your own man and all," the colonel said, after a hearty greeting. Christian nodded, even as he wondered just how ill equipped the stables at Sibel Hall had become. No wonder the colonel hadn't visited the village recently. And on the heels of that thought came another. When they arrived, Christian wondered just how welcome the old fellow would be.

MILLFIELD WAS A typical little town, with a pleasant green and a small church and various shops for bread, cheese, tea, and shoes, among other things, as well as a small inn. After posting his letter, Christian poked his head into the common room, for such places were well known as gathering spots for locals. Here his title served him well, for it made for effusive greetings when he ordered a late luncheon in hopes that the food was better than that of the Hall. The colonel received more wary treatment, and that's when Christian saw the whispering begin.

He had planned to pose several general questions while they waited for their food, leading up to more particular ones concerning Sibel Hall and its environs, and finally, the rumor of the haunting. Unfortunately the colonel once again ruined his plans.

"The viscount's here to roust the ghost, you know," the older man exclaimed loudly, and Christian cringed. Didn't the old fool know any better, or had he deliberately revealed Christian's purpose here in order to foil it? "He's the one who exposed the Belles Corners business."

Christian stifled a groan. So much for his subtle probing into local opinion. Everyone in the vicinity, including any who might be hammering away in the cellar at Sibel Hall, would soon be fully aware of his mission. He managed a laugh and a shrug. "Just taking a look, you might say, and enjoying the Devon countryside as well."

Despite Christian's efforts to gloss it over, the colonel's bald announcement quite naturally cast a pall over the gathering. Some of the fellows, even big, strapping workmen, ducked their heads, as if in fear, at the very mention of the ghost, while others laughed aloud.

"Don't you be mocking the devil, Tom Green, or you'll find yourself walking home without yer head some dark night," said a heavyset woman, presumably the owner's wife.

"And who shall take it from me? Will it be you, Bess?" the fellow hooted.

"You best not jabber about what don't concern you, Tom," the owner said, defending his spouse with a fierce swipe of his towel.

"Well, I've lived here all my life," a sharp-faced young man put in, "and I've never heard a thing about any specter! It's my thinking that the new owners have been drinking to their good fortune a bit too often, if you take my meaning."

A series of hoots followed, and the colonel whirled around. "Now, see here, young Kendal," he sputtered, launching into a lengthy outraged protest, to which Christian turned a deaf ear. Instead, he leaned close to the owner and pursued his line of inquiry as quietly as possible. He discovered only that no strangers had been lurking about, no reports of unusual doings (beyond the phantom) had been heard, and no one (in his right mind) had been up to Sibel Hall in some time.

For Christian, his efforts were not unlike his dissection of homes and their structure, only these were focused on the history of the house itself, its environs, and the people of the area. Usually the pasts of all were intertwined, but it seemed that the previous owner of Sibel Hall, Bascomb Averill, hadn't been on good terms with the villagers for many years—something to do with an old quarrel over payment for services rendered to some workmen.

After the owner of the inn left to tend to some other customers, Christian listened as best as he could manage, when he could escape the colonel's interference, to the gossip and the rumor and the various conjectures on spectral visitations, including the notion that Bascomb had been so mean he was probably up there tormenting anyone within his reach, or that he was so tightfisted he kept watch over his hoard even in death. Of course, no one knew what that hoard might be or where it had come from (these fellows not having been privy to Cousin Mercia's theories), but Christian thought that might explain the housebreakers chipping away at the cellar walls.

Despite buying several rounds of tongue-loosening drinks for the loungers, he really didn't come away with anything noteworthy except a fine, leisurely meal of rustic meat pies and potatoes, topped off by a sweetened currant pudding and attended by a decent ale. All in all, Christian could hardly call it a wasted trip. But he still had one more thing to do.

When the colonel proclaimed, loudly, of course, that he was going to see about the coach, Christian hung back and scanned the room until his gaze lighted upon the sharp-eyed young man with whom the colonel had argued. With an inclination of his head, he drew the fellow off into the shadows in the corner.

"You're young Kendal?" Christian asked.

"I am," the young man answered. His voice and his stance were cocky, but his expression was guarded. "Alf's the name."

"And you aren't afraid of the phantom?" Christian asked.

"Me? Not a whit, my lord, especially since none have seen him except doddering old fools," he declared, then paused uncomfortably. "Begging your pardon, milord, but you ain't seen him, have you?"

Christian laughed. "No, but I'd like to. I'd like to catch him in the act, if you get my drift."

"Ah, so you don't believe in him any more than I do," Alf said with a smirk.

Christian shrugged noncommittally. "There are those who firmly swear by him, and I wouldn't want to disparage them," he said, giving Alf a sharp look.

"No, milord," the young man answered readily.

"However, I wouldn't mind having a stouthearted fellow with another pair of eyes and ears to assist me in my investigation," Christian said.

"Ah! Then I'm your man, milord!" Alf said without hesitation.

"You can be discreet?" Christian asked.

"Silent as a lamb, milord!" Alf assured him.

Christian paused, then said to the young man carefully, "And you have no fear of night noises or strange lights, fiery-eyed dogs, that sort of thing?"

Alf snorted. "Why, I'll be happy to go out to the churchyard and sleep on old Bascomb's grave if you want!"

"I don't think that will quite be necessary. But you would have no qualms about staying at the hall?" Christian said.

Alf shook his head. "It'd be a nice change from the old place, and I expect my granddad can manage for himself for a few days."

"Very well," Christian said, obviously surprising the fellow. "Pack some things and come round when you are ready. Tell the girl who answers the bell that you are to settle in and wait for me."

"Right, milord," Alf said with a grin.

Christian nodded, then slipped out of the building, well satisfied himself. He couldn't be everywhere at once, so he could use some assistance. And this fearless young fellow might prove quite an effective spy. Or an extra fist, should things come to that.

Chapter Nine

FULL OF GOOD food and with a scheme afoot, Christian returned to Sibel Hall in far better spirits, determined not to let his hostess ruin his good mood. For one delightful moment, he imagined her greeting him with open arms in the manner of his last mistress, who had quite a fondness for his money, if not for himself. But he knew such a reception was not in the offing, and in a way he was glad. Miss Parkinson had already proved that, despite her straitened circumstances, she could not be bought. It would take more than coin to stir her interest. But what?

True to form, his hostess bestowed upon him no shining smile at his return. The colonel received a rather reserved one, while Christian got a set of pursed lips and a brief nod before a rather accusatory report that nothing, as yet, had been found in the library and that dinner would be served presently.

"Oh, we already—"

Christian managed to elbow the colonel hard enough that

he gulped for air, then slapped the old fellow on the back for good measure. "I'm hungry as a horse, and the colonel is as well!" he said in his most disarming manner.

"Well, I . . . oof!" the colonel grunted at another soundly placed nudge.

"And how was the village?" Mercia asked.

"Delightful!" Christian answered. "You should have joined us," he added, flashing a grin at his hostess.

"Some of us have work to attend to," the Governess replied rather stiffly.

"And was there much talk of our Sir Boundefort?" Mercia asked.

Christian assumed she meant the specter, for he didn't care to contemplate the alternative. "Not really," he said, hoping against hope that the colonel hadn't been paying attention when he had interrogated the company at the inn— or, at least, that the old fellow would hold his tongue for once. But whether the colonel feared another poke or simply hadn't caught his breath from the last one, he wisely kept his mouth shut. Christian was so pleased that he wondered why he hadn't started elbowing the man days ago.

"No doubt they were too agog over our visiting nobility," Emery put in, his tone caustic.

"Why, yes, of course!" Mercia exclaimed. "I suspect that Lord Moreland was the topic of conversation and all were speculating as to his visit."

Not likely, with the colonel around to give away all the details, Christian thought.

Mercia turned to Miss Parkinson. "Perhaps they think he has come to call upon you, dear."

To Christian's surprise, his hostess blushed and turned her head away. "Foolishness," she murmured.

"I don't see why not," Mercia said, ignoring Miss Parkinson's obvious discomfort.

"Yes, why not?" Christian said, ignoring it just as easily.

Emery snorted. "Because no one would believe a titled

gentleman would search for a bride among the gentry, let alone here at Sibel Hall."

His words, true though they might have been, struck Christian the wrong way, perhaps because of the speaker or, more likely, the disparaging tone in which they were uttered. "As far as I know, titled as well as untitled gentlemen can look for their brides wherever they wish," he said.

Miss Parkinson swung round at that. "What utter nonsense!" she sputtered, apparently taking umbrage at his words, not Emery's. "I am not the least bit interested in marrying," she proclaimed, her color still high. Delightfully so. Luxuriantly so.

"Oh, really? And why is that?" Christian asked, genuinely curious. He had never encountered any woman, let alone one in the financial straits of his hostess, who rejected wedlock out of hand.

"If you must know, I see no advantage to a female in such an arrangement—beyond the monetary. And as soon as Sibel Hall is sold, I shall set up my own small household, which is all that I have ever wanted. I have no need of additional funds."

Christian grinned. "Surely you can see *some* advantage beyond the monetary?" he asked, his brows lifted slightly. But if he had hoped to fluster the Governess, he should have known better. Indeed, his provocative question only seemed to harden her expression—and deepen her determination.

"And if I ever did entertain the notion of taking a husband, it would hardly be a man with a reputation as a . . . a rake, titled gentleman or not," she announced baldly.

Christian winced at the barb, as well as Emery's snort of derision. "And just what sort of ideal fellow would you consider?" Christian asked, studying her with interest.

She paused, hesitant, as though she had never even imagined a mate. What an odd creature she was! "Well, he would have to be an upright, serious sort of gentleman," she said.

"Like your father," Mercia put in.

"Yes," Miss Parkinson agreed.

"Who was your father?" Christian asked, suddenly alert.

"He was a man of science," Miss Parkinson proclaimed. "A scholar, as was his father before him. Indeed, as I understand it, the Parkinsons have always been thinkers, explorers of knowledge."

Christian frowned. His family had been founded by an explorer of another kind, one Black Jack Reade, a genuine pirate who, after being caught in a tight spot, decided to share his spoils with the crown and in so doing won himself a tidy little estate and a barony. In the years since, the Reades, showing a shameless knack for self-aggrandizement and marrying well, had parlayed that small holding into a vast earldom, several lesser titles, and a hefty bit of land.

They had never lost the craftiness of their ancestors, and Christian had always been grateful for a bit of that tainted blood. But now he rather wished he'd been born to a family a little less cunning and a lot more . . . studious. If only his dear grandfather had been an inventor or a dilettante or a connoisseur of anything but women. If only his father had spent his youth digging for ancient treasures in Greece and arraying his prizes at the family seat, instead of being a great wit and an even better gambler. Somehow Christian didn't think either skill would be high on the Governess's list.

"Indeed, I could not respect a gentleman who did not devote himself to some sort of study, not necessarily science but perhaps philosophy, literature, the arts," she was saying. Having grown more confident with the recitation of each holy trait, she seemed to be eyeing Christian directly now. "So many men are idle creatures, devoted solely to gambling and drinking and the, uh, pursuit of feminine companionship."

"How right you are, my dear!" the colonel said, with a harrumph of disapproval. At a sharp glance from Christian, he cleared his throat. "I beg your pardon, my lord. Not you, of course."

"Of course," Christian murmured sarcastically.

Warming to her topic, Miss Parkinson continued her depressing litany of virtues. "He need not be a researcher or experimenter per se, but a man of learning who continues to read and enrich himself."

Did she know how much he hated books? Christian wondered.

"Such a man would have to be scrupulously honest, of course," she said.

Christian winced again. Did that mean he should admit he knew nothing about ghost routing? It wasn't as though he had *lied* about his experience, not exactly. No one would call him dishonest, *really*.

"He would treat me with the utmost respect, a true gentleman in thought, word, and deed," she said.

Christian nearly groaned at that one, for her ideal certainly wouldn't corner her on dark stairs. Hell, the poor sod probably wouldn't dare touch her, Christian thought sourly. An heir would surely be the result of immaculate conception.

"He wouldn't have to be handsome, merely of a pleasant aspect," Miss Parkinson continued.

Christian, who had variously been described as "incredibly handsome" and "gorgeous" by swooning females, clearly could not claim to possess a "pleasant aspect." He scowled.

Apparently enjoying herself, Miss Parkinson paused, as if mulling over the coup de grace. Then she smiled faintly. "In fact, I would suspect he would wear spectacles, which I find indicative of a man of thoughtful character."

Well, that did it. Christian certainly would never qualify as a scholar. He'd frittered away his time at Oxford, totally uninterested in the deadly dull lectures on ancient times. He despised poetry, didn't care much for literature, and the extent of his reading was usually limited to his correspondence.

As Christian watched with an admittedly surly expression, Miss Parkinson smiled and calmly excused herself to see if dinner was ready to be served. There was something in the curve of that mouth that annoyed him even more than the ridiculous recitation of virtues of her intended. Her *imaginary* intended, Christian reminded himself. Some fellow too perfect to exist.

Indeed, he suspected that the wily woman had purposely described characteristics she knew he did not possess, that no one could possess, just to irritate him. Obviously his hostess was totally unimpressed by Christian's own many stellar qualities, namely his money, lineage, title, and good looks. It was almost as if she had taken pains to quote everything that he was not. Deliberately.

Christian frowned. At first, he'd thought her . . . diffidence rather amusing, the justifiable wariness of a woman facing a stranger she had invited into her home. Over the course of his stay, however, he had come to see her manner differently. It wasn't outright contempt but more of a subtle sneering, as if he were both ineffectual and a fool. Maybe he had spent a few rather aimless years in the typical *ton* pursuits, which included gambling and a certain appreciation of the ladies, but a lot of the stories that were told about him were pure exaggeration and embellishment, the Belles Corners affair being a case in point. Hell, if he'd done half of what was reported, he would have become prematurely exhausted.

Perhaps Miss Parkinson believed all the gossip, but even if she assumed the worst of him, it would hardly explain her attitude. It wasn't as though she treated him rudely, but there was that something, a distance, a look in her eye that told him he didn't measure up. To what? Some sap from the Royal Society? He'd met some of those fellows, and they were queer cards indeed and not any smarter than he. So, if he joined them, would that make him suddenly more appealing? More deserving of her respect?

Christian was tempted yet again to quit Sibel Hall for good, leaving Miss Parkinson to her own devices, but instead he was seized with an unusual desire to prove himself, to show her that he wasn't an empty-headed rogue, though why the Governess's opinion should matter one whit was a mystery to him. He only knew that it did.

As he glanced about the room and saw Emery's smirk, the colonel's downcast gaze, and Mercia's vacant smile, Christian's eyes narrowed. He wasn't normally vindictive, but his hostess had definitely roused some sleeping beast with her little performance. It wasn't as though he was too vain or arrogant to accept a rebuff, but this had become something else entirely. Miss Parkinson not only had taken off the gloves, she had tossed one in his face. And Christian was never one to resist a challenge.

"If you will excuse me, I must change for dinner," he said, abruptly rising from his seat.

But instead of heading upstairs, he searched out the servants' quarters, where he found Alf cheerfully ensconced in a tiny but tidy room. If it's a scholar she wants, it's a scholar she'll have, Christian decided.

"Hello, my lord. I've settled in quite nicely, thank you," Alf said.

"Good," Christian murmured. He swung toward the sharp-eyed fellow with a resolution that had nothing to do with the ghost.

"What shall I do now?" the young man asked. "Take a look around? Spy upon the company? Quiz the servants?" He pounded one fist into the other as though his brand of questioning would involve more force than persuasion.

"No," Christian said, shaking his head. "Your first assignment is to find me some spectacles!"

ABIGAIL FIDDLED WITH the sewing in her lap. She knew she ought to be going through her great-uncle's papers, but she had been reluctant to closet herself away from the others yet again, especially when that would leave Mercia alone in the drawing room. Dinner had been a singularly silent affair, with even the all-too-voluble Lord Moreland strangely quiet. As she picked at her food, Abigail had the odd feeling that everyone was put out with her, though she had no idea why. Except for Lord Moreland, perhaps. But what had she said to him earlier beyond the truth?

She lifted her chin. If the viscount had not contributed his usual amount of flippant observations and witticisms to the table, the party had not suffered. Rather, dinner had been more peaceful, an atmosphere she preferred. And if the stillness that followed had become positively oppressive, it was only because Emery had gone to his room to study, while the colonel and Lord Moreland had left to continue their search of the library.

Perhaps she should join them, simply to aid in their efforts, Abigail thought, her heart racing in sudden anticipation. Frowning at her own reaction, she told herself that her obligations as a hostess demanded that she keep Mercia company here, even if she could not share the woman's love of needlework.

"Are you so certain you never wish to marry, my dear?" her cousin asked, abruptly breaking the silence.

Abigail drew a breath of surprise at the unusual topic before she answered. "Yes, quite certain," she finally said. She knew that men, arrogant beings that they were, could not understand, but Mercia, of all people, surely must.

"Believe me, I have had enough of waiting upon another person's whims, and I look forward most fervently to my own household," Abigail said. "I have always wanted a little house like the cottage I grew up in, the old rectory at Haverfield. Did you know it?"

"I'm afraid not, dear," Mercia murmured.

"It was a lovely place. Peaceful and cozy, with a garden that nearly ran wild every year," Abigail said, smiling in fond remembrance. "That is my idea of a home."

"But with no family to join you there?" Mercia asked.

Abigail glanced over at her, startled, but Mercia remained engrossed in her sewing. "It would be wonderful to have my family around me once more, but they have been gone many years now," she said, firmly tamping down the emotions that threatened to surface at that admission.

"I'm sorry, dear. I knew that. But I was referring to a family of your own."

For a moment Abigail was at a loss as to the older woman's meaning. And then she realized that Mercia was referring to children. *Her* children. She nearly laughed. She had never even considered the possibility, so busy had she been fending for herself. She could not imagine being responsible for someone else as well, and the youngsters with whom she had come in contact during the last few years had all been such wretched, spoiled creatures! And yet, she did recall her own childhood warmly. If only . . .

Abigail paused and drew a deep breath. "I'm afraid children would involve a husband, and I am not interested in acquiring one," she replied firmly.

"It sounds like a lonely life to me," Mercia commented.

Abigail stiffened, hurt somehow by the aspersion cast upon her dream. "But what of you? You never married."

"I never had the opportunity, my dear, and so cannot regret a choice I did not make."

"Surely you don't regret being independent?" Abigail asked, genuinely shocked.

"There are varying degrees of independence, and few at all for women, as you well know," Mercia said. "But you are attractive and young yet and could easily garner a proposal."

Abigail made a dismissive sound. "Thank you, Cousin Mercia, but I beg to differ. I am firmly on the shelf!"

"You are not exactly an ape-leader, my dear," Mercia said with a chuckle.

Abigail smiled at the compliment, but she knew she was no beauty. Older, with a limited income and no impressive connections, she knew what sort of prospects she could expect on the marriage market: a gentry widower looking for a hard worker to raise his children or a shopkeeper who needed help, perhaps. In other words, she could look forward to a lifetime of toil with little reward. She had already been through that and did not care to undertake it again.

But Mercia continued, undeterred. "And you have certainly not lost the attention of the gentlemen."

Abigail stifled a laugh. "Thank you, but I hardly think conversation with my male relatives qualifies." She wasn't even sure she could count Emery as a gentleman or his sullen sulks as civility, let alone attention.

"I wasn't speaking of our cousins, but of our dear visitor, Viscount Moreland."

The older woman spoke in the same casual tone that she always used, but Abigail could not react quite as carelessly. Indeed, she was so startled by Mercia's comment that she poked herself with the needle she was using and bit back a cry of dismay.

Mercia, engrossed in her own sewing, must have thought the sound signaled dispute, for she continued blithely, "Now, my dear, I've seen the way he looks at you, and it is not in the manner of a disinterested man."

Against her will, Abigail felt her pulse pick up its pace. Lord Moreland, interested in her? For one giddy moment, she allowed herself to savor Mercia's words—until she remembered that her cousin also claimed to have seen Sir Boundefort's specter and believed that an old rhyme held hidden references to treasure. Mercia meant well, but she had a tendency to embroider more than tablecloths.

"Perhaps you could adjust your rather rigid list of desirable attributes to include Lord Moreland as a possible suitor," Mercia suggested.

She and Lord Moreland as a match? Ignoring the sudden fierce pounding of her heart, Abigail told herself that she had never heard a more nonsensical notion. And if there once had been a child who believed in such farradiddle, that dreamer was long grown and wiser in the ways of the world. Indeed, Abigail was hard-pressed to believe that any reasoning adult could imagine such a preposterous connection.

Although not suspicious by nature, she glanced at Mercia

sharply, seeing a pattern in the course of the household conversation. Perhaps the three cousins—or two of them—had
concocted this fantasy to save themselves from ruin, or at
least from having to leave Sibel Hall, to which they all
seemed unaccountably devoted.

In this rich piece of whimsy, Lord Moreland, a handsome, wealthy, and powerful viscount, destined someday to
be an even wealthier and more powerful earl, takes leave of
his senses and offers for a plain spinster, a former companion with nothing to recommend her except a threadbare old
manor and a ghost. At which point, presumably, the witless
man magnanimously provides for every one of her relatives.

Someone in the house had been reading too many novels.
Now, it seemed, she must nip this absurd scheme in the bud,
adding that to all her other responsibilities and concerns.
With a sigh of annoyance, Abigail poked herself again, then
stared down at her work in disgust. She hated sewing, having taken it up only on the orders of her godmother, who
thought every female ought to be usefully occupied.

She had brought it with her out of habit, but now she
wanted nothing more than to fling it to the floor and stomp
upon it. Alarmed at the violence of such feelings, Abigail set
the needlework aside carefully and rose to her feet. She felt
restless, filled with a sudden inexplicable, reckless yearning.
Obviously she was growing impatient for her new home and
its freedom from duty.

"Although I appreciate your concern for my future, I am
hardly a suitable match for a nobleman, and Lord Moreland
is certainly not the sort of man I would consider, should I be
thinking about marriage—which I am not," Abigail said.

"It seems to me, dear, that you are predisposed against
him."

Startled, Abigail glanced at her cousin sharply, but the
older woman was still bent over her needlework.

"Considering your circumstances, I suspect it is only natural for you to feel some resentment of the wealthy and privileged," Mercia added.

Abigail blinked in surprise. Resentment? Certainly not! She was not one of those female philosophers who wished to overthrow the country's class structure. She had no wish to trade places with the empty-headed, spoiled, vindictive females of the upper orders, and she opened her mouth to say as much. But a niggling sort of doubt, along with a predilection for the truth, made her shut it once more.

Perhaps she did harbor some small bit of prejudice against the very rich. She had seen her godmother's friends and relatives waste their time and money in idleness, gambling, or drink, an observation that undoubtedly had colored her opinions, and not for the better. It seemed to Abigail that so many of the *ton* had everything handed to them and squandered it, while other worthy people, be they tradesmen or soldiers or churchmen, struggled just to feed their families. It was entirely unfair, she admitted. But was it fair of her to lump all noblemen together when there were some who worked for the betterment of the populace, through Parliament or their own devices?

As if reading her mind, Mercia spoke again. "I hardly think it right to judge the viscount solely on the basis of his position in society, a birthright he can help no more than you or I."

Abigail frowned. Perhaps she was a bit biased concerning Lord Moreland and had raised her expectations concerning his achievements accordingly. In contrast, Emery hadn't accomplished much with his life so far, and yet she didn't belittle and belabor his shortcomings. Unsettled by the idea, Abigail was not sure how to respond.

"Just think about it, dear," Mercia advised. "His lordship could be your chance for real happiness. Don't throw that chance away merely because of preconceived notions."

After years of attending her godmother, it took quite a bit to overset Abigail, but Mercia had managed to do it with a brief, fantastical conversation. Abigail stood there staring at her cousin's bent head, torn between the urge to laugh out loud at such preposterous nonsense and the urge to weep for the loss of the girlish dreams that might have let her believe it.

"I think, dear cousin, that you are letting your imagination run away with you," Abigail finally managed. Straightening her shoulders, she turned on her heel. "Now, if you will excuse me, I think I will look over some accounts."

Hardly lingering long enough to hear Mercia's murmured good-bye, Abigail hurried from the room. But even though she had every intention of heading for the study, her feet seemed to travel of their own accord toward the library instead. She ought simply to retire, she told herself. It was growing late, and the gentlemen probably had abandoned their search for the evening. Yet she knew that Lord Moreland kept no regular hours, and for some reason her breath quickened.

She paused to take a deep, calming draught of air, telling herself that she would find the room empty and the object of her unaccountable anticipation applying himself to a bottle in the cellars. Yet she saw the thin glow of lamplight through the doorway that meant someone was still about. Perhaps the colonel had fallen asleep in an armchair there, she thought. It would not be the first time.

When she reached the threshold and looked in, however, both men were still there, awake and occupied with the search. "I say, take a look at this," the colonel said, pointing to a book he held in his hand.

"Let me see." The low timbre of Lord Moreland's voice sent unwanted shivers down Abigail's back, though she had once thought it as straight and impervious as the rest of her. Apparently not. The tremors seemed to travel throughout her body down to her fingertips even as she paused in the shadowy entrance, like a thief in the night stealing a glimpse of him. Surely she hadn't been affected by Cousin Mercia's lunatic suggestions?

Determined to disprove that notion, Abigail lifted her chin and prepared to announce her presence, but at that very moment Lord Moreland, who had walked over to where the colonel stood, reached into his coat and pulled out a pair of . . . spectacles! Abigail was held fast, stunned to silence by the sight of him carefully putting them on, then leaning over to study the volume that the colonel tendered.

He wore spectacles? She tried to still the sudden clamoring of her nerves at the revelation. She had never heard that he did, but she was not exactly privy to the habits of the *ton*. And perhaps they were strictly for reading, an activity in which she had never seen him engage. Indeed, in her less charitable moments, she might have suspected him of lacking the skill altogether.

But he was reading now, right there before her eyes, and despite all her efforts to the contrary, Abigail's heart tripped, her breath caught, and her pulse pounded as she saw him casually, elegantly, lift a hand to the page before him. His features were aglow in the lamplight, his golden hair falling forward, gilded to a burnished sheen, and Abigail was sure she had never seen anything so beautiful in her life.

When he had asked her what kind of man she would consider marrying, Abigail had deliberately stressed certain attributes just to prove a point—that Lord Moreland's high opinion of himself was not shared by all and sundry, that other, more important characteristics were valued by discerning people. But now all her heart's desires coalesced into this one perfect vision. He wasn't a scholar. She knew that, and yet what did she have to base her judgments upon? Her own prejudices? A first impression? Hearsay? Casual manners and a bit of erratic behavior?

All her presumptions seemed to melt away in the heat of the moment, and Abigail felt a soaring feeling in her heart, accompanied by a sinking feeling in her head. Both parts of her recognized that the sight of him here and now had caused some sort of shift in the current of her life. She had been treading water before, trying her best to ignore a certain undertow, but now she was drowning. Sunk. Lost forever . . .

Chapter Ten

CHRISTIAN STARED AT the long line of dusty old volumes and tried to appear scholarly. As difficult as it was, his technique must be working, for Miss Parkinson seemed to have thawed just a bit since he had first donned his new spectacles the other night. He had seen her, of course, lurking in the doorway, but it had been his good fortune that the colonel chose that particular moment to point out some useless bit of information which required him to put on the damn things.

He had practically felt her reaction from the doorway and had tried not to look too smug. Although she hung back, never entering the library that night, Christian noticed the difference, subtle yet delicious, in her manner toward him. She still wasn't what he would call warm, but her smiles weren't quite as forced, her expression as disapproving, or her demeanor as forbidding. He liked the idea of thawing things out even more, though he wasn't quite sure what he would do with an overheated Miss Parkinson.

Christian shuddered as a sudden very real inferno gripped him, and he grabbed a book, any book, for a needed distraction. After a glance at the cover, he paused in surprise. It looked as though he had finally found something interesting, a period piece on how to build a manor house. Just like Sibel Hall.

Leafing through a few pages, Christian admired some exquisite wood-block renderings of late medieval architecture before his attention was caught by the delicate sprawl of old ink. He squinted through the spectacles, which were little more than clear glass, and was delighted to discover handwritten notations in the margins. Some long-ago owner must have felt compelled to comment on the author's work.

Pushing at the rims perched upon his nose, Christian read, "None at the Hall" next to a reference to oriel windows. At last he'd found an observation, however unenlightening, about the place!

Christian flipped through more pages, searching now for the elusive script, and he turned the book to see the next one more clearly. "Blocked off after the tragedy," it said. Tragedy? What tragedy? Against his better judgment, Christian felt the tickle of curiosity. He had just begun reading the small text beside the notation when he heard someone approaching.

In the unlikely event that the noisy arrival might be Emery, Christian quickly tucked the volume behind his back, not willing to share his find with the so-called scholar. He straightened just in time to see Miss Parkinson burst into the room, startling him so that he nearly dropped his prize. The Governess never hurried, never skipped, never danced, and certainly never *burst*. Christian was even more surprised to discover that her face was flushed becomingly and her eyes bright. He wanted to ravish her right then.

"There is a buyer interested in the house!" she announced, the cause of her enthusiasm putting a bit of a damper on Christian's own euphoria.

"I have just received word from a Mr. Smythe of London.

He is in the village and wishes to come at once to have a look!" she said, waving a missive, presumably the one just received, in one hand.

Christian watched excitement—or the closest he had ever seen to excitement—light her face, and he felt a twinge of guilt. Of course, no one here, including his hostess, knew that Mr. Smythe was Christian's solicitor and that no sale would ever materialize from his viewing Sibel Hall. Christian fought against the odd sensation that he had betrayed the woman, beating it down with a cudgel of good sense. After all, his hand had been forced. As much as he disliked deceiving Miss Parkinson, the ghost had driven him to desperate measures.

Christian couldn't remain here forever. He had other responsibilities, other tasks awaiting his attention. Yet how could he leave without completing his charge here? And how could he even begin to rid the place of a specter that failed to show itself? Since Sir Boundefort's past appearances seemed to be connected with potential buyers, presumably for the express purpose of driving them off, the only thing to do was to dangle a buyer before the old haunt. Thanks to Sir Boundefort's efforts, however, no real purchasers were interested in the place, so Christian had to manufacture one. And just in case anyone in the household might give away his game, Christian had kept his scheme to himself.

When he had written his solicitor, it had seemed a clever enough plan, but he hadn't counted on the odd feeling of duplicity that nagged at him. Only the knowledge that he was also misrepresenting himself as a scholar and a ghost router saved him from blurting out the truth. He decided that since he was lying about pretty much everything, at least he was consistent.

"Of course, I have sent word that he is most welcome to come at his convenience," Miss Parkinson said. She sat down hard upon a Grecian sofa, a frown creasing her brow.

"But what about Sir Boundefort? What if he decides to show himself?"

That's just what I'm counting on, Christian thought. Aloud, he said, "I'll take care of the specter."

She glanced up at him, as though startled by his sudden determination, and then paused, her gaze arrested. Christian realized he was still wearing his spectacles, and he had to bite back a grin of triumph. Really, this was all too easy. He said nothing, waiting as she stared at him rather dreamily before catching herself and straightening.

"I don't suppose you have found anything?" she asked. If the question had a negative ring to it, at least her tone lacked its usual bite.

"I'm afraid not," Christian said, trying to adopt a scholarly manner. "The library is, uh, very well stocked." Although he had made a concerted effort to search the shelves, he was too restless to keep at the task for long, and his labors had been interrupted by walks through the house, inspections of the cellars, and the like.

Still attempting his best impression of a studious sort, Christian strolled past his hostess, gesturing at the bookcases, as one of his old instructors often did. "There are many, uh, interesting volumes. But so far we have found no records of the house itself, no history, no plans, no family memoirs." He paused to shake his head. "That is odd in itself. Where is the family Bible? Where are the deeds and accounts and anecdotes of generations? I can't even find any reports on the village or the area."

His own family histories, grossly embellished, of course, were ensconced in a favored position in the portrait gallery at the earl's seat. Christian paused to deliberately furrow his brow, as it seemed the sort of affectation his new persona might adopt. "Is there another place where these things might be stored?"

Miss Parkinson shook her head. "I have no idea. I haven't run across anything of the sort in the study, but I have yet to go through all the clutter in there. And I haven't even begun to inventory the rest of the rooms. Perhaps what you are looking for is scattered about the building or has gone missing long ago."

Christian rubbed his chin in what he hoped was a thoughtful manner. "That is always possible, but the complete lack of these materials makes me wonder if they haven't been stored elsewhere. Or if someone else isn't hoarding them." Emery and his so-called studies came to mind, and Christian wondered if a search of the scholar's rooms might be in order.

Miss Parkinson shook her head again, not following his hint. Perhaps she wasn't as cynical or suspicious as he. Or perhaps she actually trusted that weasel cousin of hers. Christian frowned, unable to comprehend that possibility.

"Have you asked the cousins?" Miss Parkinson asked. "I will, but first I must make certain that all is in readiness for Mr. Smythe's arrival." She rose to her feet with sudden purpose. Christian was hard-pressed not to scowl. Although he sensed a certain softening in her attitude toward him these past few days, he still never seemed to see much of her.

He realized that she was busy with Sibel Hall, but it wasn't as though she could actually do anything to improve the place at this late date, certainly without putting plenty of money into it. Yet, as always, she would not linger in his company, especially when they were alone. It was almost as if she possessed some kind of timing device concealed on her person that rang out a warning after a spare few minutes.

Christian eyed her sharply, tempted to search for it, and to his surprise, her gaze met his and slid away as she lifted a hand to her hair. He paused in surprise. Was the woman actually concerned about her appearance? Christian felt a surge of triumph that waned as soon as he wondered whether her unexpected awareness was connected to him or to the potential buyer. Suddenly he wanted to pound the daylights out of his own solicitor.

But when his hostess excused herself, her eyes downcast,

Christian realized he was still wearing his spectacles. And he grinned.

MR. SMYTHE ARRIVED directly, and Christian made it a point to be in the drawing room to greet him. The three cousins were there, as well, and Miss Parkinson introduced everyone graciously. True to Christian's instructions, Mr. Smythe pretended ignorance of his employer and all else to do with Sibel Hall. He had a client who was interested in a nice, older property within a certain price range, such as this one, the Londoner explained. And he even made a show of looking forward to touring the dreadful structure, with that client's interests in mind.

"Well, we are most delighted to meet you," Miss Parkinson said. "But I'm afraid that the solicitor who is handling the estate is occupied elsewhere and will be unable to join us." Apparently, the fainthearted fellow could not be induced to return to the Hall on any account, but there was no need to mention that small point.

"Quite understandable," Mr. Smythe said. "I must apologize for appearing on such short notice."

"Not at all!" Miss Parkinson protested, most sincerely. Christian had no doubt that she would welcome any interested party who showed up on her doorstep, at any time of the day or night.

"I will, however, be guiding you about myself, and since I haven't lived here very long, I must beg your indulgence," Miss Parkinson said. Christian took a moment to wish she would beg *his* indulgence, then glanced around in surprise as all three cousins remained mute.

Apparently the Governess had given them strict instructions not to join the tour, and Christian made a mental note to question her about it, as well as to ferret out the details of the previous showings. Just who had been involved during those instances? He seemed to remember Mercia claiming to have seen a specter on one such visit, but he needed to know exactly who was where each time. This time, he himself would be there.

"I'll join you," Christian said. Flashing a smile at his hostess, he moved forward without giving her a chance to argue. She could hardly do so when the specter might make an appearance at last. Christian practically rubbed his hands together in anticipation, perhaps of getting them around the old knight's throat.

Smythe proved to be well worth his fees as they trooped through the sprawling structure's rooms. He was knowledgeable about houses and even managed to point out a few selling points that had escaped Christian's notice. But despite the man's enthusiasm, Sir Boundefort remained elusive.

By the time they reached the great hall Christian was growing impatient, particularly since the Governess spent several minutes extolling the virtues of the space when it was clear that she knew nothing whatsoever about its architecture. Having held his tongue as long as he could, Christian was about to break in, even though Mr. Smythe could hardly care one way or the other, when a noise drew his attention to the fretwork.

Alert at once, Christian stepped closer and cocked his head to the side, straining to hear the odd keening sound. It was sort of a whistle or a wail, although why a ghost would make such a curious din, he had no idea. Then again, he was no expert on the phenomenon. Glancing covertly at his companions, Christian saw that Miss Parkinson continued speaking, while trying her hardest to ignore the interruption, and Mr. Smythe, though politely paying attention to her, kept darting glances toward the fretwork.

Finally, Christian walked directly to the dark partition, hoping to better determine the source of the noise, but the large hall, with its vaulted ceiling, made that task difficult. This time he was fairly sure it wasn't coming from below, which puzzled him. Where else would the ghost hide except in the cellar—or in the formerly locked rooms?

Christian hurried behind the fretwork, only to find that someone had closed the door he had left standing open. Reaching for it, he jerked hard to no avail. The damn thing was locked again! He patted his pocket, but the hairpin was long gone, presumably removed by his efficient valet. Muttering a curse under his breath, Christian turned to retrace his steps and beg his hostess for another when he heard Smythe's gasp.

"What the devil is that?" the solicitor asked, his normally steady voice wavering ominously.

Hurrying now, Christian emerged from behind the partition to see both Smythe and Miss Parkinson still as stones and staring somewhere above his head. The solicitor looked rather white-faced, while his hostess gaped, as if amazed, her luscious lips parted delightfully. Swinging around, Christian glanced upward, unable to see much of anything except the heavily carved wood dissolving into the darkness. For one wild moment, he wondered if the ghost made himself visible only to certain people, himself not among them, then he stepped backward, working his way toward his transfixed companions.

And finally he saw it.

High up behind the fretwork there was a flash of white. Christian squinted, stepping back once more to obtain a better view, and there, seemingly floating in thin air, was *something*. It was pale and diaphanous and rather shapeless—not exactly Sir Boundefort come to life but definitely more interesting than a few knocks from under a bed. Of course, it was too dark to see well, but Christian had prepared for that possibility, having instructed Alf to secrete a couple of lanterns about.

Hurrying behind the fretwork, he conducted a cursory search that told him the lamp he was seeking wasn't there. He rushed out again and went quickly to a side table, where he found the requested lantern tucked underneath. Lighting it, he stepped back to where his companions were standing

stock-still and held it high, but the glow did little to illuminate the upper reaches of the shadowy end of the hall.

Irritated now by both the elusive phantasm and the keening noise, Christian stared up at the thing for a long moment
before coming to a decision. The only way to get a closer
look at the specter was to get closer to it. Gazing up at the
intricately carved partition, Christian wondered if the steady
footwork of his pirate ancestors would serve him if he tried
to climb the fretwork. This was certainly no rigging, and he
hoped fervently that the old wood had not rotted away as he
grabbed hold and started up.

But he hadn't counted upon Miss Parkinson, who took
sudden, violent exception to his plan. Just as he managed a
foothold, she gasped in horror. He could only assume that
the Governess didn't approve of her guests climbing the
walls.

"My lord, what do you think you are doing?" she cried,
rushing toward him. "Stop that at once!"

Christian might have ignored her, except for the fact that
she managed to grasp his coat and tug on it in an attempt to
keep him grounded.

"Miss Parkinson, let go of me!" he said, only a veneer of
civility keeping him from throwing her off. Or over his
shoulder.

"I will not!" she replied, in her usual stubborn, argumen-
tative fashion. Why was the woman so damned difficult?

"Stand aside, I tell you, or you may be hurt," Christian
warned.

"I may be hurt?" she echoed, as if incredulous.

Christian turned his head to glare down at her, only to become aware that the keening had stopped, replaced by a
rather loud noise that sounded like throat-clearing. He
glanced behind him to find Smythe trying to get his attention.

"Uh, I believe the, uh, thing has vanished," the solicitor
said, pointing upward with a pudgy finger.

Christian looked up but could see only darkness. Cursing

under his breath, he swung his gaze back to his hostess. "Now see what you've done!" he snapped. For a long moment, Miss Parkinson simply stared at him while clutching his coat, and for once, Christian was too angry to wish her touch elsewhere. Finally, as if coming to whatever senses she might possess, she released her hold, and he dropped lightly to his feet.

But his mood was not so light. Without pausing to consider his course, Christian took a menacing step forward, while his hostess stepped backward accordingly. He had only an instant to relish that satisfying response before *she* lashed out at *him*. "See what *I've* done?" she said, echoing his words. "What I've done is probably save your life, you, you *idiot!*"

Christian stared at her, dumbstruck. Her face flushed, her eyes flashing, her breasts heaving, his hostess looked far more attractive than her usual dowdy self, and he felt a most primitive reaction. His lust was tempered, however, by her words. Christian couldn't remember anyone, even his grandfather, ever calling him an idiot.

"Now just a moment," he said, reaching out to grasp her arms. He glared down into her face as she glared up at his, the two of them locked in angry silence. Then her mulish expression gradually gave way to something else entirely, and Christian felt a kick in his gut. Or was it his groin? He wasn't certain what he felt or what he intended to do about it, but given the heat of the moment, his response probably would have centered on the luscious mouth that was parted slightly. Indeed, he was just about to give in to an urge that had nothing to do with the scholarly image he was trying to assume when he heard another loud clearing of a throat.

"Uh, if you'll excuse me, I think I'll go out for a breath," Mr. Smythe said.

Glancing over at the solicitor, Christian couldn't tell, but he had the uneasy suspicion the man was laughing. At *him*, the *idiot*. And while he was gaping at Smythe, his hostess slipped from his fingers. Christian didn't know whether to be relieved or disappointed when he found himself grasping thin air.

For her part, Miss Parkinson looked decidedly flustered, presumably because she had actually raised her voice. With a sigh, Christian glanced away, suddenly unable to look at her. The pounding heat had passed, but its intensity left an indelible impression, at least upon him. He told himself that anger at her interference had driven him to such strong emotions, but there was much more involved, so much more that Christian couldn't begin to understand.

He told himself he was lucky to avoid what surely would have earned him even more contempt, but his fingers tingled at the loss of her. He wanted her back in his arms, no matter what the consequences. Even as he tried to still the indecent clamoring of his heart, Christian was seized by the rather daunting notion that if he ever really did lay claim to this woman, he would loose an array of emotions far more fierce than his usual remote dallying, far more exciting than simple sex, far more sustaining than friendship.

That union loomed before him, as deep and changing and fascinating as the seas that had lured his ancestors, and Christian knew he could take a breath and plumb the depths. Or he could simply skirt the issues and skim the surface, a temptation for a man who was accustomed to taking all that life offered with ease.

Over all the uproar inside himself, Christian heard Mr. Smythe clear his throat yet again, and he knew that now was not the time to make any sort of life-altering decision. His solicitor was waiting, a specter might be lingering, and the subject of his conundrum looked as confused as he felt.

"There is no need for you to leave, Mr. Smythe," Christian said over his shoulder. He lifted his hand once more to extend his palm to his hostess, who eyed him warily. As well she should. "I need . . ." Christian paused, a wealth of hidden meaning in those words. "Another hairpin," he muttered.

"What? Why?" It took the flushed Governess a full

minute to gather her composure, which pleased Christian no
end. Finally, she lifted her delicate brows in disbelief. "Do
you mean to tell me the door is locked again?"

Why else would he want her hairpin? Christian thought.
If he was the type of man who desired a memento of their
recent encounter, he would certainly take something far
more substantial. Swearing under his breath, Christian deliberately turned his thoughts from that path once more and
nodded curtly. "Yes, the door is locked again."

Miss Parkinson's eyes widened in surprise, and she lowered her voice. "You don't suppose that Sir Boundefort did
it, do you?"

Christian realized that he had abandoned all attempts to
appear scholarly, but he couldn't help it. He had no idea
what those in the scientific community thought, and as for
himself, he could neither prove nor disprove the existence of
ghosts. But he would swear by anything that this specter, at
least, was not otherworldly.

"No, I don't. I assume that he could pass right through
the oak without bothering with lock or key," Christian answered. "This business is the work of some mischief
maker." As he had thought all along, someone here at the
Hall was up to something. He would love to get his hands on
the culprit.

For once his hostess did not argue with him, but lifted
pale fingers to her hair. Before he embarrassed himself gaping like a hayseed, Christian turned his head away. This time
he didn't feel up to watching her remove the pin, not
after . . . whatever . . . had just happened.

When she laid the piece of metal in his outstretched
palm, Christian tried not to notice its warmth or anything
else. Taking it up, he hurried behind the partition without a
backward glance. But even as he knelt in front of one of the
doors, he swore that this time would be his last. As soon as
he got a chance, he was going to have Alf remove the damn
things from their hinges.

When he heard the click of the lock, Christian grabbed up

his lantern and rushed through the passage, only to find an empty room and the door to the outside firmly locked. Rather than waste time there, he turned and headed to the other door and the cellars, Miss Parkinson at his heels.

"Please stay at the top of the stairs," he said. But of course she ignored him, following behind as he searched for any signs that someone had been this way. His lone lantern did little to dispel the darkness, and with a sharp surge of annoyance, he realized that he was too late. If he had managed to get down here right away or if the door hadn't been locked perhaps he could have caught a glimpse of something.

Now he looked at the vast, shadowy space, cluttered with all manner of items, and knew there was little he could do. If anyone had passed this way, he or she had plenty of places to hide—behind heavy furniture or even in old cupboards—and it would take more than one searcher to find the culprit. Cursing under his breath, he turned back toward the stair.

"Aren't you going to look around?" Miss Parkinson asked.

"Why bother? We'll never find anything in this jumble. Meanwhile, no one is guarding the door," Christian reminded her. "I don't know about you, but I don't care to be shut down here."

If he expected her to cringe, as usual, at the prospect of his company, unchaperoned, she proved him wrong. "You could simply pick the lock again," she said fearlessly. "I have plenty of hairpins."

Was it his imagination or did her lips curve into some semblance of a smile before being lost in the darkness? A heat spread through Christian at the thought, and as he climbed the steps, he grinned. In another setting, he might have pursued the possibility of that smile further, perhaps with a stroll in the garden or a tryst in some private parlor, but here the way led to a dark stone passage and a drafty great hall, where Mr. Smythe stood waiting nervously.

For a moment, Christian paused to watch Miss Parkinson's attempts to mollify the man she thought was a prospective buyer, but then he seized his opportunity to slip away. As much as he disliked parting with his hostess, he had someone else to meet. And a ghost to rout.

Chapter Eleven

CHRISTIAN FOUND HIS quarry lurking not far from the great hall, but instead of watching the suspects as instructed, Alf Kendal seemed to have his eye on one of the maids—at least until he saw his employer.

"Milord! Now, don't have at me!" the fellow said, holding up a hand to stave off Christian's wrath.

"Well?" Christian prompted, crossing his arms over his chest.

"Well, you see, it's this way, milord. I tried to keep an eye on all of 'em. I truly did! But they were too slippery for me! That colonel, he took off right away, kind of following you, like. Hanging back, but close enough to hear what was said, for a while at least. I figured he would stay put, so I checked on the others. That puny young fellow was gone, and that old lady, she thought I was the solicitor. Me!" he said, shaking his head at that. "Then she demanded to know exactly who I was and what my business was at the Hall! Right fierce she was, too!"

Cousin Mercia fierce? Christian began to think he had misjudged his man. How could Alf be counted upon in a fight if he was intimidated by an eccentric elderly female?

"By then, I'd lost both the gentlemen. Looked down by the hall here, but saw no sign of either one of them," Alf said. He shook his head again. "I'm sorry, milord, but if you want all three of them watched at once, then we're going to have to have some help."

Christian sighed. The young man had a point. But even the oafish Emery presumably would notice the sudden appearance of a legion of spies. And they would need a veritable army to watch all the doors, inside, outside, and below in the cellars, let alone any hiding places he had yet to discover. Christian scowled. This ghost-routing business was turning out to be far more difficult than he had expected.

Conceding the problem, he nodded to Alf. No man could be three places at once. But now he knew no more about the movements of the three cousins than before the specter's appearance. Had one of them managed to sneak ahead to reach the great hall before he and Mr. Smythe and Miss Parkinson arrived? But how could anyone manage to dangle . . . whatever it was . . . from the vaulted ceiling?

"I take it old Boundefort showed himself?" Alf asked, canny lad that he was.

"He did indeed," Christian said. "Or rather, something did. It was hard to see up there in the shadows."

"Up there?" Alf asked.

Christian nodded absently. "Yes, he was sort of floating around the rafters."

"He was *floating*?" Alf asked, even his hardened voice rising a bit.

"*Something* was floating," Christian amended.

"Well, how the devil did it get up there?" Alf asked.

"That's what I intend to find out," Christian declared. Alf gave him a sidelong look as if to say that he didn't envy that task. Christian was none too keen on it himself. Either the specter had disappeared into thin air by virtue of his other-

worldly abilities—a possibility that Christian found unlikely—or someone more substantial had put on quite a
show, then made a clean escape, probably to the outside.

Or perhaps there was some other hidey-hole that Christian had yet to find. These old houses were often riddled
with priest's holes, secret passages, and the like, and such
places might not be described anywhere. Not that he had
found any accounts of the house at all, Christian thought
sourly. That observation reminded him of the book he had
found, the only record, however feeble, of anything to do
with the damned structure. Now where had he put it?

"Well, I can't say whether any of those three you set me
to watch was up to something or not. But I can tag after one
of 'em now, milord," Alf offered, eager to assist once more.
"Personally, I'd have a go at that military fellow. Never
knew one that was trustworthy," he added, nodding sagely.

Christian was more inclined to suspect Emery, but he
wasn't sure how much of that suspicion sprang from his gut
dislike of the so-called scholar. He caught himself scowling
and turned his attention back to Alf. "And just how do you
intend to shadow anyone about the hall undetected, especially after being caught out this afternoon?"

Alf turned red-faced, obviously embarrassed at having
been trapped in the act, and by an old lady no less. He
cleared his throat. "I'm thinking you can say I'm your valet
or some such."

Christian eyed the young man askance. "I already have a
valet," he said, not bothering to add that Alf did not resem-
ble one in the slightest. The village youth looked more like
a groom or a driver, but what possible reason could someone from the stables have for wandering about the house?

"You shall just have to say you are a manservant," Christian said. "But right now I'd like you to take a look in the
cellars. See if you find any signs that someone has been pok-
ing around down there. And, for God's sake, do something
about the door locks, so that no one can keep us out again."

"Yes, milord! I know just the thing," Alf said with a

wink. He hurried off, presumably to fetch whatever he needed for the job, while Christian headed back to the great hall—and Sir Boundefort.

MUCH TO CHRISTIAN'S disappointment, the vast space was deserted, but he told himself it was just as well. He had difficulty concentrating on the task at hand when Miss Parkinson was around. Perhaps something about that lilac scent affected his brain, and other parts of him, as well.

Crossing the old tiles with a swift stride, Christian stopped before the partition to stare up into the darkness. No telltale signs of the spirit lingered, at least from what he could see, but he remembered very well where it had been. The placement had been a nice touch, making the thing difficult to catch while amazing the onlookers. Of course, Christian didn't believe anyone or anything was capable of hovering in midair like Montgolfier's balloon. Indeed, he thought it no coincidence that the specter only showed itself conveniently close to the fretwork.

He studied the screen with a critical eye. Although the carved wood looked sturdy enough, he wondered if he ought to have Alf fetch him a ladder, if only to placate his hostess. But even as he stared upward, considering his options, something nagged at the edge of his awareness. What?

While he struggled for an answer, he heard a noise behind him and whirled, his body tense and alert. It might simply be Alf or . . . Christian was pleasantly surprised to recognize the drab skirts of his hostess. Had she actually sought him out? That heady conjecture was quickly tempered by her expression, which made him certain he wasn't going to enjoy this encounter.

The Governess was back in full force. Fighting an urge to straighten up and check his hands for cleanliness, Christian smiled graciously, a waste of good teeth, no doubt. The Governess halted several yards away.

"If I may have a word with you?" she asked.

Christian made a show of glancing around. There was no one else in the hall. "Certainly," he said, tempted to throw up his hands in exasperation. Or throw her over his shoulder and then stop her mouth with his—before she could say anything annoying.

Too late. "I hesitate to interrupt you," she said. That old tone was in her voice, intimating that he was frittering away his time simply gawking at the ugly hall. "But I'm afraid that I've received some disturbing news."

Uh-oh. Had Smythe broken under pressure exerted by the mistress of Sibel Hall, telling all? Christian tried to look suitably innocent. "Oh?" he asked in a casual voice.

"Indeed," she answered, her hands behind her back, as though preparing for a good, stiff lecture. "It seems Cousin Mercia was quite startled by a rather . . . unsavory person wandering through our private rooms."

Mercia startled? From what he had heard, it was the other way around. The old woman had scared poor Alf, probably tormenting him with tales of ghostly sightings and paranormal activity.

As if she could tell he wasn't appropriately serious, the Governess pinned him with a gimlet eye. He wondered if misbehavior warranted a spanking, and then grew positively warm at the thought. Lud, his tastes were becoming bizarre. Next he'd be begging her to take a switch to him in some sort of de Sade business. The tutor and the naughty boy? Christian nearly laughed aloud at the notion of the upright Miss Parkinson participating in any such nonsense.

"I hardly know where to begin," the Governess said.

Me either, Christian thought wickedly. He arched his brows slightly, which made Miss Parkinson's lower. She drew a deep breath. "Since Mercia does have a tendency to . . . embellish, I hesitate to accuse you of any . . . poor judgment," she said. And yet wasn't that exactly what she was doing? And it wasn't the first time. Christian nearly shook his head in amazement. He couldn't recall anyone ever having the temerity to find fault with him, and now he seemed to be getting more than his due.

"Well, I see I shall have to speak plainly," she declared in a huff. "Cousin Mercia claims you are employing one of the village ne'er-do-wells in some sort of personal capacity. Considering the situation here, do you really think it best that you introduce someone else into my household, especially someone of ill repute?"

Christian didn't miss her emphasis on *my*, and he wondered if Miss Parkinson weren't perhaps a devotee of de Sade after all—at least the dominance part. She certainly tried to lord her meager power over him. Did she treat everyone that way, or was he alone privileged to receive that treatment? If so, why? Perhaps he ought just to submit and find out.

His pirate blood made submitting a bit difficult, though. No matter how tempting he found his hostess, he wasn't about to ask permission to hire his own people. Nor did he feel the need to explain that "unsavory" Alf was just the type he needed for his rather furtive operation.

Christian affected innocence. *Studious* innocence, he hoped. "Well, I thought it might be wise to have some assistance."

Her look told him she thought him ineffective enough on his own. "Surely there is someone already within the household who would prove more . . . reliable?"

"I thought it better to employ an unbiased party," Christian said, trying to sound scholarly.

"But surely there are far more suitable people among the local populace," she protested.

"Ah, but I had my reasons for picking Alf," Christian said, assuming a thoughtful air.

Miss Parkinson lifted her brows, and he was hard-pressed not to grin. "I had to choose a fellow who wasn't afraid of ghosts," he confided.

That one stumped her, and for a moment he thought she might actually give way, but he should have known better.

She opened her mouth to argue further, prompting Christian to step forward and lean close. "If he lifts any of the silver, I'll pay for it myself," he assured her.

As always, Miss Parkinson seemed flustered by his nearness and pulled away even as he reached for her arm. He caught a whiff of lilacs and then heard something fall to the floor. He hoped it wasn't anything he would miss, like his good sense . . . or his heart.

They both leaned over to retrieve the dropped item and bumped heads. Not exactly the body part he would have hoped to rub up against. Reaching out a hand to steady her, Christian found himself gazing into her face, open and suddenly vulnerable. Had he actually hurt her? He opened his mouth to ask, only to watch her eyes widen and her gaze drop . . . to his lips.

Heat flooded him, along with a sort of wildness that was startling. He wanted to seize her, slide over her, and take her on the medieval tiles, here and now. Not trusting himself to move, Christian knelt there, staring, as she met his gaze. For one heady instant he felt as though she might agree, might even meet him in a headlong rush to passion. But then she broke away, and the moment passed. Like the one earlier this afternoon, it was gone forever, a chance not taken.

Miss Parkinson straightened, and Christian could do nothing else but rise as well, pummeling all his reckless impulses into a pose of civility, if not studiousness. She held something before her like armor, almost as though to fend him off, and he nearly laughed. If she thought a book would stop him, she was sadly misguided.

"I found this on a side table in the gallery, and I didn't know whether—"

Christian cut her off with an exclamation of delight. "The book!" he cried. Recognizing the volume that he had so recently found in the library and put aside in order to greet Mr. Smythe, he reached out with unfeigned eagerness. Indeed, so intent was he upon the tome that he nearly forgot to don his spectacles. Thankfully, he remembered when the pages fell open, and he reached into his pocket for them.

Moving with deliberate care, Christian made the donning of the lenses into a slow, sensual act that sent his own pulse kicking, while Miss Parkinson practically swooned. Biting back a smile of triumph, he assumed his most serious expression as he leafed through the volume, seizing an excuse to inch closer to his hostess when he found the page that had so interested him earlier.

"See this notation?" he said.

"Y-yes," she answered, and Christian was pleased to see she was not as unaffected as she might pretend.

" 'Blocked off after the tragedy,' " she read aloud. "What tragedy?" she asked, turning her head. She was so near that he could feel the brush of her breath.

"I was hoping you might tell me," Christian said. And that wasn't all I was hoping . . .

She broke away yet again, her gaze sliding from him even as she stepped back, and Christian was hard-pressed not to groan in disappointment.

"What kind of tragedy would cause you to block off part of a building?" she asked.

Christian glanced down at the printed words, trying to find an answer in the accompanying text, and then it suddenly leapt out at him. "That's it!" he cried. Slamming shut the book, he strode toward the fretwork, staring up at it in excitement. "That's how it was done!"

"What? How what was done?" Miss Parkinson asked, sounding a little alarmed at his enthusiasm.

Christian brandished the volume, but couldn't even attempt to appear studious. "They walled up the way to the minstrel's gallery!"

"What is the minstrel's gallery?" Miss Parkinson asked, her brows furrowing.

Christian pointed. "The fretwork hides a balcony where musicians once played for the lord of the hall. And I'm betting that's how our ghost managed to float through thin air!"

As Christian watched comprehension dawn on his hostess's lovely features, he had to fight an urge to spin her around in celebration of his discovery.

"If it is walled off, how did anyone except Sir Boundefort himself find a way up there?"

"That is what we have to determine. But I have a feeling that once we open up the minstrel's gallery, Sir Boundefort's haunting days will be over."

Snatching up a lantern, Christian headed behind the heavily carved wood, his hostess close at his heels. He held the light high, but as he suspected, its glow did not illuminate the upper reaches of the wall, where the gallery must lie, hidden in shadow. The space was simply too dark and narrow.

Thankfully, the door that led to the cellars still stood open, and Christian stepped inside. He had never really examined the room thoroughly, having been intent upon finding the cellars at the time. Bad lapse, that, he scolded himself. He was really going to have to pay more attention to detail if he expected to rout this troublesome specter.

Now he did so, walking the perimeter slowly, holding the lantern high, then swinging it low, inspecting one wall and then the other, peeking behind objects but moving nothing as yet, gauging the size of the space and the placement of the walls. Beside him, his companion kept blissfully quiet, and he was again reminded that despite all her annoying habits, when it came right down to it, Miss Parkinson could be counted upon to behave in just the right manner—unlike any other female he knew.

They had nearly gone round the entire room when Christian paused at a telltale sign at his feet. He knelt to examine scratches in the tiles, as if something heavy had been moved, then glanced up to see an ugly old painted coffer that might once have held medicines or stored herbs angled before him. Straightening, he pushed the monstrosity away from the wall, and there it was: an opening, dark and ragged.

Christian lifted a hand to one rough edge. Obviously,

someone had cut through the plaster that blocked the way, perhaps with the very same tools that lay in the cellars. Lifting the lantern high, he stepped through the hole to find a set of stairs curving upward. Despite his excitement at the discovery, he made his way carefully, lest he meet some pitfall, either accidental or intentioned by the specter or its minions.

The swish of skirts behind him told him that Miss Parkinson followed, game as ever. Of course, there was no point in telling her to wait behind, and that knowledge, instead of irritating him, filled him with a kind of exhilaration as they marched onward together into the thick of adventure—or as close as one could come to it in rural Devon.

The steps opened onto a narrow balcony along the wall behind the fretwork. Without the lantern, it would have been black as pitch, and even with the light, the space was thick with shadow. Christian didn't know what the flooring was like, so he reached a hand out to his companion.

"Careful here. Watch your step," he warned. When the old wood held their weight, he released her and searched the space, hoping to find . . . he had no idea what. But though he swung the lantern high and low, there was nothing to be seen except the clean-swept planks and the dark expanse of carved wood a few feet ahead of them. Although Christian ran a hand along the surface of the stone wall, he could discover no signs of any other egress, and his initial sense of triumph began to fade as he realized that the proof he had expected to uncover wasn't here.

The mystery of the specter remained.

ABIGAIL WATCHED THE play of light upon the old plaster and wood as the lantern swung this way and that and tried to look for some sign of Sir Boundefort. But her attention kept straying to the flesh-and-blood man at her side, more real and far more compelling than any ghost. Indeed, it seemed to her as though Lord Moreland was even more handsome in the near darkness than he was in the broad light of day, a truly spectacular feat, considering that his visage always was breathtaking.

Right now he was frowning, his brows drawn together in a rare display of displeasure, but it did nothing to detract from his appeal. In truth, Abigail was seized by a sudden urge to smooth that brow with her own hand, a most disturbing impulse. Deliberately, she looked away and tried to catalogue all his failings.

After all, hadn't he just unleashed some miscreant upon the household without even consulting her? But his explanation was so reasonable, she could hardly fault him. Still, he might have shared his thoughts with her. She owned Sibel Hall, and after long years of standing by powerless, she wanted to be apprised of everything. Now that she finally had a measure of control over her life, she was loath to relinquish even a bit of it.

"Come!" Abigail barely had time to draw a startled breath before her hand was seized in a firm grip, the object of her musings pulling her after him like so much flotsam. Her irritation at this type of manhandling was overwhelmed, much to her dismay, by the delicious heat of his fingers holding hers, a sensation that should not, by any means, be quite so delightful.

"What on earth are you doing now?" Abigail asked when she managed to catch her breath at the bottom of the narrow stairs. She snatched at her skirts with one hand while her companion helped her through the opening—a rather nasty, gaping hole, in her opinion. Once through, she watched while he pushed the cupboard back into place and tried not to mourn the loss of his touch.

"I'm tired of wasting my time hunting for missing records and plans. I'm going to take a look at the outside of the building myself and see if I can find any hides," he said, striding down the passage toward the door to the old kitchens that now led outside.

"I assumed you had already searched for such things,"

Abigail said a bit peevishly. It seemed to her that the man had accomplished awfully little during his time here.

"Not the right way!" he answered over his shoulder in a getting-down-to-business tone that sent an unaccountable thrill through her. Abigail told herself she was simply pleased that he was finally doing *something*.

That knowledge alone was enough to prompt her to return to her work and let him go about on his own. Mounds of paperwork awaited her in the study, and she had other pressing duties to tend to as well, including soothing Mercia's ruffled feathers about the interloper from the village.

Even without all those responsibilities, Abigail knew she ought not spend time alone with Lord Moreland, unchaperoned. Indeed, since his arrival, she had done her best to avoid him. Yet somehow she continued following him down the corridor. Considering his tendency to become distracted, she reasoned that perhaps she ought to keep an eye on him, just in case he stumbled across more wine or something of that nature.

"And just what way is the *right* way?" Abigail asked as he led her outside. She was determined to concentrate on the matter at hand, but the change from the dank darkness to the fragrant breeze made her pause, and she drew in a deep breath. The air was fresh and clean, the old courtyard overgrown with plants that had once been neatly arranged. Abigail suddenly realized she had never even explored the grounds.

Once she had loved to walk and study nature, but years pent up inside with her godmother had dimmed that joy. Now it seemed that she was still tied to habit and duty and must work to recover that delight. Perhaps when she had her own little cottage, with its own small garden, she would be able to treasure such moments again, she thought wistfully.

"The right way, barring any written record, is to walk around the outside of the house looking for discrepancies, like unexplained stretches of blank wall. Or try to envision what the place would look like without one of the walls. The chimneys are good indicators of the locations of interior walls," Lord Moreland said.

Abigail tried to follow his directions, but her attention wandered instead to the man himself. His voice had altered subtly, and there was something about his stride, suddenly so purposeful, that engaged her. And the way he stared up at the house, with the discerning eye of an expert . . . why, he was actually studying the building, she realized.

"The chimney stacks are usually in projections along the outside walls, and there's probably an internal wall between one stack and the next. Staircases are most often located in projections too, and may be indicated by smaller or staggered windows. The current central stairway here, with its open area, is clearly a later addition," he observed.

Abigail listened to his casually tossed words in growing astonishment. She could only gape as he pointed toward the side of the house not far from their recent exit. "You can tell the great hall is there because the house was originally built around this courtyard. In such arrangements, the hall is at the back, with the kitchens on one side and the family apartments on the other. Of course, that initial design has been added on to several times over the years, with disastrous results.

"And yet those additions are just the place for us to find surprises," he noted, flashing a smile at Abigail that in itself was enough to make her heart race.

Turning to walk in another direction, he pointed at an outcropping. "The timber-and-plaster framing here makes it easy to add, subtract, or alter partitions without much reference to windows or chimney stacks. And even the original roof space will have taken repairs over the years, at which point false ceilings may have been inserted.

"When I searched the interior, I couldn't find anything that looked like an attic chapel from the days when Catholics had to practice in secret. That doesn't mean there wasn't one, of course, but it makes it hard to find one without any plans. Then again, plans are most useful when the floors and ceilings are consistent throughout the house, which is definitely not the case here. And we can ignore the most modern addition, since hides passed out of fashion in the early fifteenth century."

Dumbstruck, Abigail stared at him in complete amazement. How could she have imagined that he had done nothing while he was here? Read nothing in his life? Knew nothing beyond the frivolous?

"Whoever else is looking for the supposed treasure, or whatever, obviously has discovered something. He's been up in the minstrel gallery and down in the cellars, chipping away at the foundation." Lord Moreland shook his head. "But he's not very clever. Although stone walls can be thick enough to have spaces quarried out of them, and some medieval residents kept their valuables safe from fire and theft in such small spaces, I didn't see any evidence of that sort of thing in the cellars."

He paused, as if in thought, and Abigail feared she might swoon. Not only was he the most beautiful and virile of men, but she had been very wrong in dismissing his life as wasted. Obviously he wasn't only a rake and a gambler, but possessed a mind worthy of admiration. And she was happy to admire it . . .

"No," he muttered to himself. "If there are any hides, I'll wager they're in the additions, some location where it is difficult to account for all the space, either under the roof or around the chimneys or old staircases, especially a staircase near a chimney stack." He turned to look at her, his face alight with an excitement that made Abigail shiver in response. "And I know just the place!"

Abigail was so enthralled that she could only stand there wide-eyed, and so she might have remained if he hadn't plucked her from her place as he passed her, dragging her along with him again, back toward the open door. She didn't even stop to wonder why she allowed such behavior after vowing never to be led about by anyone.

In truth, Abigail was too occupied with the feel of Lord

Moreland's hand against her back as he hurried her forward.
And if she did have one coherent thought, it was the
abysmal observation that right now she would probably follow him anywhere.

Chapter Twelve

⚜

THE STAIRCASE TO which Lord Moreland led her was an old one that Abigail could barely remember, for it opened onto rather drafty apartments that had been forsaken for more modern rooms in a newer wing. Again, she was struck by the fact that her guest had not been wandering about aimlessly as she had suspected, but had done his research. The thought made something quiver within her breast, and Abigail hoped, quite fervently, that it was not her heart.

She stood by, trying not to gaze too adoringly at his person while Lord Moreland studied the stair carefully, making rudimentary measurements with his long strides. And yet she found it impossible to ignore the way his blond hair glinted in a patch of sunlight, the way his lashes fell against his cheek, and even the way his breeches fit his rather muscular legs.

To Abigail's chagrin, everything about the man seemed twice as bright, twice as handsome, and twice as compelling as before. Her own good sense told her that was quite impossible. The man had not transformed himself; it was only her perception of him that had changed. It had all started with those dratted spectacles, she thought, wishing that she had never seen them.

Abigail had no idea how long she stood there watching Lord Moreland tap on the walls around the steps, but it was surely the most time she had ever wasted. At various moments she considered knocking at the paneling herself, but since she wasn't precisely certain what he was looking for, she deemed it best to stay out of his way. She knew logically that she should be off doing something else, yet she couldn't seem to make herself move. After all, he might very well rouse Sir Boundefort with his efforts, and Abigail did not want to miss such an appearance.

She was trying to avert her eyes from the somehow intimate sight of Lord Moreland putting his ear to the wall when he finally made a low noise of triumph. With a flourish he turned to her, and to her astonishment a heavy oak panel swung upward to reveal a dark cavity. Abigail stepped forward, but he held her back with an outstretched arm.

"Let's have a look first, shall we?" he said. When he picked up the lantern he had brought with him from the great hall and thrust it into the space, Abigail gasped aloud. Anyone trying to enter this hide would have taken a fatal step into nothingness, for behind the panel the floor dropped away into a black hole.

Alarmed, Abigail clutched Lord Moreland's arm, thankful that he had not rushed forward headlong. Stricken at the thought that something might have happened to him, she looked up at his face—a face suddenly and fiercely beloved. Luckily for her, he was too occupied with staring into the hole to notice her concern, and she removed her hand from his sleeve. But her fingers shook, and she had to draw a deep breath to regain her composure, so shaken was she by the thought of his possible injury—or worse.

It reminded her of the moment earlier today when he had started to climb the fretwork in the great hall, a piece of folly that would surely have resulted in his broken neck. But he had not thanked her for her intercession, Abigail recalled with a frown. Despite his heretofore unappreciated knowledge and expertise, Lord Moreland possessed a dangerously reckless streak. And for some unaccountable reason, instead of inciting her disapproval that observation made her pulse race.

"Ah, there's a ladder," he said, his voice filled with an enthusiasm that Abigail did not share. She dutifully peered where he pointed and saw old pieces of wood leaning against one wall in the narrow opening.

Although Abigail dismissed the discovery, to her horror Lord Moreland swung one leg across the abyss and placed a booted foot on one of the ancient rungs. Again she grabbed his arm, but it held the lantern, which swung wildly, inciting her further. "You cannot mean to go in there!" she protested.

"Of course I do," he answered, flashing a fearless grin that both thrilled and irritated her.

"But you have no idea how old that thing is or if it is even stable. Nor do you know what might await you below!" Abigail exclaimed.

"Why, Miss Parkinson, I've never known you to be fainthearted," he said, his smile now both brash and challenging.

Abigail lifted her chin. "I am not fainthearted. I am simply being sensible."

"Ah, so that's what you call it," he said. He held up the lantern as if to take it down with him, but he was hindered by Abigail's grip on his arm. When he lifted his eyebrows in that maddening fashion of his, she released him, albeit reluctantly.

"As the owner of this house, I demand that you get out of there at once," she said.

Far from obeying, her guest simply laughed. "But you are always demanding that I do my job, and this, Miss Parkinson, is it." And with that, he began climbing downward.

Stricken, Abigail leaned into the opening and watched the bobbing lantern descend with alarming speed. But before it disappeared entirely into the blackness, she took a deep breath, lifted her skirts, and swung herself into the space. Her foot found a hold even as she grasped at the worn wood, the old ladder banging against the wall with the force of her efforts.

To his discredit, her companion did not voice any surprise at her arrival. In fact, he seemed to find her appearance amusing. "I should probably warn you that this might be an old garderobe shaft," he shouted up at her.

"Garderobe? You mean a *privy*?" Abigail cried. Her voice was loud in the slender passage and sounded a bit panicked, which no doubt contributed to Lord Moreland's laughter, echoing from below.

Thankfully, the space didn't smell. If it had once been used to transport waste, it must have been thoroughly cleaned. Still, Abigail was careful not to touch anything beyond the ladder and tried to prevent her skirts from brushing against the wall.

Now that she was inside the opening, she felt no fear, certainly not for herself. She realized, with no little startlement, that she had complete confidence in the man whom she once had characterized as lackadaisical and unwise. He would protect her—she knew that with utter assurance—while she would do her best to keep him safe as well.

Somehow that idea did not seem absurd, even though she could hardly expect her presence to prevent anything untoward happening to Lord Moreland. Still, she was struck by the odd notion that together they were invincible. Perhaps such errant thoughts were based upon the homily that should something disastrous occur, it was better to have another person on hand to go for help. Or at least that is what she had heard.

To Abigail's relief, the old ladder held, and she made her way to the bottom without incident. There she turned to face Lord Moreland, who grinned unrepentantly, despite his flagrant disregard for her wishes. And instead of giving him a lecture on personal safety and adherence to civil behavior,

Abigail felt an answering jolt of awareness run through her, his high spirits somehow infectious.

Neither could she ignore his light touch upon her back and his presence beside her, so close in the narrow passage. Down here they were completely alone, so cut off from everything else that the darkness seemed to enclose them in a secret world all their own. The isolation fostered a sense of connection between them that was only heightened by Lord Moreland's mood.

Apparently he thought that exploring some old and possibly dangerous passageway was the height of exhilaration. And perhaps it was. Abigail realized that she had become so entrenched in a life of drudgery and duty, so deadened to emotion, that she had forgotten how to react with anything other than numbness.

Lifting her chin, she took a deep breath and tried to feel, opening herself up to experience, and when she did so a sharp sense of anticipation pierced her, so bright and fierce that she nearly stumbled. Lord Moreland's hand was there, at her elbow, to keep her from mishap, and she felt a distinct surge of something run through her, as though passed from him through his touch. Breathless and giddy, Abigail was struck by the notion that in that moment he had reanimated her as surely as one of Mary Shelley's corpses.

Indeed, all reasonable concerns about their journey into the depths fled as she reveled in this sudden sensation of *life*. Everything around her seemed more poignant, as though all her senses had sharpened. The darkness held an exotic mystery to it, and the glow of the lantern a brilliance that dispelled the shadows. The air was stuffy and close, but she caught the pleasing scent of her companion, a heady mixture all his own that made her heart pound frantically.

"It looks like this is the end of the road," Lord Moreland said, his voice so low and compelling that Abigail shivered.

"Don't worry," he said, misconstruing her response. "There must be an exit. I just have to find the catch."

Abigail watched as he moved toward what appeared to be

a solid wall and ran his beautiful hands over the surface. Drawing in a sharp breath, she realized that any sensible woman would be worrying about their egress. Instead, she stifled a strong desire to have those beautiful hands run over her.

Shocked at such thoughts, Abigail wondered if perhaps being numb and dead had been so bad after all. But it was too late to go back now. She had emerged from her tomb and would not be induced to return, no matter what manner of dangerous ideas her rejuvenation produced. In fact, she found those dangerous ideas so appealing that she stood watching Lord Moreland with a kind of breathless wonder.

He moved within the pool of light, tapping here, pressing there, making low sounds of disappointment or discovery, just as her father had when working on some scientific study. His features were alive with excitement and such bright intelligence that she wondered now how she could ever have thought him less than brilliant. Enthralled, she took the opportunity to admire his dedication, his grace, and well, yes, his body. After all, it was hard to ignore in these close confines, especially when he leaned this way and that and stretched upward and bent down, presumably looking for trapdoors or openings of some sort.

He was tall and solidly built, though Abigail could not find an inch too much flesh anywhere within view. And she looked. Well, who could blame her? There wasn't anything else to do at the end of the narrow corridor except to study her companion. And when he moved out of the lantern light, Abigail had to stifle a cry of dismay.

It was not simply because she could no longer peruse him at her leisure. Seeing him disappear into the blackness dredged up old fears from her youth when the loss of her parents had taken her from a safe, comfortable, loving world into another, far less appealing one. There had been other desertions, as well, one especially that made her nearly call him back. But at last a shred of reason prevailed, reminding her that no man, not even Lord Moreland, would leave her here alone.

Abigail relaxed slightly, forcing her breathing to ease as she concentrated on the sound of his taps and bangs while he searched. But without the distraction of his delightful form, her worries returned. What if he couldn't find a way out? What if the panel by the stairs had fallen shut, and they were trapped in here? Abigail tried to dismiss such fancies. She hadn't escaped from her godmother, her heart's desire finally within reach, only to expire in some musky old tunnel.

Still, the possibility nagged at her, especially now that she would least welcome it. She had spent all those years as a companion half dead, eking out an existence that might have sustained her body but not her spirit. Now, when she was free and truly alive, she would not succumb to an old passage. Nor would she stand idly by and watch life pass her. Drawing a deep breath, Abigail vowed to seize each moment. No more hours spent closeted with old papers. She would go out, even in the most inclement weather! She would visit the village! She would go riding! She would . . .

Abigail's silent declarations were interrupted by the movement of Lord Moreland, and she stepped out of the way, as best she could, as he brushed past her. Her response was automatic, but while she pressed her back against the wall, Abigail wondered why she bothered with petty courtesies at this point. After all, she was cooped up here alone with the man. Why even bother with his title? Abigail knew his name, and the knowledge suddenly made her giddy.

"Christian," she whispered. The sound, loud in the silence of the gloom, sent shivers up her spine.

It caught Lord Moreland's attention as well, for he stilled immediately. He was so often moving that his sudden quietus was arresting in itself. He wasn't facing her, but while Abigail stood watching, he turned his head slowly to gaze at her with an intensity that made her want to hide. But she remembered her recent vow and chose instead to meet his gaze directly, losing herself there. Who could forget his eyes, such a deep green as was possessed by no other? It was sinful for a man to have such eyes, Abigail decided.

"Yes?" he asked softly.

Whether spurred by the darkness or the danger or the nearness of him, Abigail felt emboldened, reckless, desirous of some experience beyond the mundane march of her days, some memory to take with her either to the tomb or back into the world. Outside this passage, she had been trained to a life of duty and dullness, but here in the shadows she felt a wild freedom, along with an urgency that could not be denied.

"Kiss me," she whispered.

The words slipped out, as if wrung from her by some unseen power, and for one horrible moment Abigail thought he might refuse her. She saw the surprise upon his handsome features. What if he should laugh in her face? Deny her? Argue that she had rebuked him for untoward behavior? Suddenly Abigail was assailed by a multitude of worries and fears. But they melted away as he slowly lifted his hands to cup her face.

Although his weren't the smooth hands she expected of the idle rich, she welcomed their roughness. There was strength in them, Abigail knew it, yet his thumbs stroked her cheeks in the gentlest of caresses. She watched, enthralled, as he bent nearer and nearer . . . Then her head tipped back, her lashes drifted closed, and he kissed her.

His lips were so soft, so welcome that Abigail made a small sound of joyful greeting, and she leaned into him, sliding her hands up his waistcoat, feeling the breadth and heat of him before she locked her arms around his neck. His mouth moved over hers, tasting, exploring, and when she felt the sweet, insistent pressure of his tongue, she welcomed it as well, reveling in the warm invasion.

Abigail heard herself moan blissfully, but she didn't care. Instead of withdrawing in horror, she kissed him back, clinging to him shamelessly, and to her utter delight, he, too, made a low sound of pleasure as he pulled her into his arms.

The press of his body made her breathless and giddy. Her head swam, her blood pounded, and her spirit sang, for surely this was all she had ever dreamed. Now she was truly alive in every sense and glad of it.

Abigail whimpered when his mouth left hers, but it was only to rain kisses along her cheek and against her neck, in hidden places behind her ear and in her hair. She murmured her approval and then was shocked to realize he was removing her hairpins and tossing them away, releasing the heavy mass down her back. She gulped, both jolted and elated by his action, then watched wide-eyed as he drew back to study her, running his fingers through the thick strands and arranging them around her face. When he did so, the look in his eyes was so fierce and hungry that Abigail nearly quailed before it.

But something inside her rose to meet that hunger, and she lifted up on her toes, took his face in her hands, and kissed him, holding him steady, entwining her tongue with his. He groaned, the sound rumbling up from his chest through his throat and into her veins as he pushed her back against the wall. He seemed anything but scholarly now as he took her mouth with near violence, his hands roaming over her body with shocking familiarity. And Abigail welcomed his touch, forgetting all concerns about dedication and study, remembering only that this was Christian, Lord Moreland, the only man who could ever move her in this way.

Nothing else mattered except the feel of his hard body against hers, the taste of his mouth upon her own, and the desperate, driving need to know him better—in every way. Abigail seized her chance in the shadowy passage, running her fingers through his silky hair, gilded golden by the lantern light, pressing her lips against the heated skin of his throat, and moving her palms over his shoulders and chest. Somehow she ended up tugging at his coat, and he shrugged it off so that she could feel the strength of his arms through the pale linen of his shirt before he seized her again.

Wishing that one of her own garments might be so easily discarded, Abigail rued her usual companion's clothing, dark and ugly, long of sleeve and high of neck to hide her from the world and its denizens. The material, which had suited her well before, now seemed too heavy, too thick, a barrier between her needy flesh and Christian's caress.

Christian. She whispered his name, and to her surprise, he answered her in kind. The sound of his voice, deep and low, murmuring *Abigail* against her hair, nearly made her swoon. Her head fell back even as he pushed her higher against the rough plaster, his lower body, hard and pulsing, finding a niche between her thighs.

At her gasp, he lifted his head, and she peered through a fringe of lashes at his dark gaze, intent upon her. "You . . . You make me . . . I've never . . ." he whispered brokenly, in a manner wholly unlike his usual glib self. "Oh, hell," he swore, and then he seized her again. He moved, and the world upended. Literally.

One moment Abigail was pressed up to the wall, the next she was dropping through space, Christian with her. The man possessed amazing reflexes, for in the span of that instant, he turned her to take the brunt of the fall himself. Abigail felt him land with a thud, his arms round her, and then they rolled, coming to a stop in sweet-smelling grass. Her head spinning, she thought at first that she was imagining another's voice, crying out, but then she heard it again, and she knew she wasn't dreaming—or alone.

"I say! What the devil?"

The voice, exceedingly loud, was impossible to ignore, and Abigail slowly opened her eyes to the sight of a pair of men's feet. Men's bare feet. Ugly, bare, men's feet. Surely they weren't Christian's? Gulping in surprise, she followed the line of the toes, past a thick ankle to a pair of hairy, bandy legs and, thankfully, the hem of some sort of banyon.

"Abigail? Lord Moreland? By Jove!" Glancing just a bit higher, Abigail realized the bare feet, bandy legs, and banyon all belonged to her cousin, the elderly colonel, who was standing before them clutching his robe in one hand and some sort of cudgel in the other.

Having identified them, the colonel apparently no longer saw the need for the makeshift weapon, so when he lowered it, Abigail took the opportunity to sit up. After attempting to smooth her disordered skirts, she lifted a hand to her head, only to recall that her hair was loose down her back, her pins gone. Her face flamed, and her only consolation was that the colonel's was just as red.

"I say! I was just about to have a bath when I heard the most peculiar noises emanating from the hill here. Rather alarming, I must say." He looked a bit sheepish as he put the cudgel, a rather hefty branch, to one side.

A bath? Abigail glanced about her and realized that they were in some sort of valley that apparently housed the Hall's plunge bath. She vaguely remembered the solicitor pointing out the spot when giving her a tour of her property, but she had dismissed it, having no desire to trudge outside to cleanse herself. A small tub in her room suited her much better, thank you.

And well she had been proved in her decision, for now the colonel stood before them looking utterly ridiculous and indecently unclothed. As Abigail saw the folly that housed the bath nearby, she could only be thankful that they had not come upon the man ensconced in it! Of course, their own precipitous arrival had to look extremely odd to her cousin, and she tried to find some kind of suitable explanation.

It eluded her, however, and she simply stared blankly at the old gentleman while Lord Moreland rose to his feet, dusted himself off, and reached for her hand. With his help, Abigail managed to stand, but her legs were shaky, and she was far too aware of the warmth of his touch.

"Are you all right?" he asked.

She nodded swiftly, unable to meet his gaze.

"Nothing broken?"

Just my pride, Abigail thought, as she abruptly became

aware of the ramifications of the situation. She shook her head glumly.

"Very good," he murmured, before turning to address her cousin. "I beg your pardon, Colonel! We had no intention of interrupting you, or indeed, coming outside at all, but we seem to have stumbled across a hidden passage in the Hall."

"Really?" Completely disregarding his state of undress, the colonel was all curiosity, shuffling past her to peer into the blackness that they had but recently vacated.

"I say! I had no idea!" the old fellow marveled, though he evinced no interest in actually stepping into the opening.

"I suspect it is an old priest's escape route," Lord Moreland said. He swung round as if to study the area in which they now found themselves. "I would imagine it was already here, buried in that hill, when the plunge bath was built and was simply incorporated into the design. Perhaps for the purpose of midnight trysts," he added, flashing a grin that made Abigail recoil.

Although seemingly amused by her reaction, Lord Moreland sobered as he turned back to the colonel. "However, if you don't mind, I would prefer to keep the discovery of the passage among just the three of us."

The colonel gave him a bewildered look.

"Part of my research and all that," Lord Moreland explained, with an air of confidentiality.

"Oh! Of course!" the colonel said.

"Besides, the other cousins might worry, or take it upon themselves to have a look," Lord Moreland said. "And I would hate to see anyone hurt or trapped. Why, we barely made it out ourselves."

"I can see that!" the colonel said with a glance at their disheveled state. Although he seemed quite happy to accept that excuse, he was eyeing her hair a bit quizzically, and Abigail had no idea how to account for the loss of her pins—unless she claimed Sir Boundefort had plucked them out.

"The place is quite narrow and low and frightfully confining," Lord Moreland said, surprising her with the lie.

"Miss Parkinson's hair was caught on a nail, and I, uh, lost my coat, as well."

The explanation sounded feeble even to Abigail's ears, but the colonel seemed to swallow the falsehoods with equanimity. "Dreadful business!" he muttered. "Ought to have the place shut up or blocked off!"

"Yes, of course, but in the meantime I think I shall try to close it myself," Lord Moreland said. Ducking inside, he returned, thankfully wearing his coat, and proceeded to push the stone face into place with apparent ease. But then he did everything with ease, didn't he? Abigail reflected.

Turning back toward them, he flashed a smile. "Now, we must be off, so as to close the other end of the passage and to allow you to continue your ablutions."

The colonel, reminded of his state of undress, turned red-faced and pulled his banyon tighter around his body. "Yes, of course. Most unseemly."

Abigail was glad to escape any further scrutiny from her cousin, but when she felt the light touch of Lord Moreland's hand at her back, she drew in a ragged breath. Suddenly she wasn't that eager to leave the area and her relative, no matter what he might think of her. The colonel's company now seemed eminently preferable to being alone with Lord Moreland, considering what had gone on between them. Swallowing a groan of dismay, Abigail looked back with longing to where her cousin stood awkwardly by one of the pillars.

If the old fellow hadn't been half naked, she would have rejoined him in an instant.

Chapter Thirteen

CHRISTIAN HEADED TOWARD the nearest entrance to Sibel Hall, aware that he must close the opening to the passage before someone else stumbled upon it. However, his thoughts kept darting from the hiding place to what had happened there, and he felt a new rush of heat and want and . . . wonder. What else could he call it when the Governess who so often looked upon him with disapproval, the woman who had once spurned his advances, whispered his name in the darkness and became a lilac-scented creature of desire?

His heart thudding anew, Christian glanced at the woman beside him, half convinced he had imagined the whole thing, but her hair, tumbling down her back in glorious disarray, told a different tale. He grinned, pleased with his handiwork, then shook his head. He couldn't believe how his previously dismal luck had turned, how the formerly standoffish Miss Parkinson had changed, or how incredibly passionate their encounter had been.

He was still hot. Just a whiff of lilac was enough to tighten his breeches, and he groaned as he shortened his stride. Beside him, Abigail wore a more circumspect expression, at odds with her rather wild coiffure, and he wondered how the devil he was going to prevent the Governess from reappearing. It was this woman, the one who had whispered his given name in the darkness, he wanted. Abigail.

What had caused her transformation? Christian wondered. All he could think was that his spectacles must be working, though he found the realization rather jarring. Holding the door open for her, he leaned forward to draw in a deep breath of her delectable scent. To hell with the passage. His immediate inclination was to haul her upstairs to his bed or at least somewhere where they could continue what they had begun.

But would a scholar do that? Christian frowned and forced his steps toward the open panel even as he wondered what course to take in this extraordinary situation. A scholar would do . . . what? Christian tried desperately to remember all he knew of studious types, but he could recall only how dreadfully boring they were.

"I, uh, really must repair my, uh, myself." The sound of Abigail's voice, low and breathless, brought Christian from his musings, and he glanced over to see her looking rather stricken as she tried to put her hair into some kind of coil.

"Here," Christian heard himself saying as he pulled the lone hairpin from his pocket and held it out to her.

She smiled rather nervously, and he knew a fierce urge to keep her with him, perhaps forever . . . only because once out of his sight, she might change back into the distant creature of scorn and rules and rigidity.

"Thank you, though I don't think one will be much help," she said. At least she took the pin, anchoring the heavy weight of her hair precariously at her neck, where it hung half unbound.

Christian swallowed hard, fighting the need to spread the silken strands across her breasts and rub his palms over their softness. He sucked in a harsh breath. He wanted to rub her all over. Hell, he wanted to *lick* her all over, tasting every inch of the delicious body hidden beneath her dowdy garments. Opening his mouth to say as much, Christian paused. A scholar would never say such a thing, he realized, and he grimaced, suddenly finding his new persona constricting. Far too constricting, as he gave a surreptitious tug at his breeches.

Having secured her hair, Abigail turned to go, and Christian frantically sought some way to stop her. Besides tossing her over his shoulder. "Wait," he said, hurriedly shutting the passage entrance. "Did I close the way to the minstrel's gallery, too?" he asked, uncertain. His mind was in a muddle, a lust-crazed delirium.

"I, uh, don't remember," she answered, in her Abigail voice. Low, soft, and so sensual it made Christian feel as though her hands were running over his body. If only they were. Gooseflesh rose as he imagined himself naked and . . .

She eyed him uncertainly, and Christian shook his head. "Let's make sure. Walk with me," he said, inclining his head. He was afraid to touch her, afraid to scare her away, afraid, for once in his life, to take what he wanted. Should he say something about what had happened between them? Should he apologize? Hell, no! Not when he was aching to do it all over again.

What would a scholar do? Christian wondered rather desperately. For perhaps the first time in his confident existence, he was at a loss, so they moved along in silence that seemed to grow more uncomfortable by the moment. Although he had no idea how some studious type might behave, Christian was fairly certain this was not the way to hold any woman's interest. When they finally reached the great hall, he poked his head into the unlocked room and saw that he had indeed pushed the cabinet back into place, where it hid the opening behind it.

When he returned to the great hall, Abigail lifted her brows in question, and he nodded while trying to think of something—anything—to keep her with him. Should he drag her back into the darkness? Simply reach for her? But when he took a step forward, she took a step back, suddenly wary.

"I, uh, really should go," she whispered.

"No!" Christian tried to put some order to his careening thoughts. How to stay her? Words of admiration? Words of love? Words of poetry? Christian balked. He wasn't really a scholar—or even a ghost router.

"That's it," he muttered to himself. Then he flashed a grin at Abigail, who eyed him uncertainly. "Before you go," he said, intimating that he would let her leave . . . someday, "I wanted to remind you not to mention our little discovery to anyone else, including your relatives. And while we're on the subject, I'd like to ask you a bit about them, as well."

Before she could refuse, Christian continued, assuming his most thoughtful expression. "Just how well do you know these cousins of yours? What can you tell me about them?"

Although she sounded surprised, Abigail answered in a matter-of-fact tone. "I had never met them, as I can recall, before my arrival here, so I'm afraid I can't tell you much about them at all."

Christian frowned. Not the answer he cared to hear. "They all lived here until the death of the previous owner, Mr. Bascomb Averill, your uncle?"

"Great-uncle," Abigail amended. "And they weren't all living here. I think the colonel has made Sibel Hall his home for some time, but Emery was just visiting, down from school, and as I understand it, Mercia simply came for the funeral."

"And stayed on?" Christian prompted.

"Yes, well, you can hardly blame them," Abigail said, though her expression seemed to belie her words. Christian had to struggle against an urge to kiss her practical yet luscious mouth.

"I know you are eager to sell the house, but should you succeed, what will become of them?"

"They each were left a small stipend in the will."

"But they won't be staying on here?" Christian prompted.

Abigail shook her head. "None of them has that kind of money, I'm certain. Nor have they evinced any interest in purchasing the house, no matter how attached they are to it."

Christian paused, then strode across the tiles as he spoke. "So each of the three has either visited here before or even lived here and has some attachment to the place. And yet you are the one who now owns it."

Abigail stiffened. "I was as surprised as anyone by the inheritance."

"Obviously, your great-uncle had some good taste," Christian said, flashing Abigail a grin that seemed to catch her by surprise—and put her back at ease. "Yet his choice would seem to cause some resentment among the other relatives, wouldn't it?"

Abigail paused, as though to choose her words carefully. "I suspect they were as surprised as I was by the contents of the will, though I don't think anyone could claim to have held Bascomb's affections. However, if they are resentful of me, I have never seen any sign of it."

"Still, it's not a good situation," Christian murmured, half to himself. "You are the one who will benefit from the sale of the house, yet someone is preventing you from doing so."

"Someone or something," Abigail amended.

"Perhaps," Christian acknowledged, though he didn't believe for one moment that anything otherworldly was responsible for Sibel Hall's haunting.

As if reading his thoughts, Abigail looked at him quizzically. "But if it truly is not Sir Boundefort, then what could someone hope to gain by such nonsense?"

"I'm not sure, but I don't like it. I don't like it at all." Christian turned to her sharply. "If anything should happen to you, who would inherit?"

She blinked at him, as though astounded by the question. "Well, I have never had the need to make out a will, so I assume my next of kin, and, before you ask, I'm not sure who that would be."

Christian swore under his breath. So far, nothing untoward had been directed at Abigail herself, simply the interested buyers, but what if whoever was behind those incidents decided to scare the lady of the house? Or worse? Christian's dormant protective instincts rose to the fore, and he was seized by a sudden desire to take her away—from Sibel Hall, its resident ghost, and all her relatives.

But to where? He didn't even have a home. Of course, he could take her to the family seat, but what would his grandfather say? Hell, the earl would probably welcome her with open arms. It was Christian who felt a certain uneasiness about the plan, the kind of uneasiness that came from sudden, irrevocable life change. Still, he was tempted, driven by a need to keep her safe, above all else.

He opened his mouth to make the suggestion, only to shut it again. One look at Abigail's face told him she would never leave. The woman was nothing if not resolute, an admirable trait . . . sometimes. Christian frowned. "Do you have a firearm?"

Abigail arched a lovely brow. "Am I supposed to shoot the ghost or my relatives?" she asked, displaying the acerbic wit that Christian appreciated more fully when it wasn't directed at himself.

He answered her sardonic look with a grim one, well aware of the role reversal. "I am serious. What if our specter, whoever or whatever it is, decides that you're standing in his way, that you're expendable? I don't like the idea of you running around here, revealing yourself to some unknown assailant at every turn, without any way to defend yourself."

"Who says I can't defend myself?" she retorted.

Christian sighed. Why was the woman so damned difficult? Before he could argue, she turned toward the wall of weapons and removed one of the decorative swords from its perch. Did she think to defend herself with that? Christian burst out laughing, though his laughter died away when she brought the point to his throat.

"You find me amusing?" she asked, her lips curled into a challenging smile that made his blood heat. The Governess as swordsman? Would she ever cease to amaze him? With a grin, Christian dragged the other foil from its place and prepared to put her in her place. Or at least show her a few tricks.

Flourishing the blade, he bowed low, both his confidence and his excitement high. Abigail chose that moment to hike her skirts so as to widen her stance, and all Christian could do was gape as the gown inched upward. Although the elegant fashions that women wore often hid a wealth of defects, that was not the case here. Abigail's ankles were small and well turned, and the sight of her shapely calves made Christian break out in a sweat. To some degree he was aware that this glimpse of Abigail's lower limbs was arousing him far more powerfully than the naked forms of his last three mistresses, but that awareness did not stop him from staring, transfixed, his body responding accordingly.

Only the slap of her foil against his own jarred him from his stupor. Startled, he looked at her face, finding it flushed and smiling as she lunged, easily knocking aside his nonexistent defense. He rallied even as he admired her skill, her form, her grace, but most of all the expression of triumph on her face, along with something he had never seen there before. Delight. Freedom. Exhilaration. Christian realized he was faltering again, so enamored was he of his opponent, and he struggled to deflect her surprisingly effective attacks.

She was skilled and aggressive . . . and distracting. He would give her that. In the end his strength would prevail, but in the meantime he was thoroughly enjoying himself. He had never fenced with a woman before, and he found the experience thrilling. And stimulating. Already he was considering the boon he would demand when he eventually won this little match . . .

As if well aware of his lack of concentration, Abigail

lunged. Damn, but the woman kept him on his toes. And well entertained. Christian laughed in pure pleasure as she repelled a particularly well-placed attack. She was laughing as well, her face flushed a delicate rose, her hair loose about her in a dark, inviting tangle. Christian wanted to throw down his weapon for another, taking her right here on the old dais in a mess of skirts and half-undone clothing. Who was this woman, and why had he never met anyone like her before?

Christian nearly asked the question aloud. Instead, he said, "Where did you learn to fence?"

Abigail smiled. "I made my father give me lessons after y—," she began, only to stop suddenly, as though she had said too much. Her defense faltered, but she came back even more forcefully. "I begged my parents for lessons, and my father, being unable to stand my pestering, finally gave in, although Mother was against it."

Christian grinned, diverted from his swordplay by the shared confidence. Somehow he had harbored the notion that she had popped from the womb, full grown, dressed in her dowdy colors and ready to disapprove. But she had been a child once. Christian felt an odd sort of revelation at the notion. He wondered what she had looked like. What kind of girl had she been? He couldn't imagine her as dainty. More likely she had been a tomboy with a fierce will and passion besides. What had turned her into the Governess?

Suddenly Christian was filled with a desperate thirst to find out all about her, to know her as he had never known anyone. She had fallen silent, and he prompted her. "You prevailed over the objections, obviously, and received your lessons."

"Yes. Mother deemed it unladylike, but I didn't particularly care to be a lady," she recalled, a sparkle in her eye and a curve to her lips. Defiance, just as he had surmised, shown quite brightly on her exquisite face. "I wanted to be a . . ." Again she halted, and just as she was becoming imbued with a delightful animation, her expression faltered and her words trailed off.

"What did you want to be?" Christian asked.

"Nothing. A child's whim, nothing more. We all put away such follies, don't we?" she asked, her voice suddenly hard.

As she spoke, Christian thrust, but this time his opponent gave way as though tired of the game. He could hardly crow triumphantly or beg the boon he had imagined would come with his hard-won victory. What had happened? He watched, dissatisfied, as she calmly returned her foil to the wall. And when she turned back to him she was remote once more, as though the two of them had never engaged in either the swordplay or the love play.

Baffled, Christian could no more explain this transformation than he could the earlier one. All he knew was that he felt bereft—as if the woman he desired more than any other had left the room. And indeed she had, in spirit. It took only a moment more for her to do so literally.

"If you will excuse me, I have neglected my duties far too long," she murmured, as she swung round.

Christian leaned absently on the foil. "Abigail . . ."

He called to her again, but she already was hurrying away, as if she actually feared his pursuit, and so he simply stood there dumbly, wondering what a scholar would do.

Hell, what would anyone do?

PLEADING A HEADACHE, Christian sent his excuses down to dinner. Although he half expected the Governess to come marching up to complain of his apparent sloth, he suspected she would not want to discuss his . . . condition. Nor was she ever likely to appear at his bedroom door. More's the pity.

Still, he set Hobbins to keep the household at bay while he slipped out the rear of the house, hoping that no one except his own groom would know he mounted one of his horses and rode alone to the village to meet his solicitor.

As instructed, Smythe had secured the private parlor at the inn, and Christian hurried in as quickly as possible to avoid notice. He was counting on the lack of communication between the villagers and the Hall to keep his visit quiet, although he had a story at the ready should his movements be discovered. And even should Miss Parkinson herself burst in upon them, his little outing was well worth the risk. For once, he was actually going to dine on something edible.

"My lord," Smythe said with a bow. "It is a pleasure to see you, as always." Smythe was solid and gray-haired, having started out as a young man working for Christian's father; he was clever and skilled and devoted to the Reades.

"Thank you, Smythe. I'm sure you find the surroundings an improvement over this afternoon's encounter."

The solicitor chuckled. "A most unusual assignment, if I may say so, my lord."

"You may, as I find it just as ... unique," Christian replied. Motioning for the older gentleman to take a seat, he pulled up a chair to the laden table and took a deep breath of the mingled scents of beef pie, pheasant, and bread, hot from the oven, with honeyed butter. Not as delightful as lilacs, perhaps, but just the thing for a man's other appetites.

It was only after Christian had done justice to the landlord's excellent meal that he was prepared to discuss business. Leaning back, he fixed Mr. Smythe with a direct gaze. "I need you to do a little research for me." When the old gentleman nodded, Christian continued.

"Find out anything and everything you can about the former owner of the Hall, Bascomb Averill. Contact the solicitor who handled the estate. Also, I need information on the other three residents, a Mercia Penrod, Colonel Averill, and Emery Osbert, all supposedly relatives of the deceased. I want to know who they are, where they came from, and what sort of stipends they received in the will."

Christian paused uneasily. "And see what you can discover about the current owner, a Miss Abigail Parkinson, lately companion to a Lady Holland, also of Devon. Find out what you can about her, as well as her connections to the others and who might be next in line to inherit."

"Ah, Miss Parkinson. A very gracious young woman," Smythe remarked, and Christian had to bite his tongue. Of course, she was gracious to Smythe. She thought he was going to buy that monstrosity of a residence. Christian frowned. From the moment of his arrival, his hostess had seemed to disapprove of him, but not the others who took advantage of a good nature he rarely glimpsed. It was almost as though she held a grudge against him. But why? Christian could swear that he had never met her before. But if he had, Smythe would ferret out the truth.

"You'll pardon my saying so, but I find such a combination of intelligence and good sense and practicality in a young woman quite refreshing," Smythe observed.

Smythe would. He was probably used to seeing the spoiled, grasping ladies of the *ton* at their worst. Christian knew he himself was. "She was a companion," Christian heard himself blurt out.

"Ah. That would explain her fortitude." Smythe nodded. "That's a very difficult position, for one is not accepted by the servants and yet is not a member of the family. Belonging to none and yet beholden to all," he added, shaking his head. "Of course, it all depends on the employer. I've seen some who provide a pleasant environment for all their staff, while others work their dependents to the bone."

Christian shifted, suddenly uncomfortable with thoughts of Abigail being worked to the bone. But what did he know of her? Something had turned her from a sword-wielding young tomboy into the Governess. What? And when? Christian wondered how long ago her parents had died and how many years she had been toiling as a companion. And just what kind of employer was this Lady Holland?

Even as he wondered, Christian felt a certain disquiet with his carefree existence. Although his own parents had died, he had not been forced into near servitude. Instead, he had been taken in by his loving grandfather, pampered by a life of luxury and wealth and privilege. The comparison did not cheer him, for Christian had always accepted his place in society as his right, taking for granted his good fortune as easily as the next breath when he owed it all to an accident of birth. The realization made for some very sobering thoughts.

"That also explains her urgency," Smythe was saying, dragging Christian out of his introspection. "Miss Parkinson is quite eager to sell the Hall in order to establish her own, far smaller, household. A practical female indeed."

Practical. That certainly described Abigail, though Christian had never used the word in reference to someone he lusted after. Either his tastes were changing, or the Governess and her stellar attributes represented just one side of the elusive Abigail.

"Well, I shall let you know my findings," Mr. Smythe said, shuffling some papers on which he had been taking notes. "Do you want me to come myself?"

"No," Christian said. Even he would find it hard to explain should the solicitor return to the village. And then, for some bizarre reason, Christian felt guilty for his demands, even though he was paying the man well enough. "I'd come to London, but I can't leave here," he muttered.

He didn't bother to explain, even to himself, why he couldn't come and go as he pleased or why, despite all, he felt the need to return to the Hall even now. Although he had set Alf to keep an eye on Abigail, Christian preferred to keep his own eyes on her—and anything else he could manage. At that thought, need blossomed in him so hot and fierce that he deliberately stayed, to prove himself its master.

But it was late, and he had eaten his fill and said his piece, and Mr. Smythe, probably eager for his rest, watched him expectantly. And so Christian took his leave, wishing that the prospect of his own bed did not seem so uninviting.

• • •

ALTHOUGH CHRISTIAN WANTED to head straight to Abigail's room, he decided against such a rash action, guessing that he would not be welcome. He realized he could not continue what had developed in the hidden passage, for he had done something to disturb the delightful harmony of the afternoon. He wasn't sure of the nature of his transgression, but he suspected that swordplay did not qualify as a studious pursuit.

The realization annoyed him, for although he had set out to prove that any fool could wear spectacles, his plan was working far too well. Although he had gained the attention of his hostess, Christian found that he didn't care to be admired for attributes that were not his own. Indeed, he was wondering if Abigail's scorn wasn't preferable to her admiration gained dishonestly.

Oddly enough, he felt rather deserving of her scorn, a sensation of which his grandfather would, no doubt, approve. He began to wonder if his entire visit to Sibel Hall was the old man's idea of teaching him a lesson. If so, he liked the instructress too much, by half. So, why hadn't he tried to find out more about her? He'd been too busy strutting about and sulking. Gad, what a combination!

Christian shook his head at his own heedless behavior, then cocked it when he heard a sound ahead. He was approaching Abigail's room, and he tensed, instantly alert for all manner of intruders. Slipping around the corner, he saw a shadowy form, lounging opposite, then relaxed as it evolved into Alf.

"There you are, milord! Like to scare the life out of me," the villager whispered as he crossed the corridor.

"Did you think I was a ghost?" Christian asked, flashing a grin in the darkness.

"No. Thought you was a dangerous character, and I wasn't far wrong," Alf said, with a canny nod.

Christian grinned again. "Have you seen anyone else?"

"No. Unless the old specter can float through walls, no

one's come about since the miss herself went in nigh on an hour ago."

"Good," Christian said. If only he could enter as easily. Just to keep watch over his hostess, of course. "Nothing unusual to report?"

"Not a whit, milord. Boring evening, all around, I'd say. All they did was eat dinner, sit around, and go to bed," Alf said, his voice heavy with disappointment. Apparently he had envisioned a livelier experience here at the Hall—if not hauntings, perhaps bacchanalian delights. Which reminded Christian . . .

"I realize there was some feud between the villagers and the previous owner, but what about before? Surely you can tell me some history of the place?"

Alf shook his head. "I'm afraid I'm not much for history, milord. All that fighting and powermongering. It's hard to keep track of who's doing what."

"There was fighting over Sibel Hall?"

Alf looked surprised. "Not that I know of," he said, and Christian had to bite back a sigh of impatience. Apparently, the young man was talking about history in general.

"All I know is that some old knight built the Hall way back when, and the owners have always done all right for themselves, without sharing much of it with the townsfolk," Alf grumbled.

This was getting him nowhere. "What about your grandfather? Perhaps he has some knowledge of the past?"

Alf snorted. "Aye, but not the sort of stuff you be wanting, I'll wager."

Christian was ready to throw up his hands. It seemed he'd have better luck ferreting out state secrets than learning anything about this wretched structure.

"But old man Abbott might know a thing or two," Alf said. "He knows everyone's business, though I'm not sure you'll like what you'll be hearing. He says those that live up here are balmy, which is why all this talk of ghosts didn't surprise me any." Although the two men were alone in a dark corridor while the rest of the household slept, Alf leaned close, as if to impart a vital confidence. "Says madness runs in their blood," he whispered, nodding sagely.

Christian didn't find that prospect too alarming. So far the only resident he might qualify as "balmy" was Cousin Mercia, although he could very well include Emery, just for his own amusement. Abigail, on the other hand, was as far from madness as anyone could get. Christian wondered if old man Abbott was acquainted with the Governess, who undoubtedly would not approve of his description of the household.

Christian grinned. "Very well. Tomorrow, let's pay a visit to old man Abbott."

With a nod, Alf disappeared into the shadows, off to his tiny room below, but Christian remained where he was, deep into the night, watching, waiting . . . and wanting.

Chapter Fourteen

AFTER SPENDING HALF the night watching outside Abigail's door, Christian groggily decided there must be a better way. If only he could stand guard inside her room, then maybe he could get some sleep. But if he were inside her room, he probably wouldn't be sleeping. He sighed. Either way he wouldn't be getting much rest.

His late arrival downstairs guaranteed him no breakfast, so he ducked into the kitchen, where he coaxed an apple from a giggling servant girl. He was just exiting the room when he chanced upon his hostess, who made no effort to hide her displeasure at his tardiness. Or was it simply the sight of him that pained her so? Christian decided her breathless whispers in the secret passage had been the deluded fantasies of a sleep-deprived man. As her gaze slid away from him, presumably in censure, he thought about explaining himself, but the admission that he had lurked outside her bedroom door half the night probably wouldn't earn him any approval at all.

Besides, it wasn't the sort of thing a scholar would do, Christian realized. Even though what little success he could claim with his hostess seemed due to that persona, he was already growing tired of it. He had the nagging sensation that she had been kissing someone else in the passage, some bespectacled, studious sort masquerading under his name.

Christian shook his head. All this bookish business, false though it might be, was affecting his mind. That's what happened to people like Emery. Too much thinking made a man not only dull but half mad, as well, Christian decided. He wondered just how far gone Emery was at this point and just what that madness might make the boy do.

"I am glad to see you abroad at last," his hostess said, though her tone lacked its usual sharpness.

Christian ignored the rebuke. "I was going to have another look for hides today," he said before taking a bite of his apple.

His hostess eyed him strangely, and Christian wondered if he should apologize for eating in front of her or eating standing up—or even eating in general. But his only other option was starvation.

"I wonder that you have anywhere else to look," she said, in a sort of breathy whisper.

"Oh, I suspect there might be one or two more surprises in the old place yet."

A long silence followed, in which, no doubt, she was judging his abilities or his devotion to duty, and he was coming up wanting. "And just what do you hope to find in all these places?" she murmured.

The girl you once were, the woman I glimpsed yesterday, Christian thought, but he didn't say it aloud, for he realized that she was staring at him, rather intently and most specifically at his mouth. He licked his lips, catching a bit of errant juice, and watched her eyes grow wide and her cheeks flush. Perhaps Abigail was somewhere in there, after all, straining to get out of her Governess costume . . .

"Care to join me?" he invited, as casually as he could with his body straining his breeches.

Unfortunately, the giggling servant girl chose that moment to hurry past, and as though recalled from some spell, the sultry seductress disappeared once more behind the stiff facade of his hostess.

"No, I, uh, I don't think that would be . . ." she trailed off, blinking as though dazed, and then recovered herself. "I have things I must do. Please excuse me."

With that she turned and fled like a frightened rabbit. Interesting. Christian had half a mind to pursue her, but that was not the role of a scholar, he thought, frowning. Later, he promised himself, as he turned to stroll through the house, looking for another secret passage into which he might lure his hostess.

Really, she was such a unique and infuriating being, Christian mused as he took a bite of his apple. His attraction to her, so mystifying at first, was beginning to make a bit more sense. She was no frivolous, empty-headed, grasping young female of the *ton*, but an individual, a genteel, well-mannered, honest woman with a backbone of steel and a clear head in any situation.

He had always been drawn to strong, independent women, choosing his mistresses accordingly. It was a preference that probably went back to his mother, a beautiful creature who had managed to hold her own against a Reade male. Christian smiled fondly. He remembered his parents sparring, but never actually fighting. There had been a lot of shouting, but even more laughing and loving. Theirs was a different sort of marriage than what he saw today. Perhaps it had always been different.

Christian's father had claimed he knew the moment he saw her that she was his. "You'll know, son. You'll know," he always said with a laugh. Christian frowned. Maybe that was why he had never married. None of the ladies he'd met had ever struck him like that, and so he kept waiting, for something that seemed just out of reach . . .

Popping out a side door in order to toss away the apple core, Christian realized he hadn't inspected any of the out-buildings, and so he headed toward the first one that he saw, which appeared to be an old chapel or perhaps a parish church, long abandoned.

Interesting. It looked as if it had been built after the orig-inal hall, which was unusual. More often the chapel had been part of medieval dwellings. Christian tried the door and was glad to find it unlocked. He had returned Abigail's hair-pin to her and would have to get another. Just in case. The place was small and dusty, apparently untouched for years, but there was a lovely window at the one end, which Chris-tian paused to admire. Otherwise, the space was unremark-able.

Or so Christian thought until his eyes grew accustomed to the dimness. Then he noticed that the plaster walls on ei-ther side of the narrow seating area were unusual, to say the least, for they appeared to be decorated with some sort of carvings. Christian walked to the wall on the left and stopped to examine it, only to shake his head in bafflement. Across the surface were scattered several circles of various sizes and designs. Lifting a hand to one, Christian ran his finger over the indentations. This one was plain, but others were more elaborate. He squinted at some writing, Old English or some kind of runes, but he could make no sense of it.

Tilting back his head, Christian saw that along the top were faded figures, painted cherubs frolicking, perhaps. He crossed to the other wall and found it much the same, except aligned above the circles here were saints, or so he assumed because of their halos and lack of wings.

Odd. Was this the striking bit of architecture his grandfa-ther had eluded to? Christian doubted it. The earl probably had never even been here. No, it looked to Christian as if he had stumbled across the only thing of interest at Sibel Hall. Excluding its owner, of course. Grinning, he walked around the inside of the small building, but he could find no clue to the purpose of the strange carvings. Perhaps it was some old Celtic tradition he knew nothing about or a bit of whimsy Boundefort had carried back from the Crusades. Yet Christian felt the nagging sensation that he was missing something.

With a shrug and a sigh, he moved on to the stables and the gardener's shed and what appeared to have once been a dog kennel. Christian decided that the estate, although neglected, could be refurbished. His explorations did not reveal any further hides, however, and he finally wandered back to the library, where he hoped to find some book to prop in front of his face while he took a nap. Perhaps that was what Emery did behind all those thick covers.

Christian found the room deserted. Apparently the others had given up their search for any mention of the Hall's history. He could hardly blame them. He walked over to where he had found the volume with the notations in the margins. Now, what had he done with that? With a shrug, he tugged a large tome off the shelf, only to reject it. After all, he had to at least look like he was reading.

His next choice, a book on classical design, was a definite improvement. In fact, Christian was thoroughly engrossed in the text before he remembered to don his spectacles. Slipping them on, he dropped down onto an old damask-covered chair and opened the book again, feeling once more that familiar surge of interest in his pet passion.

After his parents' accidental death, Christian had spent several aimless years playing at being the typical Regency buck, but he soon had found the life sadly lacking. He'd never thought of himself as particularly talented or intellectual. Although he had enough sense to keep the family fortunes going, juggling businesses or entering politics left him cold. But after Bexley Court burned down, Christian's initial horror had turned into something else. As he pored over blueprints and sketches and spoke with builders, he discovered that all facets of the planning interested him in a new and stimulating way. Here, at last, was an endeavor that held his attention far more than jumping fences, turning cards, or tipping bottles. And he had enjoyed it.

At least until now.

Christian grinned. Although Sibel Hall was an abysmal example of form and structure, there was something uniquely satisfying about the place. And with that thought, he turned the page and settled in to read.

ABIGAIL FOUND HIM there, his head tilted back, his spectacles slipping over his elegant nose, the open book upon his lap, and she thought her heart would melt. She had peeked in earlier to find him so engrossed in his reading that he never even noticed her presence.

She lifted the volume from his fingers and set it aside. Architecture. So that was what interested him. And she was well aware of his expertise after listening to him talk about where to find secret places in the house. Unable to help herself, Abigail reached a hand toward his brow, but snatched it away before she actually touched him.

Why was he so tired when he slept so late? Was he up each night wandering the rooms, searching for clues to the hauntings? The thought of him walking past her chamber in the late hours made Abigail's heart trip. Only strength of will had kept her abed last night instead of heeding her own wanderlust, her desperate yearning to seek him out in the darkness.

Stifling a sigh, she sat down, hard, on the Grecian sofa, unable to deny the truth any longer. She was lost. Totally lost. Sunk. Drowned. Beyond all hope of rescue. For no matter what, she wanted to see him, to be with him, to touch him with a feverish intensity that frightened her. This morning she had found excuses to linger around the dining room, eager to catch a glimpse of him, and when she did she had to fight the urge to throw her arms about him in fervent greeting. She could barely trust herself to talk with him, for

when he took a bite out of his apple, it was all she could do
not to take his face in her hands and eat from his mouth.

Abigail stared helplessly at his sleeping form, admiring
the hard line of his cheekbone, the soft curve of his lashes,
the golden sheen of his hair. She studied the broad arc of his
shoulders, the wide expanse of chest and the long line of
muscular thighs, and drew in a sharp breath. Was there ever
any man more exquisite?

Although never one to indulge in drink, Abigail felt like
one of those fellows who, after one sip, returned night after
night to the bottle, unable to stay away. Her desire for the
viscount, for his presence, for his voice, for the sight of him,
was like some kind of compulsion. He had unleashed something in the hidden passageway that could not be reined in,
and it rose up in her, needy and wanting, driving her here to
his side.

But how would she ever appease it?

AS IT TURNED out, old man Abbott was visiting his sister,
so Christian was left with nothing to do but kick his heels at
Sibel Hall, waiting for some news from Smythe. The days
passed in dismal monotony with poor food and even poorer
progress—with either the ghost or his hostess.

After a particularly disappointing dinner, Christian
slipped away to meet with Alf, hoping that the villager had
fared better than he, but one look at the young man's face
disabused him of that notion. Before Christian could reach
his side, Alf was hurrying forward and shaking his head.

"I don't know if I can stand another day of it, milord."

"What? The boredom?"

Alf scowled. "Some of us aren't bored, milord, but suffering from a bit of the shivers," he said, shuddering as if to
illustrate his condition.

"What? Don't tell me you're afraid of the specter?"
Christian asked, incredulous.

Alf shook his head with a snort, his pride obviously warring with his unease. "It's not him, but *her*, milord!"

"Her?" Christian might allow that the Governess was a bit intimidating, but he would hardly deem her the sort to frighten a hardened young man like Alf.

"Aye, milord," Alf said, leaning close to lower his voice. "It seems like every time I turn around, there she is!"

"Abigail?" Christian asked, startled. "I mean, Miss Parkinson?"

Alf snorted again. "Not the young miss, milord. The old one! She's as queer as Dick's hatband," he whispered.

Christian was hard-pressed not to laugh. He tried to school his features to solemn concern, but his lips kept twitching, a circumstance that Alf, no doubt, noticed.

"You might think it funny, milord, but I swear that *she* is spying on *me*."

"A turnabout that would be enough to unnerve anyone," Christian said in a sober fashion.

"Aye, that it is, milord. That it is," Alf muttered. "I'm telling you, there's something unnatural about that old woman."

"Yes." Anyone could see that Mercia was short a sheet, but hers was a harmless eccentricity, certainly nothing to make a grown man quail. Keeping that observation to himself, however, Christian cleared his throat. "Have you noticed anything suspicious, anything else, that is?"

Alf shook his head. "If you'll pardon my saying so, milord, nobody here seems to do anything, except the young miss, of course."

Of course. "Well, try to stay out of Mercia's way and keep an eye on Miss Parkinson, especially today while I'm off to see this old man Abbott of yours," Christian said. As much as he enjoyed his few escapes from Sibel Hall, he didn't really like being away from Abigail. Just for her protection, of course.

"Aye, milord."

Although nothing untoward had occurred as yet, Christian didn't like the situation one bit. He paused to stare at Alf directly. "I don't want anything to happen to her."

The villager balled his hands into fists, as if to prove his resolve. "Anyone what wants to get to her will have to go through me first," he said, striking a threatening pose.

"Good," Christian said, trusting to the young man's mettle.

"I can even keep guard later, if you want me to, milord," Alf added.

Christian shook his head. "I'll take the night watch."

"Same time tonight, then, milord?"

Christian nodded and slipped away, a new alertness about him as he took his leave. Just in case Mercia was lurking about, he didn't care to have her reporting his actions to his hostess.

OLD MAN ABBOTT was a grizzled elderly fellow with an observation about everything. He was both a gabster and a gossip, but he wasn't stupid, and Christian enjoyed listening to him talk. That proved to be a good thing because it was extremely difficult to steer Mr. Abbott to the subject in question and keep him there.

After a good half hour of hearing about assorted shopkeepers and their various failings, Christian gamely tried again. "I'm puzzled by the fact that I can't find any histories of Sibel Hall or even the area. Do you know where I might find any?"

Old man Abbott shook his head. "Never did learn to read. Highly overrated, if you ask me. My sons and grandsons, even my daughters, can, but where does it get them? Worked up over the latest broadside or paper."

"Well, then, perhaps you can tell me what you know of the building's history?"

Old man Abbott sighed. "If I were you, I'd hightail it away from that place, my lord, and its people. Never been liked, those Averills, nor the ones that came before 'em."

"And why is that?"

"A bad bunch, full of tempers and passions and misdealings, which is to be expected, considering that the place was built upon the blood of others," he said, nodding sagely.

"And whose blood would that be?" Christian asked, wondering if some other family had owned the land upon which the Hall was constructed.

"Those heathens, them that the Crusaders went all that way to kill!"

Nodding slowly, Christian refrained from mentioning that most of the country was stained with someone's blood, whether Celt or Viking or Saxon. "But surely that counted as war."

Eyeing his guest meaningfully, Abbott declared, "That old knight killed, and not just in foreign lands. He murdered his neighbors! Lover's quarrel, I gather. Did her in whilst in a jealous rage and then her brother as well!"

Now the old fellow had Christian's attention. "Really? What neighbors? What happened?"

But apparently Abbott had shared the extent of his knowledge. To all further queries he simply shook his head, professing no knowledge of the details. "I'm just telling you what I heard, and I'm not surprised to learn of more ill doings at the Hall."

"And why is that?"

Old man Abbott leaned forward dramatically. "The Hall is tainted, and all the blood of its owners is tainted as well," he whispered.

Christian shook his head too, even as he decided that the old fellow would make a great addition to the house party. Between the two of them, old man Abbott and Mercia could surely conjure up enough doom and gloom for several hauntings.

•   •   •

ABIGAIL TURNED HER head to glance back along the dim corridor, but she saw nothing moving in the shadows. Why, then, did she feel as though someone was behind her? She frowned. Lately, she had felt the presence of someone or something. At first she had thought Sir Boundefort was finally making contact, but with a growing sense of unease, she wondered if a very real person was following her about the house, watching her secretly, perhaps with evil intent.

But who? One of her cousins? One of the servants? Some nameless person who had snuck into the rambling building and was roaming its rooms in comparative freedom? Abigail realized that this was not her godmother's home, where a huge staff kept the place not only running smoothly but well protected. They were isolated here, with their few maids and rumors of a specter driving away all visitors and tradesmen.

When Christian had asked her if she could handle a weapon, she hadn't believed in any threat, but now she wasn't so sure. The memory of that day gave her pause, and Abigail drew in a deep breath. She had not lied about her skills—or her fortitude. She had faced her intemperate godmother, importune gentlemen, and a specter. She wasn't going to quail in the face of some unknown lurker who didn't have the courage even to show his face.

Squaring her shoulders, Abigail turned and headed toward the great hall—and its wall of weapons. She knew exactly what item she wanted, and she hurried into the hall, keeping her back toward the way she had come as she surreptitiously removed the piece from its place. Sliding it into the sleeve of her gown, she then crept back toward the entrance and waited.

It wasn't long before she heard the faint rustle of movement, then saw a face peeking out from around the corner. Without hesitating, Abigail stepped forward to confront her pursuer, a nine-inch blade in her hand.

•   •   •

CHRISTIAN WANDERED DOWN too late for breakfast yet again, his stomach already protesting the small portions and ill servings to be had at Sibel Hall. He knew he ought to seek out Alf, having missed him the night before. Indeed, he had been surprised to arrive at his post in time to see Abigail retire for the night, and he had wondered what had kept her up so late. But his stomach was growling, so he turned his steps toward the kitchen, hoping to catch the same giggling maid he had yesterday.

Unfortunately, she wasn't there, Christian realized as soon as he entered the room. In fact, the only person occupying the large space was his hostess. Drat! Caught out again! No doubt she was here to prevent him pilfering from the larder. Since her back was to him, Christian was about to duck out, but she spoke before he could make his exit.

"What would you like?" she asked in a gentle tone.

Christian gaped. He glanced around, certain that she was speaking to someone else in that voice, not cold or tart but soft and low. "Who, me?" he asked, baffled.

"Yes, you," she answered, proving to Christian that he was still asleep and dreaming. "What would you like?"

Christian grinned at the leading question. "Oh, I can think of lots of things," he murmured as he walked slowly toward her.

Her dark brows inched upward slightly. "I meant, what would you like for breakfast?" Christian's disappointment was tempered by the realization that she was slicing bread. She stood at the long oaken table that occupied much of the kitchen, a long fork at her elbow. She was going to make him toast? With her own hand?

As if unaware of his confusion, she continued speaking. "I have a bit of cold ham, and I can make you some eggs or a plum cake. No, I don't think we have any plums. An apple tart, then."

"You can cook?"

She gave him a look that questioned his wits, but Christian was questioning them anyway. "Of course I can cook."

Christian remained skeptical. If she could, why the hell didn't she teach the kitchen staff here how to do it? He had never had more wretched swill in his life. And he loved his food. He wasn't a connoisseur by any means, nor did he employ a French chef. He just wanted good, solid English food, and plenty of it. With some flavor. With some variety. With some . . . dessert.

Christian watched as she poured some flour into a large bowl and tossed in other things until it was a big, gooey mix. Then she plopped it down on the table and began rolling it out. Her hands were covered with flour, and although most of his friends would have wrinkled their noses in disgust, Christian was drawn to the sight. As always, she was competent and efficient, and Christian stared, rapt, even as he imagined those hands upon him, the two of them rolling around in the flour . . .

He was just about to seize her when she picked up a knife and began to peel apples with the ease of an expert. Was there no end to her talents? Here was a woman who could balance books, run a household, serve as a companion, fearlessly explore secret passages, fence better than some men, and bake an apple tart. Christian felt dizzy with discovery. Who would want a spoiled, grasping, gossiping creature with no skills beyond a few social graces and the ability to dabble at watercolors or the pianoforte when he could have a real, genuine woman?

Seized by a sudden certainty, Christian opened his mouth to say as much, when she turned toward him. A lock of hair had fallen loose to brush against her lashes, and she blew it away. He grew hard in an instant. Spying a smudge of flour on her cheek, Christian decided to lick it off. And continue on from there. He leaned close.

"Would you like a bite?" she said.

Convinced he was imagining things, Christian blinked, only to see she was proffering a piece of apple. Now he was sure he was dreaming. Instead of lifting the fruit from her fingers, he bent his head toward it, looked directly into her eyes and took it, taking her fingers into his mouth as well and sucking the juice from them.

Her eyes widened, and Christian leaned forward to seize his chance, but she turned away, back to her work. "You may tell your man to stop spying upon me."

Christian blinked, the change in subject—and mood—taking him aback. Had he heard her correctly? "What?"

"You may tell your man, the villager you felt the need to hire, to quit following me about. I find it wholly unnerving, and as I told you before, I am capable of defending myself."

Christian felt like one of Montgolfier's deflated balloons, the ardor sucked out of him all too quickly by the casual unmasking of his plan to safeguard her. He should have known. She was too clever by half not to notice Alf's presence. Christian shifted uncomfortably as she set her creation in to bake.

"Although I do appreciate the thought behind your actions," she added. "You also need no longer keep watch outside my room at night. I assure you that it is locked and secured against all intruders."

As Christian gaped, she smiled. "Now, perhaps, you can get some sleep at night and avoid missing your breakfast."

He was right. She was too clever by half. Christian struggled to keep up. "I'm concerned that whoever is behind this specter of yours might try something else, something more dangerous."

"I do not see what he—or it—can gain from harming me."

"We still don't know who would inherit, should something happen to you," Christian protested. "A convenient accident might eliminate the need for hauntings to halt the sale of the house."

She looked startled, but still she argued. "And just how is anyone here going to maintain Sibel Hall on a small stipend?"

"Perhaps they are counting on the so-called treasure to fund their stay," Christian suggested.

Abigail frowned. "A foolish hope indeed." She dismissed the idea with a shake of her lovely head.

"Crimes have been committed based on worse follies," Christian warned. Why did she have to be so stubborn? How was he going to protect her? And, more important, how was he going to get into her bedroom if she objected to him being outside of it?

Ignoring his comment, she put the toast on the fork and bent to the fire, and his disgruntlement slipped away. There was something about the picture of her there, beautiful despite her dowdy clothes and cooking for him with her own hands, that made his heart catch. He had hardly ever entered a kitchen, any kitchen, and yet now this room, the purview of the servants, seemed the coziest of spots.

Christian took a deep breath, only to sigh in pure pleasure at the incredible smells. Baking cinnamon, nutmeg, and apple wafted through the air. And he'd thought the lilacs were wonderful! He was drooling, and he couldn't tell where the hunger was coming from. It no longer was his belly crying out to be filled, but all of him, desiring to fill and be filled. He wanted to lay Abigail across the floured surface of the table and have his way with her. He would have, too, if he hadn't wondered whether one of the maids might wander in or if his hostess might take a meat cleaver to his more tender parts.

Still, need pounded out a drumbeat in his blood, making him yearn not just for the sex but for *her*, every inch, every breath, every thought, every dream. The awareness of her as a singular being and his desire for her struck him uncommonly dumb. He stood staring, like a fool, for the longest time, even as he searched for words to tell her, to let her know that she was tastier than anything that could be concocted in this kitchen or any other, with her lilac smell and her smooth skin and her heavy hair.

How was it that she was here, within his reach, this living, delectable, treat of womanhood? How had he stumbled across such a treasure, his for the taking? Or at least the attempt? As she gingerly laid his toast onto a plate, Christian shook his head in puzzlement. "Why aren't you married?" he blurted out.

He was startled by her response, a low laugh. "Who on earth would marry me? I have spent my adulthood as companion to a demanding elderly woman who continually pointed out the magnanimous charity of taking me in. She made very clear her expectations for me, and they did not include socializing with those in her company, or anyone else, for that matter." She dipped a thick-handled knife into a crock of butter and slathered it upon his toast.

"I can do that myself," Christian murmured.

She glanced up, as though in surprise, then smiled. "Sorry, old habits," she said, sliding the plate and the butter toward him. "Where was I?"

"Why you did not marry," Christian prompted.

"Oh, yes. Believe me, no one likes a companion who draws attention to herself, by word or deed or appearance. Younger women see you as a threat, older women as a temptation to the gentlemen. So you try your best to make sure no one takes notice of you, to become invisible." As if she had revealed too much of herself, Abigail paused. "I assure you that the men who came into my orbit did not have legally sanctioned liaisons in mind."

Christian set his teeth, angry once more at the nameless, faceless denizens of the *ton* who dared to make unwanted advances toward her, but before he could speak out, she shook her head.

"But all that matters little, for in truth I have no wish to be married. As I said before, all I want is my own little cottage, with no one, especially not some loutish fellow, commanding me about," she added with a crooked smile.

Before Christian could protest that he, for one, was not a lout, she paused to lean upon the table and stare off into the distance. Her face, limned by the light from the tall windows, looked positively angelic, and Christian was struck dumb once again.

"It will be a cozy place, small, but neat and tidy and comfortable, with lots of windows and fresh paint and a garden in the rear." She spoke as if reciting some long-cherished hope. Indeed, she looked so dreamy that Christian could almost feel her yearning, and it struck him to the core. Obviously, that dream owned her heart, and a man had no place in it.

"And what of your paragon mate?" he asked sarcastically.

She looked at him and blinked, as though awakening from a daze. "My what?"

"The only sort of man you would consider marrying, a man of science, of study, a buttoned-up, deadly dull boor, whose pompous droning puts the whole room to sleep," Christian said, aware of his resentment but unable to stop the flow of it. After all, he was only speaking the truth. The scholarly sorts he knew were awfully similar to Emery, if not as rude. They always had their head stuck in a book and never made for good company, which was why so few of them were married. At least that's what he had always thought.

"You know, someone like . . ." Christian paused, pleased to see a blush climb her cheeks before he finished his sentence with a vengeance. "Emery!"

She stared at him in stunned silence, and Christian lifted his brows. "Well, isn't that the sort of fellow you want?"

She blanched, and Christian flashed a grin, enjoying his bit of retribution. "After all, Emery's a scholar, though I've yet to see exactly what he studies or where all of it is getting him. I'm not sure a man without any other resources can support a family on eclectic reading," he continued, his brows furrowing.

"But he does meet your other criteria. He's certainly not handsome or too robust." Indeed, Emery looked like the kind of young man who'd been perpetually sickly as a boy and would want his wife to tend him during his frequent relapses. His frequent, *whiny* relapses.

"Of course, he doesn't possess even the most rudimentary of social skills, but that wasn't on your list, was it?" Christian grinned evilly. "And you know exactly what you want. You recited it all quite well."

Abigail chose that moment to take an inordinate interest in checking the progress of her baking. Finally she inhaled deeply and spoke, without glancing up at him. "Emery is not . . . without his merits."

Christian burst out laughing at that bit of hedging, and when he saw Abigail's lips curve suspiciously, he wanted to kiss her mouth. Hell, kiss her all over. So much for Emery. Now if he could only forward his own cause.

"And why aren't you married?" she asked, still seemingly too occupied with watching the tart to look up. It was probably a good thing, as the question caught Christian unawares. "Too much of a rake, no doubt," she quipped.

Christian opened his mouth to give his standard prevarication, but it seemed too flippant, not in keeping with the mood of precarious truce between them. But what other answer to give her? The one he gave his grandfather. That he was waiting for someone special. He didn't know who, but he would recognize her when he saw her, and he would know, deep down inside, that she was his bride. She might not be one of the select ladies presented at Almack's. She might be different. Unexpected. She might smell like lilacs and have eyes of that same vivid hue . . .

Christian jerked upright, startled by his own thoughts, only to find Abigail eyeing him quizzically. His gaze slid away. "I was nearly married once," he admitted.

Hearing her swift intake of breath, Christian glanced toward her, surprised to see her staring at him with a stunned expression that hardly seemed a fitting response to his disclosure. Did she think that no one wanted him? Christian frowned. Just because she had odd tastes did not mean he wasn't on the list of every other woman, especially those who valued wealth and a title more than arcane attributes like scholarship and honesty.

"Who?" she asked, her voice odd.

Christian shrugged. "One of the duke of Bedford's innumerable daughters. Lily, or was it Jonquil? All of them are named after flowers, and each is more spoiled and scheming than the last." Christian couldn't help tensing at the memory of his close escape. Too close.

"What happened?"

"Unfortunately she took a fancy to me, and since none of the duke's daughters have ever been denied anything, she fully expected me, and my grandfather, to fall at her feet, prostrate with gratitude at the opportunity to join her family. When I did not, she used all her wiles to trap me."

Christian's expression hardened. "She arranged for us to be 'discovered' in the garden, she in a state of dishabille that would require me to do the proper thing. Thankfully, I sent my regrets in answer to her invitation by way of a young man who was eager to take my place. You could hear her shrieks all the way to the ballroom."

"I see," Abigail said softly.

Did she? Christian wondered. Then perhaps she might excuse some of his worst behavior. He had become wary after that, wary of women and flirtations and invitations. While he tried to find the words to explain, she set the steaming tart upon the table before him, and Christian gave up all attempt at speech. The scent made his mouth water and his stomach growl, and he wasted no time in cutting into it. He popped the first piece, still hot, into his mouth, and then closed his eyes. Heavenly.

He was tempted to propose right then and there, but the prospect of an abrupt rejection stopped him. Instead, he gazed up at her longingly. "I don't suppose you'd be willing to take over the cooking here, at least during my stay?"

Chapter Fifteen

ABIGAIL FOUND HERSELF wandering the rooms of Sibel Hall, seized by a restlessness that made working in the study impossible. Instead of doing her duty, she found herself longing for . . . adventure, or at least the exploration of some secret passageways. But Christian had found no other hides and seemed unlikely to do so. And what other sort of adventure could she expect to find here in Devon?

She flushed as the memory of what had happened in the priest's escape returned in all its lurid glory. It wasn't as though she was looking for . . . *that*. She was simply bored, not with the deadly dull tedium she had known as a companion but with books and correspondence and such. It was all Christian's fault. He had awakened her from her stupor, and now she wanted . . . life. But life usually consisted of obligations and work, not heart-thudding excitement.

Yet even as Abigail reasoned with herself, her steps led her through the house, seeking something. Or was it someone? Perhaps, she admitted. But who could blame her for forgoing the isolation of the study and the tepid conversation of her cousins for the dazzling company of her house-guest? Abigail frowned at the thought, aware that since she had changed her mind about him, Christian had become far too appealing to her. Now, instead of cataloguing his faults, she could do naught but admire everything about him, even the teasing wit she once would have dismissed.

Abigail had the uneasy sensation that her feelings for the man were becoming far too particular, which could only lead to heartache, as well she knew. That sort of pain had been one of the reasons she had cut herself off from the world, and she didn't want to go through it again. And yet the reckless embrace of life that had been roused in the passage drove her forward, overriding her reservations.

She told herself that theirs was a harmless flirtation, the kind that she had never had the chance to engage in before. Who could blame her for wanting to enjoy a more light-hearted existence, that which had been denied her after the death of her parents? And if she stole a few kisses? Well, that, too, was an experience she had never known.

Except that she wasn't getting any kisses.

Abigail stifled a discontented sigh. Since his first aborted efforts to woo her on the stairs, Christian had not approached her again. She could have sworn that a man like the viscount would be undeterred by her refusal, and yet he had behaved like a gentleman. Such conduct proved that he was different from the usual fellows who importuned her, and a woman could hardly find fault with a man who took her at her word, for that was just the sort of man she wanted, wasn't it?

It was, Abigail confirmed. And yet, she knew an absurd yearning to be importuned once more. Certainly, there had been that time in the passageway, but she had been the one to instigate that, and though she hoped for some kind of repetition, days had passed and nothing had happened. When she had learned that he was lurking outside her bedroom during the night hours, it had taken all her strength not to fling open the door and seek him out. She had lain abed, sleepless and breathless, listening for any sound of a knock, but Christian had remained a gentleman.

Truth be told, Abigail was growing rather disgruntled by the whole thing. For the first time since she had expounded on male virtues—virtues she admittedly had deemed lacking in the viscount—she began to wonder if the traits she had listed were as desirable as she had originally thought. Perhaps there was such a thing as too much studiousness in a man, for a devotion to books left little time for . . . adventure.

The tinkle of piano keys drew her from her thoughts, and she wondered if Sir Boundefort was up and about, now trying to communicate his wishes through music. Although Christian seemed to believe the ghost wasn't real, Abigail wasn't so sure. She had no evidence of his existence, and yet she could hardly imagine anyone perpetrating such an elaborate hoax here at Sibel Hall. It was baffling, but she had no doubt now that Christian would solve the mystery. Impatient at first with his seeming lack of progress, Abigail no longer chafed at the delay. In fact, she rather dreaded the prospect of his success, for to whom would she look for adventure then?

Frowning, she told herself she would not need any spurious entertainments, for she would at last have her heart's desire, her cozy cottage, peaceful and private. But somehow the recitation of her lifelong dream didn't cheer her as it once had. Dismissing that thought, she turned and headed toward the snippet of melody, uncertain of what she would find and even more uncertain of what she hoped to find.

Abigail entered the music room warily, but she saw no formless phantom, only Cousin Mercia and . . . Christian. Drawing in a sharp breath, she tried to throttle the rush of pure pleasure she felt at the sight of him. Now that she had seen for herself that no specter pounded the keys, Abigail knew she ought to leave, but like a drunk eyeing a bottle, she moved forward, unable to help herself.

"Cousin Abigail, hello!" Mercia called out, and Abigail knew a terribly impolite wish that her cousin would disappear, at least for the moment. To make up for such traitorous thoughts, she greeted the older woman twice as warmly.

"I was on my way to the drawing room when I heard the pianoforte and had to come investigate," Mercia said. "I must admit that I hoped to catch a glimpse of Sir Boundefort."

"Alas, it was only me, tapping the keys," the viscount said.

He wore his spectacles, and Abigail wondered if he was a musician as well, such talents often being the outlet of a creative mind. Her gaze met his warm one, then slid away, and she cursed the blush that rose in her cheeks. Her hands moved restlessly, and she lifted her fingers to the brooch that hung inside her gown.

"Oh, but we are always pleased to see you, your lordship. Aren't we, Abigail?" Cousin Mercia said.

Abigail could only nod stupidly, emulating the foolish young ladies of the *ton* she so despised. Perhaps she had better slink back to the study.

"Do you play, my dear?" Mercia asked.

It took Abigail a moment to realize the older woman was talking to her, and she blinked, uncomprehending.

"The pianoforte," Mercia said.

"Oh, no!" Abigail exclaimed, with no little alarm. She had a rudimentary knowledge of the instrument, to be sure, but questions like Mercia's were usually followed by requests for a demonstration.

"Surely you are being modest," Mercia said, obviously surprised at the lack in Abigail's education.

"Miss Parkinson has other . . . skills," the viscount said, and Abigail glanced toward him with mingled disbelief and gratitude. "But perhaps we can induce you to play for us," he added, flashing one of his heartstopping grins at Cousin Mercia.

Apparently the older woman wasn't immune to Christian's charm, for after a few protests she took a seat and began to play a lovely waltz. Smiling in encouragement, he turned and bowed to Abigail.

"May I have this dance?"

Abigail stared at him wide-eyed. Was he mocking her? He stood awaiting her answer, one hand outstretched, just as though he were inviting her on some new adventure. But Abigail shook her head, unable to join him.

Christian stiffened, his handsome face losing its open, lighthearted expression, and Abigail drew a deep breath. "I've never actually waltzed, just watched," she explained, though it pained her to do so.

He smiled slowly, but it was not a smile of amusement at her expense. It was a gentle, impossibly seductive invitation to join him, to learn from him, to become a part of his world, just as though she had been born to it. And Abigail was helpless to refuse.

Without waiting for her demur, he reached for her hand, taking it in his own. This was no formal ball, so neither of them wore gloves, and Abigail reveled in the warmth of his skin against hers. He put her other hand on his shoulder, then rested his upon her waist, making her remember all too vividly the other occasion when he had touched her—and the way he had touched her. Her face flamed, and her breath came short.

"Easy," he whispered, bending his head close. "Now, take a step back."

Abigail blinked, then looked down at her feet and obeyed.

"To the side," he prompted. "And then forward." When she followed his movement, he murmured his approval. "One, two, three. See how easy it is?"

Abigail disagreed, for she found it hard to concentrate on her steps when Christian was this close, his hands upon her, his face so near to hers, his body only an arm's length from her own. But she followed as best she could. At first he counted out the steps in a low voice, then, as she grew more confident, he simply took her with him, sweeping her about the room as if they were born to dance together.

All awareness of her surroundings faded away, and the music seemed to swell beyond Mercia's pianoforte to a full orchestra, playing inside her heart. Abigail felt breathless and giddy as he whirled her round and round, across the floor, then slowed his steps until they were barely moving at all. She glanced up at him in question and saw the heat in his eyes. It passed between them, ignited an answering warmth in her body, and Abigail wondered, dizzily, if he was going to kiss her, at last.

She waited, breathless with anticipation, for the first touch of his lips, but as she watched, his expression changed gradually until he looked . . . uncomfortable. With a sinking heart, Abigail realized that the man she had thought a rake was too much a gentleman to act upon his impulse. Frustration rose up inside her.

What was the matter with a few kisses? She had experienced little enough enjoyment in her life. Why not seize this small pleasure? But seize it she would have to, for they had completely stopped now, and in a moment her opportunity would pass, just like the one in the kitchen when he had taken the apple from her. Helplessly, Abigail realized that if she wanted to be kissed, she was going to have to do it herself, taking the bull by the horns, so to speak.

Eyeing her partner with new purpose, Abigail drew in a deep breath and lifted her hands to his face. She saw surprise cross his face at her touch, but she didn't hesitate. Pulling his head down even as she stretched up onto her toes, Abigail brushed his lips with her own. It was easy, really, she noted, before surrendering all thought to the white-hot taste of his open mouth upon hers as he drew her into his welcome embrace.

"Shall I play another?"

The sound of Mercia's voice, rising above Abigail's thundering heartbeat, must have caught Christian's attention, for he pulled away and stepped back, shielding her with his body. "Yes, do play something else. A minuet, perhaps?" he said over his shoulder, his easy tone revealing none of Abigail's agitation.

He was going to ask her to dance again, but Abigail could not. Had Mercia seen them? She was all too aware that she had no one to blame but herself for her indiscretion. Face flaming, she whispered her excuses and fled.

CHRISTIAN FULLY INTENDED to follow Abigail and . . . do what? Say what? He wasn't sure, but she had looked so stricken that he felt he ought to do something. But Mercia chose that moment to query him about his investigation and to extol the virtues of her cousin, just in case Christian hadn't already noticed them. By the time he managed to escape, Alf was waiting outside the music room with a message for him.

"There's a fellow at the back of the house, milord. Says he's got a letter for you, and he won't hand it over to anyone but you personally."

At last Smythe must have something to report, Christian thought, with no little elation. He had told the solicitor not to use the post, for fear any information directed to him might fall into the wrong hands, ghostly or otherwise, and so had instructed him to send a messenger.

Hurrying to the servants' entrance, Christian found a young man waiting just inside the door whom he recognized as one of Smythe's young clerks. The fellow obviously knew Christian as well, for he swiftly handed over the missive.

"Shall I wait for a reply, my lord?"

"Yes, but give me a moment to have a look," Christian said. The servants' hall was deserted, so he walked toward a tall bank of windows and shook open the foolscap. His eyes scanned the page, and he grunted at the information contained there.

"What is it, milord?" Alf asked, suddenly at his elbow.

"Well, it isn't good," Christian muttered. He glanced up from the letter. "All three of the cousins receive stipends in the will," he said, mentioning the amount to gauge Alf's reaction.

The young man whistled. "Wish some wealthy uncle would leave me that! It's not a fortune, but a man could get by on it," the canny fellow observed.

"Perhaps, but with much smaller accommodations than those available at Sibel Hall," Christian noted. He read further, only to swear under his breath. "And not one of the three now living at the hall has any accommodations at all to return to, as far as Mr. Smythe has been able to discover."

"No wonder they're none too eager to leave," Alf said.

"No wonder, indeed," Christian mused. "The colonel has made no secret of the fact that he has lived here for some time, but Emery was supposedly down from school, yet Mr. Smythe has found no record of him at Oxford or Cambridge and is now searching the rolls of lesser institutions. And as for Mercia, he can't trace her at all. The address the solicitor had was a room that is now otherwise occupied."

Christian tapped the paper against his chin and stared out the window. Had the older woman actually claimed she had her own household? He couldn't remember. He would have to ask Abigail. Lowering the sheet once more, Christian read the last few lines through fully, then again, in disbelief.

"Now what?" Alf asked.

Christian glanced up, his brows furrowed. "Surely this is the oddest thing of all. Mr. Smythe can't find any record of Abigail's—Miss Parkinson's—relationship to Bascomb Averill."

Alf's eyes narrowed. "Are you saying the miss ain't who she says she is?"

"No." The answer came from his gut.

"Well, that's a good thing, seeing as how she's as dangerous a female as I've ever come across. I'm telling you,

the woman pulled a knife on me!" Alf said, his tone a mixture of awe and outrage. "I was fair scared out of my wits!
After all, it's not as though I could give the lady a bruiser,
now, is it?"

"Certainly not," Christian replied. He had heard all this
before, including Alf's claim that should his village cronies
hear of him being bested by a woman, he would never be
able to show his face there again.

Before Alf could work himself into a froth over the incident yet again, Christian broke in. "Thankfully, you need
not worry about any future threat from our hostess. Mr.
Smythe says she is the Miss Parkinson named in the will,
which even mentions her employment as Lady Holland's
companion. However, he cannot discover her relationship
to old Bascomb, through either her father's or her mother's
side. Odd," Christian murmured, tapping the paper against
his chin again.

"Beg pardon, milord, but maybe she's a by-blow, born
on the wrong side of the blanket, if you get my meaning,"
Alf said in a hushed voice.

It would be difficult not to understand Alf's bald suggestion that Abigail was illegitimate. "I believe that Mr.
Smythe has the wherewithal to explore all avenues," Christian said dryly.

"Oh. Yes. Of course," Alf said, looking a bit perplexed.

Straightening, Christian stepped away from the windows
and pulled a coin from his pocket, which he gave to the
grateful messenger. "I have no reply, except that I wish you
would return, whether you have any additional news or not,
just in case I have any information of my own to share."

Nodding in agreement, the young man was gone, and
Christian was left with more questions than before his arrival. With a sigh, he turned away from the door and went
off in search of Abigail, in the hope that she might provide
him some answers.

●   ●   ●

HE FOUND HER in the study, dark head bent over a stack of papers, and he was surprised by the swell of feeling that coursed through him at the sight of her. He wanted to cross the expanse of carpet and step behind her, to lean over her and breathe in her scent. He wanted to remove her hairpins, one by one, and release the heavy mass of her hair into his hands. He wanted to lure her from her work, to show her the delights to be found in play, to lay her across the desk, to seat her upon his lap, to take her in every way a man can.

But he hadn't the right.

The knowledge came to him, unbidden and unwanted, for surely a scholar would not be so bold. Christian scowled. Not being himself, he hadn't the right to do anything, his new persona standing in the way as surely as another man would have. He had donned it in a fit of temper, but the guise could not be as easily shed. Now he felt trapped by it, ensnared in lies of his own making.

Christian bit back an oath at the bitter reality that he was consigned to playact at being some meek milksop, while Abigail was thrust into the role of aggressor. Although he had no objection to the latter, particularly, he was ready to take matters into his own hands, both figuratively and literally. But those hands were tied.

Christian cleared his throat in a scholarly effort that came out sounding disgruntled instead.

"Oh, Chri–, Lord Moreland, you startled me," Abigail said, flushing delightfully. Then those delicate brows of hers lowered. "Did you knock?"

"Of course," Christian lied. "I need to speak with you about something important." He advanced toward the desk.

Although she drew back warily, she nodded her head, game, as always. Christian spared a moment in admiration of the fact before he took his seat across from her. He had her attention now, and he was tempted to tell her all, but somehow he didn't think an admission of his numerous falsehoods would further his cause. He pictured a return of the Governess, stiff and disapproving, and he shut his mouth.

"Yes?" she prompted.

Christian sighed and tried to appear studious. "In the course of my, uh, investigation, I have asked for some assistance outside Sibel Hall, so that I could devote all my time and energies here." To you. "As you know, I have been most interested, concerned even, with the fate of the other residents should you succeed in selling the building."

Abigail nodded her encouragement, apparently pleased to hear he was doing anything at all, so he continued. "Therefore, I asked my solicitor to look into the backgrounds of those residents, and I must admit that what he found out disturbs me."

"What is it?" Abigail asked, leaning forward.

Christian leaned forward as well. "None of them has any other residence or income as far as he can deduce." He held up his hand to forestall any argument. "Now I know that the colonel has made his home here for some time, but Emery's background is a mystery, as is Mercia's." Christian slanted Abigail a glance. "Did she actually say she had a place of her own?"

Abigail paused to consider the question, then shook her head. "I'm not really sure. Perhaps I simply assumed so when I should not have. But where was she living, and, oh, dear, where will she go?"

Christian shrugged.

"This is a dreadful coil. Sometimes I wish I'd never inherited the Hall," Abigail murmured.

"Then you could not fund your dream."

Abigail eyed him in surprise. "Quite so. But why on earth does it have to be so difficult and complicated?"

Christian shook his head. "I don't know, but it gets more difficult and complicated, or at least more odd. Sm–uh, my solicitor said he can't find any record of your relationship with Bascomb Averill."

"But he's my great-uncle," Abigail protested.

"On your mother's or your father's side?"

Abigail looked pensive. "I'm not sure. I thought he was one of Mother's relatives."

"Did she ever talk of him?"

Abigail paused, as if in thought. "No," she finally said, her expression clouded. "In fact, the first I heard of him was when he approached me at my parents' funeral. He introduced himself as my great-uncle Bascomb. Although we had little contact with my father's relations, they had arrived to take over the house, so I met most of them at that time.

"I guess I just assumed Bascomb was Mother's relative. He wasn't very pleasant, so I certainly didn't wish for further acquaintance with him. He told me I would have to make my own way in the world, which I did."

"What about the cousins? What did they say? Were they with him?"

Abigail's brows furrowed. "No. None of the cousins were there. I had no idea they even existed until the solicitor told me about Sibel Hall. He introduced them as cousins, so I thought we were all related. And they called me their cousin as well."

Christian frowned. "Let's not bring up the subject with them just yet," he suggested, meeting Abigail's eyes. For once she nodded in agreement. At last they were working together, but toward what? Christian had come seeking answers but found only more questions.

CHRISTIAN WAS DREAMING, vivid visions of the Governess shedding both her guise and her clothing and coming to him, all soft and round and passionate. Had he once been unable to imagine such a thing? Now he could picture her in all her glory, for he had touched her, molded her body with his hands, rocked himself against her . . .

"Milord! Milord!"

Why wasn't she calling him by name, as she had in the passageway? "Christian," he corrected, reaching for her.

"Milord!"

With a start, Christian awoke to come face-to-face not with the delectable Abigail but with Alf Kendal, a quizzical expression on his pinched face. Christian sat up abruptly, nearly bumping heads with the man.

"What is it?" he snapped.

"You were dreaming, milord," the fellow observed.

And a man's not allowed to? Dreams were all that Christian had. And spectacles. "Well, I'm not now," he grumbled.

"No, milord." Alf cast a critical eye over the neglected state room, far from the occupied part of the house, then turned back to Christian. "What are you doing here? It took me forever to find you."

"Obviously, I was sleeping," Christian answered, as he swung his feet to the floor and tugged at his cuffs. The ornate couch had wrinkled his coat, a fact that would irritate his valet no end.

Alf's curious look told him that the boy wondered what he had been doing to exert himself to exhaustion. "I'm still keeping watch during the night, without Miss Parkinson's knowledge, so keep that information to yourself," Christian explained before the lad jumped to any conclusions.

Although Christian got little enough rest, he had Hobbins wake him early, so no one, especially his clever hostess, would be the wiser. Then, during the day, he sought some secluded spot within the rambling structure to take a nap.

"Ah." Alf shook his head as if the habits of the *ton* were too baffling for his comprehension.

"What is it?"

"What's what, milord?"

"Why were you looking for me?" Christian asked impatiently. He had been driven from his dream for this?

"Ah, that! Well, I've been wanting to tell you about

something suspicious that's been going on, that I've been keeping my eye on."

"Yes?"

"It's that scholar fella, that Emery," Alf said, leaning close.

Christian straightened, suddenly alert. "Yes?"

"I've been watching him pretty regular, and I've been noticing him skulking outside."

"Yes?"

"Around the plunge bath."

"Around the plunge bath," Christian repeated, dully, his initial interest dampened. Undoubtedly the boy was availing himself of the amenities of the house while he still could. What was so suspicious about that?

"It is refreshing. I've used it myself," Christian told him. On those days when it didn't rain, the summer weather turned hot and sultry, making the outdoor facility a pleasant experience—indeed, one of the few to be had at Sibel Hall. Christian paused in thought, his brows furrowing. Then, again, Emery didn't look particularly clean . . .

"I didn't say he was using it, milord."

Christian stiffened. "He's not spying on Ab– Miss Parkinson, is he?" If so, Christian would be happy to crush the little weasel once and for all.

But Alf shook his head. "No, milord. That Emery, he only goes out there by himself, but he doesn't use the water at all."

Christian lifted his brows. "What does he do?"

Alf leaned close again, as if to impart a confidence. "Well, that's the suspicious part, milord. He sometimes goes into the bath, but he never puts any water in it, just knocks about the walls of the thing."

Understanding dawned at last on Christian, who could be excused for being half asleep. "Damn! Does he stay in the bath or look around the whole area as well?"

"He's all about the place, milord."

"But he hasn't found anything, has he?" Like the secret passageway?

Alf shook his head. "Not as far as I can see, and I've been keeping a pretty close watch on him."

Although Christian had dismissed the passage as an old priest's route, it wouldn't hurt to examine it again. And, no matter its significance, he certainly didn't want Emery to find it. The idea of the scholar spying on him in the bath made the hair on the back of his neck stand up. The idea of him spying on Abigail made Christian surge to his feet.

"I think I'll take a look out there myself. You keep an eye on Emery and let me know if he heads my way."

"Aye, milord. I'd rather stay away from there, if I can."

Christian looked askance at his stalwart villager, who was proving to fear eccentric old ladies, young ladies with knives, and now plunge baths. "Why the devil? Are you afraid of a bit of a wash? These cold baths are supposed to be medicinal."

Alf seemed insulted. "I ain't scared of any old water," he mumbled.

Christian's brows inched upward. "What, then? Do you think it's haunted? Have you seen anything odd out there?"

Chagrined, Alf shook his head. "Now, milord, you know I don't believe in any of that ghostly business. It's just that there's bad blood out there. That's what caused the feud, you know."

"Between Averill and the villagers?"

"Aye. He hired a lot of 'em to do the excavation work for that whole fancy bathing place and thereabouts, then never paid them what he rightly promised," Alf explained.

Christian felt the blood rush from his head. "Excavation work?"

"Yes, milord. You know, digging."

Christian muttered an oath. "Do you have any idea where they did all this digging?" he asked, his voice rising.

Alf shrugged. "But one of the older men might."

"Don't tell me, let me guess. Old man Abbott." Christian

groaned. He doubted he had the patience for another go-round with that grim fellow. "Why don't you just ask your granddad?"

"Will do, milord!" And with a nod Alf was gone.

But Christian wasn't about to wait for an answer from the village. The excavation work Alf mentioned might simply refer to the hole that was dug for the plunge bath and the surrounding landscaping, no mean feat to carve out of the countryside.

Or it might mean something else altogether.

Chapter Sixteen

ABIGAIL WASN'T LOOKING for Lord Moreland. Not really. It was simply that she hadn't noticed him recently, and her discreet inquiries had revealed that no one else had seen him either. Naturally she was concerned, especially when she thought of all the mishaps that could befall a man alone in this old house, rife with mysterious happenings.

He could have fallen down some hidden passage, or been struck by something in the cellars, or worse yet, been the victim of some sort of foul play. Although Abigail couldn't really picture Christian as a victim, she nonetheless continued her search, anxious to find him, simply to assure herself that he was well.

Moving into one of the unused wings, Abigail caught a flicker of movement ahead and hurried forward. Either the ghost was abroad or someone else was roaming these rooms. But who? And why? Perhaps his lordship was exploring some new hide. Her heart thumping, Abigail turned the corner eagerly, only to nearly collide with the young man

Christian had hired from the village. He uttered a startled sound, a look of alarm upon his face.

Was the fellow up to some mischief? He had given her a wide berth since she had accused him of following her, although her initial outrage had been tempered by his explanation that Lord Moreland was concerned about her safety. Now, however, the fellow looked concerned for his own safety. Apparently he thought she carried upon her person the dagger with which she had threatened him, even though Abigail had made it quite clear at the time that she was only defending herself.

For a moment she thought he was going to turn and flee, and her brows furrowed. What, exactly, was he doing here in a deserted section of the Hall? But then, perhaps sensing her distrust, he held up his hands, as if in surrender. "Now, miss, I haven't been following you about at all. I swear!"

"Then why are you here?"

"I was looking for his lordship."

Christian! "And did you find him? Where is he?" Abigail asked, immediately diverted.

"He's gone out to have a look about the plunge bath, miss."

Abigail felt her cheeks heat at the image of Christian, clothed only in a heavy banyon or perhaps even shrugging it off to step into the water, totally nude. Although she had never seen a naked man, she had glimpsed pictures of statues, and she could imagine . . .

"Oh, he's not going to take a bath, miss," her companion said, as though reading her mind—or her expression. "He's looking about for anything, well, suspicious. Something to do with excavation, I believe."

Excavation? Did that mean he had found some other passage, a tunnel perhaps? Curiosity, concern, and a sudden yearning for . . . something, made Abigail's pulse race. "Thank you. You've been most helpful." And without waiting for his reply she hurried toward the nearest doors.

Once outside, Abigail skirted the side of the building, ig-

noring the overgrown shrubbery, and finally emerged at the
rear of the house to take in the full view of the grounds. She
paused in wonder. Had she ever really seen the vast expanse
before? Perhaps not from this location. Perhaps not on a hot
summer day when sunlight glinted off the tall oaks, their
leaves fluttering in the breeze. Perhaps not with an uncriti-
cal eye that looked beyond the superficial signs of neglect to
the lovely arrangement of trees and gardens, gentle slopes
and lush valley, where the folly that housed the plunge bath
was located.

It was an open-air structure, meant to capture the En-
glishman's idea of warmer climes, Abigail suspected, with
the inevitable pillars. Knowing little of architecture, she
vowed to ask Christian, but that thought brought her mind
back to her mission. She hurried forward, craning her neck
even as anticipation beat a rapid rhythm within her breast,
yet she could find no sign of him.

When she reached the folly, Abigail slowed her pace. She
had not been here since the day she had fallen out of the secret passageway at the feet of the colonel, and she felt her
cheeks heat in remembrance. What if the villager had been
wrong? What if Christian was inside, bathing? Abigail
opened her mouth to call out, to warn him of her approach,
but only a hoarse croak emerged as she mounted the stairs.
When she reached the top, she covered her eyes with one
hand, then peeked through her fingers, only to see nothing
except the inside of the small structure, still and quiet.

Sighing in relief, or perhaps disappointment, Abigail
looked around the area with a frown. The cold stone held no
appeal for her, nor did the prospect of washing here, away
from the house, out in the comparative open. Whatever daring she might have possessed when she was young had been
replaced by wariness and a need for privacy that years of
serving on demand had instilled in her.

Although there was a changing room, Abigail couldn't
imagine shedding her clothing there or exiting it wearing
only her shift. Why, anyone could come upon her once she

emerged! She flushed, her breath coming quickly as she stepped toward the plunge bath itself. It was so deep that steps led down into the recess, and Abigail was struck by the uneasy sensation that someone could drown in it.

When she had nearly reached the bath, Abigail heard a noise that made her pause, and her disquiet grew. None of the mysterious happenings at Sibel Hall had truly alarmed her, and she had dismissed Christian's concern for her safety as touching but unfounded. Now, however, she realized just how alone she was within the confines of the folly, tucked into the valley behind the house.

Other estates were staffed with innumerable gardeners, footmen, groomsmen, and the like, but Sibel Hall boasted few servants and none to oversee the grounds. Abigail's nerves strained at the thought—but what could possibly threaten her? The specter? A stray animal?

She feared neither. And having never been one of those fainting females who cowered in the corner, Abigail straightened her backbone, determined to discover the source of the sound. It was probably only a few rustling leaves caught in the recess of the bath, she told herself and she moved to the edge, only to rear back with a gasp as a figure loomed up from the depths. Off balance, she would have fallen if the form had not reached for her just as her dazed mind recognized it as that of Lord Moreland.

"Christian, you startled me!" Abigail said, but whatever outrage she felt was soon overwhelmed by her awareness of him, his closeness, and the hands he used to steady her. Her rapid breathing did not ease, but increased its pace at his nearness.

"I'm sorry, but I was down there." Much to Abigail's disappointment, he released her and gestured toward the marble steps that led down into the bath. "When I heard someone coming, I didn't want to be caught unawares, especially by a well-aimed rock or anything else that might land upon me."

Abigail eyed her ghost router with fresh admiration.

Surely he was more alert than any scholar she knew, and probably far better at protecting himself—and others. Trying to ignore the little hitch of excitement that her discovery incited, Abigail assumed a serious air. "If you wish to return to your study, I will be happy to stand watch," she offered.

He flashed her a white-toothed grin in response that nearly turned her knees to jelly. "Thank you, but I don't think there's anything to be found down there. It must be somewhere else," he said, pausing to scan the inside of the structure. He wore his thoughtful expression as he gazed at the ceiling and the floor in turn, then he paced the space, his long, muscular legs striding with elegant grace across the stone. Abigail felt light-headed.

"What are you looking for, another hide?" she managed, as she tried to keep her mind upon business, not upon the way he filled out his breeches.

"Perhaps," Christian answered over his shoulder. He was obviously possessed by the excitement and determination to discover that she had seen seize him before, the enthusiasm that fired her own passions for life—and for him. Abigail swallowed hard.

"Alf claims that the bad blood that exists between Sibel Hall and the villagers can be traced back to when this plunge bath was built and the landscape altered. Apparently there was a dispute over payment due—for excavating." He stepped into the changing room, looked around, and emerged again to peer into all the nooks and crannies.

Abigail frowned. "The folly hardly appears large enough to cover any excavation, except that done for the plunge bath." She glanced into the marble-lined depression, which looked as though it could easily accommodate two people or more. Suddenly warm, Abigail walked away from the edge and across the stone floor to the steps that led down to the grass—the very same grass where she and Christian had rolled about not that long ago. She lifted a hand to fan her heated face.

"I suppose you're right," Christian said from behind her.

He walked onto the level ground and looked around. "It would have to be something larger, more elaborate, like a grotto or a tunnel." Then he paused, turning to flash her another grin. "Or a passage."

Abigail watched him walk toward the rock that hid the exit to the secret route from the house and tried not to lose herself in the memory of their encounter inside. She cleared her throat. "But I thought you said the passage was an old escape for priests, here before the plunge bath was built."

"I did." After glancing at the rock face, he turned his back to it and stared directly across the greensward, where another, identical stone stood in perfect reflection of its counterpart. "But what about over there? Don't you think it a bit odd that the slopes meet at the same point? That the two rocks are placed exactly opposite each other when the rest of the landscape tends toward the wild?"

Abigail couldn't answer. The rocks, when she noticed them at all, had seemed some sort of rugged natural gate to the little valley. But Christian, of course, would see more. He always saw more, Abigail realized, with sudden insight. He didn't brag about his knowledge, like Emery, or devote most of his time to his work, as her father had. But he possessed intelligence and learning and, perhaps even more important, an innate sense, an ability to discover things in the world around him and put that knowledge to use.

It was a skill that served him well, certainly better than all of Emery's studies, and Abigail felt the now familiar wash of admiration for him, mixed in with a heady dose of desire. She watched, enthralled, as he walked over to the opposite stone, studying it as though it would yield up its secrets to the force of his will.

"But what do you hope to find? What would Bascomb be digging beyond the bath?"

Christian shrugged. "Perhaps a hole for this supposed family treasure of yours."

Not mine, Abigail thought to herself, though she did not give voice to the argument. She still didn't know what to make of Christian's claims that the man she had known as her great-uncle Bascomb had not been her great-uncle at all. She had mulled over every memory, sought out every old piece of correspondence, but had found no reference to the man among what was left of her parents' personal things.

Accustomed to reason and order, Abigail didn't care for the odd sensation that something didn't fit where it should. And now she was wary not only of the ghost but also of the possibility that her precious inheritance was not her own and would suddenly vanish, as swiftly as her childhood home had.

Such a frightening prospect brought a new urgency to her efforts to be rid of the specter, and Abigail couldn't help wondering what finding Bascomb's supposed excavations would accomplish. But how could she object to Christian's explorations when he was so obviously excited by them? And his excitement fed something deep inside her as well, some previously untapped yearning for adventure that she hesitated to acknowledge. No doubt her godmother would have called it a reckless streak.

"I wonder if the mechanism is the same," Christian said, drawing her attention to him once more. And as she watched, he put his beautiful hands to the stone, running them over the surface. She grew heated once more, for she knew just how those hands felt, touching, caressing . . .

She drew in a sharp breath just as the face of the rock swung outward. Astonished, she hurried forward to where he stood, in front of an opening into the slope itself. Not quite as tall as Christian, it was black as night inside and smelled of dank earth.

"You cannot mean to go in there," Abigail protested, though she had the sinking feeling she would not be able to stop him.

As though divining her thoughts, Christian laughed in outright dismissal of her caution, and Abigail reached out a hand to clutch his arm. "At least take a lantern. What if it plunges downward like the other passage? You could be killed!"

Christian paused. "If it is like the other one, it would go upward," he argued, turning to incline his head toward the opposite slope, which led up to the house. Although this hill was similar, there was no building within sight.

"Perhaps it led to some structure that is gone," Abigail suggested.

Christian shrugged, but he must have seen the panic in her eyes. "I'll go get a lantern. Don't go in yourself," he said, his green eyes bright. Apparently what was all right for him was not all right for her, which just showed his own heedlessness, she thought. But before she could protest, he issued another order. "And shut it up if anyone else comes round." And then he was off, his long legs eating up the ground on his way to the Hall.

Abigail watched his graceful strides until he disappeared, then frowned at the gaping hole in front of her. She had not particularly cared for the other secret passage at first, especially after all that business about it being a sewage shaft, but it had never seemed as repulsive as this one.

According to the gothic novels that were all the rage, the discovery of something like this, even those leading to hideous dungeons and the like, was considered romantic. Abigail had never understood the appeal of the books, however, and she certainly saw nothing appealing in the blackness ahead of her. It looked to her more like the abode of a giant worm, all damp earth and, well, dirty. She wondered if that explained its proximity to the plunge bath.

Before she could muse upon the place any further, Christian was hurrying back to her, lantern in hand. For a moment she entertained the delightful fantasy that he was rushing to her side for the sake of herself, not some ugly cavity in the ground, but then she dismissed that delusion with a sigh.

"No one came about, did they?" he asked her, his face bright with expectancy.

"No."

"Good. Now, if you would kindly keep watch, I'll take a look." He lifted the lantern and plunged into the darkness as though he were on some great quest.

Abigail was not as enthusiastic, and she watched him step inside with no little trepidation. The lantern's glow illuminated a long, narrow passage that resembled drawings she had seen of mine shafts. "Perhaps it is an old mine," she called out.

When Christian didn't answer, she took umbrage. He was getting too far away already. And, of course, she had no intention of letting him go in there alone, so she lifted her skirts and followed, swallowing a rather moldy stench that made her wonder if the bodies of those who had gone before might be, well, ahead of them.

This wasn't at all like the other secret passage, which had been finished in stone and plaster. Here, the ground beneath her feet was just that and timbers that braced the earthen roof were the only thing Abigail could see besides dirt. Christian ducked as he moved forward in the low tunnel, but she still worried that he might strike his head or trip or fall. She resisted the urge to tug at his jacket in an effort to make him sink even lower. After all, she wasn't really supposed to be here.

"I thought I told you to stay outside," Christian said, as though reading her thoughts. "What if someone locks us in here? I have no idea where this ends or if there is any other exit."

His warning made Abigail shiver, but she refused to leave him. If anything happened to him, she would never forgive herself, for she was the one who had invited him here and badgered him to do something. She would be responsible, and she would not be able to live with herself, especially if she were waiting outside when he might need her.

They were in the bowels of the earth now, the entrance a faint pinprick of light behind them, and Abigail became concerned about the amount of air. Did miners put shafts into their tunnels? Suddenly she wondered if the reason Bascomb hadn't rendered payment to his workmen was because it wasn't built correctly. Airless. Dangerous. With poor supports.

Abigail knew enough to realize that the bracing timbers were the only thing that stood between the two of them and a ton of dirt, and she had read about cave-ins that had buried miners alive. It was not a fate she was inclined to tempt, not even for the sake of the sale of Sibel Hall or the pursuit of her dream.

Heart pounding, she was just about to beg Christian to turn around when he suddenly lurched backward with a groan and an oath. The lantern swung wildly, and soil fell from above, dusting her head and shoulders. With a low cry of alarm, Abigail reached for Christian, certain the earth above was crumbling down to crush them.

"Hurry!" she yelled, pulling him along with her as she raced back toward the light, the blessed air, and the open green spaces that she swore she would never forsake again. Once they were outside, she gulped in deep breaths of relief and gratitude, but one glance at her companion told her all was not well. He had dropped the lantern and was clutching his shoulder.

"What happened? Are you hurt?" Abigail asked.

He muttered something about ramming into a joist, and she felt a new rush of concern. "Here, sit down," she urged, forcing him to lie back against the grassy slope.

"Yes, Governess," he murmured, and Abigail wondered if he had struck his head as well. What if he was delirious?

"Shut the tunnel," he said through gritted teeth, and Abigail spared a moment's irritation for his single-mindedness. But she swung the rock face into place before kneeling beside him.

"Let me see," she said, lifting his hand away from the injured area. His elegant chocolate-colored jacket was torn, but she couldn't see beyond that.

"Let's get this off you." She carefully tugged the sleeve from his good arm and then down the injured one and away.

The edge of his waistcoat at his shoulder was dirty, and there was a bit of blood on the shirt there, so she reached for his waistcoat, intending to remove it as well.

"I'm all right, really," Christian said, but his voice held an odd strain to it. Abigail glanced up in concern only to find his eyes upon her, dark and intense.

Her fingers, poised at the top button on his waistcoat, faltered. Flushing, she tore her gaze from his and put her mind back to her task, but now her hands trembled, and she noticed the hard heat of his chest when her knuckles brushed against it. Her breath came more quickly, and when at last she opened his waistcoat, she felt dizzy at the sight of the linen shirt plastered against his body.

As if sensing her dazed state, he helped her, sitting up to shrug out of the waistcoat, and Abigail put it aside, trying not to notice how well he filled out his shirt. Belatedly, she remembered her duty and leaned forward to inspect his shoulder. There was blood showing against the white linen, and she took herself to task for letting her mind wander elsewhere.

To truly inspect the injury, however, she needed to remove the shirt as well, and she sat back on her heels, looking helplessly at where it was tucked into his breeches. She hesitated only a moment, then leaned forward to tug at the linen until it sprang free. Lifting it upward, she carefully removed his good arm from the sleeve, then paused before freeing the injured shoulder. But he helped her again, lifting the shirt over his head and tossing it aside. Then he lay back against the grass, his upper body utterly naked.

Abigail drew in a breath at the sight of his chest. It was impossible to ignore, so wide and golden and hard with muscle. She had known he was strong, but his arms were laced with muscles. They filled out skin that was smooth and gleaming, as was his chest, except for the two nipples, dark and hard, that made her mouth suddenly dry. With a start Abigail jerked her attention back to his shoulder, where a small amount of blood lingered.

"I'll get some water to clean that up. I think there are some towels at the plunge bath." Then she glanced at his face, expecting his assent, only to stare at him, her pulse pounding.

The expression he wore was not that of a suffering man, but rather that of a wolf, lean and hungry and casually waiting to devour its prey. And Abigail had no doubt that she was his intended victim. Rising unsteadily to her feet, she realized that she ought to flee to the house and never look back.

Instead, she headed toward the folly.

CHRISTIAN WAS IN agony. It wasn't his shoulder, which was just bruised a bit and maybe scratched. No, his pain came from farther down. His groin was throbbing so, he wondered how Abigail could have missed the rise in his breeches. Innocent that she was, she probably didn't know what it meant, or else she would have realized he was not an injured man but a man who, after one brief protest, had surrendered himself to her ministrations with the same duplicity he had shown her in all else.

He had let her do what she would to him, not because his injury needed tending but because he wanted her to touch him, to remove his clothing, and, oh, God, to bathe his shoulder. Christian groaned aloud as he saw her approach with a wet cloth. At the sound, she hurried forward, probably under the impression that he was in pain. He was. And he had a feeling it was going to get worse before it got any better.

He watched as she neared him, an expression of both wariness and determination on her face. When she knelt beside him, he caught a whiff of lilacs and rested his head back against the grass to avoid reaching for her. At the first touch of the cool water against his heated flesh, he shuddered. She washed it tenderly, then paused to examine her work.

"There's a long scratch here, but not too deep," she said.

"I think the bleeding has stopped, but perhaps we should bind it."

She looked at Christian for confirmation, and he shook his head. Lifting a hand, he closed his fingers over her own, pressing them against his shoulder. The cloth was in the way, but nonetheless he felt her skin against his, warm, gentle, and oh so arousing. She must have seen the desire in his eyes for she stared at him, her pupils huge, her breath coming swift and shallow, her cheeks flushing.

Then, her gaze never leaving his own, she dipped her head and moved his hand aside to place a kiss against his bruised flesh. It was as though she had applied a spark to tinder. Christian had been waiting too long, holding himself back too tightly, playing the scholar too well, and when her lips touched him, he sounded his need in a near-feral growl. Before she could draw away, he flipped her onto her back and rose above her.

Thankfully, she made no protest, just watched him with those wide eyes the color of flowers, so Christian leaned down to take her mouth with his own. He had no patience to be gentle, and his fierce need made him thrust his tongue into her mouth in heady exploration, but she met his passion with her own, the lilac-scented passion of the woman she had been and would be again only with him.

Christian felt both a surge of triumph and a hot swell of possessiveness. Tossing the pins from her hair, he fisted his hands in the heavy mass, holding her head still for his kisses. His heart pounded, his lower body throbbed, and his head swam. He needed more, and he slid a hand over her shoulder, down to her breast, feeling the weight of her, but the stiff material of her gown stood between them, and he tugged at the fastenings, pulling it down over her shoulders, with her shift as well, until her breasts were exposed to his gaze.

Heavy, round, pale white and tipped with rose, they were more beautiful than he could have ever imagined. Nestled between them on a thin chain was a round piece of jewelry, surely an anomaly on the Governess, but not on his woman. Though she needed no such adornment, Christian liked the location of the golden circlet, his groin throbbing at the exotic decoration. Drawing in a harsh breath, he lifted a hand to trace the edges of the cool gold against hot skin, smooth and creamy.

His fingers were trembling like a novice's, Christian realized, but he couldn't steady them, couldn't detach himself from the raw excitement that flooded his veins. Cupping her with his palm, he caressed her softness, rubbing and kneading and then lifting the crest up to his lips. Abigail closed her eyes and moaned, low pleasure sounds that urged him on as he suckled first one and then the other. She writhed beneath him in an unwitting movement that only fed his desire, and when his groin brushed against her leg, he felt his restraint spiraling out of control.

"Christian. Christian." She whispered his name in that luscious voice of hers, and he lifted his head in answer only to stare, arrested by the picture she made. Flushed rose, she lay against the slope, her eyes dazed with desire, her dark hair spread upon the grass, and her gown pushed down to her waist. He wanted to see all of her, to strip the ugly garment from her and shed his own clothing, to take her in the most important union of his life.

But before he could move beyond the thought, she lifted her hands to his face and pulled him down for a kiss, moaning into his mouth when his naked chest met her soft breasts. Christian jerked against her instinctively, then wrapping his arms around her, he held her close, drugging himself with long, lush kisses so he couldn't think about the reality that he was outside, in the open, making love to his hostess, a genteel young woman who had begged for his aid. She was begging for it now, too, he thought wickedly, as she rubbed her nipples against his chest in a movement that fed his desire for another, far more intimate, rhythm.

"Christian, Christian," she called out in a breathy whisper that roused his conscience along with his senses. If only she wouldn't say his name, which had an annoying tendency to call him back to himself. It wasn't as though he didn't love to hear it on her lips, but right now it brought a bitter, guilty tang to the proceedings, for the simple reason that her idea of Christian didn't have one bit to do with the real man.

She didn't even know who he was, he thought, the realization cutting through the daze of his ardor. She thought him a ghost router, a scholar, a man who wore spectacles, for God's sake! And she was succumbing to that man. What happened when she discovered she had made love with a stranger? Christian shuddered and set his teeth against the white-hot lust that had claimed him.

He had woven his bed of lies and now he could not bear to lie in it. Loosing a harsh breath, Christian broke the kiss. He lifted his head. He removed her hands from about his neck. And he pulled her gown back into place, putting her unresisting arms into their long sleeves and securing the fastenings with gentle thoroughness.

Then he held her close for a long moment. "I'm sorry," Christian muttered. "I . . . lost control of myself." With a rather embarrassed murmur, she accepted his apology at face value, never imagining his true meaning. He was sorry, all right, sorry for having to stop, sorry for all his lies, sorry for everything.

Surely he was the sorriest man on earth.

Chapter Seventeen

CHRISTIAN SAT STILL in a straight-backed chair while Hobbins poured alcohol into his cut with what seemed like inordinate zeal. He flinched. "Do you have to be so cold-blooded about it?"

"The wound must be cleansed," Hobbins intoned even as he attempted to rub the flesh raw. Christian remained skeptical. After all, his shoulder hadn't hurt like this when Abigail tended it.

Abigail. Christian set his teeth against the memory. Flinch? He felt like kicking himself when he thought of what he had given up. Hell, he couldn't even think about what he had given up without growing painfully hard and throbbing, as if his prick wanted to flog him for his misjudgment.

"I found your, ahem, spectacles, I presume?" Hobbins said, carefully setting the lenses on a nearby chamber table.

Christian glanced at the hated accoutrement and frowned, then jerked backward. "Ouch!" he said, pulling away from

Hobbins, who appeared to be amputating his arm with a binding cloth. "Take that thing off me."

"Very well, my lord," Hobbins replied.

"One would think you care more about my clothes than my person," Christian commented, blowing out a breath in exasperation.

"My responsibility is to your wardrobe, my lord," Hobbins replied, gathering up the bottle and the linens.

Ignoring his valet's gibe, Christian flexed his arm in relief, then glared at the spectacles, hating the man who wore them until he realized that he'd become jealous of himself, of his own success with them. He hadn't been wearing them this morning, Christian told himself, trying to take comfort in that fact. Yet there was no denying that every other piece of evidence pointed to his hostess's preference for that other man, the one who pretended to like books and who reined in his piratical impulses. At least until today.

"I assume you are endeavoring to entice Miss Parkinson with that bogus accessory?" Hobbins asked in a disdainful voice.

Christian frowned. He hated when his own valet passed judgment on him. "It was a bit of a lark," he mumbled. Sort of like his entire visit to Sibel Hall.

"I see, my lord," Hobbins said, in a tone that declared he did not. "You were, in effect, mocking someone else's hopes and dreams."

Christian glanced at his valet in startlement. "No," he said, though he supposed one could view his actions in that light, especially if one were his hostess. He scowled. Perhaps he originally had acted out of . . . a fit of pique, but he had meant to prove a point, that spectacles did not make the man. Unfortunately he was now caught in a coil of his own design, for he had succeeded all too well. He had made his hostess fall for the man she thought him, but not for *him*.

Meanwhile, Christian had been taking a bit of a tumble himself. His initial wish for her affections may have been misguided, but now he was deadly earnest about it. Every time he saw her, it seemed as though he discovered some new delight about her, some additional facet to rouse his interest—and his passions. When she confessed that she had never danced, in that soft admission Christian had heard a world of hurt that tore his heart out. He wanted to give her the waltz, to give her everything she had ever missed, everything she had ever wanted.

But his new persona, indeed, all his lies, stood in the way. What would happen when she found out he was a fraud—no scholar, no wearer of spectacles, not even an expert on ghosts? Christian shuddered. For the first time in his life he felt a twinge of fear, and he didn't care for it. He couldn't go on like this, getting himself in deeper and deeper, with no end in sight.

"Perhaps you should take to your bed and rest from your . . . injury," Hobbins suggested in a dry tone that bordered on sarcasm.

Christian ignored it. "I can't. Smythe's messenger is coming today, and I have to meet with him." He hoped the fellow would have some information that might aid his investigation, which was still proceeding at a snail's pace. Despite all his discoveries about the house, Christian was no closer to unmasking the specter than the day he had arrived. He scowled.

"And what are you going to tell him, my lord?"

Christian glanced at his valet's impassive countenance, and his own expression hardened with sudden resolve. "I'm going to tell him to have Smythe return immediately with someone—anyone—to pose as a potential buyer." Maybe that would force the villain's hand, at least.

Meanwhile, he had a tunnel to explore.

CHRISTIAN'S MEETING WITH the messenger was brief and uninformative. Smythe was still looking for information on both the Averill family and Abigail's line, but he had nothing further to report as yet. The clerk did pen a letter, however, at Christian's directive, in which he claimed that Mr. Smythe's client was most interested in Sibel Hall and would soon return.

"Post it before you leave the area, and it should arrive this afternoon," Christian advised. He was standing at the servants' entrance, bidding good-bye to the fellow when Alf hurried up, looking a bit chary.

"What's the matter now? Has Mercia been bothering you again?" Christian asked, tongue firmly in cheek.

The villager reddened. "No, my lord. And Emery went off to his rooms, so I got myself a bit to eat. Did you have anything?"

Since when had the fellow been interested in his dining habits? "No. I haven't had time today. But I'm glad you're here. I may need your help. Do you know anything about mines?"

When Alf shook his head, Christian explained about finding the tunnel. "It isn't the most pleasant of passages, but I think it's sturdy enough. Although I ran into a joist and dislodged a bit of earth, the place didn't cave in. I'd like to take another look at it, if you'll keep watch at the entrance."

Alf nodded, though his expression was still oddly wary. "You're not afraid of going underground, are you?" His fearless villager was turning out to be spooked by everything *except* ghosts.

But Alf shook his head. "No, milord. I ain't afraid of a bit of earth or even narrow spaces. If you want, I'll take a look through the thing, while you keep watch."

Christian frowned. "No. I'll go." He wasn't about to order someone else into a possibly dangerous situation, while he idly stood by. Besides, he was curious to find out where the tunnel led.

"Well, if you say so," Alf said, again in a rather nervous tone. "I'll just fetch some lanterns and meet you there."

Christian's brow rose, but he finally decided to ignore the villager's behavior. Perhaps the canny Alf had an assignation with a housemaid to cancel before manning the tunnel.

With a nod, Christian took his leave, striding out into the gardens that led toward the folly.

When he reached the rock face, he tried not to think of what had happened here not that long ago. But when he glanced at the hillock, he saw the grass matted down, evidence of two bodies entwined in the sunshine, and he swore under his breath. At least Abigail wasn't here to remind him in person of just what he had given up.

The thought had barely crossed his mind when he saw her exiting the house and coming toward him, with Alf in tow. What the devil? Christian had worried that their first meeting might be awkward after what had gone between them, but now he didn't feel awkward. He just felt angry.

"Miss Parkinson, what a surprise!" He greeted her with a nasty smile. "I assume you just happened to run into my friend here when he was getting his lanterns," he added, inclining his head toward a red-faced Alf.

"No," Abigail answered without prevarication. She was wearing her determined face, and Christian stifled a groan. "Actually, I had asked Alf to let me know if you recklessly decided to pursue this exploration again."

Reckless? Christian set his teeth, all attempts at a scholarly demeanor falling by the wayside as he faced off against the Governess. He opened his mouth to argue, but Alf managed to insinuate himself between the two of them.

"Now, milord, don't take on so. The miss here, well, she, uh, pulled me aside and warned me that I was to tell her if you tried to go underground. She didn't want you to go in there alone, but she figured you'd want to do just that." Alf flashed a crooked grin. "All I can say is she knows you well, milord."

Christian flinched. She didn't know him at all, and that reminder took the heat out of him. He glared at Alf. "And just what is your excuse? Who pays you?"

"You do, milord, but this is her house." Alf shrugged. "And she carries a big knife."

Christian threw up his hands. He was obviously outnumbered, so he gave in as graciously as possible. But there was still the question of who was to explore and who was to stand watch, and since all three wanted to do the former and none wanted to do the latter, an argument ensued. When the Governess swore she was coming with him, Christian explained that Alf was smaller and wiry and fearless.

Abigail was not appeased. "Two men plus danger equal recklessness in my opinion," she said, her arms crossed in front of her. And for all he knew she had a dagger ready to push her point.

With a sigh, Christian finally had Alf fetch his groomsmen to stand guard, while he, Abigail, and Alf all carefully entered the passage, which wouldn't be secret much longer. "If we get any more people involved, we'll have to charge admittance," Christian grumbled.

This time he was careful to keep his head and shoulders low as he crept through the narrow space. He made his way nearly doubled over, and after a while, his back began to cramp. Instead of thinking about the kind of ministrations he might beg from his hostess, Christian began to question just how long the excavation continued. No wonder the tight-fisted Bascomb hadn't wanted to pay for all this work.

All during the long trek, Christian noted that despite the tight quarters, the rather moldering smell, and the dirty environs, Abigail never uttered a word of complaint, drawing his admiration yet again. Here was a woman to stand at a man's back, in dark alleyways and crowded ballrooms alike. And although her stubborn refusal to leave his side had irked him, Christian couldn't help feel a slow swell of pride—and something else, a determination of his own.

After a mile or so underground, they finally reached the end of the passage, much to Christian's relief, but Alf cried out in dismay. "Why, it's nothing but a blind alley, and after coming all this way!"

"A tunnel this long doesn't just go nowhere," Christian replied, and he ran his hands over the surface in front of him, as well as the sides and even the timbers. But he found nothing except the rough texture of tree roots encroaching on the passage. Then he looked up, where a bunch of old roots dangled, and grinned. Giving them a hefty push upward, he felt the ceiling give way until he managed to poke his head out of the hole.

But his efforts were met with disappointment, for Christian realized he was in no hide, surrounded by Sir Boundefort's hoard. Nor was he in a building of any kind. Indeed, he was out-of-doors again, just as he had begun, the only difference being the tall trees that loomed above him. After all that crawling about below, they had not reached any treasure trove that might explain Sibel Hall's many mysteries. Instead, they appeared to be in the middle of nowhere, surrounded by old oaks and undergrowth.

"What is it, milord? What do you see?" Alf called impatiently from behind him. Christian glanced around to discover that the exit, such as it was, consisted of an old stump, which had fallen to the side, and he climbed out onto the ground. Reaching back down, he helped Abigail and Alf out, as well, so that all three of them stood in the shade of the ancient trees, taking in their surroundings.

"Why, it doesn't go anywhere," Abigail marveled, as she surveyed the area. "Perhaps, like Walpole, Bascomb was enthralled with gothic novels and simply wanted a secret tunnel of his own."

Christian frowned. A gothic novelist of the last century, Walpole had built himself a castlelike home called Strawberry Hill, which was rumored to house all sorts of nonsense from his books. "Somehow I can't picture the tightfisted Bascomb spending money for romantic ornamentation."

"What a minute, milord! I know where we are," Alf said. "And we aren't on the Sibel Hall property anymore."

"What?"

"See the long line of oaks?" Alf noted, pointing west. "They continue all the way up here, behind us and go past us, on the east. That marks the edge of the Averill estate. The trees have been here forever, dating back to the first dispute between the neighbors, or so it's said."

Christian glanced around with some surprise. "So the tunnel actually goes between the trees? No wonder there were so many roots pushing at the sides."

"Look there, you can see Dowsett Manor," Alf said, pointing once more. Christian followed the line of his arm until he spied a stone structure, its windows glinting in the sun, nestled far below in a green valley.

"But why tunnel all the way here when he could just ride or walk?" Abigail asked.

"Madness. Madness in the blood, I tell you," Alf muttered. He shook his head before jerking a startled glance toward Abigail. "Beg pardon, miss."

"She's not one of them," Christian pointed out.

"Oh, that's right! That's good. Well, then, madness," Alf repeated. "Madness in the blood."

IT WAS ABIGAIL'S idea to visit Dowsett Manor, with the hope that the occupants of the house might shed some light upon the tunnel between the two properties. And Christian, always eager to escape the confines of Sibel Hall, was only too glad to join her. Soon, however, he was to regret the outing.

The drive—in his own coach—was pleasant enough. Christian would have preferred to ride, but hesitated to suggest it, since he was unsure of both Abigail's skills and the state of the stables. Besides, he wasn't sure if he trusted himself to be alone with her in the countryside, where they could stop at any moment and make a bed in the grass again.

Trying not to think about what he had given up, Christian vowed to quit sneaking glances at the woman who sat across from him. Such flirtation had always been a part of his liaisons before, so the effort to pretend that nothing had changed between them was giving him a headache, as well as a pain lower down. It throbbed even as he told himself that this was not a liaison. Nor was Abigail like any of those other women.

By the time they reached Dowsett Manor, Christian was pressing his temples, even though he never suffered from the megrims or any kind of discomfort, at least above the groin. If Abigail was going to give him aches higher up, then perhaps he ought to leave while he still could. Unfortunately, he suspected it was already too late.

They were greeted at Dowsett Manor by a butler who took one look at Abigail's dowdy clothing and lifted his big fat nose in the air. She didn't even flinch, but since Christian suspected it was because she was used to that kind of treatment, he grew even more annoyed. He lifted his own noble nose in the air, along with his eyebrows.

"Your neighbor, Miss Parkinson, along with Viscount Moreland, to see the residents here," Christian said, putting the servant in his place. With a flicker of interest, the fellow became more obeisant, showing them to a parlor and assuring them that while Mr. Milner was not at home, Mrs. Milner would be happy to receive them.

Afraid to bring up the topic of their treatment and her past grievances for fear he might lose his temper, Christian set his teeth and put his mind to the task at hand. "Did you tell anyone we were coming?"

Abigail shook her head. "I did ask the colonel, casually, mind you, whether he knew any of the surrounding families, and he was very vague. I admit I find it odd that the three cousins are so reclusive."

Surely that wasn't all she found odd about them? Christian bit his tongue because at that moment the mistress of the house rushed into the room in a flurry of silk and feathers. And like a bee to honey, she made directly for where Christian stood.

"My lord! What an honor and a pleasure to have you call upon us! I vow, we are so secluded that the society here and abouts is simply abysmal. However, now that I know that you are in the neighborhood, I shall have to gather a group together for some dancing and cards, of course!" she gushed, engulfing him in a cloud of perfume.

Christian nearly choked, and he felt like choking her. Amid all her chatter, she had never even acknowledged Abigail's presence. "Mrs. Milner, I presume?" he said, tilting his head.

"Why, yes, of course, my lord," she simpered. "Such a pleasure! Such a surprise! As I said, we simply must get together. My husband will be so sorry that he missed your impromptu call!"

"I am here with your neighbor, Miss Parkinson, the new owner of Sibel Hall," he said, sweeping an arm toward Abigail in a gesture that even Mrs. Milner could not ignore.

"Ah, yes," the woman said, nodding in the briefest of acknowledgments. Before she could launch into another lengthy ramble, Christian took his seat.

"I wonder if you could give us some information about the former owner of the Hall."

She looked at him blankly.

"A Mr. Bascomb Averill?" Christian prompted.

"Oh, my, no!" she said, fluttering toward the door, where she rather loudly called for tea.

Christian rubbed his temples. He did not want tea—or anything else—from this woman.

"Did you see much of him?" Abigail asked.

Mrs. Milner hesitated, and for a moment Christian thought she would refuse to reply. He half rose from his chair, his anger barely leashed. But whether she suspected his intent or simply feared he might leave, she answered, though she looked at him, not Abigail, when she did so.

"Mr. Averill? Oh, my, no! We had no dealings with the man whatsoever. We found him quite discourteous, even belligerent. Why, he said we had no right to be here!" she said with a sniff. "Can you imagine? Just as though we hadn't paid good money for the house!"

Money and the position it bought were obviously important to Mrs. Milner, whose husband, Christian suspected,

was in trade. He'd seen these social-climbing, grasping females before. He could only be thankful that she didn't look
old enough to have a daughter to throw at him.

"So you recently purchased this property?" Abigail
asked.

Again Mrs. Milner hesitated, and Christian didn't know
what irritated him more, her treatment of Abigail or Abigail's composure in the face of it. He didn't trust himself to
speak.

"Yes! It was a bit small and out of the way, but Rupert—
Mr. Milner, that is—insisted upon a country place," she said
coyly.

"Can you tell us anything about the previous owner of the
house?" Abigail asked.

Mrs. Milner didn't bother to hide her annoyance.
"Dowsett Manor? Why, no. I'm afraid I know nothing about
those . . . people. I suppose they fell upon hard times."

"Or bought something larger," Abigail put in, and Christian had to bite back a laugh at the subtle gibe.

Their hostess appeared startled. "Why, yes, I suppose
that's possible. No!" she said, shaking the feathers in her
hair. "Now that you mention it, I believe it was owned by a
widow, a Lady Chestleham, who passed on. No one to inherit, I assume. But her misfortune is our gain, so I say."
Mrs. Milner waved a hand in obvious dismissal of the subject.

But Abigail, despite her treatment, was not to be dismissed so easily. "Do you know if this widow was a member of the original family that founded the place?"

This time Mrs. Milner made her displeasure obvious.
Turning to Abigail, she lifted her chin and looked down her
nose, perhaps in imitation of her own butler. "I have no idea.
Whatever personal items that were here were removed and
sold at auction, I believe," she snapped, shuddering as if
with distaste. But Christian was willing to bet that some of
those things were right here staring him in the face, as well
as stuffed in the attics. Unfortunately, he hadn't the time or

energy to go through someone else's house as well as Sibel Hall.

"Ah, here is the tea at last," Mrs. Milner said, with a wave of her hand. Turning her shoulder toward Abigail, she gave Christian a long-suffering smile. "Servants are so difficult to find these days, especially in this rural area. I vow, I don't know how I shall survive!"

Christian rose to his feet. "I'm sorry, but we haven't time for tea today," he said, without any further explanation.

Mrs. Mimer practically shrieked in protest. "Oh, but, my lord, you simply must have something!" Another time Christian might have been eager to eat anything not served at Sibel Hall, but right now he didn't have the stomach for it.

"I'm sorry, but no," Christian said, turning to Abigail. She had a puzzled expression, presumably because he was leaving without mentioning the tunnel, but he simply shrugged. He could tell Mrs. Milner had no knowledge of the passage and would not be happy to learn of its existence. The first thing she would do was fill it in, and Christian wasn't about to give her the pleasure.

"But Mr. Milner will want to meet you, and we must arrange for a soiree!" the woman protested, following Christian to the door like a frantic puppy.

"I am staying with a party at Sibel Hall, but I'm afraid I'm too busy with my commission there to have any time for amusements."

Mrs. Milner looked at him blankly.

"I'm trying to rout the specter that haunts the place," Christian explained, while Mrs. Milner gaped. He flashed her a smile. "When I do, I'll try not to send it over this way."

Christian brushed past the butler, then turned on the threshold. "Oh, you are right, Mrs. Milner. Your servants are terrible."

As he stalked toward the waiting coach, Christian heard the sputtering of the woman he had left behind, as well as a stifled sound from beside him. But even the rarity of Abi-

gail's laughter could not rouse him from his ill mood, and
after helping her inside, he threw himself into the seat opposite with more force than necessary, jarring his throbbing
head.

"A pox upon that wretched female!" he muttered, lifting
a hand to his temples. "I can't believe the way she treated
you."

"I'm used to it," Abigail replied with a tight smile.

"Well, I'm not," he retorted.

"It doesn't matter," Abigail said, and all traces of laughter faded away, to be replaced by the Governess, in full
form.

Christian frowned at both her transformation and her dismissal of the subject. It *did* matter, and he wanted to protest
her acceptance of such treatment with a shout, raging at the
injustice. But, of course, that would not be very scholarly, an
observation that made him even angrier. He felt like snatching the spectacles from his pocket and smashing the damn
things beneath his foot. They were probably what had given
him the headache.

Christian set his teeth. Suddenly he was furious—with
that idiot woman, with Abigail for her steadfast composure,
and with himself because he could do little except return
Mrs. Milner's rudeness. Yet even as he fought against his
frustration he realized that there was something else he
could do.

He could make sure that Abigail never received another
cut like that one. He could make her his viscountess, his future countess, take her to court, lavish her with jewels and
fine clothes and servants to grant her every whim, and build
her a house, the most beautiful, tasteful, modern house ever
created. And then let anyone disparage her!

Yet instead of easing his frustration the plan only pained
him, for Christian knew Abigail would never agree to such
a proposal. She didn't care about any of that and didn't want
to marry anyone, least of all him.

●　　●　　●

WHEN ALF HEARD about Christian's disappointing trip to Dowsett Manor, he snorted. "Of course the owner's not going to know anything!" he said, shaking his head. "You have to go to the people in the know, the ones who wash the dirty linen, if you get my meaning. Let me pay a visit to the servants' hall, and I'll find out more than a dozen calls upon the witless gentry will get you."

Christian took him up on the offer and was not disappointed. When the villager returned a few hours later, he had a satisfied grin on his face. "The house has changed hands several times over the years, so there's no sense looking for any more of the bad blood between the original families."

Alf paused, to grin wickedly at Christian. "In fact, our Bascomb didn't seem to have an aversion to his old neighbor. Quite the opposite." When he leaned close and lowered his voice dramatically, Christian hoped whatever he had to impart didn't involve any more mention of madness in the blood.

"I heard from an old stablehand who's been there since he was a lad. Lady Chestleham used to go out riding, always to the line of oaks near the edge of the property. And she didn't want anyone to attend her. Well, our man being curious, one time he followed her and found nothing but her horse standing there, the rider nowhere in sight.

"Well, he fussed and worried and didn't know what to do, but knowing he wasn't supposed to follow, he didn't say anything. He went back to the stables, and lo and behold, the lady of the house rode right up later that day. Knowing his betters, or at least human nature, our man figured she was meeting someone up there, and he was glad that he didn't come upon them, doing the deed right there in the woods!"

Christian frowned.

"You see?" Alf asked, as though he were dense. "Lady Chestleham was meeting old Bascomb, going through the tunnel he had specially made for her. Probably had that bath put in for just that sort of dallying, too!" Alf winked.

Christian held up a hand to stop the flow of information

from the villager. He had no interest in the affairs of the neighbors. Nor did the report of their antics help him in the slightest. Instead, he felt the now familiar swell of aggravation at the knowledge that the tunnel seemed totally unrelated to the haunting, as well as yet another waste of his time.

For a man who had once pursued life with ease, Christian found himself facing a whole slew of disappointments. Although the whole house was abuzz with the prospect of a buyer returning with Mr. Smythe, the specter had not shown itself, making Christian's effort to force the villain's hand unsuccessful. He cursed under his breath. The days were passing, each more frustrating than the last.

Sensing his mood, Alf slipped away, leaving Christian alone near the servants' hall, where he remained lost in thought until a small, stout female in an apron and cap came barreling into the room. At first he thought Alf was chasing her in some misguided romantic pursuit, but she was too hysterical for that, wailing and jabbering nonsensically. Christian tried to stop her, but she flailed like a wild thing, knocking him aside on her way to the door. She flung it open with a screech, then fled, and it was only then that Christian made sense of her screaming.

It was something about a ghost.

Chapter Eighteen

CHRISTIAN SKIDDED TO a halt on the tiles of the great hall, only to glance around in disappointment. He had half expected to run right into the specter, corporeal or not, but the space was just as dim and deserted as usual. He swore under his breath, pacing the area until Abigail arrived, breathless, behind him.

"He's gone." Christian cursed, unable to hide his frustration with a scholarly pose. Just once, he'd like to get his hands around the neck of the formless thing or, better yet, around the neck of the person responsible for it.

"Wait. I think I see something up there," Abigail said, pointing to the fretwork. "Put your spectacles on, and perhaps you may see it, as well."

"I don't need my spectacles," Christian said through set teeth. But he moved closer to the carved wood and looked upward. There was something. It appeared to be a bit of white, perhaps a piece of the ghost's costume that had caught and held.

"I'm going up for a closer look," Christian said to Abigail over his shoulder. Grabbing a lantern, he headed toward the door that now had no lock at all, thanks to Alf. He grinned at the sight, then moved the coffer that hid the stairs to the minstrel's gallery. Of course, as soon as he stepped through the opening, he heard Abigail behind him. Without bothering to tell her to wait behind, he hurried upward, anxious to see a piece of evidence at last.

He walked nearly the length of the minstrel's gallery before he spied it. A slip of something, probably material of some sort, it dangled from a space in the fretwork, tantalizingly out of reach. But Christian was more determined than any specter.

"I think I can reach it." Ignoring Abigail's protest, he leaned forward as far as he could. At another time he might have been more gratified to feel Abigail's arms round his hips. Now he simply ignored her attempt to anchor him and reached even farther, only to fall back with an oath. Finally he lunged, catching the edge of the cloth and tugging it loose. With a grunt, he landed on his feet, straightening as Abigail released her hold upon him.

Drawing in a deep breath, Christian opened his hand to examine his precious clue. But the evidence, such as it was, made him swear aloud. Although he wasn't sure what he had hoped to find, this definitely was not it.

"Nothing," Christian muttered as he fingered the piece of material. "Nothing but a linen napkin stuck into the fretwork." It was almost as though the specter—or its perpetrator—was deliberately taunting him. Christian felt a surge of angry frustration.

Apparently Abigail wasn't very pleased either, for while he stood there staring at the napkin, she smacked him on the back with her fist. Hard. It could not be considered a love pat, even by someone as desperate as himself. And then she did it again. Harder.

Christian swung round before she could land another blow. "What the devil?"

"You idiot!" she cried, her face pale in the lamplight. "You could have been killed!"

Oh, no. Not that again. Christian groaned. He appreciated her concern for his safety, but why did she always have to insult his intelligence? "I wasn't going to fall." Did she think him wholly without any physical skills? He could name a few . . .

"And just what if this was a trap? What if the specter had tampered with the railing? You could have gone headfirst into the fretwork or the tiles below! Did you stop to think of that?" she demanded.

Well, actually, no, Christian admitted to himself. He flashed her a grin in appeasement, but the Governess was not appeased. This time she clouted him upon the arm. Apparently she struck out at whatever part of his body was closest, and in a cautionary move, Christian turned slightly so that the lower part of his anatomy faced the railing. No need to endanger himself unnecessarily, he thought, more threatened now by Abigail than by the ghost.

But even as that thought went through his head, her words returned to nag at his brain. Something about a trap? Christian froze. Maybe the napkin hadn't been placed here as a taunt, but as a lure. Grabbing the lantern once more, he ran to the steps and hurried downward, Abigail on his heels, only to stop at the bottom.

It was as he feared. The opening was blocked.

Christian cursed his own folly. He had been careless, so desperate for a clue that the culprit had outwitted him. The realization both shocked and enraged him, and he felt like smashing his fist into whatever covered the way out. Instead, he forced himself to think, not the scholarly-type thinking, either, but the pirate type.

Thankfully, Abigail remained quiet behind him, offering no suggestions and placing no blame. Taking a deep breath, Christian lifted a hand to the wall before him, running his fingers over the edge of the plaster, then into the opening, where he felt the smooth surface of wood. Presumably someone had set the heavy cabinet back into place to block their exit. However, since he had moved the thing before, he ought to be able to shove it out of the way again, even from this awkward angle.

Raising both palms to the surface, Christian pushed, but the thing didn't budge. He tried again. And again. And again. In disbelief, he finally struck the surface hard with his palm, then leaned forward to rest his head against it as he gasped for breath. Although he hated to admit that anyone, particularly anyone here at Sibel Hall, could best him, he could do no more. No doubt another piece of heavy furniture had been moved in front of the coffer or a chair wedged against it, effectively preventing their escape.

"Perhaps Sir Boundefort is holding it closed," Abigail whispered from behind him.

Frustrated and disgusted with himself for not anticipating this predicament, Christian answered in a voice heavily laden with sarcasm. "Oh, I'm sure that's it."

"Perhaps you can reason with him," Abigail suggested.

How a perfectly logical woman could spout such nonsense was beyond Christian's endurance, especially in his current mood. He set his teeth. "I can't very well reason with him when I don't believe in him!"

Naturally, his companion answered in kind, her tone that of the Governess in high dudgeon. "Well, you are the ghost expert!"

Christian blew out a breath, his patience exhausted. "I hate to tell you this, my dear Miss Parkinson, but I am no ghost expert," he said. And it felt good.

"But—but what of your reputation?" she sputtered.

"My reputation, as it were, is mostly a tissue of fabrications and exaggerations." With a sigh, Christian dropped his arms and turned to face his hostess.

"But what of Belles Corners?" she asked, her expression one of disbelief. "Why, it is the most famous debunking of paranormal phenomenon since the Cock Lane ghost."

"The Cock Lane ghost?" Christian asked, his brows inching upward.

The Governess eyed him as though he were an imbecile. "Yes, the Cock Lane ghost. Surely you have heard of it?"

Christian shook his head with deliberate firmness.

The Governess sighed in exasperation. "In the latter part of the last century, the landlord of a house in Cock's Lane coaxed his daughter into using a piece of wood to make rapping sounds, which he claimed were caused by the ghost of a previous tenant," she explained. "Various personages, including Samuel Johnson, investigated before it was discovered to be a scheme to discredit the previous tenant. Why, the case is infamous! Surely you remember it?"

Christian grinned, overcome by a kind of unholy elation at the admission of his ignorance. "I hate to tell you this, but I was dragged by friends on a lark to Belles Corners." And often had he regretted it since. "All I did was look at the bed more closely than most and found the boy inside rapping."

Christian paused to flash a wicked smile. "Perhaps he got his idea from your Cock Lane business!"

The Governess crossed her arms across her chest.

"Perhaps not," Christian muttered. "But because of that one fateful afternoon, I am now viewed as the premier expert on hauntings when I assure you that I know nothing more than the average man—probably even less."

As the truth dawned on her, the Governess looked horrified and more than a little outraged, making Christian thankful that no weapons were within her reach. But he knew she also wielded a mean fist, so he stepped back, coming up against the blocked exit.

"So your trumped-up expertise consists of nothing except happenstance?" she demanded.

Christian frowned. He would rather claim he was more intelligent than the rest of the rabble at Belles Corners, but instead he simply shrugged.

"Why, then, did you answer my summons, wholly misrepresenting yourself and your abilities?" she demanded, her lilac eyes huge in her pale face.

Christian threw up his hands. "Believe me, it wasn't my intention! Most of that correspondence, and I get plenty of it, goes to my town house, where my secretary has instructions to toss the lot of it."

"But mine was addressed to your family seat."

"Exactly," Christian said. "It arrived at the family seat, where my grandfather managed to snatch it up and determined that I should come take a look."

He saw no need to add that the old man had cajoled him with tales of Sibel Hall's nonexistent architectural delights. Besides, for some reason, he found himself loath to admit his passion for building to Abigail, who would no doubt scorn him for a fool, one of those arrogant noblemen who played at being his own architect, especially since she scorned him enough already.

"I see," she said dully.

Christian waited for the inevitable blow, or, at the very least, a long lecture from the Governess on duty and responsibility and honesty, but it never came. Instead, she simply turned on her heel and ran up the steps, disappearing into the darkness of the top, without any light to guide her.

"Abigail, wait!" Snatching up the lantern, he hurried after her. She was the one who had warned of traps, and yet she was racing up there, recklessly, just to avoid his company. He would rather have faced the lecture.

"You have to admit that I've been of more help than anyone else!" Christian yelled. "You don't have to know anything about ghosts to know that someone is trying to scare away buyers and worse!"

He emerged at the top of the stairway to see her standing at the balustrade, shouting out into the shadows. "Hello! Is anyone there?" she called.

Christian set the lantern down. "What are you going to do? Keep yelling until you are hoarse? Unless someone chances into the great hall, you'll never be heard."

Ignoring him totally, she leaned forward. "Hello! Can anyone help me?"

Christian swore under his breath. The only thing worse than being trapped up here was being trapped up here with a woman who ignored him. He had half a notion to take her in his arms and make his presence felt, most keenly, but the thought of another rejection on top of everything else was too much. Besides, righteous guilt gnawed at him, forcing him to take the blame for this debacle, despite his grandfather's schemes and all the circumstances that had conspired to make him into a ghost router, a scholar, a wearer of spectacles.

Christian scowled, then winced as Abigail's shouts echoed in the narrow space. With a glance at the fretwork, he decided that now was as good a time as any to find out just how sturdy it was. Walking to the railing, he put a booted foot onto the ledge and launched himself forward.

"Christian, no!"

Now she noticed him, Christian thought, as Abigail's shriek echoed behind him. But he had already latched hold of the carved wood. He struggled for a moment, wondering just how far it was to the floor and what his chances were of surviving a fall, before he found a foothold. The fretwork, no doubt carved out of solid oak, didn't even sway, and as he made his way downward, he didn't encounter any broken pieces or rotten wood. Thankfully, his pirate blood came in handy, along with a lot of tree climbing in his youth, and he made his way nearly to the bottom before dropping easily to the tiles.

"Christian! Are you all right?" Abigail called from above him, her panic obvious.

Slightly mollified, Christian grinned. "Yes! As soon as I find a lantern, I'll get you out of there." He grabbed one from its hiding place and headed into the old buttery. Sure enough, a heavy casket was wedged in front of the coffer. With a couple of mighty heaves, Christian dislodged it, then managed to push the cupboard away from the wall. He had barely moved it when Abigail, who never burst or leapt, flew out of the opening into his arms.

Half expecting violence, Christian blinked in astonishment as he was enveloped in lilac scent and warm, soft woman. Was she crying? He was definitely mollified. Murmuring something unintelligible into her hair, Christian pressed his lips against her forehead. And from there, it was only a brief, tender trip down to her mouth, where all the heat between them blazed forth . . . until Abigail broke away.

"You idiot! You could have been killed!" she whispered breathlessly, still locked in his embrace.

"What did you want to do, cry for help for days?" Christian asked lightly. She was pressed up against him so tightly, he found it hard to think, let alone speak.

"Someone would have come, eventually," she answered.

"Well, if you want to go back up there . . ." Or somewhere more comfortable, like the nearest bed . . . Without waiting for further argument, he took her mouth again, and she answered in kind, all their disputes lost in the passion that rose between them, fast and furious.

Christian might have pushed her up against the wall or the cupboard or anything, his oft-thwarted need was so great, but a noise, over and above their frantic breathing, penetrated his fevered brain, and he broke away, putting a finger to Abigail's lips. He barely had time to enjoy her dazed expression of disappointment before he heard something else coming from the great hall.

"Hello? Sir Boundefort? Are you there?" Christian bit back a groan at the sound of Cousin Mercia's quavering voice. He was tempted to stay where he was, but Abigail was already slipping from his arms and brushing her skirts. And he supposed it might be awkward to be caught in the act (or as close to it as possible) with his hostess should someone actually venture into the darkened room.

Without bothering to cover the opening to the minstrel's gallery, Christian followed Abigail into the great hall, where he saw an eager Mercia with a sour Emery, and a rather nervous Colonel lagging behind.

"Hallo? Oh, it's just you two!" the old fellow bellowed, sounding relieved.

"I told you it was nothing," Emery snapped.

"The little maid—Becky, I believe—came to the drawing room, fussing and wailing that the ghost was abroad. Said it chased off one of the servants, then set about torturing people in the great hall. Said she could hear your screams!" the colonel said, shaking his head in disgust. Then he paused. "You weren't screaming, were you?"

"Certainly not," Abigail replied in her most prim tone. Christian loved it. He wanted her to use that tone just before he made her scream with pleasure.

"I was calling for assistance, however," Abigail said. "We saw something behind the fretwork and found a way up to the minstrel's gallery, but someone blocked our exit, trapping us up there." She pointed toward the area in question.

The colonel and Mercia made the appropriate noises of distress, while Emery just looked disgruntled. "However did you manage to escape?" Mercia asked.

"Oh, his lordship is quite . . . resourceful," Abigail said, making Christian's heart hammer in his chest and other body parts stir as well. He flashed her a grin, grateful for both her praise and her discretion. He didn't want anyone tampering with the fretwork, just in case he needed to climb it again.

"But, I say, what is this minstrel's gallery?" the colonel asked, moving toward them. "I have no knowledge of it."

"Apparently it was blocked off years ago," Abigail explained.

"Oh, my, yes," Mercia piped up. "I do recall something about someone falling or being pushed from the ledge."

Christian exchanged glances with his hostess over this bit of information. "You knew about the minstrel's gallery?" Abigail said, in a sharper voice than usual.

"Why, yes, dear," Mercia said.

"Why didn't you say anything about it?" Abigail asked.

"Why, I didn't think it was important," she answered.

"But that's right where the ghost . . ." Abigail trailed off, either afraid of saying too much or aware of the folly of reasoning with the older woman.

The colonel cleared his throat. "Well, let's all have a look, shall we?"

All three cousins crowded into the shadowy room to view the ragged hole in the wall that covered the stair, though none actually braved the opening. Presumably, the colonel was too leery, Mercia too delicate, and Emery . . . well, no doubt Emery knew exactly what the gallery looked like, Christian thought darkly.

"It's all part of the family history and the legends of Sibel Hall," Mercia said, as everyone trooped back out into the great hall. "I believe it was Sir Boundefort's wife or lover who fell to her death. Perhaps he threw her off in a fit of rage, and that's why his soul is not at rest. And he might not like you trespassing upon his domain," she added.

"It wasn't Sir Boundefort, but someone alive and hardy who trapped us up there," Christian corrected, with a sidelong glance at Emery.

"Well, I warned you about the dangers of the Hall," the so-called scholar said. "I think you got whatever you deserved, wandering about uninvited."

Christian stopped to turn toward the boy. "And who should be invited, if not the owner? Why shouldn't she go wherever she wants in her own house?"

In the face of Christian's implacable questioning, Emery sputtered, and perhaps they might have had a reckoning at last, but Christian felt Abigail's hand upon his arm, restraining him. Presumably she did so out of civility, something Christian thought highly overrated, especially after what had happened there today.

Although Christian hadn't felt particularly endangered in the minstrel's gallery, the incident put all his instincts on alert. What if he and Abigail had been trapped somewhere else, like the secret passage? As much as he enjoyed her company, the threat of being buried alive with her would definitely damper his enthusiasm.

The villain was growing bolder—of that there was no doubt. Just how desperate was he? What might he do next? Would he target Abigail in particular? And if so, how was Christian going to keep her safe?

ALTHOUGH CHRISTIAN REMAINED on alert, nothing out of the ordinary occurred, and he was again reduced to kicking his heels—until Alf hunted him down to say that Mr. Smythe and the "buyer" had arrived. The news filled him with a rather unholy glee, for he was certain the specter would make an appearance. And this time Christian was going to catch him. If by doing so he proved to Abigail that he could accomplish his task better than any of her men of science, then that would suit him just fine.

Alf in tow, Christian strode toward the great hall, determined to take out all of his many frustrations upon the specter that had haunted his existence for far too many days and nights. He found Abigail already there with Mr. Smythe and a short, rotund man in a garish waistcoat, who was smiling much too avidly at her. Couldn't Smythe find a buyer who wasn't a lecher? Christian wondered, setting his teeth.

"Ah, Lord Moreland! How nice to see you again," Smythe said. Christian nodded curtly in greeting, ignoring the flicker of surprise in the solicitor's eyes.

"My lord, I would like you to meet Mr. Gaylord, a man with a fine eye for a property," Smythe said.

"Gaylord," Christian muttered, barely acknowledging the fellow, who seemed to have an eye for the ladies as well.

"Mr. Gaylord is quite pleased with the house," Smythe remarked, though from the looks of him Gaylord was more interested in its owner. Christian ground his teeth. He tried to insinuate himself between the interloper and Abigail, but Gaylord refused to move. Christian was about to knock him aside forcibly, when he realized that the fellow had gone rigid. His lips worked, but nothing came out as he stared upward.

Following his stricken gaze, Christian looked toward the fretwork, and there it was, a pale, formless thing floating in the upper air, weaving and wailing. Sibel Hall's specter had just made his latest—and last, Christian vowed—appearance.

"Alf! Cover the exit to the minstrel's gallery," Christian yelled. He heard his man rush into action even as he bounded forward and grabbed hold of the fretwork.

"Christian, no!" He heard Abigail's shout of distress, but ignored it. She was too far away to catch him, and this time no one was going to hold him back. He climbed the now familiar carved wood with confidence, his eye on the specter above. It continued floating and wailing, apparently unaware of his movements directly below, and he hurried onward until he was right beneath it.

Then, before it could move, Christian reached up, grabbed hold of the thing and pulled. It gave way instantly and, thrown off balance, he nearly fell. Vaguely he heard Abigail's cry ring out through the hall, but he righted himself, clinging to both the fretwork and what he clutched in his hand as he began his descent. Although it was an awkward business, Christian managed to hang one-handed from the partition while making his way down.

When he dropped to the floor, Abigail rushed toward him, her face pale and stricken. He had the feeling that she might have struck him—or kissed him—if not for their audience. Instead she simply stared at him wide-eyed as Christian held out his prize.

"Here's your ghost," he declared, shaking out the bundle that he carried. Stripped of its seeming ability to float upon the drafts high in the hall, the specter didn't look very frightening. Indeed, it didn't look like much of anything at all. Christian realized it was nothing but strips of old, nearly transparent linen, sewn together haphazardly and attached to a pole. A pole long enough to reach from the minstrel's gallery through the fretwork.

"Mr. Smythe, Mr. Gaylord, would you please keep a watch back here?" Christian commanded as he hurried behind the partition. Although he didn't think anyone except himself had ever climbed it, he didn't want whoever was up in the balcony to escape it the way he had.

Mr. Gaylord remained immobile, but Smythe and, of course, Abigail, followed him, positioning themselves at either end of the screen. Christian shook his head at her stubbornness, but he didn't have time to argue. He rushed into the small room behind, where Alf was standing by the cabinet, watching it rattle and inch forward.

At a nod from Christian, Alf pushed the furniture away from the opening while Christian stepped into the breech. He was just in time, for the piece had barely moved when he was nearly knocked over by someone intent on fleeing the stairs at all costs. But Christian wasn't about to be struck aside. He had spent far too much time with Gentleman Jackson and other boxers less inclined to follow the rules. With a few well-placed blows, he had the miscreant gasping and doubled over.

Locking an arm around the fellow's neck, Christian dragged him out of the buttery, past a startled Abigail and into the great hall. But he didn't need the light from the tall windows to know with whom he had struggled. Throwing the fellow down into a straight-backed chair, Christian kept him there with a firm grip upon his shoulders.

"Emery!" Abigail cried as she hurried toward them. "What on earth were you doing?"

"Nothing," the young man muttered, still sullen despite a lip that was beginning to swell.

"Nothing except scaring off potential buyers," Christian said sarcastically.

Emery squirmed in the chair. "I didn't do any harm."

"But why? Why would you do such a thing?" Abigail asked.

"It was just a jest," Emery mumbled, trying to shrug beneath Christian's grip.

"But why?" Abigail repeated.

Emery slunk down in his seat. "I just wanted to stay here. That's all."

His explanation was so patently false that Christian grabbed him by the neck, ready to wring the truth from him, but a gentle hand on his arm restrained him. Abigail, looking stricken, obviously didn't want him to beat the facts out of the boy. Why? Because he was a scholar? Christian blew out a breath of exasperation. He was betting that Emery had never even been to school.

Turning toward Alf, Christian nodded at his prisoner. "Would you do the honors?" he asked, stepping aside.

With an evil grin, the young villager took his place.

"Where are you going?" Abigail asked.

"I'm going to do what I should have done a long time ago," Christian declared. "I'm going to go to search his room to see just what sort of studying he does up there."

Ignoring Emery's shout of protest, Christian strode from the great hall, Abigail on his heels. Although he had a feeling that she didn't approve of his tactics, he was determined to prove that her faith in the weaselly youth, who wasn't even her cousin, was misplaced. Kneeling before the boy's door, he picked the lock and swung it open.

It was a mess, a jumble of clothes and books and papers that made even Christian wrinkle his nose. Obviously, the boy had been reading something, but what? He stepped over to a heavy writing desk, piled high with several volumes, and smiled smugly. Turning to Abigail, he gestured to the titles.

"What is it?" she said.

Christian smiled grimly. "The missing family histories."

Chapter Nineteen

ABIGAIL FOUND DINNER to be an odd, rather uncomfortable business, for she presided over a table with an empty place, that of the young man she would always think of as her cousin Emery. Christian had insisted that the boy leave, and though she still felt a certain guilt over her inheritance of the house, Abigail had reluctantly agreed to his ouster.

She and Christian had spent hours going over the materials in Emery's room, evidence that his elaborate hoax had been more than a prank. Indeed, he had deliberately forestalled the sale of the building while he searched for that ridiculous treasure supposedly mentioned in the family rhyme. Although Abigail was inclined to forgive his foolishness, Christian pointed out that he had locked them in the minstrel's gallery and with his motives unmasked, he might be driven to more desperate measures.

So he was gone, and now Abigail faced the other two cousins, abuzz with questions, and Christian himself, who had succeeded beyond her expectations. She drew in a shaky breath at the thought. Seeing him this afternoon, leaping into the fray, clever and handsome and bold, had only strengthened her feelings for him.

As always, Abigail had tried to reason with her treacherous heart, and this time she had a definite grievance. He had lied to her. Well, not lied outright, perhaps, but through the sin of omission. Yet Abigail found it hard to be angry with the man who had brought her back to life, who had introduced her to a world of freedom and adventure and pleasure, carrying her away until she was a hairbreadth from surrendering herself to him. That she hadn't was not due to her own good sense but to his gentlemanly withdrawal, for the man she had often thought heedless had possessed the wherewithal to call a halt to what she had started.

If he wasn't an authority on ghosts, what did it matter? Abigail had never considered such expertise a great achievement anyway. What was more important was that he was gentle and kind and bold and reckless and . . . Abigail frowned, amending her thoughts. He was gentle and kind and studious . . . and he wore spectacles.

And when he had swung from the fretwork, nearly falling to his death or injury, all the misunderstandings, everything he was or was not, didn't seem to matter anymore. Once he was back on his feet, Abigail had nearly thrown her arms around him in relief, her heart overflowing. The viscount might have accepted her invitation under false pretenses, but he had solved the mystery and more. He was her hero.

"I still can't understand it!" the colonel boomed out from his place at the head of the table. "Why an intelligent boy like that would waste his time chasing after an odd bit of poetry, and disrupting the whole household to boot, is inconceivable. I would never have believed it!"

"And you say that you found all the family histories, everything relating to the legend in his room?" Mercia asked.

"Yes," Abigail answered. It had all been there, the plans to the house, the elimination of the old kitchens, the blocking up of the minstrel's gallery, and the intriguing story of Sir Boundefort himself, told in bits and pieces tucked away in records and letters and diaries.

Abigail drew a deep breath. "According to the accounts we found, our ancestor was in love with a young lady but hadn't the resources to marry her. So he went on the Crusade and returned a wealthy man, knighted, only to find that the young lady's brother had forced her to marry another."

"How despicable!" Mercia said. "What happened?"

"She was a widow, so he still had hopes of marrying her," Abigail said. "He bought this land, next to where she lived with her brother and her daughter, and he built the Hall as a paean to her. Her name was Sibel," she added.

"He even named his house after her!" Mercia said. "How romantic!"

"Yes, well, he also built it to show off to her brother the mistake he'd made," Christian noted.

"Do go on," Merica urged.

Abigail frowned. "There are varying opinions on what happened next, but apparently they met in secret and he lavished her with gifts, but the brother found out. He was spying on them from the minstrel's gallery and was discovered, so Sir Boundefort confronted him there. They fought, and the young widow tried to intervene."

Abigail sighed, still shaken by the sad tale. "Some say she fell to her death, others that the brother deliberately threw her over the ledge. But whatever the true circumstances, she struck her head on the tiles and died. Mad with grief, Sir Boundefort killed her brother."

"That was probably when the stairs to the gallery were closed off," Christian mused.

"And no doubt that was when he made up the rhyme, as some sort of tribute to his lost love, not as a clue to lost treasure," Abigail pronounced, quite firmly.

"Isn't there some line in that thing about singing?" Christian asked.

"'Neath the angels singing fair,'" Merica quoted, eyeing him curiously.

"Obviously Emery discovered the minstrel's gallery, where musicians played and songs were sung, and thought to find the treasure below it," Christian said.

"That explains why the room where the steps are hidden is in such a jumble. He must have been searching there as well," Abigail added.

"And that's probably why he was digging around in the cellar, too, below that whole area. "'Neath the angels singing fair,'" Christian muttered thoughtfully.

For a moment Abigail thought he might offer up a solution to the rhyme. She would not put it past him, for hadn't he single-handedly accomplished almost everything else? Gazing across the table at him, she smiled in heady admiration of her guest, certain that she could continue to do so indefinitely. But the thought brought her up short, for she realized then what she had been too busy this afternoon to notice. Her smile fled, and with a gasp of dismay Abigail faced the truth.

Having routed the specter of Sibel Hall, just as she had requested, Lord Moreland had no reason to remain.

CHRISTIAN STALKED THE dark rooms of Sibel Hall, listening for signs not of the specter but of its perpetrator. He didn't trust Emery as far as he could throw him, and although he had put the boy on a mail coach, he was concerned that the so-called scholar might return. He was all too aware that nothing could prevent the angry young man from coming back with a new pick to attack the foundation—or the owner.

Christian winced, his heart lurching within his chest. Yet what was he to do? He could roam the house tonight, but what of tomorrow and the day after that? His work here was finished. He couldn't linger, no matter what the pretext. He frowned. Although the threat of Emery was hardly a pretext, there was no denying that he would seize any excuse to remain. He had routed the ghost, but he couldn't exorcise Abigail as easily.

A heavy wind sent rain lashing against the outer walls, and Christian welcomed it. The storm, which had begun after nightfall, suited his mood. He felt edgy, full of energy in a dangerous way as he prowled through the darkness. The mantle of his scholarly pose weighed heavily on him, and he wanted to throw it off, like the veneer of civilization that stood between him and his pirate ancestors.

Their legacy was a tempting lure. If he were one of them, he would simply break down the feeble piece of wood that barred his way and march into Abigail's bedroom. Would she scream and hold the sheet to her luscious breasts or would she indignantly order him to leave? The vision of her in some sort of nightdress—any sort—made him hard, as did the thought of finally subduing the Governess.

Like a formerly caged tiger on the loose, Christian paced the corridors, restless and hungry, only to find himself, finally, before her door. No matter what he willed, all steps led him here—all his thoughts, his hopes, his dreams, his desires lay behind that portal. Although he longed to break it down, if only to relieve some of the tension that had driven him, he did not. Instead, he knocked. And he waited.

At first Christian thought she hadn't heard him. She might be a heavy sleeper, or the sound might have been lost in a roll of thunder. But, at last, the handle turned, and the door swung inward. Without pausing for an invitation, Christian stepped inside and shut it tight behind him.

"You might have asked who was there before welcoming me in," he muttered. "I could be any manner of intruder." But his anger at her lack of caution faded away at the sight of her, tall and straight and wearing the same robe she had worn that night on the staircase. When she had spurned him. Would she spurn him again?

"Christian," she said, her voice a lush feast for his senses.

She wore no guise of disapproval, no hint of the Governess as she watched him wide-eyed. "What is it?"

What is it, indeed? Christian stared at her, and all the frustration and want and need of the last few weeks boiled over. Lifting a hand to his face, he tore off the hated spectacles and threw them to the floor.

"I'm no scholar, and I don't wear spectacles." The words came out in a harsh growl. Drawing a deep breath, he stepped forward. As usual, Abigail held her ground even though she gaped in surprise at his admission.

"My family wasn't founded by a Crusader or a knight of any sort, but by a pirate, and his descendants have all been plunderers of one kind or another, giving allegiance only to their own. That's the blood that runs in my veins." Christian stopped but a few inches from her. He offered no apologies, only the truth, at last.

"I know," she whispered.

Christian didn't pause to consider her reply; he only knew that she had not denied him. And then he did what he had always wanted to do. He picked her up, cradling her in his arms, and covered her gasp with his mouth. He tasted her long and thoroughly, branding her as his own, breathing in lilacs and Abigail, and reveling in the heady feeling that came only with her. *Love.*

Carrying her to the bed, he tossed her down, looming over her like the pirate he was. She gasped, half in outrage and half in laughter, then grabbed the front of his shirt and tugged him down on top of her, demanding a kiss. Her eagerness, her touch, the feel of her beneath him only fed his rampant hunger. He had never before been more alive, more aware of everything around him, and more true to himself. His pose was at an end, and yet here was Abigail accepting him, welcoming him into her bed.

And this was no dream. As if to prove that, Christian rose over her, stopping her teasing with his mouth, and opened her robe, sinking against the luscious body clad only in a thin nightdress. He groaned. Releasing her hair from its braid, he spread the thick mass over her shoulders, then paused to admire his work, dark silken strands glowing in the lamplight.

But Abigail grew impatient beneath him, and she tugged at his shirt until Christian lifted it over his head and tossed it aside. He shuddered at the feel of her pale hands upon his chest, and while she dragged him down for a kiss, he stripped the robe from her shoulders. Gasping for breath, he pushed it aside, reveling in the sight of her, both the Governess and his Abigail, in nothing but white linen.

With trembling hands, Christian explored her body, rubbing the soft material against her, seeking out her curves, and then slowly lifting the hem. His heart hammered in his chest, his breath coming fast and hard like some boy at his first lesson in love, but no amount of control could dampen his fevered excitement. The feel of her skin, warm and smooth, made him dizzy, and he followed the trailing material with his hands and his mouth, tasting every inch of her as he had desired to do for so long.

No timid girl, she explored him as well, her tentative touch growing more assured and more demanding. "Take off your breeches," she ordered, in a breathy sigh that made his body jerk in response. Christian fumbled with his fall only to realize that he was still half dressed.

"Oh, hell, my boots," he muttered, swinging to the side of the bed. Yanking them off, he dropped them on the floor, then stood and stripped off his breeches. When he turned to face her, he was totally nude and suddenly uncertain. Would she look at him with the maidenly horror of a Governess?

Their gazes met across the few feet that separated them, and in her eyes Christian saw a feverish desire to match his own. Instead of shying away from him, she rose to her knees and lifted a hand to his chest, and he drew in a harsh breath as her fingers trailed across his skin. Then she moved closer, pressing kisses to his heated flesh, imitating his own techniques with alarming skill and amazing nuance.

When she ran her tongue over his nipple, Christian

groaned. When her hands roamed along his back down over his buttocks, he shuddered. And when her breasts brushed against his genitals, he swore aloud, tossed her onto the bed and rose over her, subduing her shrieks of laughter and protest with his body.

"Abigail," he whispered, and her expression softened, her lips ripe, her eyes wide and dreamy, her body yielding to his own.

"Christian," she answered, and this time the sound of his name on her lips only brought him joy.

"Say it again," he said. "Again, and again, and again."

Her breathy whisper urging him on, Christian mounted her, probing and testing, but she welcomed him with such moist heat that he set his teeth against an urge to plunge deep. Instead, he moved slowly, rocking his hips, carefully making his way until he felt the last barrier between them give way. He exhaled then, a long, harsh breath as he stroked her, coaxing forth her passion, holding himself back until he felt the first tremors of her release. And when he shuddered uncontrollably with the force of his own, Christian knew he had met his fate, and no conquest this, but an alliance.

Like his pirate ancestors, he had captured his woman at last, and made her his. Yet while doing so he had surrendered himself, his very heart and soul, into her keeping.

Christian had thought to hold her close, to finally sleep here in her bed beside her, but he soon found out that Abigail had other ideas. The woman he had once thought stiff and unyielding wouldn't hold still. She stroked his arm and his back, nipped at his ear and whispered questions about his anatomy that made him grin.

"Can't a man get some rest?" he teased.

Smiling wickedly, she swung over him, and Christian reached for her, only to spring back with an oath as something struck his nose. "That necklace of yours is lethal," he complained, lifting a hand to grasp the deadly piece. "What is this, your own personal cudgel, for use upon any importune male?"

She laughed softly, a throaty sound that, impossibly, managed to arouse him again. "No, it's an old brooch of my mother's, handed down through the family."

"Yet you always keep it hidden," Christian said, glancing up at her face. She colored, the faint tinge of rose making her even more beautiful. Then she shrugged, a gesture Christian found wholly endearing.

"The clasp is long gone, so it is easier to hang on a chain. And, as a companion, I thought it best to keep it hidden away," she explained.

The implication that Abigail was prey to the petty jealousies of other household members, or worse, theft, was evident in her tone, and Christian felt a rush of anger that she had ever been put in such a position. He closed his fingers tightly around the golden circle only to pause in surprise at its heavy weight.

"As well you should have," he said. "It might be worth something."

"Oh, I doubt that," Abigail said. "It has no jewels or stones, and is rather plain. But that is why I like it."

Of course. The Governess would not be dazzled, which was one of the reasons he loved her. Even showered in jewels, she would never be garish or tasteless, but always herself. And this piece, odd though it was, seemed to fit her, Christian thought, examining it more closely. Cast all in gold, it resembled a large, flat ring, with a gold bar across the center and unusual indentations along the outer rim which might be some sort of Old English or runes.

Christian paused, rubbing his thumb over the surface, while something nagged at his thoughts. "The pattern looks . . . familiar to me somehow."

"Oh, I don't think so. It has been in my mother's family for years and years."

But Christian still struggled with a memory. He knew

nothing of jewelry, particularly antique pieces, and yet . . . "Do you know what it says?"

"Something about true love, I imagine," she said.

Christian glanced up and grinned. She was blushing again, and he decided that he had a definite fondness for that delicate rose hue. Indeed, he began to think of all the ways he might induce that lovely flush all over her body. Loosing his hold on the jewelry, he let it swing free, only to grab it suddenly again.

"Ah! I'll take it off if you are going to choke me with it," Abigail said indignantly.

"I have it!" Christian crowed, unable to contain his excitement.

"I know. Now please let go of it," Abigail said tartly.

"No! I know where I've seen that design before! Get dressed!" he urged, releasing the brooch from his hold. Even as she protested, Christian was already on his feet, tugging on his breeches. The mystery of Sibel Hall, having taunted him so long, now felt tantalizingly close to solution.

ABIGAIL WAS STILL protesting as Christian took up a lantern and hurried her downstairs, through the darkened rooms of the old house. "But you routed the ghost. What on earth are you looking for now?"

"The answer," Christian said as he raced to the great hall, still and silent except for the crash of thunder and the lash of rain against its walls.

"What answer?" Abigail asked.

"The answer to everything," Christian said, pulling her behind the fretwork. But this time he moved past the first door to the one that led to the old buttery and the kitchens that were no more. He paused at the end of the passage, where stout oak prevented their exit.

"You are talking in riddles," Abigail complained. "And . . ." Her words trailed off when he bent to pick the lock. "I am not going out-of-doors in this weather!" she cried.

"Oh, come on. It's only a few steps," Christian argued as the door swung wide.

"We're liable to be struck by lightning," she said in her Governess voice. At least that's what he thought she said as the sound of rain and wind swallowed her speech.

Christian flashed her a cajoling smile. "We won't be out there long enough. And it's warm. Wet and warm. You don't mind getting a little wet, do you?" he coaxed in his most seductive tone.

"Oh, very well," she muttered, her color high. With a triumphant laugh, Christian took her hand, and they ran pell-mell across the overgrown grass to the next building.

"Where are we?" Abigail asked when they stepped inside.

"The chapel," Christian explained, running a hand through his damp hair. "I should have guessed it, of course. But I knew the chapel was built after the original hall because it wasn't attached. So I didn't think Sir Boundefort had a hand in it. After learning his story, I'll wager he built the chapel himself after his lady died."

Christian lifted the lantern high and pointed to the left wall. "See? I don't know if they're singing, but there are angels."

"'Neath the angels singing fair,'" Abigail murmured. She turned to Christian. "The line about blessed care must refer to the chapel. I suppose we ought to have realized that meant a holy place, but the words were all so cryptic, I thought them nonsense."

Christian walked to the wall below the painted cherubs. "And look here. Does this remind you of anything?"

Abigail stepped forward to examine the strange carvings, lifting a hand to run her fingers over the indentations in wonder. Then she turned to him with an expression of astonishment. "Why, they remind me of my brooch."

"Exactly," Christian said in triumph. "May I have it?"

While Abigail tugged the necklace from the bodice of her gown, Christian walked the length of the wall, studying the various circles and pausing to touch each in turn. He knew the brooch would match only one, and finally he stopped before it. He held out his hand, and Abigail dropped the circlet into his palm, the gold cool against his heated skin. Turning the brooch carefully, he lifted it to the wall and set it into the recession. With one small adjustment, it fit to perfection. Then he pressed the face of the brooch hard against the surface. There was a creak, followed by a click.

"What on earth?" Abigail whispered.

Feeling rather proud of himself, Christian grinned. "I have a friend who knows quite a bit about locks."

"The one who taught you how to pick them?" Abigail asked wryly.

Christian nodded. "This is an old type of puzzle lock. Sometimes the keyhole is concealed by a pivoted cover or elaborately hidden in decoration. Or sometimes, as in this case, there is no keyhole. The secret here is pressure, either on certain parts of the design or, as it turned out, on the entire design, triggered by the front of the brooch, the ring brooch."

" 'The ring when set against its mate, Sweet kiss! Shall unlock the gate,' " Abigail murmured. "But why my brooch?" She turned toward Christian with a puzzled expression.

Christian shook his head. "How does the rest of it go?" He was hard-pressed to remember one word of the rhyme, even though it had been rammed down his throat for weeks.

"There's only one more verse," Abigail said.

"Then start at the beginning. Give me the whole thing again," Christian urged.

Abigail drew a deep breath and recited in a low voice,

My grief is such I cannot bear,
So must my worldly goods despair.
All my treasures sacred keep
In stone abode and darkness deep.

There shall they rest in blessed care
'Neath the angels singing fair,
Untouched by all but she who wear
Mine own love token in her care.

Thy ring when set against its mate,
Sweet kiss! Shall unlock the gate
For only her, all others spurning
Until my lady's love returning.

"'Mine own love token,'" Christian repeated. "This must be the brooch that Sir Boundefort gave to his lover."

"But how would I have it?" Abigail asked, obviously baffled.

"Because you are the one who will return!" Christian exclaimed with sudden insight. "That's why we could find no record of your connection to the Averills. There is none! You are not a descendant of Sir Boundefort, but of his lady. Wasn't she a widow, with a daughter?"

Blinking in astonishment, Abigail lifted a hand to her throat, groping for the brooch that was no longer there. "But that would mean that Bascomb solved the rhyme. Why didn't he ask me for the brooch? Or bring me here?"

Christian shrugged. "He was an old man. Perhaps he wasn't interested in the treasure, just the answer to the puzzle. Or maybe he felt that no one except you could actually unlock the so-called gate."

"And just what have we unlocked?" Abigail asked.

With a flourish, Christian pushed on the end of the wall, which swung inward at his touch.

"Another hide?" Abigail asked.

"The first and yet, the final, one," Christian answered. "It's larger than the occasional space used by medieval homeowners to safeguard their wealth, and, may I add, far more ingenious, as well. Sir Boundefort was a clever character," he added.

"Very nicely done, my lord."

The sound of another voice in the dim chapel made Christian whirl around, poised and alert. He half expected to see Emery smirking in the darkness, but the shadowy form was smaller and female. Mercia. Christian breathed a sigh of relief. After all his cautions, he had let excitement over their discovery distract him from potential dangers.

"Oh, Mercia! You startled me," Abigail exclaimed.

The older woman, eccentric as always, remained just outside the lantern light, and Christian wondered what the devil she was doing out and about at this hour.

"Again, very nicely done, my lord," she said. "For someone our dear cousin, or shall I simply say, our dear Abigail, dismissed as her Last Resort, you have proved to be surprisingly clever. Far more clever than Emery with his books and studies. Far more clever than I, even, for though I knew the rhyme held the key, I failed to unlock its secrets."

Christian eyed her quizzically. Why was she skulking in the shadows? The woman was damned peculiar at the best of times, but something about her behavior now roused all of his instincts. He inched toward Abigail, although outwardly he maintained a casual pose.

"Well, perhaps your treasure is in here. Shall we have a look?" Christian asked the older woman. He had hoped to draw her out, but she remained where she was, her sometimes peculiar presence turning downright eerie.

"There is something! It's a chest!" Abigail announced, obviously unaware of any undercurrents. And perhaps she was right. These last few weeks might have left him overly suspicious. After all, what could a little old lady really do? Christian turned his head to see some kind of trunk secreted inside the opening.

"Drag it out here, and then step back," Mercia said.

Surprised at the older woman's demand, Christian swung back around only to gape in shock. Mercia had moved forward finally, but the lantern's glow revealed that she held something in her hand, specifically a pistol, which she was pointing at them in a rather deadly fashion.

"Mercia!" Abigail cried from beside him. "What on earth are you doing?"

"My dear Abigail, whether you are related to some long dead doxy or not, you have no claim to this treasure. As a true descendant of Sir Boundefort, I am taking my rightful share," the older woman said.

"What of the others?" Christian asked dryly.

"To the clever—and the persistent—go the spoils," she said. "I have toadied up to Bascomb all my life, living in near poverty, counting the days until I could come into my own. That day, unfortunately for you, has finally come."

"Mercia!" The Governess was back in full force, scolding her elder in tones of stunned disapproval.

"I'm sorry, dear, but once I realized that I wasn't going to get the house, I knew I wouldn't have the luxury of a lifetime in which to solve the mystery, as Bascomb had," Mercia said. "I knew the old devil was close to the solution, but I didn't realize how close. I assumed that I, as his next of kin, would inherit. Alas, he foiled me, even in death, the bastard."

Christian heard Abigail's low gasp from beside him, even as he wondered if old Bascomb had died unassisted, or if he'd had a little help from the cold-blooded Mercia.

"I had not counted upon the cousins hanging about, either, but I soon discovered that Emery was quite intent upon finding the treasure, and I trusted to his efforts. Obviously, my faith was misplaced. But you, my lord, have proved yourself beyond anyone's expectations," she added, though Christian took no comfort from the compliment.

"Now, if you would please use those underemployed muscles of yours to drag the strongbox into the chapel, I will hold my fire," she said, her grip on the old pistol surprisingly steady.

Christian studied the weapon, which looked suspiciously familiar. "You surely cannot believe that old firearm from the great hall is still in working order," he said, hazarding a guess.

"I'm certain it is, my lord, for I keep it primed and at the ready. What better place to hide something than in plain sight? I wouldn't want to have anything incriminating in my possession, lest anyone search my room, like you did Emery's," she explained. "Now, we have wasted enough time. The chest, please."

Christian moved into the dark cavity, but he gave the contents a wary look. Sir Boundefort might not be able to haunt the place, but he'd been a crafty character, clever enough to keep his hoard out of anyone's hands for centuries. Christian gave the chest a nudge with his toe, just to make sure it wasn't covering up some trapdoor or other devilry.

"I said drag it, not kick it," Mercia called out. She was impatient, obviously, and Christian took heart, for impatient people made mistakes.

But he couldn't trust to that adage. He needed a plan. And quickly. He couldn't very well toss the chest at her, for it was too damn heavy. He was just going to have to leap for the pistol, but he'd have to be sure Abigail was out of the line of fire. The old woman could shoot only one of them, and he was going to make certain it wasn't Abigail.

With deliberate care, Christian pushed the chest forward. He still wasn't sure that Sir Boundefort was done with his tricks, and he was buying time, as well, time to come up with a better plan. Stepping in front of the piece, he slowly pulled it from its hiding place, across the old stone floor. If he could just get closer to . . .

"That's far enough, my lord!" Mercia ordered. "Now, if you would please step backward. You, too, Abigail, dear." Christian heard Abigail's gasp of alarm and realized the old woman wasn't going to shoot them. She was going to shut them up in the hide, and since the brooch was the only way to unlock it, the two of them would be trapped there forever.

"But surely you are going to open the chest?" Abigail said, her voice even despite their circumstances. Once more, Christian could only admire her steady strength, her courage under fire, her intelligence. Only the Governess could reason with a madwoman like Mercia. "I should at least like to see the treasure that Sir Boundefort took such pains to hide, that has been secreted here for centuries," Abigail said.

The older woman hesitated, but then greed, as it so often does, overwhelmed her caution. Impatient, she stepped forward to kneel before the chest, the pistol still held in one hand. "All right, but don't make a move, or I'll shoot."

She paused to study the chest and ran her other hand over the dusty surface. "There's no lock."

Obviously she was pleased by the discovery, but Christian grew more wary. After such an elaborate scheme to hide it, the chest wouldn't just be open for the taking, would it? He inched closer to Abigail even as he waited for inspiration to strike him—with a new plan. He still held the brooch, a feeble weapon at best, but if he aimed it at Mercia's hand, he might knock the pistol aside, or at the very least cause her aim to go awry. Never having excelled at ninepins or the like, Christian broke out in a sweat, for he would have only one chance.

The lid of the chest fell back, and in the glow of lantern light Christian saw an empty tray fitted neatly into the top of the opening.

"There's nothing in it!" Abigail said from beside him.

"Yes, there is, stupid girl!" Mercia answered, excitement rife in her voice. "This comes out. See the finger holes?" she said, pointing to the tray. Still holding the gun in her right hand, she reached into the tray with her left. But as soon as her fingers slipped into the holes, the older woman jerked back wildly. The pistol flew from her grasp, and she began screaming in agony, her cries echoing through the chapel in a horrific wail.

"What on earth?" Abigail said, rushing forward, while Christian retrieved the weapon skidding across the stone floor.

"Help me! Help me, you stupid girl!" Mercia cried.

"What is it?" Abigail asked, bewildered and frantic.

Christian knelt next to the chest. "It's Sir Boundefort's last safeguard," he said, running his hands along the exterior of the chest, searching for the release catch. "The unsuspecting thief reaches into the tray, setting off a spring trap that closes over his fingers, like those set to catch animals in the wild."

Trying to concentrate amid Mercia's writhing and shrieking, Christian felt something give and heard a snap. Presumably the tray could be removed now without danger. Either that or the wretched trunk would release darts at them next. Glancing about, Christian searched for something to pry out the tray, but Mercia was already pulling her hand out, bloody and mangled, along with it.

She sank back onto the stone, clutching her injured hand with a wail, just as a shadowy form appeared in the doorway. Christian seized the pistol, determined not to fall prey to either an evil Emery or a crazed colonel. He could not make out the figure, but above the sounds of Mercia's whimpering and Abigail's soothing whispers as she bound the injury, he heard the familiar clearing of a throat.

"Yes?" Christian said.

Hobbins stepped into the light. "I heard a commotion, my lord, and wondered if you were quite well."

Christian grinned at the sight of his old family retainer, for in his hand the valet held the other pistol from the wall of the great hall. "Thank you, Hobbins. You are well prepared, as always."

"I try, my lord," the man said.

"I do believe we need a physician, if you can have one summoned," Christian said.

"Very good, my lord," Hobbins replied with a nod. And without comment upon the bizarre sights before him, the valet turned to attend to the matter.

Leaning back against a heavy wood bench, Christian loosed a sigh of relief and decided his ghost-routing days were over, this little adventure having come far too close to an exploration of the other realm, firsthand. Frowning, he glanced toward the space that had nearly been his tomb, only to realize that Sir Boundefort's chest stood open and seemingly disarmed. But no glint of gold or sparkle of jewels gave hint of the treasure within.

"So what have we here, Sir Boundefort?" Christian asked softly as he leaned forward.

"Don't you touch it! It's mine!" Mercia wailed, struggling to sit up despite her wounds.

Abigail kept her still with a restraining arm. "Be careful, Christian," she whispered. "Whatever it is, it certainly isn't worth getting hurt."

Spying something shiny within, Christian snapped it up. Thankfully, nothing tore off his arm, and he rubbed the object against his sleeve. "A portrait," he murmured, looking down into the face of a medieval gentlewoman, dark-haired and sad-eyed. "This is Sibel, I'll wager. Yes! She's wearing the brooch," Christian realized, for the circlet at her throat was small but familiar.

Abigail leaned close, and Christian handed the portrait to her. "Your ancestress," he said, feeling an odd sort of hitch in his chest. Glancing away, he turned back to the trunk, pulling out a small drawstring bag.

"Mine! Mine!" Mercia cried. Proving surprisingly agile, she snatched at the pouch, spilling its contents onto the floor, then shrieking in disgust.

"Dust!" she shouted, outraged at the sight of what looked like brown earth. "Dust! Where is the gold? The jewels? The spoils of the crusaders?" Rummaging wildly in the trunk, she tossed aside a faded piece of cloth with her good hand, grabbed up something else, then flung it down as well.

Christian watched as what appeared to be part of a bone rolled across the stones.

"Tell me that's not someone's finger," Abigail said, eyeing him askance.

Christian grinned. Was there ever such a woman? "Well, at least it's not the finger of anyone we know," he said, picking up the piece to study it.

A large chunk of wood followed, nearly striking Christian. "Hey!" he shouted to the frenzied Mercia. But the woman was past all reasoning. Throwing a tooth and several pieces of parchment to the floor, she buried her face in her good hand and wept.

"What does it all mean?" Abigail asked, carefully retrieving the discarded items.

"I'm not sure, but I suspect it is Sir Boundefort's treasure, all right, just not the kind his ancestors were expecting," Christian said. "He put his wealth into the building of the hall, but kept hidden that which was most dear to him, his most valued possessions and the spoils of his journeys in the last Crusade."

Christian picked up the chunk of wood and held it up to the light. "Not every good knight returned with silks and plunder. And those were different times—when other things were revered. Perhaps our pious soul thought this a piece of the true cross?"

He carefully replaced the wood in the trunk, then bent to return as much of the earth as he could to the small sack. "And this might well be soil from the Holy Land," he said, putting it back in the chest. Unfurling the faded cloth, he saw a cross upon a field of pale green that once must have been vibrant.

"Our man's device," Christian said. He tucked it back in place, along with the other items. "Some saint's tooth? Another's bone?" he asked, then shrugged. "Perhaps these papers will tell the tale, but I think what we have here is a hoard not of worldly worth but of spiritual."

"Religious relics," Abigail said, and silence fell over the chapel but for the muffled weeping of Mercia and the pounding of the rain outside its walls.

Christian nodded. The mystery of Sibel Hall was finally solved, if not to everyone's satisfaction, at least to his own. His task here was completed beyond any measure of a doubt. But now what?

He glanced toward Abigail and wondered.

Chapter Twenty

ABIGAIL LOOKED OUT over her little garden and sighed, unable to believe that its profusion of blooms would soon fade. Although the days were still warm, summer was waning, and before long it would be giving way to cooler breezes and falling leaves. And then what would she do?

Abigail winced at the question she had been trying to ignore. She had her cottage, finally, her heart's desire, so naturally she would spend her time in it, enjoying her privacy to the fullest. Cooped up, all alone?

Again Abigail ignored the question, concentrating instead upon the home that meant so much to her. After all those years of yearning and dreaming, she had come into it quite quickly and easily. Once the specter and everything that went along with it had been revealed, Mr. Smythe had been eager to purchase Sibel Hall for a client, though not Mr. Gaylord. And, bless him, Mr. Smythe had even found a delightful property for her in exchange, which left her with far more money than she had hoped.

Abigail sat back on her heels and admired her home, thankful for her good fortune. The cottage itself was lovely, a picturesque bungalow with fresh paint and lots of little windows and a beautiful view of the rear garden, to which she had been adding her own touches. Weeding took time, of course, but Abigail most enjoyed those days she was able to spend out-of-doors tending to growing things, her appreciation of nature fully renewed.

She didn't have to, of course. She could have paid a gardener, but she liked to do it herself. The work gave her a sense of accomplishment, and without it years of duty made her, well, fidget. Although she treasured her freedom, she was ill prepared for a life of leisure, and when she wasn't working in the garden, she was somewhat at a loss. Oh, she had her reading and her correspondence, but she still despised needlework, couldn't play her small pianoforte very well, and grew bored. Restless. Yearning . . .

With a frown, Abigail wondered if she ought not involve herself more with the neighbors. Things here at the cottage had grown a bit quiet, especially after her day girl complained that she couldn't sit and chat if she was to be about her work. Obviously, the girl didn't have the good sense to enjoy her position, for she had even had the temerity to suggest that Abigail hire a companion!

She wasn't lonely, Abigail told herself even as she cocked her head at the sound of someone in the drive. Rising to her feet, she turned and shaded her eyes, heart racing, pulse clamoring, only to see that one of Farmer Morrison's cows had wandered away again. The sight of the lumbering beast, walking toward her as if in greeting, made Abigail's eyes ache with the pressure of unshed tears.

All right. She *was* lonely. But she didn't miss her godmother's household or her cousins who had turned out not to be cousins. Although he was not even a distant relation, she still corresponded with the colonel. He was happily living with one of his old military cronies and had written glowingly of the fellow's widowed sister. He had even heard

from Emery, who might *really* study with the monies left
him in Bascomb's will. As for Mercia, Abigail had made
sure the woman was taken care of, her stipend assuring her
a cozy berth with a caretaker who would make sure she was
clothed and fed, while keeping all weapons out of her possession.

Abigail couldn't say she longed for any of them. One person and one person only occupied her thoughts, and she was
finally forced to admit that she missed that someone with a
desperation that grew ever stronger. The long days of her
freedom had given her plenty of time to relive every moment spent with him, including the last—when he had
proposed to her.

Like everything else, Christian Reade, Viscount Moreland had offered marriage with a cavalier shrug and a flash
of white teeth, hardly the most romantic of gestures. And
then, instead of whisking her off her feet, he had told her
that he realized she did not want to wed, that she valued her
independence and her dream of her own home above all
else.

But think about it, he had said. Think about it! You know
how to reach me, he had said, just as though she would pen
him a polite note admitting that she loved him, passionately,
endlessly, helplessly, and, by the way, would he please come
for her?

Abigail snorted. She had her pride, and, truth be told, she
had clung to her vision of her future, coveting her little
house and garden. And, yes, she had to finally admit that she
had been hurt when he hadn't remembered her, had forgotten their initial meeting that, although so long ago, still res-
onated in her heart. She had stored up a lot of resentment
over those years, years spent dreaming of him riding up to
her parents' house and, later, rescuing her from her godmother's and whisking her off to a life of adventure and
freedom and love.

In her naïveté, she had expected too much from their
chance encounter. Abigail knew that now. But no matter

how she might dismiss it, the painful death of her dreams still haunted her. And when she had penned the letter asking him to rid her of the specter, she acknowledged now that she just might have been thinking of more than his reputation with ghosts.

But even those last tattered hopes had been dashed when he arrived at Sibel Hall and didn't know her. And Abigail had held that against him, nursing the old grudge back to life. She had told herself she was disappointed that he had accomplished so little in his gilded existence, that he was not the sort of man worthy of admiration, that he was a rake and a liar, when really she only faulted him for one thing: his abandonment of her.

Abigail lifted a hand to her face, shocked to feel the scalding heat of tears. Had she turned into a sour old spinster, without even a real suitor in her past to blame for her bitterness? For how could she hold Christian accountable for a brief encounter in his youth, a boy's play promise?

The real man, the adult Christian, a chameleon of light and dark, had proposed to her, perhaps more out of duty than desire, but what kind of fool would she be to let pride stand in the way of her happiness? Even half a loaf of life with Christian would be better than none, far better than what she had once thought her heart's desire. For without him her carefully planned existence was empty, certainly better than the long years she had spent with her godmother, but lacking in love, excitement, passion . . . and adventure.

Blushing, Abigail recalled the night in her bed that had, to her disappointment, put no child in her belly. She wanted that child. And others. She wanted a home that was filled with a family, not empty rooms that ensured a stultifying solitude. And, most of all, she wanted Christian Reade, Viscount Moreland, a scholar who wasn't studious, a pirate who wasn't a cutthroat, a wonderful, reckless, caring, witty, glorious man who had broken her heart once only to piece it back together, reviving her dreams and breathing life into her weary existence.

Drawing in a deep breath, Abigail wiped the stain of long unshed tears from her face and squared her shoulders. She knew what she must do.

CHRISTIAN STRODE INTO the house, looking for his grandfather. Having just returned from London, he wanted to assure himself that all was well—and to check the post, of course. He had been to the City for a meeting with his architect, but the afternoon had not gone well. Although he had tried to resume his previous life upon his return from Sibel Hall, nothing felt the same. Oh, his interest in building was still there, but he kept thinking he should ask Abigail's opinion.

Christian laughed, a humorless sound, at that notion. Abigail was happily ensconced in the cottage he had chosen, unbeknownst to her. No doubt she was living her dream and never even thought of him, except to rue the night she had let him into her bedroom. Christian knew that. He recognized it as fact, and yet, try as he might, he could not dismiss that evening or the woman he loved so easily.

And so he went through the motions, studying plans and drawings, making halfhearted decisions, and spending time with his grandfather, with whom he shared a new bond. Now, the highlight of the day for both of them was the arrival of the post. Christian just couldn't stop hoping for a letter from Devon.

"There you are! Where have you been?" the earl said, an expression of such expectation on his face that Christian hated to disappoint him by complaining about his architect.

"Just talking with Bramley," he replied. "Where's the post?"

"Forget the post," his grandfather said, with a wicked grin. "There's someone here to see you."

Christian started, his heart lurching in his chest, before reason overcame his hopes. More than likely it was some designer or builder, seeking his business.

"Out in the garden," his grandfather said. "By the old lilacs. I ought to have Thompson plant some new ones. We need more of them about the place. Perhaps a whole line of them."

The minute he heard *lilacs,* Christian was on his way. Hurrying to the tall doors that led out onto the elaborate grounds, he ran down the stone steps of the terrace, past the carefully tended beds to where the countryside encroached and several enormous lilac bushes basked in the fading sunlight. There was Abigail, poised before them.

When Christian saw her standing there, a memory came back to him slowly, like a dream, a memory of his younger self, visiting his grandfather's house with his parents. Adults were coming that day, and he was admonished to behave himself, but he tugged at his neckcloth and hoped the couple would bring sons with them.

To his disappointment, their only child, though about his own age, was a girl. Since he was going through his pirate phase at the time, Christian had no intention of sitting still for any tea and cakes. Brandishing a wooden sword, he had yelled something like, "I'm Black Jack Reade, and you're my prisoner."

To his surprise and delight, she had responded with, "You'll have to catch me first." And then she ran away. Naturally, Christian gave chase, but she was fast, for a girl. He finally found her under the massive lilac bushes at the back of the gardens, one of his own favorite spots. Impressed with her daring and her hiding skills and her good taste, nevertheless he dashed in, sword in hand, and claimed her.

"And what do you do with your prisoners, my lord pirate?" she had asked, not one bit intimidated by his swagger.

"Why, I usually make them walk the plank," Christian had replied. "But you being a girl and all, I expect I shall have to ravish you!"

"And how do you do that?" she asked.

"Why, I kiss you, of course," Christian replied, laughing his bold pirate laugh. But it had faded away as he looked at her, cheeks flushed, hair like spun chocolate, silky bits flying away from her face, and her eyes . . . They were the color of the lilacs themselves, soft and sweet and bluer than blue. And in that moment she was the first girl he had ever really noticed, ever really looked at, certainly the first one who made his pulse pound.

Surprisingly, she did not demur as he leaned close, but only watched him with rather wide-eyed fascination. And so he had kissed her. His first kiss. It was just a brush of the lips, but he thought his heart would fly from his chest. He pulled back slowly, reluctantly, and saw that she had closed her eyes. Watching her open them had been what he now recognized as an erotic experience of the first order. Of course, he didn't know it at the time; he knew only that she suddenly was beautiful and he wanted to give her the world.

And, then, startled at the discovery of his vulnerability, he had reverted back to the game. "You're my wench now!" he had shouted, standing up to brandish his sword.

Christian half winced, half smiled at the memory of his young bravado. He had turned round and round and collapsed in a heap beneath the lilacs, their fragrance heady and sweet. Her voice, low and pleasing, followed him down. "Very well, my lord pirate," she said. And she, too, lay back, and they looked up into the branches above, locked in their own world until her parents called for her.

When she left, Christian had darted into the house, taking a place at one of the long windows, where he watched their carriage move away. His parents were outside, tendering farewells, but his grandfather was seated by the fire, and Christian remembered with startling clarity how he had turned toward the earl with utmost seriousness and announced, "I'm going to marry that girl."

"Who? Parkinson's daughter?" his grandfather had said, never for one moment dismissing Christian's youthful determination.

"Yes," Christian replied.

"Good choice," his grandfather had said, nodding.

The poignancy of the memory washed over him, catching at his throat and squeezing at his chest. That was why she was familiar. Those eyes! Who could ever mistake them? And, abruptly, he realized why his grandfather had sent him to Sibel Hall. The earl had remembered her name. The old man wasn't growing senile at all, but was sharper than ever.

And now, the child Christian had once kissed stood before him, a woman full grown, and he cursed himself for not recognizing her the moment he'd seen her, for letting years of wary bachelorhood make him too blind to see that he had found her again at last.

"I've been talking to your grandfather, and apparently I owe you my thanks," she said, presumably driven to speech by Christian's long silence. "He says you scoured the countryside before settling on the cottage that Mr. Smythe conveniently offered me."

Was she angry? Christian shrugged. "I had to give you the choice. I didn't want you settling for me because you had no other options."

Her lips quirked. "Would I settle for anyone? Only the most intelligent, most clever, most resourceful man could tempt me to wed."

Christian lifted his brows. "Do I know him?"

Abigail shook her head. "No, you don't realize all that you are, but luckily I appreciate every single one of your talents," she said, pausing to tick off these supposed attributes on her fingers.

"Your knowledge of architecture, your quick thinking, your ability to unravel the most complex of mysteries, your love of adventure, your boldness in the face of danger, your bravery, your strength, your cleverness, your skill with locks, your physical prowess, your passion. You think you aren't a man of learning, but you know things you don't even know you know," she said in a breathless rush.

Christian blinked at that cryptic remark, but she went on. "Truly, you are a man of many talents, far too many to list.

And I love you in all your guises, ghost router, scholar . . . and scoundrel."

Christian felt his pulse pick up its pace. "And I love you, not only the Governess, the woman who served as a companion, the most reasonable and practical of females who had the courage to call me an idiot to my face, but Abigail as well, the lady who longs for adventure and sword fights . . . and passion. And let's not forget Abby, who stole my childish heart and held it in her keeping all these years."

She smiled, so softly and sweetly that Christian felt a hitch in his chest. "You remembered."

He nodded, not trusting himself to speak.

"Maybe deep in my heart, I still harbor a yearning to be swept off my feet and overwhelmed by a pirate in gentleman's breeches. Or out of them," she said, her lips quirking.

Christian laughed. "I am that pirate, and as I recall, you were once a pirate's wench. *My wench*." And with that, he stepped toward her and did what he had always wanted to do. He tossed her over his shoulder and carried her back to the house, where he lay claim, at last, to the woman who would be his wife. And his wench.

Keep reading for a sneak peek of Deborah Simmons's wonderful new historical romance, coming from Berkley Sensation May 2004

London 1820

There was a severed hand in the ballroom.

Lady Juliet Cavendish, pausing at the entrance, gaped in horror, for the blackened flesh was perched precariously atop a canopic jar, hardly the proper place for such a specimen. Indeed, one glance told Juliet that the entire ballroom was piled high in disarray, and she loosed a sigh of disgust.

Had she been present to oversee the arrival of her father's latest acquisitions, this clutter could have been prevented. But, apparently, the shipment had been unloaded during the night, and no one had thought to wake her. Now, her task of sorting and cataloging would be doubly difficult. Usually she would catalogue the heaviest objects first, but a glance told her they were scattered about, so she decided to reverse the order of her study, beginning with the small pieces on the table.

So absorbed was she in her task that at first Juliet heard nothing beyond the scratching of her pencil in the stillness of the vast room. But gradually she became aware of another sound, a low rumble, like the drone of a bee, and Juliet glanced about her in puzzlement, for surely no insect could flourish in the dismal chill of a London autumn. Juliet felt the hairs on the back of her neck rise.

Suddenly, her quiet morning of study turned eerie, the ancient objects surrounding her transforming the ballroom of her father's town house into an alien landscape of ominous portents. Her gaze settled unerringly upon that which occupied most of the area within her line of sight, the largest and most valuable of her father's acquisitions, an alabaster mummy case.

A vast reliquary with a majesty above and beyond the more ordinary discoveries, it stood alone, as if even the loutish workmen dared not mar its gleaming surface, carved with a multitude of figures, precise and elegant. Juliet stared for a moment, transfixed, before reason asserted itself. The case was uncluttered and lay separate from the other items, except for a wooden crate that leaned against one side. Juliet frowned at the sight, and when a particularly odd noise assaulted her senses, it appeared, for one wild moment, as though the mummy was making known its displeasure at the encroachment.

Drawing a deep breath, Juliet took firm control of herself. Obviously, there was a reason for the continuing, if sporadic, sounds that were emanating from the mummy case, or rather, from that general direction. Juliet stopped beside the crate and looked down. Although unsure what she would discover, she certainly was not expecting a pair of boots.

For a moment, Juliet feared that a dead body, or at least one that was not mummified, had somehow been transported into the ballroom. But that outlandish supposition did not explain the noise that had interrupted her work. She moved before the crate and peered into it. The owner of the boots was reclining inside as though in his own boudoir, and he was definitely not dead, for a hideous cacophony issued from him, a behavior commonly known as snoring, but with which Juliet was not very familiar. Undoubtedly, he had found this niche early on and slept off a drunk instead. Only such an ignorant ruffian would dare make a bed in something used to transport antiquities, then tilt it against a priceless artifact.

"You there! Come out at once!" she demanded. When the fellow didn't stir, Juliet moved to the rear of the crate and pushed, trying to dislodge it, as well as its occupant. As soon as the crate began to tilt, the slumbering figure erupted from the interior so swiftly that before Juliet could blink, he was crouching before her in a threatening stance, a knife in one outstretched hand.

"Who the devil are you?" he demanded.